Timothée de Fombelle

ALMA

The Wind Rises

Illustrated by François Place

Translated from the French
by Holly James

Europa
editions

Europa Editions
8 Blackstock Mews
London N4 2BT
www.europaeditions.co.uk

This book is a work of fiction. Any references to historical events, real people, or real locales are used fictitiously.

First Publication 2022 by Europa Editions

Translation by Holly James
Original title: *Alma. Le vent se lève*

A catalogue record for this title is available from the British Library
ISBN 978-1-78770-401-5

de Fombelle, Timothée
The Wind Rises

Art direction by Emanuele Ragnisco
instagram.com/emanueleragnisco

Cover and inside illustrations by François Place

Prepress by Grafica Punto Print – Rome

Printed and bound in Great Britain by Clays, Elcograf S.p.A.

Timothée de Fombelle is a Paris-based playwright and author of award-winning fiction. His Toby Alone series has been published in twenty-seven languages and is the winner of numerous awards, including France's prestigious Prix Sorcières, and the Marsh Award.

Holly James is a translator, writer and editor from the UK. She translates from French, German and Spanish. She currently lives in Paris.

François Place has written and illustrated many prize-winning books. He is also the author of several novels, a memoir, and the children's illustrated series, Lou Pilouface.

Contents

"Follow the tree flowers [. . .]
Only the tree flowers. As they go, you go.
You will be where you want to be
when they are gone."
—Toni Morrison, *Beloved*

PART ONE

I

When Lions Become Kings

There's a zebra with no stripes standing in the yellow grass. Two children are lying in its shadow.

"Look how tall he is."

Her name is Alma. She's talking to her little brother, who's stretched out next to her.

"Look!"

They're lying on their backs, side by side in the sprawling savanna. When the sun shifts across the sky, the animal takes a step forward to keep the children in the shade. They're looking at him, laughing together. Alma doesn't know it yet, but she'll treasure this memory later: the coolness, her brother by her side, the ripples of his laughter.

"See? I told you. You didn't believe me," says Alma.

The boy doesn't reply. All the zebras of the valley are small, stripy, and timid. This one is very tall, so tall you can't reach his head even if you stretch your arm up and stand on your tiptoes. He has a leather collar fastened around his neck, but he doesn't have a single stripe. He stands there quietly, keeping watch over them. He's not afraid of anything.

"Where did you find him?" asks Lam.

"I didn't find him. He's the one who found us." Her brother goes quiet, his eyes sparkling.

"What are you thinking about?" asks Alma. Silence. He considers for a moment.

"I'm trying to see if I can remember a day that was nicer than today," says Lam.

Alma smiles. Just a few moments ago, she showed him how to climb up onto the animal's back. She held onto the leather collar, and her brother climbed up behind her, wearing the blue hat he never goes anywhere without. Galloping towards the trees, they sent the gazelles flying in all directions like butterflies. Then they slid off the animal's back into the grasses, overcome with joy.

"His name is Cloud," says Alma, breathlessly.

"How do you know?"

"Because he's white all over."

"Can we choose any name we want for new things?"

"Yes," she replies proudly. "We can do whatever we want."

But Alma knows that before Cloud and his whiteness, the last new thing to arrive in the valley was her little brother. Nothing else has appeared on the horizon since Lam was born when she was three.

The valley is completely enclosed by cliffs. It's hot and beautiful, a kind of paradise. It's like a gigantic hand, brimming with savanna, trees, and wild animals. It's an open hand that gives them everything they need to live: food, starry nights, and little monkeys up in the branches for entertainment. It gives them torrential rain to run into with no clothes on, afternoon snoozes curled up between their parents, and tall grasses that bow down to make way for the lions and the wind.

But nothing exists for them outside of this protected,

secluded world. One family, alone in a valley that stretches as far as the eye can see. Nothing else comes in from anywhere to be given a new name. Unless you want to give a name to every passing cloud!

And then, out of the blue, came the zebra with no stripes. Standing there above them like an apparition. It was a year ago exactly that Alma first saw him. She spent whole days wandering through the valley all alone with her bow and arrows on her back. She wanted to find him to make sure it hadn't been a dream.

Gradually, she learnt how to approach him, but for months she didn't tell a soul. She kept him all to herself.

"Cloud!" Alma shouts.

Cloud bows his head and looks at her with his gentle eyes.

"Does he answer to you?" asks Lam.

They're still lying in his shadow. Alma rolls onto her side, smiling, and a cloud of tiny birds shoots up from the grass into the air. She turns her back to her brother.

"Where did he come from?" asks Lam. "From over there?"

Silence.

"Aam. Tell me."

He calls his sister Aam. He drags the word out, like the noise you make when you're eating something delicious.

"Did he come from over there? Aaam! Tell me."

The little boy rolls over towards his sister. He asks her again.

"Aaaam . . . where did he come from?"

Even in paradise, you have to tell stories and create imaginary worlds for children. So Alma created a land she calls "over there" for her brother. She tells him stories about it every night. She's filled it with black flowers, little girls who smell of roasted sugar cane, tall grasses that sparkle in the dark, houses with wings as tall as the cliffs. She says "over there" in their mother's language, the language of stories and songs.

But something unexpected has happened, something that's beginning to scare her. Her brother has built his own hut in the world she created. Little by little, Lam has been setting up camp over there, in that imaginary land. It's all he's been thinking about, day and night, for months.

He refuses to move on.

Lam hears a murmur coming from his sister. It sounds as though she's smiling and humming at the same time. She likes being the queen of this land she created for him. She likes telling these beautiful and dangerous stories that come tumbling from her lips without her quite understanding how.

Time passes. The sky is closing in, casting darkness over the valley. Cloud is still standing over them. He hasn't moved a muscle. There's a little bird with a silver beak perched just above his eye, and he doesn't want to disturb it. He doesn't even blink.

Alma's still humming, her mouth closed, keeping all of her mysteries to herself.

"Stop," begs Lam, "please stop . . ."

Suddenly, Alma goes quiet. She can feel something shivering behind her. It's making the sound the trees make when they drip dry after the rain.

It's her brother crying.

"Lam . . ."

She turns to him and presses her forehead against his. Their noses rest one on top of the other. Two faces that fit perfectly together. It's impossible to tell which of them the tears belong to.

This is why Alma thinks they'll never leave each other's side. She has an older brother, Soum, whom she loves dearly. But little Lam is the other half of her.

He stops crying the moment their skin touches.

"Is he from over there?" he asks again. And then: "Will you take me one day, Aam?"

There's a long silence.

"And what about us? Where do we come from?"

Alma doesn't reply. She only knows that she was born here, thirteen years ago. She grew up with her parents and Soum, free to roam the vast land where Lam would later be born.

There's just one limit to their freedom, one rule their father repeats over and over again, looking them straight in the eye: nothing and no one must enter the valley. And nothing must leave. When he says these words, his stare becomes a black arrow, unrecognisable. She's afraid of this look. It's the reason why she didn't breathe a word about Cloud until today. Because when he arrived that day in the pouring rain and she saw the iron crescents on his feet and the leather collar around his neck, she knew he must have come from somewhere else.

Alma and Lam stand still as statues, listening to the wasps buzzing as Cloud bats them away with his tail. Then the little boy lets go of his sister. He rolls onto his side.

"Are you okay?" asks Alma.

But Lam isn't really there anymore. He's lying on his back, clutching his blue hat in one hand. He's peering at the zebra with no stripes, white like the morning mist.

Only he can't be a zebra. He's too thin, too tall, his mane too long. Perhaps, just yesterday, he was still *over there*, playing in the sparkling grasses. Lam looks into Cloud's glistening eyes. He'd like to dive into those eyes and come out on the other side. Leave the valley and finally see what lies beyond.

Then the rain begins to fall. The raindrops make a crackling sound as they hit the grasses and the hot earth. It sounds as

though they're falling onto embers. The first rains of monsoon season have arrived. In one or two moons, almost a whole year's worth of water will rain over the valley. Lying on their backs, Alma and Lam open their mouths to try and feel those first few drops of magical rain on their tongues.

But before long, the rain starts to pour down hard, and they get up. They pick up their hunting bows from the grass. Attached to the curve of each wooden bow is a quiver for the arrows.

In the distance, a herd of antelope dashes towards a row of trees. Cloud shivers as though he's waking up from a dream.

"Stay here, Cloud! We'll be back tomorrow."

They each press a cheek to his neck to say goodbye. He shivers again, either because he's happy or because he's cold.

On another rainy day, just a few months ago, Cloud escaped from a world where moments like this didn't exist, where no one even remembered freedom anymore, where people would stick their heels into his sides to make him gallop after fugitives who smelled like fear. Here, he's discovering the smell of the earth, the feeling of peace, and the sounds of the children's joyous cries as they run in the rain.

But deep down, he knows he'll have to leave again soon.

"You mustn't mention Cloud. Okay, Lam? Not to anyone."

Lam is running by Alma's side, blinded by the raindrops. Their bows are strung across their backs.

"Promise?"

He doesn't answer. He just smiles. He knows what he has to do. He has a plan. He's ten years old now. Ten monsoons exactly. By this age, wild animals have long been able to hunt alone, and some lions have even become kings.

2

A Passage to the Rest of the World

They're so happy together, they could stay this way for the rest of their lives.

The rain has been falling now for forty days and forty nights.

The family gather around the fire, which floods the house with light. Outside, night has fallen. They have furs wrapped around their shoulders, and there are more carpeting the ground. Sheets of rain slide down the stacks of grass that make up the roof above their heads. The walls are made from branches and straw, stuck together with golden earth.

Lam is leaning against his father. He's fast asleep. Alma is sitting opposite them, next to her big brother, who's crouching over the fire. Soum is smiling, his head tilted to one side. Their mother watches as he stokes the fire with a stick. Each spark that rises from the flames is reflected in her eyes.

The streams in the valley are flooding, but their house is higher up on the savanna, wrapped in the embrace of the giant branches of a fig tree. In the arms of that tree, they feel protected from everything. Like survivors of the Flood.

Alma loves moments like these when they're doing nothing,

together. That's why the rainy season is always a time for celebration. Outside, the water does the hard work for them, filling the water basins, transforming the valley, ploughing the earth, and making the buds on the trees burst into blossom. All they have to do is listen to the chorus of the fire and the wind. All they have to do is enjoy the feeling of being alive and the warmth of the fire on the soles of their feet.

Sometimes they all start laughing softly in unison for no particular reason—simply because it's so sweet, so wonderful, they're overflowing with joy.

Alma is thinking about Cloud. She can imagine him standing under his acacia tree. She and Lam have gone out in the rain every day to see him.

Lam has learnt to ride Cloud by himself, holding on tightly to his leather collar. The little boy is so light that the animal forgets he's there as he gallops. Alma watches as they cross the waterholes, frightening away the dopey warthogs that stand in their way. Lam is almost lying flat on Cloud's back as they bolt into the undergrowth. They cut through the leaves at lightning speed. Then they disappear completely.

Hours later, Alma takes Lam in her arms and holds him tight. They crush the little white carnations in the grasses beneath their feet. Lam's body is tired, but there's a fire in his eyes and his skin is glistening in the rain.

"You need to know when to stop, sometimes," she says.

"Why?"

He looks at her, smiling. She puts on her best stern expression.

"You're crazy."

Lam plays dead in her arms. Nearby, the animal looks on innocently, though he can barely stand, either.

Alma is watching her little brother sleeping by the fire,

pressed up against his father. She's the only one in the house who knows why he's so exhausted.

But suddenly, she remembers that there are two lionesses that roam around Cloud's sleeping spot, hunting for the whole pride. There are little jackals that gather at the spring nearby, too. Once the water covers up the carcasses left behind in the grass, they start attacking live animals.

Alma is afraid for Cloud, who doesn't yet know about all the dangers in this dazzlingly beautiful valley. She'll go and look for him tomorrow. She'll bring him closer to the house. She'll finally tell her father about him. If he meets this visitor from the outside world, perhaps he, too, will dream of venturing out beyond the cliffs.

But she won't reveal the whole truth. Her big secret.

She won't tell him she knows how Cloud got in.

It was a year ago exactly that Alma discovered Cloud. It was during the same heavy rains that come before each summer.

Alma was climbing the rocks, out of breath.

From up there in the cliffs, she watched the white waterfalls tumbling down, barely making a sound. A herd of buffalo, disoriented by the floods, had been chasing Alma, and she'd lost her bow in the commotion.

She only likes to see buffalo from afar, scattered across the golden savanna. Up close, they're ugly, hunch-backed, and dangerous. Once, a buffalo had almost killed her older brother, and sometimes others would attack the house. In an attempt to shake the beasts off that day, Alma had climbed the little pass leading to Thorny Ravine in the pouring rain.

The ravine is the only way through the cliffs encircling their valley. But its depths are full of prickly vegetation—spiky trees intertwined with vines and thick, thorny bushes. The remains of a few reckless birds impaled on the spines act as a warning to anyone who dares try and cross. The ravine is a narrow passageway between two cliff faces. One hundred feet deep and covered in a thick carpet of thorns, it's impossible to cross, so Alma and her brothers never go near it. They're afraid of falling in and suffering the same fate as the antelope whose bleaching skeletons will forever line its depths.

But that day, as she reached the edge of the ravine, Alma saw a new landscape unfolding, one she'd never seen before. Tired and soaked to the bone, she retraced her steps to peer at the buffalo waiting beneath her. Then, turning to face the ravine, she saw not thorns, but a vast expanse of water.

An ephemeral lake had engulfed the prickly trap. She couldn't believe her eyes.

Because of the rain, the torrential downpour that had fallen, the abyss had been transformed into a lake stretching far into the distance between those steep cliffs. And there, just below her, was Cloud.

She could just make out his strange silhouette amidst the eddies forming in the current. He was trying to swim, colliding with the cliffs as he struggled to get out of the water. She hadn't named him yet, but there was a cloud of mist surrounding his mane. Alma heard the poor creature panting. The water level was beginning to drop. Cloud was going to be trapped in the thorns.

Alma understood there and then that he'd come from somewhere far away. He'd been transported there by those magical rains. The flooding and the waterfalls had filled the ravine to let him pass, as though flying, over the thorny hell below. He came from over there—from all the way over there.

His hooves continued to scrape against the same rock. His breathing was becoming weaker and shallower. Alma felt her breath falling into sync with his.

Then, a little further along, she spotted a pile of black rocks that had tumbled into the ravine. Part of the cliff had collapsed. The rocks created a steep bank, the only possible way for Cloud to get out.

If Alma had known how to swim, she'd have jumped into the water to guide him. Instead, she began to grab objects around her to hurl in his direction: pieces of wood, rock, roots torn from the earth. The bombardment forced Cloud to edge his way towards the bank of black rock. That was exactly what Alma intended.

She began to jump up and down and, hoping to drive him further towards the rocks, shouted the most terrible words she could think of in all the languages her mother and father had taught her.

Alma couldn't tell what was working best: the stones, her screams, or her frantic movements. The important thing was that, slowly but surely, Cloud was inching towards the bank. Finally, as he reached the rocks, he was able to hoist part of his body out of the water. Astonished, Alma saw for the first time his mane, then his leather collar, then his tall, white body, without a single stripe.

But she sensed he was beginning to falter, that he could fall back in at any moment. She picked up one final stone and threw it with all her might into the water behind him. This time, he managed to get out and clamber up the rubble.

He stopped when he reached Alma. He looked at her and gave a snort, wondering what to think of this frenzied creature that had saved his life. Then down into the valley he went, and after scattering the buffalo with a few kicks of his hind legs, he disappeared.

This first encounter probably explains why it took so long for Alma to get near him again.

Three days later, when she returned to the scene, the water had vanished from the ravine, and the thorny barricade had reappeared. Not a trace remained of the phantom lake.

Alma went down onto the bank formed by the black rocks. She'd never dared to go that far before. It was the edge of the abyss. Rocks slipped away beneath her feet. Gently, she called Cloud, hoping he was hiding somewhere nearby.

Then she noticed a gap in the rocks, a very low and deep cave, no wider than a tomb. She entered. It took a few seconds for her eyes to adjust to the darkness.

A little canoe with two paddles had been stowed there. It was very slim, carved from the trunk of a kapok tree with bits of bark still intact. The canoe was covered with moss. It must have been in the cave for years.

Water . . . and a boat. Now Alma knew that for a few hours each year, the day after the heaviest rains, a passage appeared: a passage to the rest of the world.

3

A Heart in the Grass

At home, sheltered from the rain, a thick fur wrapped around her shoulders, Alma thinks back to that life-changing day a year ago. Suddenly, a window to the unknown had been opened. First Cloud, then the canoe. Two big windows carved into their isolation.

Alma watches her parents, who are sitting on either side of the fire.

Nobody is making a sound. Her father's hand is resting on little Lam's forehead. Their mother, Nao, looks at her husband from across the flames. When their eyes meet, they share the same peaceful joy, the joy that has come to nest in their home.

Alma can imagine them speaking to each other.

"It doesn't get better than this," says her mother. "Look at them."

"You think so?" Her father always smiles at the right moment.

"Look how beautiful they are."

Nao doesn't need to speak these words. Her eyes say it all. It's not that she's proud. It's just that she can't believe it. Nao's eyes are shining so much that she has to wrinkle her nose a little to hold back her tears.

Nao's face, her heart, remind Alma of a summer night's sky. It would take more than a lifetime to count all the stars. So when you gaze up at them, it doesn't matter how tired you are; you try to fight sleep just a little longer. You don't want to close your eyes. You don't want to miss a drop of all that beauty.

But suddenly, everything stops. Alma watches as a shadow begins to form in the lingering gazes of her parents—a shadow she knows only too well. It passes over their faces when they think the children aren't looking. The shadow of a great mystery.

"Not yet. Don't say anything."

"Are you sure?"

"Later. Let them be, just a little longer."

Alma turns to look at her brothers. Is she the only one who senses the mystery? She's known for a long time that something is looming ominously over her parents' happiness. Sometimes the past returns to haunt them. Alma has a feeling her parents are on the verge of telling them everything.

She looks at each of the faces around the fire in turn until her gaze falls upon Lam, his closed eyelids as delicate as silk. When he sleeps, Lam's face is the face of a child. He stops pretending to be something he's not. Alma doesn't want these nights to end, ever. She wants him to stay a child just a little longer.

She's the last one to fall asleep. She sees the glow of the embers slowly fading before her. But what she doesn't see as she finally drifts off are the words forming on her little brother's lips. A bubble bursting in silence.

Over there.

Lam's eyes snap open, as though he's been waiting a long

time for this moment. He looks around him. He untangles himself from his father's arms and gets up without a sound.

By morning, the rain has stopped.

Alma thinks she's the first to rise. She still thinks it's an ordinary day. The flames have died and she goes out into the darkness, stretching. Outside, the grasses are glistening. Alma takes her bow and heads down a pathway of grasses that are lying flat against the ground, as though sleeping.

Leaping gazelles ricochet through the darkness. Alma loves the beauty that comes with the new day, when everything begins again and the world is fresh and damp like a newborn animal. Further down the valley, the rainwater has collected, creating mirrors of pink and blue.

Daylight is beginning to break all around her. The water reaches her thighs as she crosses the streams, surrounded by green birds camouflaging themselves in the treetops. When she reaches the river, the earth turns her bare feet red.

She stops at the top of the hill beneath Cloud's acacia tree. The branches sketch out a canopy high above her head.

She sticks her tongue between her teeth and lets out a high-pitched whistle. The sound is so high, so steady, that it's almost impossible to hear, almost indistinguishable from the whistling of the wind in the grasses. This whistle is her signal to Cloud. She stops. She looks out onto the infinite landscape around her. The sky has turned violet. Far off in the distance, towards the west, the buffalo and elephants are taking advantage of the break in the rain and heading for higher ground. Though they know a storm is never far off, the animals begin to spread across the plain.

Another whistle. Alma breathes softly. The cicadas are waking up. There's no sign of Cloud. Where has he got to?

Her fears from the night before come creeping back. Usually, if he isn't waiting by his tree, he comes as soon as she whistles.

A herd of antelope has gathered nearby. Alma recognises the three vertical black lines just below their tails and their white lips. They're impalas. They turn to her with their big eyes as if they know something she doesn't.

Alma leans against the tree.

"Cloud?" she whispers.

Where could that funny little zebra be?

She looks down at the ground. There's a black iron spike lying in the grasses at her feet. She bends down to pick it up. It's her father's hunting spear. The antelope take flight as she brandishes it in her hand.

She recognises the pattern that's been burnt into the wood below the spearhead. There's a long black line coiled around the spear like a snake. Her father must have been here during the night. What has he done with Cloud?

Alma runs back down the hill. She jumps over the little streams and climbs up the hills through the glistening bushes before emerging onto the plain again. The grasses reach up to her shoulders, and only her head, her big bow, and the tip of the spear can be seen poking out. Way up on the hill, she can see the green outline of the sycamore fig. The house isn't far now. Alma wants nothing more than to see Cloud appear in the morning light.

"Alma?"

There's someone behind her.

She turns around to see her father standing before her. He's already grabbed the spear out of her hand. He holds it out in front of his daughter and asks in a low voice:

"Where's your brother?"

"Which one?"

"Where's Lam? I thought he was the one who took the spear."

In an instant, Alma realises that nothing is as she first thought.

"Isn't he with you?" asks her father.

"No."

She looks at him in silence. Now she understands everything. It wasn't her father who left his spear on the hill beneath the tree. It was Lam. He must have woken up before her. He must have gone to see Cloud.

"I didn't mean to frighten you, Alma," says her father, smiling.

He's switched languages to reassure her. He's speaking in Fante, the language he spoke as a child.

He goes to take her hand.

"Are you okay?"

"Yes."

She turns away and starts walking into the distance.

"Where's Lam?" her father asks.

"I'm not his keeper."

Alma continues up the hill towards her house alone. She can see her brother Soum and her mother in the distance, working in the muddy yam field. With all the greenery surrounding them, they look like little terracotta figurines.

The house is empty. Alma goes to pick up the stack of folded blankets piled up against the wall. She calls out to her brother:

"Lam!"

Some mornings, he goes back to sleep in this nest of fur. But today, there's nobody there. There's just the smoky scent of last night's fire hanging in the air. When Alma goes outside, she sees dark clouds rolling across the sky. Maybe it's started raining again over the cliffs.

She goes round the back of the house and slips between the creeping branches of the fig tree. There, at the base of the trunk, is where her little brother hides his treasure. It's in a wooden box he shines with black grease. Alma's the only one who knows what's inside: two green stones, a horn bracelet, a bat skull no larger than a thumb, some seeds in a leather pouch, and a few other little treasures.

She kneels down, feeling reassured. The box is there, between the roots of the tree. Alma smiles. She knows Lam. He wouldn't have gone anywhere without his treasure. She picks up the box.

When she opens it, she immediately drops it again, as if it were on fire.

She gets up, trembling.

The box is empty.

Lam is gone. He's left the valley and taken his treasure with him.

And it's all because of her, because of the stories she told him.

Now everything has become clear. The facts are set in stone, hard and fast, as the truth always is.

Lam has left and taken Cloud, the only one who knows the way to *over there*.

A cold fear washes over her, starting in her throat and creeping down into her belly and her legs. The fear trickles slowly beneath her skin.

Standing beneath the branches of the tree, Alma can feel she's about to fall. As she hits the ground, she almost thinks she can see her heart roll out of her chest and onto the grass.

4
Wild Fortress

Nao scoops Alma up from the roots of the fig tree.

"Sweetheart . . . Alma . . . *Lilim* . . . "

Nao calls her daughter Lilim.

She calls all her children Lilim when she's alone with them. It's the most tender word she knows.

Nao's eldest son Soum comes to help her carry Alma into the house. Soum stays with her a while, smiling as he watches her sleep. Soum has never spoken a word in his life, but his collection of smiles is infinite.

Alma has been sleeping beneath the dried grass roof for hours. Soum has gone off to find his father. Though it's the middle of the day, three lamps are lit around Alma, and the smell of the oil burning on the wicks fills the room.

"Where's Lam?" Alma asks, opening her eyes.

Nao leans towards her daughter. "Your father and brother have gone out looking for him. He must be out on the savanna. They'll bring him back."

"Lam . . . "

"There's no use worrying over nothing," says Nao in her

deep voice. "He'll be back, just like the two little monkeys in the tree outside the house. We always think they've gone missing until the bread goes on the fire."

Nao is smiling as she says this. She goes back to kneading the flour and water in a wooden bowl, but Alma sees that dark cloud creeping across her face again, that shadow that Alma has come to know well. Nao is also talking a lot without stopping, which she never does.

"Just wait until the smell of the bread in the ashes fills the air. You'll see. A certain somebody will come jumping down from the branches or pop out of his hidey-hole!"

"Is it raining?" Alma asks suddenly.

"No. I don't think it will rain again now for a long time. The earth is full. It can't take any more rain."

Alma shakes her head. There's panic in her eyes.

"I'm going to get up."

"Rest, Lilim. Stay here for a while." Alma sits up, in pain.

"It's fine. I was feeling feverish, but I'm fine now. Look! I'm fine. I'm going to help them find Lam."

Nao looks at her daughter, who is already on her feet. Alma jumps from one foot to the other to demonstrate that her body can hold itself together. But her lips are trembling, and there are beads of cold sweat on her forehead.

"Look! It's fine. I'm all right."

Nao doesn't try to stop her. She knows how stubborn her daughter is.

Among the Okos, the word "alma" means "free." But it's a kind of freedom that doesn't exist in any other language. It's a rare word that describes an indestructible sort of freedom, one you hold inside you forever. Alma's father says that in his language, the translation would be "branded by the red iron of freedom." Alma has no idea what he means by "branded," or "iron." In her mother's language, the Oko language, there is no such thing as "iron." There are only words for the things that are important. Words to describe the colour of each hour of the night or the way you laugh when you're sleeping and a blade of grass tickles your ear.

"Maybe Alma's right," thinks Nao, looking at her daughter. "Alma and her freedom. It's better for her to work off her fever in the hills than to sit around here waiting."

Nao's eyes follow Alma around the house.

She takes her bow and arrows, which have been put to one side. She heads towards the door but then hesitates for a moment and retraces her steps. She buries her head in the crook of her mother's neck, just above her shoulder. They hold each other tight. It's the same old gesture, but Alma's voice begins to crack.

"Mama."

"Hurry home, Lilim."

Nao feels her daughter's hot eyes on her skin.

"Hurry home, otherwise Lam will eat up all the bread!"

Alma lingers a little longer in the nook she's always loved to snuggle up in, ever since she was tiny.

"Mama."

They stay like that for a long time. They can't hold each other's hands because Alma is holding her bow and Nao's hands are covered in millet flour. Finally, Alma pulls away. Later, when they each think back to this moment, as they so often will, neither will be able to say how long it lasted. Perhaps it was a second. Perhaps it was a lifetime.

Alma looks out over the flooded ravine. The water level has already dropped several feet. Some of the leaves that were caught up in the current have been left clinging to the cliff face, and just below the surface, the tallest branches of the thorny forest are beginning to appear in the crystal-clear water.

The water level continues to drop before her eyes. Alma ran all the way here without stopping, and she's breathing quickly, without making a sound. She walks along the ravine, inspecting the ground beneath her feet. She stops.

They're here. She can see Cloud's tracks in the mud. He must have come here after it stopped raining. But was Lam with him? She covers Cloud's tracks with her feet.

Now Alma's footprints are the only ones left in the mud.

She walks along the stones leading down into the water. From here onwards, the ground is too hard to make out any tracks. There's nothing left to follow. But there are no tracks heading back into the valley, either. Cloud's hoofprints stop here.

Alma stays on the bank. Her heart is beating so fast, the pulse on her neck, just below her ears, is visible. She looks at the narrow stream of water winding into the distance as far as the eye can see.

Where did Cloud go?

She can see the water level dropping even further on the cliff face. The prickly jungle below the surface is becoming clearer and clearer. In an hour or two, the valley will be closed off again for another year. The barrier of thorns will spring forth from the waters.

Alma approaches the cliff face. The canoe is still there in its stone tomb. Before she arrived, she decided she would go into the water if she could be certain that Lam had gone. She'd take to the watery ravine and go looking for him. But how can she be sure he's gone?

Cloud has left them. But Lam? Perhaps he's already sitting on her father's shoulders. Yes, maybe Soum and her father have finally found him, and they're all walking together with the sun on their backs. Alma imagines the fig tree appearing in the distance, the house sitting among the green grasses, and beautiful Nao at the front door, shielding her eyes from the sun with one hand, squinting in the evening light. Then she'll spot the little black silhouette wriggling on her husband's shoulders. Perhaps she'll shake her head, thinking to herself: "It's Lam! It's him. I knew it. They found him. Curse that child!" Then, laughing, she'll sweep the air in front of her with one hand to brush away the curse. Then she'll walk towards them, holding her hands high in the air to express her joy to the arrivals and to bless the ancestors watching over them. Then she'll glance over her shoulder because it would be nice if Alma came back too, from the other direction, to make the happiness complete.

Alma shivers as the daydream fades. The dream of everything being okay, of Lam jumping down from his father's shoulders and snuggling into his mother's neck as she says the words she always says:

"There you are, my little meerkat! There you are, Lilim."

Alma turns, ready to climb the black stone bank and run home. The bread will be browning in the fire. The two monkeys will be back in their tree, lying in wait for the feast and clinging to the branches with their little pink hands. But that very second, Alma sees something blue floating in the water. An island drifting above the sunken forest. It's her brother's hat.

Lam has left the valley with Cloud. There's no doubt in her mind. They left the valley together.

At the same moment, Soum finds his father standing in the silt of a stream.

There's no sign of Lam anywhere. They've been searching for hours.

They're already splitting up again to search new terrain towards the east, as if it were a game. Soum runs off as fast as his legs can carry him. If he could, he would shout out a war cry, but he's never made a single sound.

Behind him, his father stays put. He knows this is not a game. Mosi has turned to stone in the middle of the stream. His gaze falls upon the cliff far off in the distance, at the point where it splits in two.

The ravine. There might still be water in Thorny Ravine.

No sooner has he thought it than he sets off in that direction, all alone, at a hunter's trot, moving in a straight line. He doesn't go around the bushes; he cuts right through them. Nothing can stop him. He crosses the flooded valleys. He dispels the herds of zebra with his spear raised above his head. He doesn't slow down. But as his body speeds through the hills, his mind slowly sinks into despair. He thinks of Lam's determination, how his child is capable of anything. He thinks of the stubborn expression that's appeared on his face over the last few days. Why has he been disappearing all the time since the heavy rains began? Why was he always so tired when he came home in the evenings? What was he up to?

Mosi climbs the hill that leads to the edge of the ravine. All around, the waterfalls are disappearing from the cliffs. They might have already been dry for several days now. Mosi hopes with all of his heart that this is true. He likes it when the valley closes, protecting his family from everything.

But as he reaches the summit, he sees that the water is still there. There are barely a few feet left above the first thorns. But it's just enough to get through.

Then, in the mud, he sees a child's footprints.

He stops for a few seconds before the ravine.

He remembers the first time he arrived here in the rain, a long time ago.

He and Nao ran ashore in their canoe and walked up the black beach. They had no idea where they were. The two exhausted fugitives had only known each other for a few days, but it was as though they had already become one person.

Mosi goes down towards the opening of the cave where they spent that first night, almost twenty years ago. They slept there together, as though stranded on an island. The next day, all the water had disappeared from the ravine. The valley had closed them in.

Nao had looked out in the light of the early morning.

"Isaya," she said.

That's how you say "the hand" in the Oko language. The valley would be called Isaya.

It was morning. They had no idea where they'd ended up. They were hungry and thirsty. In the distance, a leopard standing on a rock watched them emerge from their cave. But that morning, thinking back on everything they had been through, on the world they had escaped, Nao and Mosi knew that this place would be paradise to them if for the rest of their lives they only had to fight hunger, thirst, and wild animals.

And they were right. For so many years, once they had built their home beneath the sycamore fig tree and the children had come into the world, Isaya was even better than paradise.

Mosi steps into the cave.

He lets out a cry, shattering the sweetness of those memories.

The canoe is gone.

Who could have taken it if not Lam?

The child is gone. He's left their wild fortress.

5

What Lies Beyond

Nao didn't hear her husband approaching, but now she can feel his shadow on her back as he walks through the door.

She turns around.

Mosi is standing against the light of the setting sun. He's holding a black leather bundle covered in soil. The remnants of his past, wrapped up in a coat and tied together with a belt. Nao tried to erase this bundle of things from her memory, but she recognises it straight away. These are the things Mosi buried when they arrived in the valley.

Nao gets up slowly. She can finally make out his face against the blinding evening sun. "Lam is gone," he says. "He found the canoe."

Nao looks at him, lost, as though he were speaking a language she doesn't understand.

"If I don't get to him before night," he continues, "the passage will close."

Nao would prefer not to understand the words tumbling down on her, but it's too late. They're already there in her heart. Leaving the valley now means leaving for a whole year. There's no way of coming back before the next heavy rains.

"I'll bring Lam back," whispers Mosi. "Tell the children they must take care of themselves now. Tell Alma . . . where's Alma?"

Nao shakes her head slowly to say she doesn't know.

"Tell her I'll bring Lam back. Tell her I'm leaving her my spear."

Nao moves towards Mosi in silence. She rests her head on his shoulder.

"What about Nao?" she asks, finally. "What will I tell her?"

There's another silence. She asks again.

"What will I tell Nao if she ever wakes up from this nightmare?"

"You'll tell her what she already knows. That she must keep the legacy of her people alive within her and keep her children close. She's stronger than I am. She must keep them all alive until I return."

He feels his wife's head growing heavier on his shoulder.

"She'll understand what I mean. She knows the secret."

Nao closes her eyes. It's true. She's guarding a treasure that doesn't belong to him. It's the memory of her people. She's the last of the Okos. She came to the valley with Mosi to protect their memory. Back then there was nothing more important to her. She was prepared to do anything.

But then the children were born, one after the other, and this evening everything hangs in the balance because of a runaway barely ten monsoons old.

"Any one of our children," says Nao, "is worth more than my people and all our secrets put together."

Mosi lifts his wife's head from his shoulder and takes it into his hands. He holds her face in front of his. He kisses her eyes, then carefully lets go, without taking his eyes off her, as though letting a bubble float away through the air on its own.

Taking tiny steps backwards, Mosi goes outside, leaving Nao behind. He grabs the large circular woven cover protecting the mouth of the well as he goes. He takes this as a shield in one hand and carries the leather bundle in the other. Nao doesn't have the strength to go outside and watch the warrior go. Nor does she have the strength to shout out one last secret she's been keeping. A secret that would have made their goodbye even more heartbreaking.

Mosi's spear is standing guard in front of the door. Nao appears to be alone in the house, but she knows she isn't really. That's the brand new secret she couldn't bring herself to tell Mosi. She isn't alone because she's expecting a baby.

Mosi is wading into the water. The branches have already begun to burst up through the surface in certain spots. He's tied his bundle of things to a floating raft made from wood and rattan. He pushes the raft in front of him and swims behind, trying to stay as horizontal as possible to avoid the thorny bushes. He can see them just below his body through the clear water. It feels as though the forest is growing all around him as he makes his way through. He's like a lost bird, flying just above the treetops.

Mosi swims. His feet never stop kicking. As a child, he grew up by the river among the Fante people of the Gold Coast, who spend their lives in rivers and the ocean. To try and coax him out of the water, his mother once told him that a blue fin was starting to appear on his back. The idea was to frighten him, but instead little Mosi began to sleep on his stomach at night to let the fin grow. Each morning, he would trace a line down the small of his back and pretend the fin was really there.

Night is beginning to fall. The water feels cooler. Mosi carries on pushing his raft in front of him.

Every now and then, he calls out Lam's name and waits. He longs to hear a croaky little voice calling back to him.

He deeply regrets never having taught Lam how to swim. He wanted to protect his children, to prevent them from exploring the ravine. Once, Mosi found a canoe that Soum had secretly been carving out of a dead tree so that he could fish in a pond full of carp, and burnt it in front of the whole family. Poor Soum had started to cry, letting out the tiniest of sobs—the only sound to have ever come from his mouth.

But now, Mosi wishes they could all swim. He wishes he could teach them everything he's ever hidden from them.

Gradually, a luminous night takes over from the day. Mosi can see pearls of water glistening at the tips of the thorns. The darkness is filled with noises. Insects and bats fly above the forest as it emerges from the water.

Sometimes he thinks he can feel creatures moving in the depths below him. One month of rain was probably enough time for water spirits and giant snakes to start settling in there. Mosi tries not to stir the water up. He takes lengthy detours to avoid getting stuck in the prickly bushes.

He'd like to stop and rest, to float on his back with the stars watching over him. But he pushes on. It's a race against time. Time goes by mercilessly, draining the water from the ravine and the strength from his body.

Every now and then, Mosi takes a sip of the pure water surrounding him.

In the middle of the night, a current appears, helping him along. The further he swims, the stronger it gets. Mosi clings to his raft and glides between the dark masses below as they claw at him, trying to hold him back. The thorns leave their marks all over his shoulders, arms, and stomach. He's moving fast now. He tries to imagine his son speeding

through this labyrinth in his canoe. The cliffs are closing in tighter on either side.

Mosi knows very well where the current is taking him tonight: the waterfalls.

He can already hear them rumbling away in the distance. He remembers how he and Nao climbed those waterfalls all those years ago, which led them to the passage, then the valley, which has been their home ever since.

He tries to swim towards the bank where the water is calmer, but each time he gets closer, little whirlpools appear, propelling him back into the rapids. Mosi can hear the sound of the waterfalls more clearly now. He knows there's a flat rock somewhere on the left—the spot where he and Nao launched their canoe into the water when they escaped. He needs to find that rock to save himself from the current.

The water is turning to white froth before him. Mosi knows that he can't get out of the water without leaving his raft behind. With one hand, he begins to untie his things. But suddenly there's a great crack, and the raft comes to a sudden halt, harpooned by a branch. Mosi snatches the leather bundle away at the last moment and dives into the depths with it.

He swims blindly through the darkness beneath the water. All of a sudden, everything is calm. He holds the leather bundle tightly. It's as though his legs are bound together, rippling as one through the black water. He lets the diving instinct of the Fante people guide him.

When his head finally emerges from the water and he catches his breath, he finds himself in a small pool that's bubbling away gently. The flat rock he was searching for is just in front of him. Mosi climbs onto it, exhausted. He crawls along on his elbows and hits his head against the trunk of a tree. He sits up, then slowly gets to his feet.

Mosi smiles to himself in the darkness, despite his exhaustion. The wood he hit his head against sounded hollow. He breathes silently, his eyes closed. It's the little canoe, lying right in front of him. Lam must have managed to cross the ravine. He must be alive.

Mosi opens his eyes again. Bending down slightly, he notices that the thin layer of earth on the rock has been disturbed. He crouches down. There are tracks on the ground. A horse's hooves mixed with a child's footprints.

A canoe, a child, and a horse.

Mosi falls to his knees.

For a long time, he's unable to move. He thinks of the horse's neigh, the sound of voices shouting, surrounding the child. He thinks of Lam's beating heart. They've taken him. He knows that terrible din only too well, those awful screams he traded in for the howling of the wind in the grasses, the trickling of the streams after the rain, the gentle humming of the Valley of Isaya.

Slowly, he pulls the leather bundle towards him. He's kept it with him all the way. He unfastens the belt, unfolds the large black coat, and spreads the contents onto the rock: a pair of trousers, a deep red jacket with velvet epaulettes, a pair of boots, a gold-rimmed hat, which he unfolds in his hands, a braided whip, and two heavy pistols. Finally, there's a brass gunpowder flask sealed with a cork plug.

Mosi puts on the soaking wet clothes. He pulls the black coat over himself and stashes the pistols and whip in his belt.

Uncorking the bronze flask, he pours a little gunpowder in his hand. The powder isn't even wet.

Suddenly, the smell of the gunpowder awakens the ghost of the man he once was, a long time ago. A man who smelt of leather and the forge, who brought fear and misery with him wherever he went. A man who was once saved by a stranger—an Oko woman—when he thought he was the one saving her.

When he set foot in the valley twenty years earlier, he thought he'd buried this man once and for all. Yet here he is once again, standing on a rock in the dead of night.

There are two eyes watching as his silhouette recedes into the darkness. Alma doesn't realise she's looking at her father.

She's the one who left the canoe on the rock next to Cloud's tracks. Then she dropped to the ground and fell asleep, despite the crashing of the waterfalls nearby.

A few seconds ago, she was awoken by a hunch. A hunch so strong, it made her sit bolt upright. On her guard, Alma crouched down with her hands to the ground and her bow strapped to her shoulder.

Just a second later, she leapt up silently like a wild animal before ducking into the shadows. She just managed to catch a glimpse of the man in the gold-rimmed hat sinking into the bushes where she was sleeping only moments before.

What's happening to her? She can feel something changing, burning through her body. She looks back at the distance she managed to cover in one leap. In the blink of an eye, she'd been able to grab her bow, load it with an arrow and take aim. She stands stock still. She can sense the slightest presence around her. Two trees creaking side by side, the tiny breaths of a cluster of hummingbirds sitting on their perch in the trees high above her. She can still hear the footsteps of the man walking off in the distance. She can smell the scent of hyenas sleeping in a den somewhere nearby. Nothing escapes her.

Alma slowly releases the string of her bow. Instinctively she knows she must be wary of everything. This instinct, this mysterious power, has come from nowhere. It was waiting to find her at the edge of the valley, a memory being stirred up inside her body.

She thinks of Lam.

Where could he and Cloud be hiding?

And who was the man she saw passing by, cloaked in shadows? How many of them are there prowling around the outskirts of Isaya? What are they looking for?

Finally, she understands why for so long, her father made her live in fear of what lies beyond the valley.

6

An Ordinary Boy

At that moment, on the very same day in August 1786, thousands of miles away, a boy almost fourteen years old is silently lifting the latch of the cabin belonging to Lazarus Bartholomew Gardel, captain of a ship named *The Sweet Amelie.*

The boy's name is Joseph. He simply slotted the blade of his knife through the gap in the door and slid it upwards. Now all he has to do is turn the handle to lift the latch on the inside and open the door. It almost seems too easy. But there isn't another sailor in the whole port here in Lisbon—not a single person across the whole Atlantic—who would dream of breaking into Captain Gardel's quarters.

It's a large room in the great cabin at the stern of the ship. The curtains have been closed for the night, and the only light visible is the lantern in the hallway. There's a faint ticking coming from a little clock hanging in a corner somewhere.

The light that Joseph let in is now spreading across Gardel's body, which is stretched out on the bed. He's asleep.

Joseph closes the door and goes towards him. The captain appears to be a light sleeper, but Joseph's footsteps are even lighter. Lazarus Gardel's thick white lace collar lights up his face, even once the room is in darkness again.

Joseph looks at the captain's face. There's a pale line quivering along each of his eyelids, as though his eyes might snap open any minute. He's breathing silently. Joseph had been expecting an ogre's snore, but instead he's greeted by the peaceful breaths of a child. And there is something childlike about the dreadful Captain Gardel. Perhaps it's his delicate skin, his pale lips, the white hair falling around his face in waves. Some days, he's like a cruel little boy toying with a bug he's just caught. Except the bugs he holds between his fingers are human beings: weary sailors, lost girls, and black captives.

Joseph knows what they say about Captain Gardel. He thinks of all the people who would give anything to be in his position, standing over this sleeping monster with a knife in his belt. Yet he resists the idea as it crosses his mind. He resists the temptation to avenge them all. He didn't come this far just to do that. There's someone counting on him for something else.

Joseph reaches for a shelf just behind the captain, skimming the hairs on the sleeping man's head, and grabs the gold chain watch and little green velvet pouch that are lying there. He stands up and listens one last time for Lazarus Gardel's breathing. Then he retraces his steps, leaving the room without a sound. He closes the door behind him.

He tucks the watch and the pouch safely inside his pocket.

The deck of *The Sweet Amelie* is deserted, and there's not a sound coming from the port. The sailors have all been out celebrating, and now they're fast asleep. A few nights' stopover in Lisbon is all they have before the never-ending journey begins. Last night was their final opportunity to spend the first instalment of their wages. Soused in Portuguese wine, they must've stumbled from one place to the next on the way back to their lodgings. There's a leg protruding from the rowboat suspended above Joseph's head, a crumpled hat trailing on the floor . . . even the ship's cat looks drunk, lying on its back in a puddle.

But Joseph is walking straight. He knows exactly where he's going. All he has in his stomach is the glass of milk and piece of bread he wolfed down a few hours earlier. Rather than running away after what he's just done, he walks calmly towards the mainmast.

On the ground in front of him lies a heap of black rope, coiled like a boa constrictor. Joseph spots the mainsail. It's as thick as his arm, brand new, and freshly rubbed with tar, ready to be hoisted the next day. The sail has been passed through a pulley at the top of the mast and then left to one side on deck. Joseph grabs a corner. He sits astride one of the starboard guns to get a better look at the cables, ropes, and shrouds stretched above him like vines in a jungle. He takes his time.

Suddenly, his gaze falls upon something. He's found what he was looking for. Way up above him, the topgallant mast has been put in place, ready to be hoisted above the mainmast. The sailors must have stopped for the night before finishing the job. This is convenient for Joseph, who jumps down from the cannon, climbs a few feet up the shrouds and connects the mainsail to another thinner sail that's rigged up to a series of pulleys. Then he comes back down to make a loop at one end.

Joseph sticks his feet through the loop.

He tightens the noose around his ankles.

"There," he says with a smile. "Hey presto."

He looks up again to make sure he hasn't overlooked any of the finer mechanical details in his plan. His eyes wander along the heights of the ship's structure for a long time. He goes over his calculations again and again. Because despite what he just did in the captain's quarters, and despite the fact that what is about to happen might seem like absolute madness, this thirteen-and-a-half-year-old boy is not crazy.

With both feet still tightly secured in the loop, he inches closer to the mast. He makes sure his pocket is closed with the captain's watch and velvet pouch safely tucked inside. He takes a deep breath, like a diver about to leap from a rock.

Then he pulls out his knife, selects one of the taut cables running along the mast and slashes it in two.

An enormous piece of wood tips over with a great crash. It's the topgallant mast, carrying with it some thirty feet of rope. The pulleys creak above Joseph's head. The snake of black rope suddenly springs up at his feet, hissing.

Seconds later, Joseph is hoisted into the air by his ankles. He narrowly misses the rowboat as he flies up from the deck in an upside-down position.

With his arms clamped tightly across his chest in anticipation of the shock that's coming, he shoots up fifty feet high, sucked up into the air with one great snap. He somersaults through the sky without making a sound before bouncing at the end of the rope once, then twice, then, more gently, a third time.

The ship is silent once more. The topgallant mast has toppled down several feet and is now suspended in mid-air. The mechanism of the pulleys propelled Joseph up into the air as the mast fell.

Hercules the cat turns over in his puddle of rum, wondering whether he just heard something. Perhaps it was a bad dream? A mouse? But he's already falling asleep again.

Still upside-down, Joseph swings gently in mid-air between the shrouds in the dark sky.

Everything is just how it's supposed to be.

The bells in the bell tower of Santa Maria de Belem chime three. It suddenly occurs to Joseph that if everything goes well, he won't hear the sound of church bells for a long time. That's perhaps the only thing he'll miss. The bells and hot bread. And the wind in the leaves. And the freshness of the forest in summertime. The sound of rain in the gutters, maybe. But that's all. Perhaps just the wet slate tiles steaming in the sun and the sound of horses' hooves on the pavement at night. But nothing else.

Nothing at all.

Soon, if all goes well, there'll be nothing but the calls of cormorants, then the creaking of the ship on the ocean, then the murmuring of the African forest. And that will only be the beginning of it all.

Hanging all alone from the end of his rope, Joseph Mars smiles as though he were just an ordinary boy.

7

The Orders of the Wind

Daylight is peeking beneath the curtains. Captain Gardel is standing in his cabin, frozen to the spot, facing the door. He's staring at the raised latch, puzzled.

"What the . . . ?"

His left eye is still sticky from sleep, and he chews on his tongue as if eating a sweet.

"What in the name . . . ?"

Gardel has just woken up. He swears he left the latch down the night before.

"What in the name of God . . . ?"

Just as he's about to turn around and inspect the room, he hears three violent knocks at the wooden door. Who dares disturb him?

The captain flings the door open.

"Captain . . . "

Before him stands his first mate, Picard, white as a sheet. His pallid face has as much to do with the late night he's had as with the discovery he's just made.

"Captain, there's something you should see." Gardel doesn't move.

"Come and look at the mainmast shrouds."

With one swift gesture, the captain pushes Picard aside and leaves his cabin. He goes up the flight of twelve steps and emerges on the aftcastle, which is bathed in sunlight. Shielding his eyes with one hand, he takes a moment to adjust to the white morning light.

Standing around on deck, seated on yardarms and hanging from the rungs tied between shrouds are thirty sailors, all looking up at the sky. They haven't even noticed the captain's arrival. Gardel throws his head back to see what they're looking at. There, swinging from the mast, is Joseph. He's dressed all in blue against the white sky, like a drop of water hanging from a piece of string.

Two seagulls swoop right in front of him.

"Where did he come from?" grumbles the captain.

"We found him here."

"But where did you catch him?"

"We didn't catch him. He hung himself up there."

"By the feet?"

"Yes."

"Who is he?"

"Nobody knows. He must be about thirteen. Maybe fourteen."

"So?" says the captain.

"So he can't be very heavy. Perhaps it was the wind," suggests one sailor, as his shipmates elbow him in the ribs to shut him up. The captain starts sucking on his tongue again. He shields his eyes with his right hand and looks further up.

"Get Dubois," he says, squinting up at the top of the mast.

Picard turns to the crew.

"Get Dubois!" he yells.

The sailors cry out one after the other: "Dubois, Dubois!"

One man sticks his head down a hatch leading to the lower deck. He, too, begins to shout:

"Dubois!"

Then he pops his head out again and says:

"He's coming."

Way up above the deck, the boy seems calm. His head is still hanging upside-down, and he smiles as a bird glides right by him. Every now and then, he brushes an invisible feather from his jacket.

Finally, Dubois' head appears through the hatch. He hoists himself up onto the deck. Dubois isn't very tall, but his shoulders are as wide as barrels. He could easily fit one of the chickens pecking away at the back of the ship into one fist. As he walks over to the captain, he shoots a quick glance at the boy hanging by his feet, then another at the top of the mast.

Jacques Dubois doesn't seem surprised by this spectacle. He's seen everything during his time as a carpenter. Once, while he was working on a Dutch ship, one of the sails tore, and a cabin boy flew off into the air with it, hanging by a thread. The poor boy was stuck up there for two days, flying behind the ship like a kite, until the wind finally died down.

When you've collected dozens of stories like that, finding a boy dangling from the shrouds doesn't have much of an effect.

"What's gone on up there?" The captain asks Dubois.

"That's the topgallant mast. One of the ropes must have snapped."

"And you think it's normal for that to happen?" asks Gardel.

"In a storm, if the waves were as high as the birds in the sky, it would be entirely possible."

"But?"

"But in August? In a sheltered port? When the water surface is as flat as a slice of ham? Impossible."

Gardel raises an eyebrow.

"A slice of ham?"

"Yes."

"Impossible?"

"Yes."

"And yet here we are."

"Indeed."

The captain looks at Dubois, who is calmly shrugging his giant wrestler's shoulders.

"Tell me, Dubois," the captain continues. "If you are incapable of preventing the impossible from happening, what should I expect from you when the inevitable happens?"

Dubois folds his arms. He doesn't reply. Gardel continues.

"In other words, could you please explain exactly what use you are to me?"

"No use," the carpenter replies. "So far, I've been of no use at all to you."

"I beg your pardon?"

"I arrived yesterday. I spent the night in the hold securing the barrels of salted meat so they wouldn't roll around. But that's all. Let me remind you that my colleague, Bassompierre, the carpenter who constructed this ship, died an accidental death along with one of his men in La Rochelle just before leaving, and that it was a miracle you found me yesterday in Lisbon to replace him."

"A miracle?"

"A miracle," Dubois replies modestly.

"A miracle?"

"Such a miracle, Captain, that if I were you, I would think it suspicious."

Gardel sniffs. He may have only just arrived, but already this man is getting on the captain's nerves. Gardel would quite like to throw him overboard with two twelve-pound cannonballs sewn into his shirt.

But he also knows that a good carpenter is the most valuable man aboard a ship. Out at sea, Gardel would sacrifice ten of his men to keep his carpenter alive. Because what use is a decent crew and a pile of goods worth a fortune if the ship is sleeping at the bottom of the sea with schools of sardines and clownfish swimming about the steerage?

Picard, the captain's first mate, has not taken his eye off Joseph. He's squinting up at him, still trying to understand. Picard has only had one eye since the day he was hit in the face by a pulley. Pulleys flying through the air during manoeuvres are so dangerous that sailors affectionately call them "widow-makers."

"So in your opinion, the boy was just hanging around on deck, and he simply tripped over the mainsail at the very same instant the topgallant mast tipped over?"

"That's right," Dubois replies.

"Unbelievable," says Picard.

"Quite unbelievable, yes."

"Get him down," says Gardel.

Picard jumps. "Get him down?"

"That's what I said. Get him down from that mast. I'll have the port police lock him up faster than you can say fisherman's hitch! I don't like people roving around on my ship. Back to work!"

Something's troubling Gardel. This stopover has lasted too long. They've already wasted three days in La Rochelle due to the mysterious death of Bassompierre the carpenter and his apprentice. The captain is afraid there'll be deserters among the crew. For as long as they stay on the coast of Europe, there's still a chance that some sailors will leave him in the lurch. The captain had to use every possible ruse to recruit them, one by one. They can't desert now.

"Hurry up, Picard! We're going."

Dubois salutes and takes his leave.

Just as the captain goes to return to his cabin, and just before the crowd of sailors begins to disperse, there's a crash of something metallic falling to the ground.

Gardel freezes.

Something has fallen out of the boy's clothes and tumbled in complete silence, before shattering on the deck.

A tall sailor rushes over to take a look. Picard goes over to the taffrail. "What is it?" he shouts. There's a silence.

"It's the captain's watch!"

Gardel's face freezes as he turns towards the ship's stern.

"What did he say?" he asks.

"It's your watch, Captain." But then the sailor corrects himself.

"It *was* your watch."

Sure enough, the object in the man's hand no longer really looks like a watch. It's more like a sort of pillbox filled with bits of metal and broken glass.

Gardel climbs down towards the sailor via a ladder leaning against the taffrail of the forecastle. He snatches the watch and looks at the inscription engraved on the case. Yes. It's his watch. It's his watch. A gold watch he bought almost twenty-five years ago, after his first trip to the coast of Guinea. He never goes anywhere without it. His initials are there on the case, in large cursive letters.

Lazarus Bartholomew Gardel has made seventeen triangular trips across the Atlantic, transporting thousands of captives and tons of goods. That's a record in his profession. The watch has survived storms, revolts, pirate attacks, looting, and wars.

It's resisted thieves on the docks of Nantes, Kingston, and Bristol. But now, thanks to this thirteen-year-old tadpole hanging from a hook, it looks more like the confetti of islands scattered in the Caribbean Sea than a watch.

Gardel closes his eyes. He doesn't even lift his head to look at Joseph. His fist is closed tightly around what's left of his watch. The whole crew are there to witness the scene, the way people watch a fire when it's too late to put it out.

Then, as if that weren't enough, a second object slips out of Joseph's clothes. It's lighter than the first and seems to fall more slowly, spinning through the air. It narrowly misses the rowboat suspended above the deck. Everyone on board has the time to watch it fall in slow motion, each filled with dread, except Gardel, who doesn't open his eyes until it hits the floor right before his feet. The velvet pouch opens up on the deck and several little white stones roll out.

This time, a hushed commotion breaks out among the crew. There's a word being whispered among the sailors. It's impossible to tell who said it first, but it's one of those words you can't hear without wanting to repeat it. A word that these men, who have never owned more in their whole lives than a hammock, a knife and a pair of breeches, say very solemnly. In doing so, they feel, if only for an instant, as though they could be the owner. *Diamonds*.

Scattered on the boards of the deck at Gardel's feet are indeed what look like diamonds.

Each time the sailors say the word, they take a step towards the pouch and the sparkling stones bursting forth from it.

Gardel has thrown himself on the ground, grasping at his treasure. The sailors back away. Nobody has ever seen Lazarus Bartholomew Gardel in such a state. Crawling around on the deck, his forehead brushing the floorboards, he gathers his scattered diamonds one by one. All the sailors can see is the little white bun coiled tightly at the nape of his neck and the flaps of his jacket sweeping the deck. He counts the treasure in his velvet pouch over and over again. Finally, he gets up, all pink and sweaty. "They're mine," he mutters. "He took them, but they're mine."

Gardel feels the sailors' eyes on him. Suddenly, there seems to be something different about them. Where before there was only fear, he can sense the beginnings of envy and disgust.

Gardel has changed beyond recognition.

"Prepare the ship. We're going," he says.

Picard goes over to him. "Aren't we handing the boy over to the police?"

"No. Lock him up in the back."

"We're taking him? I thought you said no more cabin boys on board," says Picard, as the crew finally begins to disperse.

Gardel doesn't reply straight away. He grits his teeth.

It's been a long time since he last hired children to be part of his crew. It's not a question of morals or charity. He's just noticed that cabin boys tend to get sick as soon as they get close to Africa, which makes them completely useless to him. These children are terribly resistant and never seem to die. Instead, they carry on costing him a fortune in drinking water and pea soup. At least the older sailors are courteous enough not to survive too long once they catch a fever.

"So, Captain? Are you keeping him?"

"Who said I was keeping him? I only told you to lock him up below my cabin. Hurry up, Picard! We need to get going."

He glances at the clouds that are suddenly beginning to roll across the sky.

"They're not my orders. They're the orders of the wind."

8

A Whiff of Treasure

From behind, *The Sweet Amelie* doesn't look like a ship but a little inn floating on the water with its lantern and balcony. This is the stern of the ship. Everything here is brighter and more sophisticated, from the tall windows of the captain's quarters to the painted red wooden letters spelling out the ship's name. There are imitation columns sculpted between the latticed windows. You'd almost expect to see pots of nasturtiums or geraniums and a little line of washing hanging on the balcony.

But just below the captain's quarters, there are two more windows that have been shuttered up. A hole the size of a playing card has been carved into each shutter to ventilate this dark room under the captain's floorboards. But in the late summer heat, there's no air coming in at all. The vents are about as much use as a mouse hole in a bread oven. But this morning, they at least allow Joseph, who's been left inside the room with the door double locked, to press an eye or an ear up to the hole and find out what's happening on deck.

He was thrown in after having his jacket, waistcoat, and

shirt confiscated. His bare shoulder rests against the latticed window as he listens to the sounds of the ship.

He can hear the men shouting to one another as they repair the masts, the blows of a mallet, and the clattering of water supplies and the clattering of water supplies, packages of fabric, and fresh produce being hauled aboard. Through the slats in the floorboards, he can smell the bad-quality tobacco that's just been bought from the Brazilian ships stopping over in Lisbon. He can just make out the final preparations being made, the cries of effort coming from the boatswains perched on the yardarms up in the masts as they hoist the sails and the groans of the pulleys as the little jolly boat is heaved up onto the stern. He even sees the shadow of the jolly boat being winched up right in front of the shutters. Its dripping hull is being hung just above the lantern to dry.

Finally, Joseph hears two words echo throughout the ship, the words that mean everything can begin:

"Cast off!"

Joseph feels the ship moving, that slow drift taking him away from the docks. He peers out of the little opening to watch the shoreline receding. He sees the cluster of fishing boats circulating in the mouth of the river, then watches as the water begins to get darker and bluer: the ocean! He manages to stick his hand outside to catch a few splashes of water. Only then, when he's certain the ship has left, when he's licked the salt from his fingers, does he drop to the floor and fall asleep.

"So what are we going to do with you?"

The two shutters are wide open. Captain Gardel is sitting on a chest. He's looking at the boy, who has just opened his eyes.

"Hm? What are we going to do with you now?" Gardel asks gleefully.

Slowly, Joseph remembers where he is. He has no idea how long he's been asleep. All he knows is that everything rests on these next few moments.

"Where's my jacket?" He asks groggily. "Where did you put my things?"

Gardel smiles.

"You won't be needing them."

"Why? Where are we going?"

The captain's smile cracks a little. Gardel is so used to people being frightened of him that it feels strange when they aren't. The boy clearly has no idea what's in store for him.

"Unfortunately for you," the captain begins, "you came into the wrong cabin last night."

"Seventeen diamonds and a gold watch. Doesn't seem like it was the wrong cabin to me. At least, I'm not complaining. Sometimes all you find is a chewed-up old pipe."

If it weren't for the bars across the window, Gardel would have thrown him into the water by now, even though his initial plan was to wait until they reached warmer waters so he could invite sharks to the party, too.

"I want my blue jacket," says Joseph, like a stubborn child.

"You can forget it. Seeing as you're puny as a shrimp, it won't fit anyone on board. We'll use it to plug the cannons. Can you swim?"

"Real sailors don't know how to swim," says Joseph. "It's bad luck. Give me my jacket back. It has sentimental value. I can work to pay you back for the watch."

"It'd take twenty years of work to pay me back."

"I have time and nothing else to do. But I want my jacket back. Like I said, it's sentimental."

The moment the words fall from his lips a second time, Joseph sees a glint of curiosity in the captain's eyes. It seems as though something's just occurred to him. He gets up and takes three steps towards Joseph to get a better look at him sitting on the floor.

"Sentimental . . . " Gardel repeats, dreamily.

The captain turns to leave. Joseph hears his footsteps as he makes his way across the room, followed by the door closing and the three latches locking him inside.

Up on the aftcastle, the captain walks up to the ship's wheel. It takes two men holding on to it with both hands to keep the ship on course. The large compass in front of them indicates that they're sailing southwest. A gale is blowing, and the waves are high. Gardel likes to see the ship speeding through the sea like this, whipping up a white foam. At the helm, the men tug at the wheel, making the ship dive into the troughs of the waves before straightening her up again, ready to climb the crests. Every now and then, a surge of water crashes onto the deck, and the two seasick piglets tied to the chicken coop at the stern start squealing.

Picard, the captain's first mate, has finally set the lower sails. Gardel knows that the voyage they're embarking on is, above all, a matter of speed. The shorter the journey, the more profitable it will be. Sailors, merchandise, food, and ship alike will all deteriorate over time. Even the captain is perishable. Each day that passes comes at a cost. But Lazarus Gardel has built his reputation on speed.

Three months ago, when La Rochelle's top merchant, Ferdinand Bassac, hired Gardel for the fourth time to captain one of his vessels, the two met at the shipowner's exquisite home on rue de l'Escale to sign the contract.

It was a Sunday. The iron-nibbed quill was resting on the desk next to the contract. They could hear somebody playing piano upstairs somewhere. Stirring the hot chocolate in his cup, Bassac turned to Gardel.

"What's your secret, Captain?" he asked.

"What secret?"

"Your last trip lasted just thirteen months, including the time spent in Africa and on our islands. That's no mean feat considering you'd come all the way from Amsterdam."

Gardel paused for a moment before answering conspiratorially:

"I know what slows down a ship, Monsieur Bassac. The trick is to make sure there's not an ounce of it on board."

"Not an ounce of what, Gardel?"

The captain took his time to reply. The shipowner's accountant, a young man by the name of Christian Saint-Clair, was standing nearby. A chaffinch landed on the ledge of the open window. The warmth of May filled the room, along with the scent of lilacs and freshly baked shortbread.

"Not an ounce of what?" Bassac repeated, eagerly.

"Something more dangerous than vermin or the rats that ravage the hull. A formidable force. Even the slightest trace of it must be crushed."

"Trace of what?" asked Bassac. "What is it?"

Gardel hissed the answer through his teeth.

"Humanity."

The accountant in the corner flinched as the captain uttered that word. The chaffinch took flight. Even Ferdinand Bassac felt a shiver run down his spine. He shot a glance over to the door nestled between his bookshelves, fearing that his beloved daughter, an unsuspecting visitor, the maid—or any other human being—had heard the captain. Those words felt so wrong when uttered against the backdrop of the waxed wood in his office, the sweet scent of the garden, and all those good-hearted philosophers surrounding him in his library.

Bassac and his accountant did their best to laugh off the remark, but Gardel didn't follow suit. There wasn't a trace of emotion in his face.

Ferdinand Bassac pulled the final page of the contract towards himself, trembling. He signed his initials. The quill almost tore through the paper.

Now, looking out on the horizon beneath the sails, Captain Gardel thinks of the frothy, steaming hot chocolate in the little silver pot being poured into cups, the sound of the sugar cubes being crushed with a spoon. He thinks of shoes with ribbons, of Bassac's pale hands, the servants in the corridors. He thinks of the shipowner's daughter, Amelie, a lovely creature of fourteen years, whom he went to greet on the steps on his way out.

"Good day, mademoiselle . . ."

He remembers how she whipped her skirt haughtily aside and walked straight past him, without so much as a nod.

One day, Gardel will become a shipowner. He'll command ships from the comfort of his armchair. He'll be the biggest rival of Bassac and all the others. He'll dominate them all. He's been saving for twenty years to do this. But he still needs more money. A lot more money. Sometimes, his impatience wakes him up in the middle of the night in cold sweats.

For now, he's the captain of *The Sweet Amelie*, the only master aboard for many long months. A young man climbs down from the mast and jumps onto the deck in front of him. Gardel stops him with a single gesture.

"Bring me the boy's clothes."

"Whose clothes, Captain?" the young sailor asks, breathlessly.

"The Lisbon thief. Where are his jacket and shirt?"

"The cook won them in a game of dice."

"I said bring them to me, now!"

Where did this premonition come from? Some men have a sixth sense for it. They instinctively put their noses to the ground whenever they catch a whiff of treasure.

9
The Thousand-Headed Pirate

The sailor Gardel has just spoken to is Abel Lebon. He's nineteen years old. He blushes at the honour that's just been bestowed upon him: a direct order from the captain! Abel is a brand-new addition to the crew. He's never sailed further than the river in front of his childhood home, where he used to catch frogs in his hat. He's one of those sailors who arrive fresh from the countryside with bits of straw and hay still stuck in their hair.

Abel has never had any luck in life. He comes from a poor household. The family farm was sold for a thousand pounds after his parents died when he was twelve. To console himself, he did some foolish things. He never went to school, never had a penny to his name. All he has in life are his two beloved big sisters, who live off one cow and two goats in the dunes on the Île de Ré off the west coast of France.

Over the last few days, however, he can feel his luck beginning to change. First there were the men who came into *Le Chat Rouge* inn during the early hours of the morning. The two charitable gentlemen offered to pay off Abel's drinking and gambling debts because his pockets were empty and the innkeeper was threatening to have him locked up.

It was a miracle. The men spoke kind words to him, each putting a hand on his shoulder. They scolded the innkeeper, telling him he wouldn't recognise an honest man if he saw one.

They said Lebon looked like a tough lad. They were sure great things were in store for him.

"I can see it in your eyes. You've got drive, my boy."

All he had to do was sign right there, at the bottom of the page. They said they'd pay it all off and could even offer him a job that would give him the opportunity to travel the world.

"Haven't you always dreamed of travelling, Abel Lebon?"

He just had to sign quickly, right there, and they'd get him a nightcap to toast the beginning of his new life. Now anything would be possible.

So Abel Lebon signed. He hugged them, tears in his eyes. He had a job. They gave him twenty pieces of silver upfront. He listened to the coins clinking in his jacket pocket with every step he took.

Then, one hour later, he saw the ship. A ship much bigger, much taller than the church in his village. It was still very early, but already people had gathered on the dock of La Rochelle to catch a glimpse of the ship. Lebon couldn't believe that something so miraculous had happened to him. His head spun each time he looked up at the three beribboned masts. Someone handed him a hammock to hang at the bow of the ship. They told him the ship would leave in two hours. So soon? He had no time to say goodbye to his sisters. But imagine, they said, imagine how proud they'll be when you return, arms laden with gifts.

And just like that, *The Sweet Amelie* weighed anchor, the sun behind her, parting the bright morning sea foam like a lady in a white dress cutting through a field of wheat.

Of course, Abel Lebon fell sick on the journey from La Rochelle to Lisbon. He was struck with the most terrible seasickness as they sailed through the Bay of Biscay. That probably explains why he was thinking so much about his sisters and their cow and the two little goats back in the sand dunes.

That explains why he had to keep blowing his nose, hiding in his hammock slung beneath the forecastle at the bow of the ship. But now it's time for the real departure. Now it's time for them to leave on their long voyage. And the captain has already entrusted him with a mission.

Now anything is possible.

There's a pot boiling on the ship's stove. The cook is chopping green cabbage into quarters with a machete and throwing it into the pot. He doesn't seem to realise he's on a ship, speeding through troubled waters. Abel Lebon goes over to him.

"I'm here on the captain's orders."

"What's your name?"

"Abel Lebon."

The cook is black. He speaks with an impressive English accent. When he smiles, his cheeks puff up like a frog in springtime.

"Are you a landlubber, Lebon?"

"A what?"

"Landlubber."

"Yes. It's my first time."

"*Le Chat Rouge* or the Albatross?"

"What?"

"Did they hire you at the *Le Chat Rouge* inn, or was it at the Albatross Tavern?"

Lebon smiles. His is such a wonderful tale, they're already telling it aboard the ship.

"*Le Chat Rouge*. Who told you?"

"They got me for the first time ten years ago at the Old Tower in Liverpool. It was in a street so narrow that not even two rats could cross paths without stepping on each other."

The cook bursts out laughing.

"I was just like you. Head as empty as my pockets."

He puts the machete down, wipes his wet hands and stands up.

"Lebon, my name's Cook."

He offers his right elbow, the way chefs always do to greet people, and Abel grabs it awkwardly.

"Hello, Cook."

Disarmed by Cook's soft voice, his English accent and direct stare, Abel doesn't quite understand what he's just been told: he was tricked in La Rochelle, and half the crew were recruited the same way, ensnared by tricks, debt, and despair. After all, who would volunteer to go on a voyage like this?

Cook looks hard at Abel.

"What do you want?"

"The captain is looking for the thief's clothes," explains Abel. "He needs them."

"What for?"

Abel shrugs his shoulders. He hasn't got a clue. He's obeying orders, that's all.

"I won these clothes playing dice against Rolando," says Cook.

"I know. I was there."

Cook pretends to hesitate for a moment, but he knows what he's going to have to do. He knows the captain too well.

"Take them," he says. "The blue pile by the wood leaning against the stove."

Abel grabs the bundle of clothes and tucks it under his arm.

"Anyway," says Cook, "I tried them on. They're much too small. The jacket is more like a glove on me."

Abel glances at Cook, smiling.

"A what?"

"A glove."

Cook smiles back. He's not fat. More plump, like a roast chicken. He'd need three jackets like that one just to reach around his belly.

"Hold on, boy. Where are you going?"

"I'm going up to see the captain."

Abel stops in his tracks. Cook is blocking his path.

"With the fish?"

"What fish?"

Just then Abel feels something flapping beneath his arm. He unfolds the clothes to find two sea breams wrapped in the clothes. Some of the scales have rubbed off, leaving a silvery shimmer on the jacket. Cook takes the fish back and slips one into each pocket of his apron.

"They're for the bosses' dinner. We have to make the most of the fresh stuff. We'll hardly catch anything during the voyage. Within a month, we'll be praying for a seagull to fly into the pot so we can have a bit of meat in our soup."

The smell of fish fills the captain's cabin.

Gardel has unfolded the clothes the sailor brought him and laid them out on the bed. A broadcloth shirt, a waistcoat, and a blue jacket. He's searched through all the pockets. Nothing.

All he's found is a little ball of thread wound around a cork spool in the waistcoat. The cork had a needle stuck in it. Gardel is pacing up and down in his quarters. He was certain there'd be a few gold pieces sewn in there somewhere. The reel of thread seemed promising.

The captain is still feeling the cuffs and hems. The thick fabric feels almost like cardboard. There's no sign of any coins, jewellery, or pearls stashed in the seams. But the clothes smell like they came from a fish market. Why do the boy's clothes smell so strongly of the sea?

He picks up the jacket one last time, holds it up in front of the window with both hands, and takes a deep breath. The smell is definitely coming from the jacket. The fabric is soaked in seawater. There are even streaks of white scales.

Gardel buries his nose into the collar, his eyes wide open. Suddenly, on the right shoulder of the jacket where the fabric is wettest, he sees little black spots begin to appear.

He takes a razor blade from the tabletop and begins to cut the seams around the epaulette. He works with the skill of a tailor. As a child, Lazarus Gardel earned his stripes working with the master sailmaker on one of the king's schooners. He would stitch up the sails while battles were raging on deck. He learnt to master the wind, manipulate the sails, and handle a razor blade all at once.

With a few flicks of the wrist, Gardel has taken apart half of the jacket. As he removes the lining, his eyes light up. There in the thick fabric is a sheet of paper, stained with black ink and folded in half.

The captain takes the paper in his hands.

It could be a letter from a lover, a late father's will, perhaps a cousin's address to which the boy's things should be returned if he dies. The usual things found in sailors' clothes. But Lazarus Bartholomew Gardel knows himself. His intuition didn't bring him this far just for a prayer card or the portrait of a young girl.

He unfolds the paper. The ink is a little smudged and has begun to bleed through the fabric of the jacket. The text on the parchment is legible, but the message is a perfect mystery.

Gardel sucks on his tongue, squinting at the writing.

Right in the middle of the blank page, there's a drawing of a bull's head. The tips of the horns are almost touching above the head, which in turn is framed by four arrows, indicating north, south, east, and west. It's a sort of compass rose in the form of a bull's head, only the four directions have been reversed. North is indicated at the bottom.

In the space between the horns, there's a strange little skull peering back at Gardel.

Gardel lets out a puzzled little grunt. There are also three lines of text at the very bottom that have taken a battering from the sea.

The first line consists of a series of half erased letters, the last of which are still just about visible:

. . . ET-NAV-REX

The line below contains just two words, in English: Help yourself.

The ink has run badly on the third line. It looks as though it's a signature. Gardel takes the paper over to the window and holds it up to the dim evening light. That's when he spots the name on the paper, an insolent signature scrawled in black arabesques: Luc de Lerna.

Lazarus Bartholomew Gardel's legs collapse beneath him. He staggers over towards the alcove where his bed is and sits down. The parchment is trembling in his hands.

He has just discovered a map of the sort left behind by pirates before they disappear. Mysterious directions leading to their loot. But the signature before Gardel's eyes belongs to the wealthiest, most legendary pirate of all. His name will haunt Gardel for many long, sleepless nights. It's the signature of Luc de Lerna, the thousand-headed pirate.

10

Walking a Tightrope

It's the middle of the night. Jacques Dubois, the carpenter, has just lit a lamp in the room Joseph Mars is locked in. He saluted Joseph as he entered, as though he weren't expecting to find him there.

Dubois has left Abel Lebon standing guard in front of the door while he takes measurements with his measuring rod. Outside, the wind has dropped, and the sea is calm. The ship is gliding peacefully through the night.

"What are you doing?" Joseph asks after a long silence.

"I'm working out how much wood I'll need," says Dubois.

Really, he could have started his work at the other end of the ship, but the carpenter is curious about this boy, who somehow ended up hanging from the mast like a bat, his pockets full of diamonds.

"How much wood you'll need for what?" asks Joseph.

"That's none of your business."

"I heard you saying the old carpenter died."

This time Dubois stops. He looks at Joseph, who's sitting on the floor, hugging his knees to his chest.

"Yes," Dubois replies. "He died a few days before we set sail. His name was Clement Bassompierre. He and his apprentice were found in the port of La Rochelle."

"His apprentice?"

"His fifteen-year-old apprentice."

Dubois crouches down and places his lamp on the floor. He lifts the glass and attempts to cut the wick without extinguishing the flame.

"They must have been working really hard. I know what it's like. It wasn't a new ship. They redid the whole frame, changed the masts, the yardarms, the floorboards of the lower deck. They even had to line the entire hull."

"Why?"

"Because of the shipworm that always strikes on the coast of Guinea. The copper lining alone must have cost twenty thousand pounds. It was all finished. They'd even put the final coat of tar on the copper. They did an excellent job."

Dubois lowers the lamp and looks at Joseph.

"They say the pair of them got drunk and fell off a footbridge in the port. I don't believe it. No more than I believe a boy can accidentally end up hanging from the shrouds at daybreak . . . "

Up on deck, the ship's bell rings out four times. It's time to change shifts. Some of the sailors have to get up. Others can finally rest. The two watches take turns to monitor the ship's progress throughout the voyage.

"So what do you believe?" asks Joseph.

"I don't believe anything. My job is to make sure the ship stays in one piece. That's all."

Dubois mutters something else that Joseph doesn't quite catch. Then he lifts the lamp high above his head.

"How big do you think this room is?"

"I don't know," Joseph replies.

"It's smaller than the captain's," says Dubois, "which is just above. Can't be more than 250 square feet. How many captives can be kept in here?"

"One. And even that's too many."

"Sorry?"

"One captive," repeats Joseph. "Me."

"You do know where we're going, don't you?"

"Yes."

"By winter, there'll be eighty people between these four walls. Women and children. There'll be one hundred more women in the steerage. And three hundred and twenty men at the ship's bow, in front of the mainmast."

"I know," says Joseph.

"Five hundred in total."

"I know."

But he doesn't really know. There's a huge dark cloud hanging over this voyage. Joseph has just set foot on a floating prison. It's a slave ship, whose purpose is to bring back captives from Africa. Yet Joseph is acting as though there will be nothing more on board than bags of coffee or barrels of sugar.

Since the beginning, he hasn't wanted to think about any of this. He has one goal in mind, and nothing can distract him from it.

"To fit eighty women in this room," Dubois continues, "I'll have to build two platforms, each ten feet wide, which will create a sort of balcony on each side. There'll be two layers for the captives in here and on the lower deck, too."

"That," he adds coldly, not wanting to show any emotion, "is why I need wood."

Joseph looks at him, wide-eyed. The ceiling is so low he can barely stand. If new platforms are added, the captives will have to lie down between the planks of wood to fit.

"Thirty inches high," says Dubois, as though reading Joseph's mind. "For several months."

"That's not my problem," says Joseph. "Who took my jacket?"

The carpenter is too smart to buy Joseph's feigned indifference. He holds the lamp up to the boy's face.

"What are you doing here, my boy?"

"I might ask you the same," replies a voice behind the carpenter. "Tell me, Dubois. What are you doing here?"

Dubois turns around. With a nod of his head, he salutes the captain, who has just entered.

"I'm taking measurements. We're going to need more wood."

"You'll manage," says Gardel. "Take apart the rowboat and the jolly boat if necessary. And the chicken coop. Now get out of here, you son of a barnacle! And give me that lamp."

The carpenter leaves the lamp on the floor and walks quietly towards the door.

Joseph examines Gardel's face in the dim light. The captain has a sparkle in his eye, just as Joseph was hoping he would.

Something's happened.

The door slams shut. He hears the clicking of the three latches.

Gardel throws the ball of clothes to Joseph and leans against the door, his thumbs in his waistcoat pockets.

"You're lucky. I managed to find your clothes."

"Thank you."

"They may be small, but they're made from good cotton. The surgeon could've made bandages out of them. The cook was using them to wrap fish."

"It doesn't matter," says Joseph. "It's more about the sentimental value."

Gardel smiles.

"You'll have to do something about the smell. It's hard to shake the smell of fish. I put the needle and thread back in the pocket. You'll have a bit of mending to do."

Joseph picks up his clothes and unfolds them. He looks at the unstitched fabric and turns towards Gardel, who has begun to laugh.

The light is shining on the captain's body, but it stops at his shoulders. Joseph can't see his head. It looks as though he's been beheaded, and the laughter is coming from the beyond.

Finally, Gardel comes up to him. He crouches down and whispers:

"I'm going to tell you a secret."

Joseph tries to turn away, but the captain grabs him by the neck and continues to whisper in his face.

"Don't ever underestimate people. That's my advice to you, though it won't be any use now. My name is Lazarus Bartholomew Gardel."

He gets right up to Joseph's ear.

"Lazarus Bartholomew Gardel. Do you hear? The name alone is enough to make any thief from Nantes to Saint-Domingue run a mile. But you? You weren't the slightest bit concerned."

Joseph doesn't answer.

"If I don't know a man's name, even if he looks like a nobody, I treat him like a genius . . . like the king of thieves."

Gardel continues.

"The king of thieves. Do you hear? Never underestimate people."

The captain gets up, brushing the dust from his clothes.

"And my instinct was right. My reward will be worth more than your weight in gold and precious stones."

He pauses for a moment.

"Where did you get that parchment?"

"What parchment?"

"Cut the act."

There's a silence.

"If I told you, what would you do with me?"

"Answer me!" Gardel yells. "Where did you get that parchment?"

Joseph has never underestimated the captain. He knows there's a never-ending supply of gunpowder in that man's head. He's always on the brink of exploding.

"I got it in Amsterdam a year ago," he replies. "I found it in a sailor's clothes."

"Who was the sailor?"

"Samuel Braams. He's dead."

Gardel doesn't react. But Joseph knows how important this name is in relation to Luc de Lerna's map.

"Samuel Braams? How can you be sure he's dead?"

"I'm the one who buried him."

"That doesn't mean anything."

Joseph looks up. Gardel continues.

"Braams is like his master, Luc de Lerna. And like Luc's master, Black Bart. They're invincible. Twenty times their heads have been hung at the entrances to ports around the world. Twenty different heads, hanging by the hair, their names written in huge letters to deter any pirate who might dare follow in their footsteps."

Joseph listens as Gardel concludes his story.

"The real Luc always ends up re-emerging from the sea mist beneath the four masts of his schooner."

"I'm telling you he's dead."

"How do you know?"

"I've searched everywhere for him."

"Why?"

"Same reason as you. To decipher his message."

"And?" says Gardel, trying to hide his curiosity.

"And I'm making progress."

"What kind of progress?"

Joseph hesitates for a few seconds before he begins.

"Samuel Braams was Luc de Lerna's first mate for thirty years. In the end, they were captured together."

"Spare me. I've already heard the story." Gardel heads towards the door. Joseph picks up the pace.

"Luc was hanged by the British in Barbados, but Braams was freed on the condition that he denounce ten pirates and give up their whereabouts."

"I know all this, boy."

"But it's not true."

The captain stops.

"Samuel Braams wasn't freed," Joseph explains. "He escaped. But it suited the British better to say he gave them the information. It was the best way to get him bumped off by his friends."

"So?"

"This time, it worked. He was killed in Amsterdam while trying to get a ship fitted out. His murderers didn't find anything on his person. But Braams was about to go and collect Luc de Lerna's treasure."

"And where do you come into this?"

"I was passing through. They told me to bury him and take his boots as payment."

"His boots?"

"Yes."

Gardel chews on his tongue. He closes one eye. Things are taking an unexpected turn.

"You found this in his boots?" he asks, brandishing the parchment.

"Yes."

The captain unfolds the paper and looks at it in silence.

"What's your name?" he asks, without looking up.

"Joseph Mars."

"So, Joseph Mars, you think you'll be capable of deciphering this?"

"Yes. I just need time."

The captain takes a step back into the shadows. He mutters a few words that Joseph can't make out.

He came into this cabin with the intention of finishing off the boy and keeping the promise of treasure for himself. But he also remembers his golden rule: never underestimate anyone. Joseph Mars has been working on Luc's parchment for a year. He's already come part of the way. What if the boy really is the king of thieves? An angel in disguise? You should always take advantage of an angel before burning its wings.

Just next to him, Joseph is staring into the lamplight. A single word is all it would have taken to trip him up. They say the key to lying is credibility. But that's not true. Nothing seems truer than the incredible. Surely Joseph couldn't have made up the story about finding Luc de Lerna's will in a dead man's boots? The statement was too incredible to be a lie. And Gardel bought it.

The door closes. The captain has taken the lamp with him. Alone in the dark, Joseph is relieved to find that he is still alive. For him, that's a lot to be happy about. Curled up in a ball, still hugging his knees tightly to his chest, he trembles as though he's just walked a tightrope across an abyss.

II

On Board

The next day, the door is flung open at dawn. It's Picard, the captain's first mate.

"Do you know how to navigate?"

"A little bit."

"There's no such thing as a little bit."

Picard gives him a sideways glance. Joseph notices he's missing an eye.

"Do you know how to navigate, yes or no?"

"Yes," says Joseph.

"Out."

"Me?"

"You'll be on the starboard side. Go and find Absalom. He'll be at the bow with Palardi, the surgeon. He'll give you work to do. I can't make head or tail of the captain's orders anymore."

"I'm hungry," says Joseph, pulling on his jacket, which he managed to sew up again during the night.

"Now's not the time. You'll have to wait."

Joseph leaves Picard in the room, climbs a flight of steps

leading to the officers' cabins, then continues up another set of steps just opposite.

Finally he gets to see her in the daylight with her sails set, gliding along in the wind in the middle of the ocean. Twenty-five dazzling sails. He turns around on the spot. It looks as though all the laundry from a convent or a boarding school for young girls has been hung out in the sun. Ten thousand square feet of sails stretched taut on the masts. Flying along behind the ship is the huge white flag of merchant vessels. The creaking of the hull and the masts is drowned out by the whistling of the wind, the sprays of water shooting up as the ship carves through the ocean, and the cries of a few intrepid coastal birds. An entire forest must have been felled to build this ship. Oaks, elms, and poplars—thousands of trees all gliding through the middle of the ocean.

The Sweet Amelie is over a hundred feet long and thirty feet wide. Joseph walks along the gangways that run parallel to the rowboat suspended above the deck. Anyone who saw him would think he already knew the ship like the back of his hand. He looks up towards the sky. There's a sailor at the top of one of the masts, one hundred feet above the sea. He looks like an insect resting on a bed sheet in the sun.

Joseph slows down when he spots the two men Picard told him to go and find at the bow of the ship. Just behind them, he can see the hair and shoulders of the ship's figurehead poking out. The bust is sculpted from walnut wood and painted in Naples yellow. The sculpture is of fourteen-year-old Amelie Bassac, Ferdinand Bassac's only daughter, wearing a nightshirt and bobbing up and down on the waves. She's the one the ship is named after: *The Sweet Amelie*.

The two officers watch as Joseph approaches them.

"Are you Joseph Mars?" asks Absalom.

"Yes."

"We almost didn't recognise you, now you're the right way up," the other man jokes, studying him.

"I was told you have work for me."

"Dubois said you know the ropes of his trade."

Joseph doesn't react. Why would the carpenter say such a thing?

"For the time being, you'll be working with him."

"In less than two months, we'll have arrived at the coast of Guinea. The ship needs to be ready."

"You'll have your work cut out for you," the surgeon adds unhelpfully.

"Go down the steps. You'll find him on the lower deck."

Joseph salutes the men by touching his forehead with one thumb, as though tipping an invisible cap. He climbs down from the forecastle and slips through the large open hatch on the deck. He just manages to catch a few words of what the officers are saying above him:

"He must have some kind of magical powers. How did he pull that off?"

"I thought that'd be the last time we saw him alive. Gardel isn't one to forgive."

The sound of Jacques Dubois's cutting tool drowns out the men's voices. Joseph heads into the bowels of the ship.

"There you are," says Dubois.

There are two other men with him.

"Go and see the boy over there with the saw. He can't do anything right."

Joseph does as he's told. The boy in question is Abel Lebon, and he's glad to have some help. He likes this work, and he doesn't want them to take it away from him. Woodwork reminds him of being on land and helps him forget the violence of the ocean.

Lebon and Mars each take one side of the saw. They set to work, taking turns pulling the tool towards them. Each time they stop, they can hear the fresh water sloshing around in the barrels in the hold below. They take their time, breathing in the smell of sawdust. Then, finally, their eyes meet, and they get back to work.

It's only been a few days, but the sailors are already getting into the swing of things on the ship. Everyone knows that this first stretch is the best part of the endless journey that will take them to Africa, then to the islands of America, then back to the coast of Europe.

There are currently only forty men on board. A warship of the same size would be carrying three hundred men. In a few months' time, if everything goes according to plan, there will be around six hundred people on board. So they have to enjoy the clean air and space while they can. *The Sweet Amelie* is like a large building site that the sailors are discovering bit by bit.

And they never stop. Picard is there to enforce the hellish schedule imposed by the captain. Polishing, waxing, tarring, scrubbing, carrying, climbing, tying, hoisting, hauling, furling . . . all on very little sleep and a poor diet, always at risk of being punished, always under the threat of the whip.

The captain has decided to sail directly south. He's not afraid of the pirates of Salé or Rabat, who attack any ships that sail too close to their arid coastline. Some ships take a cautious detour through the Canary Islands to the west for this reason. But Gardel doesn't believe in detours or caution. He's heading straight to Africa. He has faith in the dozens of sails pulled taut on the masts of his ship and the copper-lined hull accelerating its passage. He believes in speed.

Joseph wastes no time in telling the sailors he's made a pact with Gardel, in an attempt to explain his new-found liberty and presence on deck. He tells them he's not getting paid. By working for free as a cabin boy—a post that would normally cost Gardel twenty pounds a month—he'll have reimbursed the captain more than three hundred pounds by the time they get back to France.

Of course, this won't cover the price of the watch, and it won't even come close to making up for insulting the captain. So, because Joseph is able to read and write, Gardel is also making him to do administrative work in the chart room between his manual tasks. At least, this is what Joseph has told everyone. And sure enough, the sailors see Lazarus Gardel and Joseph Mars poring over the ship's logbook each day with several maps spread out in front of them. Joseph works alone when the captain is called elsewhere on the ship.

The rest of the time, Joseph has to keep pace with the other sailors. He knows he needs to blend in with everyone else on board. He knows that issues pertaining to privileges, clans, and jealousy are rife among sailors. He's faster and more efficient than many of the others, but he takes care to make the right mistakes at the right moments so that he gets his fair share of abuse and deprivation. Cabin boys are made to endure mockery and meanness, to be treated like plankton, to be reminded each time they attempt to hoist a sail that they're not capable of lifting so much as an anchovy.

So Joseph tries to be as average as possible. He pretends to drink a little brandy with the others, he cheats at gambling games, he sings terribly while he works.

But the real reason why they leave him in peace is that there's not a single piece of silver in his pockets. Not a penny. Everyone on board knows it.

And because he doesn't get any money, because his pockets are always empty, Joseph is worthless to them. His is the fate of the marginalised, the poor, the poets of this world. They become invisible in the eyes of others. They cease to exist.

To each of these sailors, Joseph shares the same status as the seagull perched in the shrouds, or Hercules the cat, who chases rats voluntarily and then warms himself by Cook's fire.

But when Joseph is alone with Gardel, he switches roles. In these moments, his job is to decipher Luc de Lerna's riddle. He pretends to be decrypting the message. His sole objective is to make himself indispensable for the entire journey, so he has to learn the art of taking his time, of taking out the keys one by one without ever handing over the whole bunch.

To begin with, he doesn't give anything away. Not a shred of progress in several weeks. This puts Gardel in a foul mood. He yells at Joseph, telling him he's useless, that he should have thrown him into Davy Jones' Locker.

"Anyone can turn over bits of paper under a magnifying glass!" shouts Gardel. "With the ship swaying like this, I could even do it with no hands!"

He grabs the boy by his hair, crushing his forehead against the nautical charts.

Joseph senses he won't be able to go on like this much longer. Then one night, his fears are confirmed when he's woken up at what he thinks might be his final hour.

It's the middle of the night. He tries to get up but realises he can't move. The sides of his hammock have been sewn together. He shouts for help. At that moment, the ropes attaching each end of the hammock to the beams are cut. He falls violently to the ground, wriggling like a worm. They drag him up on deck, trapped inside his body bag, and attach a hook to the foot of the hammock. He feels the wind through the fabric, hears the creaking of the pulleys up above him. They lift him up and plunge him into the water, the way that dead sailors are thrown into the sea in their hammocks to protect them from sharks. Then, after a few seconds, Joseph can feel himself being hoisted up by the feet. But with the canvas sticking to his mouth and nose, he doesn't even have time to take another breath before he's drowning again. This time, they keep him under for longer. The ship is travelling so fast, he could easily be torn from the hook. After submerging him a third time, they finally bring him back on deck, barely conscious.

Captain Gardel shoos away the two terrified sailors who helped him carry out this act of torture. He takes out a knife and cuts the hammock at one end, as though slicing open a piece of parchment paper to check on the fish baking inside. Joseph Mars' face appears. Gardel gets up and watches the boy squirm at his feet, livid and suffocating. He doesn't say a word. There's nothing to add to the warning he's given.

When Joseph is left alone again, he slowly gathers up the remains of his hammock, sniffling, before dragging himself through a hatch. He goes to hide in the small hold near the mainmast where the spare sails are stored and lies down in this nest, still trembling with fatigue, fear, and cold.

The next day, as the rain pours down on the ship, he resolves to take action right away. It's now or never. If he doesn't do anything today, it'll be too late.

It's eight o'clock in the evening. Gardel is dining with his general staff in the great cabin at the stern of the ship. Gathered around the table by his side are Picard and a few lieutenants. There's also Palardi the surgeon, Absalom the boatswain, and Morel, one of the two young trainee officers in the merchant navy, who is sometimes invited to dinner because he has stories to tell and hardly eats a thing: the perfect guest.

Those who are invited to the captain's quarters always eat

well. It's hard to imagine that just outside, the rain is lashing down on the sails, flooding the deck, and that the sailors at work in the masts on the starboard side of the ship would do anything for a cup of boiling water with a little treacle in it.

The lamps illuminating the large cabin keep everyone inside warm. In amongst all the china and silverware, next to the half-finished soup, there's Irish beef brisket, two juicy chickens on a bed of candied chestnuts, and six open bottles of wine.

Lazarus Gardel knows how to put on a spread for his inner circle. He thinks this will compensate for darker hours when food becomes scarcer.

A ten o'clock, Cook comes to collect the dirty soup bowls. Morel, the trainee naval officer, is telling a story about a penguin that fell asleep in his berth on an expedition to Newfoundland. The great cabin erupts with laughter. Palardi the surgeon sounds as though he's about to choke. As he passes the captain, Cook bends down to whisper something in his ear:

"The boy is waiting outside the door."

Gardel doesn't move, half listens to Morel telling everyone how he got rid of the penguin, then wipes his mouth. He gets up as the raucous circus act continues.

"I hope it was a she-penguin at least!" shouts Palardi, setting them off again.

"I've no idea!" says Morel. "How can you tell? I didn't go to medical school like you, doctor!"

Gardel opens the door to find Joseph Mars standing there with soaking wet hair. He must have walked all the way through the storm to get to the stern of the ship. His body is still broken by the torture he endured the night before. Gardel closes the door to mask the sound of their laughter.

"Go on," says the captain, his napkin still tied around his neck.

"Tavel, the cooper, squandered his entire salary in a card game."

"He can bet his mother and children for all I care. Is this what you've come to interrupt me for?"

"I saw him place a gold coin on the table—"

The captain grabs Joseph by the collar. He couldn't care less about sailors' tales. There are two chickens waiting on the other side of the door, along with fine burgundy wine, juicy chestnuts dripping with sauce, and jovial conversation.

"Please listen, Captain," Joseph stammers. "The letters engraved on the back of his gold coin . . . they were the same as those written on the parchment."

Gardel slowly releases his grip on Joseph's collar. They've been working night after night on this single line of smudged ink. It's the most perplexing part of the riddle. He knows the last remaining legible letters off by heart now:

ET-NAV-REX

Gardel pulls a coin from his pocket. He holds it up to the lamp. Sure enough, the boy is right. The letters are there, right under King Louis XVI's nose, on every golden coin.

"It's the quantity of treasure," says Gardel.

"And there are several numbers hidden beneath the ink blots," Joseph adds.

Seeing Gardel's eyes light up, Joseph continues. "I think I might have also cracked the mystery of bull's head. Are you familiar with the Bible?"

From Gardel's expression, anyone would think he'd just been asked if he danced the rigadoon or played the hurdy-gurdy.

"In churches," Joseph explains, "Saint Luke is represented by a bull's head."

"Who are you talking about?"

"Saint Luke is one of the Four Evangelists."

"What's gotten into you, boy? Have you swallowed a priest? Who told you all this?"

"Dubois."

"So you've been talking to Dubois about our little secret?" barks Gardel.

"I wouldn't dream of it. He tells me these things because he's trying to teach me. He's built churches in Italy. The bull's head is Saint Luke . . . "

"Luc de Lerna," says Gardel, nodding his head slowly.

Then he pays Joseph the warmest, most enthusiastic compliment he's capable of mustering:

"All right."

He goes to leave Joseph, but just as he crosses the threshold, he turns back to face the boy.

"And . . . watch out for the cook," he murmurs. "I think he's hiding something."

"Cook?"

Joseph can't help himself from smiling.

"I don't know, it's just . . . traitors. I can smell them a mile off. If anyone tries to get in my way, I take them out. I crush them. I obliterate them."

With that, the captain leaves.

Joseph Mars is left alone, lips blue, feet like blocks of ice, hair dripping. He's happy to have bought himself some time with this revelation, but he doesn't want poor Cook to fall victim to Gardel's lust for gold.

Joseph goes down to the hold. Rather than going back to the ship's bow where his mended hammock awaits him, he takes a lamp. Because at this hour, he can finally stop running across the deck in the storm and climbing the yardarms to set the sails. This is when his third life begins. His real life. The one that nobody else knows about.

He weaves through the chests of glassware and fabrics, between the copper and earthenware bowls, and goes down into the double hull of the ship's hold amidst the dried beans, biscuits, barrels of food, and drinking water. He's looking for something. He opens up trunks and rifles through piles of sacks, searching every last corner of the ship.

Because the only treasure he's seeking cannot be found on a piece of paper. It isn't buried in a hole on some distant shore. It's not the fortune of Luc de Lerna, or the dreaded Captain Kidd, Captain de la Buse, Jack Rackham, Black Bart, or any other pirate.

No. It's much simpler than that, and he knew it before he even set foot on the ship. Hidden somewhere on board the ship are four and a half tons of pure gold.

12

The Little Horse

There are a dozen men crouching beneath the trees, staring at the tracks in the mud. For a long time, nobody speaks. They part the grasses to observe the tracks, trying to understand where they lead and who they belong to.

The men are wearing strange clothes: trousers with gold stripes, hats of all different shapes and sizes, various pieces of mismatched uniforms. Some are wearing a shawl on their shoulders, while others are carrying a bag or an old rifle on a strap. Many of them are bare-chested, showing off the dark brown skin of the Ashanti warriors from the Kumasi hills.

They've never been this far from home. They've been gone for such a long time. It's late. The evening sun is beginning to peek through the leaves of the trees.

Two of the men start talking. One is very young and seems very sure of himself.

"It's a Dongola horse," he says to the others.

"We can't be sure," another man replies. "It has iron on its feet like the horses of white men."

"I'm telling you I'm sure," the young man says coldly. "It's a Dongola, maybe four or five years old. The rider must be fairly light."

"That's enough, Awoshi."

"It's missing an iron shoe on its front hoof."

The other man is getting annoyed. He's the chief, and he's thirty years older than Awoshi. He's wearing a white powdered wig, which is supposed to be a mark of authority, but instead it makes him look as ridiculous as those white men in the courts of Versailles and Vienna.

The men aren't looking at the chief. They're staring at young Awoshi in admiration. He's right. The front hoof doesn't have an iron shoe on it. They can all see it now that Awoshi has pointed it out. But how does he know the age and breed of the horse, as well as the weight of its rider, just by looking at the shape and depth of the tracks in the ground?

"We'll catch them," says the chief, unperturbed. "We'll have to follow the tracks when night falls. In the meantime, we'll sleep beneath these trees."

He looks up at the foliage, but what he doesn't see, lying flat against a horizontal branch just above him, is a shadow lurking in the darkness. Alma just has the time to lower her eyelids to hide the dazzling whites of her eyes.

For many days and nights, she's been following Cloud's tracks, her bow strapped to her back. Whenever she gets lost, she lets her body guide her, and eventually, it brings her back to the tracks. The power that took over her when she left the Valley of Isaya has stayed with her this whole time. It helps her find her way and hunt down food when she's hungry.

Sometimes, she barely recognises herself. She's able to shoot a little lapwing zigzagging through the air three hundred feet away with a single arrow. When she isn't hunting, she pilfers scraps from the pantries of wild beasts in the dead of night. She can tell if water is drinkable or deadly just by looking at it. At night she sleeps up in the trees. In the day, she rests up on the rocks and looks into the distance at the path ahead before setting off again.

She came upon this group of men a few hours ago. She'd begun to sense their presence in the air from a distance. As she flitted through the tall branches, jumping from tree to tree behind the men, the leaves rustled gently beneath her as though she were nothing more than an evening breeze passing through.

The men have finally settled in the grasses just below her. They're unrolling leaves containing a sort of translucent dough, which they then sit down to eat. They're speaking a language that Alma has never heard before. She manages to catch a word or phrase here and there: "a long time" or "tired." From what she can gather, they haven't yet found what they're searching for. Their hats are lying on the ground next to them. There's a whole range of styles, from chef's toques to tricorns to feathered felt hats.

Young Awoshi has been leaning against a tree trunk cleaning his rifle. Now he's heading towards the chief. He sits down next to the white wig lying next to his leader. It looks like a sleeping animal. The full moon is rising, but the sun is still lingering in the sky. Awoshi gazes into the distance without saying a word while the chief lights a small horn pipe. Alma is just above them, hiding in the leaves of the tree.

"We've been walking for a full moon cycle," says Awoshi.

"We have."

This time, Alma is able to understand their words, which drift upwards with the smell of their tobacco. They're speaking one of the languages she learnt from her father.

"Chief," Awoshi continues. "I don't understand. You search for days, then you find horse tracks and decide to set off in the wrong direction?"

"It's not the wrong direction. I'm going to follow the tracks. The Okos may have learnt the science of horses."

"Chief, if it's an Oko on the horse's back, you shouldn't follow."

The young man calls his leader "chief," but it's the only hint of respect detectable in his words. He's speaking to the man as though he's a child.

"If you follow the tracks," says Awoshi, "you'll only find one person. But if we go back the way we came, there may be many more. We have to find their hideout."

The chief nervously taps his pipe against the roots of the tree to empty the ash out.

"There is no hideout," he says.

He's speaking very quietly in a language that the others don't seem to understand. This lecture is only for the young man.

"Awoshi, you're the one who brought us all the way out here. Where are the captives you promised us? You're going to get us lost. You'll follow the tracks with us. That's an order. Besides, many say the Okos died out a long time ago. We have to return home before we reach the edge of the world."

His companion doesn't reply immediately. He continues to gaze out at the horizon. Above them, Alma shudders against the bark of the tree. Whether they follow the tracks or go back the way they came, their pathway will eventually lead to her loved ones.

"Listen," Awoshi says to the chief, quietly. "When you give the orders in the village, I obey. Back home, I would gladly die for you."

"Good."

"But here, so far away, it's as though I can't hear your voice, as though it stayed behind in the village. No matter how carefully I listen, I cannot hear you."

The chief turns to him with a worried expression.

"Do you understand, Chief? When you speak, I hear nothing. So now you're going to listen to me. I'm going to take two men right now and head in the direction of the rising sun. You can keep going along your path. True, you might find yourself a captive to sell on the coast. You can share your earnings with the rest of your eight men. You'll have enough to buy another wig so you can bring more shame upon your people. Okay?"

Awoshi despises anything that brings shame upon his people. His voice carries the pride of the Ashantis, who have reigned for centuries over an immense territory and can raise an army of eight thousand at the drop of a hat if they so choose.

The chief goes to get up, but Awoshi stops him.

"Don't say a word against me to the others. If they're forced to choose, they'll follow me. They'll leave you here alone. So I'm going to give you a gift . . . "

The chief waits in terror to hear what's in store for him.

"As a parting gift, I'll let you get up and announce in a loud voice that you're sending me away with two men. If I allow you to do that, they might just believe that you're still their chief."

Alma watches as the old chief hesitates for a moment, before putting his pipe away in his belt, hands shaking. Then finally he gets up and picks up his wig, brushing the hair out in the wrong direction. He walks over to his men and issues a few orders, his voice cracking. Two of the men go to join Awoshi as the others look on.

"As you requested," says Awoshi, getting up, "I'll retrace our steps. I'll find the last of the Okos."

He steps forward and grips the chief's hand tightly in his own. He gives an exaggerated bow of respect, bringing the old man's trembling fingers towards his forehead.

Alma watches as Awoshi and his two hunters head towards

the Valley of Isaya. Still crouching on the branch, she wonders about the word she just heard: "Okos." Back at home, the word simply meant "people" and was used to refer to their family, since nobody else existed.

The men had also said the word "captives."

It sounded as if they were talking about a kind of inedible prey. Alma wonders why anyone would want to catch something if not to eat it or use it to keep warm. What do they do with their captives?

She listens to the men whispering beneath her tree. They seem to be quietly complaining about their chief. The departure of the three hunters has sown doubt among them.

Alma doesn't dare move. Which direction should she take? Towards Lam or back to the valley? She thinks of her parents and Soum, oblivious to the danger they're in. She hopes the cliffs and thorns will protect them.

Alma has already made her choice. She'll never abandon Lam. Who will find him if not her? Who will bring him back home? Lam has no cliffs, no ravines to defend him. All he has is Cloud's hooves to carry him along.

"Horse."

She finally knows the name of the zebra with no stripes.

"Horse."

That's what the men called him. In her tree, she says the word a third time, moving her lips without making a sound.

"Horse."

There are so many words she's yet to learn. Some of them tender, some of them cruel. Some she'll wish she never had to learn.

Alma looks down the path that's waiting for her. She watches the moonlight streaming through the leaves and pretends that somewhere in the distance, she can already see the little horse.

13
Moses Shackle

It's one of the best-kept secrets in all of the plains.

They say the lion never hunts, that he leaves the work to the lionesses. The pride of lionesses goes hunting in the grasses while the lion waits for them in the shade. They ambush or exhaust their prey before devouring it in the blazing sun. Then the lion can be seen joining the pride, stretching before claiming his share.

But what nobody knows is that each night, the lion heads off into the tallest grasses in secret to hunt alone. And nobody will ever know because it happens in the pitch-black night, and once the lion leaps out to claim its prey, the only ones who could possibly testify are already dead.

The three men walk in single file with Awoshi leading the pack. It's been a few days since they left the others. The moon is still huge. It's risen right in front of them, filling up a whole section of sky.

The men weave through the lush green forest. There are bushes on either side grazing their shoulders. This is the first time they've seen the forest in weeks.

One of the men walking behind Awoshi is around the same age as him. Barely twenty years old. His name is Baako. He has a rifle slung across his shoulder, and he's carrying a knife on his belt. Baako's father, Eeko, is walking behind them, sharp and lively as a lizard. He walks barefoot, a red cotton cloth tied around his waist. Oddly enough, he's wearing the large beret of a long-lost regiment on his head and is carrying a dragoon officer's sabre.

Awoshi, their new chief, bends down from time to time to observe the horse's tracks in the moonlight. Not a drop of rain has fallen to muddy their path. The tracks are set in the hard ground. The horseman seems to have been changing direction at random. This strengthens Awoshi's conviction that they should trace the tracks back to where they came from rather than following them in the direction they're heading.

Sometimes, their single-file line stretches out. The two young hunters speed on ahead. They can just hear the sound of Eeko's voice humming softly somewhere behind them to the rhythm of their footsteps.

This is the best time of day for walking. They've pushed through their tiredness. The moonlight covers their bodies like a glistening oil. It feels as though there's no resistance in the air, as though they could fly if they kicked the ground hard enough. The moon has swallowed up all the stars. The only other light comes from the sparkling yellow eyes of the bushbabies—little animals with eyes almost bigger than their bodies.

The three men are walking beneath a canopy of trees. The path is getting wider, the air more humid. The moonlight pokes its way through the undergrowth. The foliage creates a ceiling above their heads, trapping the fragrant scent coming from the earth.

Suddenly, Awoshi's ears prick up. He stops in his tracks.

Just behind them, Eeko stops singing right in the middle of a chorus.

The two young men turn around in the darkness. Barely eighty feet from them, a pale mass has emerged, carrying the old man's body. With its jaw planted firmly in his hip, a lion is silently shaking Eeko like a cat toying with a mouse. Baako takes aim with his rifle but hesitates before shooting.

"No," whispers Awoshi.

If he shoots, he might accidentally hit Eeko. But more than anything, Awoshi knows that from this distance, a shot will only injure the four-hundred-pound beast and turn it against them.

Baako lowers his rifle. He watches on, trembling.

Suddenly a great commotion breaks out. It's like a dream scene: the two men watch as a black winged figure falls silently from the canopy of trees above the lion and shoots. Two loud bangs and two flashes of light explode all at once. A man rolls through the grasses with a smoking pistol in each hand, his open coat falling down at his sides.

The lion collapses in one direction and Eeko's body in the other.

Baako rushes over to his father. He cuts through the cloud of smoke billowing in the night.

Eeko is still breathing. Baako speaks to him. He moves aside slightly to let the moonlight fall upon his father's body. He lifts up the bloodstained clothes and bends over his father's wound.

"My son," the old man stammers. "Is it all over?"

Baako can't believe his eyes. He wafts the smoke away with one hand.

"It's all over. But not for you . . ."

The wound isn't deep. The scabbard of the sabre is bent in half. It saved Eeko's life.

"You're so light, so withered by the years that the lion was able to carry you as if you were his cub."

Baako's voice is calm. He smiles.

"It hurts," says Eeko in a small, childlike whimper.

"He couldn't find any meat on you! You've escaped with nothing but a few teeth marks."

The old man groans. It's not clear whether he's laughing or crying. He takes his son's hand. They can feel the warmth coming from the lion's body nearby.

Awoshi keeps his rifle aimed at the man wielding the pistols, who's now brushing himself off in the grasses. He's wearing a black coat and a gold-brimmed hat.

The man is Mosi, Alma's father. He's put his pistols down and is looking straight ahead into the night.

"Where did you come from?" asks Awoshi.

Mosi points vaguely.

"What do you want?"

Mosi doesn't answer. He'd been sleeping up in the branches, having just escaped the very same lion. That's when he heard the three men approaching. He'd have left them to go on their way if it hadn't been for the old man getting attacked.

Awoshi goes over to Mosi and kicks the pistols away with one foot so that Mosi can't reach them. He's wondering how he'll get the shackles on this man.

Meanwhile, Baako is helping his father sit up.

"See? By tomorrow you'll be walking again!"

"I don't have the strength anymore," he says, moaning in pain. "I don't want to know where the horse came from anymore."

Mosi closes his eyes. Now he understands. These Ashanti hunters are heading for the valley.

"Who are you?" Awoshi asks.

Mosi still hasn't said a word. Has the world really changed so little in his absence?

"No one strays this far from the coast," Awoshi tells his men. "Only the merchants of the desert walk these paths. And one or two men in hiding . . . "

"So which are you?" Mosi asks finally. "Did you come from the desert, or are you in hiding?"

The smoke from the gunshots has dispersed into the air. Suddenly, Eeko's deep voice cuts through the night.

"Moses Shackle . . . "

The old man has risen to his feet. He's leaning on his son for support. There's a streak of blood across his forehead.

Eeko is pointing his finger at Mosi.

"I recognise this man. His name is Moses Shackle."

14

The Path of Another Hunter

Awoshi has heard this name many times before. There was once a man who held every slave trader along the coast, from Old Calabar to the Lagoons of Assinie, in the palm of his hand. He was a young Fante who lived like a white man and had a place at the table of every governor of every fort. He was the most formidable man hunter of all.

"I saw him just before he disappeared," Eeko continues. "We'd just sold him some captives. I remember him very well."

"You're Moses Shackle?" asks Awoshi. "They say he died hunting down the last of the Okos."

"There are no more Okos," says Mosi. "It's over. I spent a long time searching. I crossed the desert and went all the way to the sea. That's when I stopped."

Awoshi is looking at Mosi. He certainly looks like a Fante. Since the dawn of time, the Fante have been the enemy of his people, but the necessities of trade have brought them closer together. The Ashantis take captives from the land, and the Fante are responsible for selling them to the forts and ships on the coast.

"What was the price of Okos back then?" asks Baako.

"One hundred barrels of powder for a male when we dealt directly with the ships. Or one and a half million shells. Women were worth much more."

"That's the price of ten captives today," says Baako.

"Some say that once they were caught, they had no chance of surviving," Eeko whispers to his son.

"But the ships were already long gone by that point," Moses replies. "And each time the captains came back for the next load, they seemed to have forgotten that detail. They'd see an Oko at Fort Ouidah or on the white sands of Anomabo and lose their minds. They'd do anything to get their hands on them."

Awoshi is listening to Moses. He's already given up on the idea of capturing him. Men like Shackle scare the merchants on the coast. They know too much. They lead revolts on the ships. And even if they make it across the sea and become slaves, sometimes their families manage to bring them back.

"You seem to remember it well," says Awoshi.

"I settled on a peaceful shore on the other side of the desert. I've spent twenty years planting a garden and hunting doves."

"And now?"

Mosi goes quiet for a moment.

"I don't know yet," he says finally. "I'm trying to work out what I'm going to do next. I followed these horse tracks all the way back. But it was no use. All they lead to is a burnt down village."

Baako watches as Awoshi bends down to pick up Mosi's pistols.

"First you saved the old man," Awoshi begins, handing the Fante hunter his weapons back. "Now you're telling us which way to go. That doesn't sound like the Moses Shackle I've heard about.

"I don't know what they say about me."

"They say you had no mercy."

"I've been away a long time."

Mosi gathers up his pistols.

"I wouldn't waste your time on these tracks," he says. "It's just a horse that's escaped from a village in flames. Why have you come all this way? Are there no more captives to be found nearer to home?"

"You have to search far and wide to find them," says Awoshi.

"Some will sell their neighbours if they happen to cross paths," says Eeko. "They fill whole canoes and take them away. The river carries as many captives away to the coast as it does grains of sand. But it's never enough to satisfy the big ships."

"All these years you've been away, you knew none of this?" asks Awoshi.

"I was busy with my garden and my family."

"Why did you leave them?"

Mosi takes a few moments to reply.

"I've lost one of my children. That's why I'm here."

Awoshi looks directly into Mosi's eyes.

"How old?" he asks.

"Half your age. If you had happened to capture one of my children, I would've paid you a very high price."

"The price we would get for an Oko child?"

"More," replies Mosi.

There's a silence. Mosi gets up and tucks the pistols back into his belt.

"Are you heading back to the coast?" he asks.

"Yes. If you say there's nothing that way," Awoshi replies.

"I can assure you there isn't. Nothing but scorched earth and blackened trees."

"What about you?"

"I'm going to cut through this way," Mosi replies, pointing behind him. "I might find my child there. I'm going to Shama."

"Things have changed a lot there."

"Things will never change enough for me," says Mosi as he goes to leave. "I'm not the same person anymore."

Eeko still hasn't taken his eyes off the man who saved his life. He watches as he disappears into the night. Then he turns to his son, who appears to be waiting for his signal. Suddenly, Baako starts running after Mosi.

"Where's he going?" asks Awoshi.

"He's going to speak to him. I didn't thank him for saving my life."

Kneeling by the lion, Awoshi pulls out his knife. He's going to stock up on provisions for the rest of the journey.

"That's definitely the Moses Shackle I knew," says Eeko, sitting down. "And yet he seems to have washed his hands of his former self."

Awoshi wipes his knife clean in the grass.

"Don't believe that. Some things can never be washed away."

Not far off, Baako slows down as he catches up with Mosi.

"There's something my father wanted to tell you," he says.

Mosi turns to look at him.

"Something he wasn't able to say back there," says Baako, catching his breath.

There's a silence.

"The child you were talking about . . ."

"Yes?"

"My father saw a child of that age. Half my age."

Mosi freezes.

"It was during the night, a few days ago. Halfway through the moon cycle. Twelve of us had set up camp for the night. My father had left the others sleeping . . ."

Mosi listens carefully.

"That's when he saw the child washing in the stream."

There's another silence.

"I'm the only person he told," says Baako.

"Where? Where was this?"

"I don't know. We've changed direction three times. All I know is the child was walking free."

"Walking free," Mosi repeats. If Lam hasn't been captured, anything is possible.

"Why didn't your father tell the others?"

"Children . . ." Baako replies, as if the word alone were enough to explain his father's silence. "He doesn't like taking children as captives."

Baako remains silent for a moment, wondering what he would have done in his father's position. Then he continues.

"She was in the stream when he saw her . . ."

"She?" Mosi exclaims.

"Yes, it was a girl."

Mosi springs towards him.

"Tell me it was a boy he saw."

Baako doesn't say anything. The look on Mosi's face is scaring him.

"Tell me!"

"I could tell you it was a boy, but I'd be lying. Even without the moonlight, there's no way he'd have been mistaken. My father has the eyes of an eagle."

Mosi begins to shout at Baako.

"Your father didn't see me coming or notice the lion right

behind him, and you're telling me there's no way he was mistaken? Your father is an eagle with the eyes of a bat! It must have been my son he saw! How many children can there be wandering out here alone, so far from everything?"

Baako backs away, as though distancing himself from someone he's accidentally injured. Then he runs. He regrets having given this man a glimmer of hope only to destroy it.

By the time he reaches the others, his father is sleeping in the tall grasses. All around them, the forest has begun to purr away again, with its soft creaking and gentle humming.

He watches lovingly over his sleeping father. In this dangerous world, the elderly are respected not because they automatically become wise with age, but because those who grow to old age, those who survive, were the wisest from the beginning.

"We'll set off again tomorrow," Awoshi tells Baako.

"To the coast?"

"No."

"I thought you said . . ."

"Shackle was the one who said it, not me. We're going to continue."

"But he told us not to follow the horse's tracks."

Awoshi smiles.

"So you think I should follow the advice of Moses Shackle? If a thief opens up his hand to show me it's empty, I look to see what's in the hand behind his back. And when Moses Shackle tells me to go one way, I take the path that leads me in the opposite direction. We're going to follow those tracks right to the very end."

Awoshi smiles at the look of surprise on Baako's face. Poor Baako was already picturing their return to the village. He could already imagine sitting his father down at the foot of a tree to spend his last days in peace.

"Don't be afraid," says Awoshi, "He survived the beast's attack. He may well outlive you. But always remember what I told you: never follow the path shown to you by another hunter."

15

Gold and Rust

"Gold?" whispers Dubois. "What makes you think there'd be gold on this ship?"

Joseph Mars' ears prick up as he catches these words on his way down to the steerage. He slips behind an oak partition to listen. Just a few steps away, the carpenter is talking to Abel Lebon. Little squares of daylight stream through the wooden grate in the ceiling onto their bodies.

"If you're looking for gold," says Dubois, "you're in the wrong place. But if you wanted to open a grocery shop, hardware store, cobbler's, tavern, a business of any kind . . . that you could do."

Joseph remains hidden in the shadows.

"With everything that's stored beneath our feet, Lebon, you could fill a whole bakery, an armoury, a fabric or crockery store. You can find just about anything on this ship except gold."

Dubois turns around suddenly.

"Is that you, Mars?"

Joseph thought he was being discreet, but apparently not. He takes a step towards them, his hands in his pockets.

"Yes, it's me."

The carpenter seems to see and know everything. Joseph can't decide whether to be wary of this man or admire him.

"Come and give us a hand," says Dubois. "The cooper has been ill for ten days. He's sleeping in the rowboat suspended up on deck. It's being used as an infirmary of sorts. I'm trying to get some of his work done while he's away."

With Abel as his assistant, Jacques Dubois is assembling one of the barrels that spent the first part of the journey bundled up in the hold. Once the ship arrives on the coast of Guinea, these barrels will be filled up with drinking water to supplement the ship's reserves, since they'll need at least 40,000 gallons on board to reach the islands without the crew and the captives dying of thirst.

"So what about you?" the carpenter asks Joseph. "Are you looking for gold, too?"

"Just like every other sailor on Earth."

Joseph smiles to hide his discomfort. He didn't think before answering. Surely nobody would suspect he's been searching the ship for weeks now in the hope of finding four and a half tons of pure gold? Joseph Mars might act as though his head is up in space, but his mind is firmly fixed on the gold.

"That's not what I meant," cries Abel Lebon, awkwardly. "I was just saying that the captain will need gold to buy the captives once we get to the coast. So I was asking, out of curiosity, whether the gold is on board."

"Out of curiosity!" Dubois sniggers.

Abel shrugs.

"It doesn't work like that, Lebon," Dubois sighs. "For one thing, it'd be too easy for men like yourself or adventurers like Joseph Mars to get their hands on it."

"What do you mean, it doesn't work like that?" asks Joseph.

Dubois puts down his tools. Up in the great cabin, the officers have just been served their dinner. The rest of the crew have to make the most of the one moment of the day when they're not being monitored.

"Listen," says Dubois.

He sits down, folding his arms across his chest. The large pine column he's leaning against is the bottom of the mainmast, whose roots plunge through the deck, cutting through the ship to its keel.

"I'm going to let you in on a little secret about this business. Not one ounce of gold ever crosses the borders of the kingdom."

He takes a deep breath.

"The gold has to be made invisible first."

"Invisible?"

"They make it disappear. Scatter it."

Dubois makes a little gesture with his hand to represent the gold magically vanishing into thin air. Abel and Joseph lean in closer, but neither of them dares to sit down.

"They start by pumping wealth into the shipyards where the vessels are built. They pay the foresters, lumber merchants, artisans, and everyone working in the port, then they pay the factories in France and abroad, the manufacturers of confectionery, bad-quality rifles, taffeta, silk, brandy, as well as the knife makers, coppersmiths, and tinsmiths. They buy everything in large quantities. That's how they get rid of the gold. It then travels up from the ports via rivers and streams, through the veins of the country, while the goods are sent back to the ports. There, the ships are transformed into big, floating bazaars. Wooden treasure troves filled up to the portholes. The ships set sail, and when they arrive in Africa, the captains exchange their goods for captives."

Abel and Joseph listen with bated breath. The night before, while they were working down in the hold, Dubois was telling them about the structure of a cathedral, comparing it to the architecture of a bird's nest. He manages to break down every subject with the same precision, the same passion.

"But before leaving," he continues, "they also give a lot of gold to insurance companies, who then sell it to other insurance companies in turn. If the ship sinks along with all its cargo, the shipowners are reimbursed for the whole lot, and they can start all over again. Like magic." He makes the same gesture with fingers as thick as hammer handles.

"It seems like a win-win situation."

"But . . . ?" asks Abel.

"But that's not to say the winnings are equal," says Dubois, turning to Joseph.

"You, for example. If I understand correctly, you're not getting paid. One day you'll have to tell me about your little arrangement with Gardel."

Everyone falls silent.

"But that's not the worst of it. There are some people who earn nothing and pay for everyone else."

"Who?" asks Abel.

"When almost everyone is getting rich, somebody has to pay. They pay for the sails and the hull. They pay the insurers of Lloyd's in London. They even pay the butcher in La Rochelle who smokes the captain's meat . . ."

Now Dubois is on a roll.

"They pay for the materials, the crew. They pay your thirty-pound monthly salary, Lebon. They pay Lord Bassac, the owner of the ship. They pay for his horses, his tobacco, the fountains in his garden. They pay for his greenhouses filled with Spanish orange trees, his daughter's lace-up boots.

They pay for the stone used to build all the big houses you see in the ports. They pay for all the candlelit dinners the plantation owners enjoy on their islands, their orchestras, the leather in their whips. They're the ones paying each time a plantation owner generously throws a coin into the collection plate when they leave church. They pay for the food Cook gives to his trusty cat, Hercules. They pay the taxes that go back to Versailles, they pay for the feathers in the king's hat, his coaches, his mistresses, the wars he wages against England. They even pay for the little farm that Queen Marie Antoinette is building for herself, and the thatched roof of her dovecote. These people pay for everything. Yet they get nothing back."

"Who are they?" asks Lebon, amazed at the generosity of these benefactors. "What are their names?"

Dubois's eyes are glazed over. His voice is getting quieter.

"By now, they no longer have names. They're walking along dirt roads. They're locked up in cattle barns or in dungeons on the coast. In eight days' time, you'll see. We'll bring them on board, one by one. We'll cram them in here, three people per ten square feet. The only reason everyone else in this game can be winners is because they've lost everything. Everything down to their names and the names of their villages that no longer exist. They've lost their children. They have nothing left. And yet they pay for everything."

Joseph has forgotten to breathe. Only now is he beginning to comprehend what kind of world he's set foot in. He's also starting to suspect that Dubois isn't just another cog in this machine like the others.

The three of them remain silent. Abel is the first to speak. He tries to bring the story to its logical conclusion.

"Then the day they're sold in the islands, when the ship sets sail for La Rochelle, when there are no more captives aboard, that's when there'll finally be gold in the hold."

"Wrong again," replies Dubois. "The captives will be left stranded in Saint-Domingue in exchange for barrels of sugar, coffee, indigo, pepper, bags of cotton, but not a single gold coin will change hands. The captives are exchanged for what other slaves have collected from the plantations in the islands. The sugar cane, the coffee . . . it's the slaves who pay for it all with their sweat and their blood. So I'll say it again: if you're looking for gold, you will never find it here. It'll reappear at the end, back on good old French, Dutch, and British soil. The goods brought back there will be worth a fortune. And all that gold will be locked up in the banks and big houses."

Joseph watches Dubois get up. He's wondering what this man is doing in the midst of all this.

"I know what you're thinking, lad," says Dubois, his eyes shining. "Listen to me. It's been twenty years since I last set foot on a slave ship. I was done with all that. I'm here on behalf of some friends."

"Friends?" asks Joseph.

"I'm giving them a hand with something."

"Are they on board?"

"No. I'm doing this one last trip for them, and then that's it."

On the deck above, there's a great stampede of feet, followed by yelling, then complete silence.

"Go and see what's happening," says the carpenter.

The young men scamper off, leaving Dubois all alone with his barrel and his thoughts.

Joseph is the first to arrive on deck. He stops when he sees all the men gathered on the port side, leaning over the rail.

"What is it?" asks Abel, sticking his head out in turn.

"It's Africa," whispers Joseph.

And sure enough, a dark line has appeared on the horizon. Something feels different. The taste of hot earth fills their nostrils and mouths. The sailors remain speechless. Their eyes are fixed on the surface of the water and the horizon. Little islands of branches and coconuts drift along in the water, bobbing up and down against the hull.

"Look!" shouts one man.

On the crest of a wave, the black dorsal fin of a shark cuts through the water, followed by another.

Joseph hears a voice behind him murmuring with a strange sort of tenderness.

"Look at that. They've been waiting for us."

It's Lazarus Gardel. He says these words upon seeing the first of the sharks, like a hunter greeting his dogs when he arrives home from a long journey.

Even the white foam spurting out from the bow of the ship has changed colour. It's the colour of fire.

On the coast, the Senegal and Gambia Rivers are churning mud out into the ocean, tinting the water with hues of gold and rust.

16

A Glimpse of Hell

The surgeon emerges at the top of the ladder, yawning. He's just finished dinner. He's the last to join the others up on deck. Joseph sees him looking out at the horizon, before rushing over to Lazarus Gardel.

"Captain, do you see that over there? Just to the right of that dot?"

"Yes?"

"That's Gorée Island."

The captain doesn't react.

"Is that so?" he says.

"You're one hundred and twenty miles too far south. We must have passed Saint Louis days ago."

"Please go on, doctor," says the captain in a sickly tone. "Do continue your explanations. I'm simply fascinated."

"At Saint Louis, you would have found captives. But in Gorée . . ."

"Are you telling me that we'd be better off not making a little stop in Gorée?"

"Well, I'm sure the fort garrison would be pleased. The

soldiers must be rather bored. But in terms of business . . . if I may give you my opinion . . ."

"I'd love to hear your opinion, Palardi! Please tell me more about Africa and its trade."

The surgeon straightens his hat. He's acting modest, not having picked up on the captain's ironic tone. Nearby, Morel, the trainee naval officer, is trying to catch his attention.

"Well, I'm hardly an expert," Palardi continues, "but I'm happy to be of assistance."

"Assistance? Why, you're more than just assistance, Palardi, you're my saviour! So what you're saying is I'm more than fifty leagues off target? Do you hear that? Morel! Picard! Absalom! A marksman three sheets to the wind would have better aim than I do! Goodness gracious. Over a hundred miles too far south! I'm about as much use as a bit of flotsam."

Gardel puts his hand to his chest like a bad actor and turns towards his audience.

"What an amateur! Gentlemen, behold the pathetic excuse for a captain you are stuck with."

Palardi is beginning to tense up at the sight of this spectacle. The captain goes over to him.

"Tell me, good doctor . . ."

"Yes . . ."

"Let's imagine for a moment . . ."

"Yes?"

"Imagine I were to open up your stomach, very gently, to operate on your spleen or liver with the sail maker's scissors, right now, in front of everyone, then stitched you back up again with a fishing line."

Palardi swallows anxiously.

"Pardon me, Captain?"

"How would you feel about that?" asks Gardel.

"I . . . that's really more a job for . . ."

"For a surgeon?"

"Yes . . ."

"You're right. It is."

The captain acts as though he's about to go. Then he stops and turns back.

"So tell me, Palardi."

"Yes?"

"Are you the captain of this ship?"

He grabs the surgeon by the ear and lifts him up without raising his voice in the slightest.

"Are you?"

"No . . ."

"So why are you trying to explain my job to me? What is it that makes you think I don't know where I'm going?"

Palardi's feet are no longer touching the ground. He's groaning quietly in pain.

"I never, for one second, had the intention to stop in Saint Louis," says the captain. "I happen to know there's nothing to be found in that part of the coast right now. As for Gorée, three ships will soon be arriving there from La Rochelle. Then there'll be others coming from Nantes and Honfleur and they'll have to fight it out over two scrawny captives and a bit of yellowing ivory."

The captain finally lets go of the surgeon's ear. He turns around to speak to his crew.

"If anyone else has any advice about the route, raise your hand!"

He looks around at them, one by one.

"You may think it's almost over, but this is only the beginning. It'll be ten more days before we arrive in Elmina. Now listen carefully. We won't be setting our feet on solid ground a day before then. That is where we'll begin trading. We'll buy every last captive we find. Then we'll continue all the way down the coast. We'll go as far as the King of Congo's house, if need be, and then we'll keep going! Until there's not even enough room for a newborn baby in the hull of this ship, until not another breath of air can fit beneath this deck. Do I make myself clear?"

The sailors up in the shrouds are clinging to the masts, trying to keep themselves from fainting. The crew appears to have got the message.

"This ship must be ready in ten days. Up until now, some of you have been shirking. But in the days to come, I'll drag you out of your little hidey-holes one by one. You're going to work until you drop at my feet. I'd rather have you collapsing now than when we have five hundred captives on board. You've just spent two months in heaven. Now prepare yourselves for hell!"

Abel Lebon steadies himself against the mainmast, trembling. He's almost certain Gardel is talking about him.

"Where's Tavel the cooper?" shouts the captain.

"He's ill," says the surgeon timidly, rubbing his ear.

"Ill?"

"He's resting a little in the rowboat," Palardi explains, pointing to the boat suspended above the deck.

"You're a doctor, Palardi. If Tavel's not on his feet by tomorrow, I'll drop you both off in the Bissagos Islands for a nice long rest on a lovely beach full of ten-foot-long snakes. Do I make myself clear?"

"Yes, Captain," gasps Palardi.

"What about Dubois? Where's he got to?"

"Here," says the carpenter, sticking his head out.

"Where's this barricade?"

"We'll need more wood to finish it off, as I told you. But three quarters of it is ready to be mounted."

"How many men do you need?"

"Eight."

"How much time?"

"Five days to put it all together."

"You'll go looking for wood on the Gold Coast when we get to Elmina or Cape Coast. For now, you can make do with what you have. I'll give you four men and three days."

"Five. I asked for five days. And eight men."

"Since you're complaining, you'll only get two."

"Why?"

"Because I can do whatever I please. And if you don't get it done in time, you'll be joining Monsieur Palardi and Monsieur Tavel on their island among the mosquitoes and the mamba snakes."

Gardel turns on his heels and shouts to the crew:

"Helm to port! Ease sheets to broad reach! Back to work, all of you. And the next to complain will get the whip."

As he leaves the deck, the whole crew leaps into action. A few men go over to the carpenter.

"Go down and wait for me in the steerage," says Dubois calmly. "There's one last thing I have to see to."

His eyes follow the surgeon, who walks along the gangway to the rowboat and steps in. Dubois goes over to him.

There, beneath a roof of tarred linen, lies Tavel the cooper, his head on a sack of hay.

Dubois watches as Palardi bends down and places his hand on the sick man's shoulder.

"How do you feel, Tavel?" the doctor asks. It's a stupid question. "You're going to have to start thinking about getting better now."

Tavel shakes his head.

"How are you treating him?" asks Dubois, pulling Palardi to one side.

"Bloodletting each morning. It should eventually do the trick."

"Bloodletting?"

"Yes. I'm draining five ounces a day from the arm."

"Where did you learn that?"

"Rochefort. At the school of surgery."

"You must have known Eugenie?"

"Who?"

"A petite, red-headed woman, about five foot tall. She lived in a little town called Doëlan off the coast of Brittany. I lived on her farm for a whole year."

"Excuse me?"

"She died a long time ago, poor thing. She was eighty years old, blue eyes. You don't remember her?"

"I . . . Doëlan? I don't know Doëlan."

"Ah, Eugenie . . . sweet but tough like an old beech tree. Does the name really not ring any bells?"

"I don't think so . . . was she also a doctor?"

"No, no. But I watched her butcher a fair few pigs."

"So?"

"So, judging by your techniques, I'd have assumed you went to the same school."

Palardi goes to grab Dubois by the throat, but the carpenter swats him away with the back of his hand, knocking Palardi backwards into the little rowboat next to Tavel.

"I'm trying to save your life, Palardi. Don't do anything else to this man. Give him the cooking water from the rice to drink. It's the only way of treating dysentery. You can ask Cook to give you some. Open the cover at night to let some fresh air in and wait. He needs time to heal. Please, give him time."

"I don't have time," the doctor moans. "Didn't you hear the captain?"

"Why do you think Gardel wants the cooper to get better?"

Palardi doesn't have to think for long.

"So he can build his barrels."

"Precisely. It has nothing to do with his health. So leave this man be. I'll deal with the captain."

Dubois leans over to the sick man and gives him a reassuring smile.

"Sleep, Tavel," he whispers. "Everything is going to be fine. You're going to get better."

Standing next to them, the surgeon tries to find something to say, but the carpenter is already gone. Palardi is left alone with the sound of the cooper's groans. He, too, feels like crying. He's never been able to heal a single person. He joined the merchant navy because he couldn't take any more on the warships, where, as the battles raged, he treated patients with a saw, a butcher's apron tied around his waist.

Dubois has gone below deck to join his men.

"The barricade splits the deck in two," one sailor is explaining to Abel Lebon. "It separates the stern of the ship from the bow. If the captives revolt, the barrier is there to save us all."

"Those of us who are on the right side," says Dubois, joining them.

Just then, Absalom, the boatswain, pops up just behind Dubois. He's looking for Joseph Mars.

"Me?"

"The captain wants to speak to you. Hurry."

Joseph does as he's told. Dubois watches him leave.

"Guess what we're going to do now?" he asks the remaining men.

"The barricade."

"No," says the carpenter.

He smiles at the expressions of surprise on the sailors' faces.

"We're going to make barrels."

Having just about recovered after the captain's terrifying speech, Abel Lebon's heart starts racing again. He's been given two days to create the barricade, but the carpenter is going to spend half of that time trying to save the cooper. There's a flicker of understanding in Abel Lebon's eyes. He's been suffering for every second of the two months they've spent on board.

As he straps an iron hoop to the first barrel, Abel goes over Gardel's awful speech again in his head. He tries to imagine what the future holds. If these last two months really have been heaven, what could hell possibly look like?

17
Good Fortune

After stopping to have a quick word with Cook, Joseph dashes towards the captain's quarters. He knocks twice on the door, determined to stay focused.

It's the first time he's been back here since that night in August when he took the diamonds and the watch. From the sound the door makes as it opens, he realises that another lock has been added. The captain has grown more wary, which is why Joseph hasn't been able to come back since.

"Sit," says Gardel.

Joseph enters. He recognises the sound of the clock right away. He sits down. In front of him is a mahogany table with two legs sawn down to keep the tabletop horizontal in spite of the sloping floorboards at the ship's stern. Gold-framed pictures line the walls. The curtains have been drawn back over their respective windows, just like at the theatre. Here, everything is refined. It's hard to believe that just a few steps away, the rest of the ship is beginning to look more and more like a prison.

High up, draped in red, the captain's bed looks like it belongs in an oriental palace. On the other side of the room, in the corner between the farthest two windows, there's a little lavatory. This is the captain's personal toilet—the greatest privilege accorded to anyone on board. The rest of the crew share an open-air platform on the beakhead at the front of the ship, where the wind and waves can strike at the most inopportune moments.

"Up on deck just before," says Gardel, "I mentioned the weak among us who've been in hiding. Do you remember?"

"Yes . . . "

The captain is pacing around the room. In his hand he holds one of his favourite toys: a folding razor blade that he flicks open and closed.

"When I said that, I wasn't even thinking about you."

"Thanks."

Joseph feels the captain almost brush past his back.

"There's no point lying to you. There are a few sailors on board I may leave behind in a cove on a Caribbean island, or perhaps exchange with another ship. But you're not one of them."

Behind him, Joseph hears the click of the razor being folded into its ivory handle.

"No . . . I don't consider you one of them, Joseph Mars."

He stops.

"I consider you to be more like the cockroaches and rats. When it comes to them, I spare myself the bother of taking the jolly boat you see hanging before this window and lowering it into the sea. With rats, the quickest way to dispose of them is to take them by the tail, when they're sleeping at the bottom of the hold at night, and slice them in two."

There's another click as the captain flicks his razor blade open again, followed by a long silence.

"You see, they're parasites. Mouths that need feeding but

serve no purpose. Now listen to me, boy. You're not doing anything I've asked you to. Not a shred of progress in a whole month. Do you know exactly what you owe me?"

"No."

"Your life. No more, no less."

Joseph doesn't say a word. The captain has stopped right behind him.

"I've been thinking a lot, my boy," he says. "I'm trying to understand what you're doing. Either you're being honest, and you haven't found a thing on the parchment the old pirate left, or you don't want to tell me what you know. In either case, your fate remains the same."

The clock is fixed to the partition right in front of Joseph. He doesn't take his eyes off it. Above the clock face, there's a carving of a little black girl with a cotton flower in her hair.

Joseph looks at her. He feels like he's counting on her. He's waiting for something.

"Would you indulge my curiosity," the captain continues, "and tell me which of these two explanations is correct? Be honest. It won't change a thing."

"The second."

"The second?"

"The second explanation is correct, yes. I don't know what you'll do with me the day I solve the riddle. So maybe I'm not telling you everything I know. It's only natural."

Gardel sneers.

"Natural?"

He circles the table, takes out a chair and sits down opposite Joseph. He waits for a moment, then suddenly drives the blade into the table just in front of Joseph.

"You think you can bargain with me?

"Yes."

"How can I be sure you know more than you're telling me?"

"What about me? How do I know you won't abandon me the day I tell you where Luc de Lerna's treasure is buried?"

Gardel laughs again, without making a sound. Then he stops. He thinks for a moment.

"What do you want?" he asks. "Some kind of guarantee?"

"Yes."

"Listen to me, boy. Do you see the hands on that clock? In two minutes, it will strike noon. If, before the final chime, you give me proof of your progress, I swear to you you'll be with me when I dig up the treasure."

"Swear on what?"

"I give you my word."

This time, it's Joseph who smiles.

"What?" asks Gardel.

"I don't believe a word you say."

The captain grits his teeth.

"So? What do you suggest?" he asks.

"Swear on the stormy skies and the seven seas," says Joseph.

"What?"

"Swear on the stormy skies and the seven seas."

Gardel's face changes. He hesitates. He's probably the only sailor in the world who laughs in the face of superstition. Yet the idea of making this oath frightens him. He doesn't believe in anything. He'd happily betray all the gods in the sky. But nobody jokes about storms at sea.

"Hurry up," says Joseph. "The clock's about to strike noon."

"I swear," growls Gardel.

"On what?"

"On the stormy skies . . ."

"And the seven seas."

"On the stormy skies and the seven seas," the captain says

finally, his face as white as the large merchant's flag flying on the other side of the window.

No sooner have they sealed the deal than the clock begins to strike. Above the clock face, the little girl with the cotton flower has started to strike the bell with a thin golden beater. One, two . . .

How could Joseph have taken such a risk? Seven, eight . . .

The clock strikes nine. The colour begins to come back to Gardel's cheeks as he looks over at Joseph. In three seconds, their pact will be worth nothing.

But just as the little girl with the cotton flower strikes the bell a twelfth time, there's a loud knock at the door.

The captain extracts the blade from the mahogany table.

"What is it?"

He gets up and goes to the door.

"You asked for me?" says the voice behind the door. Joseph can tell it's Cook even from the table where he's sitting.

"You can come in," says Joseph, as if these were his quarters.

Gardel steps aside to let Cook pass.

"I was told you were expecting me at noon."

"Sit down," says Joseph, indicating the seat opposite him.

Gardel watches the scene unfold, incapable of reacting. It's as though he's the servant of this child, who is making himself at home in his quarters.

Just as the captain goes to close the door, the cat slips through the crack, runs over to where Cook is sitting, and jumps onto his lap.

Gardel, who's becoming more bewildered by the second, closes the door and turns to look at them. Cook is quietly stroking his cat's head.

"He won't let me go anywhere without him," says Cook, apologetically.

As he smiles, his cheeks swell like sails in a gust of wind.

"What's the cat's name?" asks Joseph.

"Hercules," replies Cook, tenderly. Gardel is beginning to look positively distraught.

"Hercules?" Joseph asks.

"Yes . . . "

"Could you tell the captain why you gave him that name?"

The smile vanishes from Cook's face. He doesn't answer. He glances over at Gardel.

"Tell us why you called him Hercules," Joseph orders.

Now Cook looks at Joseph. Horrified, he slowly understands why he has been summoned to the captain's quarters.

"That was a long time ago," he says. "I paid for those years."

"What years?" yells the captain, still baffled by the situation.

"Was it Abel who told you?" Cook asks Joseph. But he doesn't wait for a reply.

"I forgive him. I like Abel. I'm the one who said too much."

"Explain yourself!" shouts Gardel. "You're not making any sense!"

"Hercules was the name of a cannon that could fire an 80-pound solid shot. It was aboard a schooner I served on for fifteen years. A single cannonball could tear through the hulls of two ships in a row."

"Don't take me for a fool," says Gardel. "There's no cannon in the world that can fire an 80-pound solid shot."

"There is. I've seen it."

"And this ship, what was it called?"

"It was a four-master named *The Hydra*," replies Cook.

Gardel turns to Joseph. This blasted boy is about to save his own skin again.

"*The Hydra*?" Gardel repeats.

"Yes . . . "

Gardel slowly turns to look at Cook. As far as he knows, there's only one four-master to have ever graced the seven seas. A ship belonging to Luc de Lerna.

"Good God," he says. He stares at Cook.

This joker, with his London accent and cheeks like cricket balls, sailed for fifteen years alongside one of the most infamous pirates in history.

Cooks looks at the ground.

"And how does Abel Lebon know this?" asks the captain.

"He saw the tattoo on Cook's back," replies Joseph.

Gardel approaches Cook from behind and tears his shirt violently. There, across Cook's shoulders, is the image of a pirate standing with each of his feet on a skull. This was the last flag used by Black Bart, which Luc de Lerna inherited from his master at the age of twenty. Cook is telling the truth. The proof is there, engraved in cannon powder on his dark skin.

The captain pulls Cook's shirt back down. He knew this man was hiding something. He's never wrong about these things.

Seeing the captain's triumphant expression, Cook stands up abruptly. The cat leaps onto the floor and scurries under the bed to hide.

"I paid my dues" says Cook. "I spent four years in the mud at Portchester prison. I nearly had my legs cut off because of gangrene. I paid for those years."

The captain goes over to him.

Unfortunately, the boy is right once again. Cook is the man they need. Who could be in a better position to help them? Fifteen years of service under Luc! All they'll have to do is question him, play it subtle so that he won't suspect what they're looking for.

Suddenly, Gardel's voice is softer than ever. He places a hand on Cook's shoulder.

"Don't worry about it," he says. "Get back to work. I had a lot of respect for old Luc. One day you'll tell me your stories. I'm glad Mars told me about your past."

But Joseph Mars seems lost in his own thoughts. His eyes are fixed on Hercules the cat.

"Mars?"

Captain Gardel watches as Joseph gets up and goes to kneel in front of the bench. He slides his hand beneath the folds of red fabric hanging from the bed. The two men listen as he calls the cat.

Joseph pulls back the bedclothes.

"Hercules," he whispers.

The mattress sits on a base made up of two single chests, each around three feet tall. Sliding his hand beneath the bed, Joseph feels the large wrought iron padlock keeping them locked shut. He grabs the cat by the scruff of the neck and pulls him close. The bedclothes fall back down, hiding the chests from view.

Joseph stands up. This is the only part of the whole ship nobody has access to. The only part he hasn't been able to search from top to bottom.

"Got it," he whispers.

"I've got him!" he says, lifting up the cat.

Cook takes Hercules from Joseph and hugs him tightly to his chest.

"Now get out!" orders the captain, who is beginning to grow tired of their nonsense.

Cook and Mars leave. The door closes behind them.

"What did you do that for?" whispers Cook when they've almost reached the kitchen. "Are you trying to get me killed?"

"Actually, I think I just saved your life," says Joseph, mysteriously. "And I managed to save my own at the same time."

Cook watches the strange boy warily as he leaves the room with a spring in his step.

"And more importantly, I found what I was looking for," says Joseph, just before disappearing.

"The cat?" asks Cook.

But the boy is gone. Cooks hears only his gleeful response:

"No! Some good fortune."

Then Joseph adds under his breath: "A huge fortune."

PART TWO

18

An Elephant in a Hat Box

You would have to be an autumn breeze to get through the enormous door of the Bassac residence on rue de l'Escale, La Rochelle, without being stopped by the coachman in the courtyard, rustle your way through the dead leaves on the ground, and brush past the last bunch of grapes on the trellis, before slipping through the crack above the glass door into the house.

Only then could you infiltrate those grand living rooms, with their ceilings covered in mermaids and schooners and tapestries representing all the gods of the sea. Only then could you slip past the servants standing guard on each landing to get to the second floor, sneak through the lock and enter the large office without being noticed by the two men talking inside, before floating gently along the mirrors towards a gallery just above the highest shelves in the bookcase. There, you would find a young girl, who appears to be sleeping amidst a pile of books.

But Amelie Bassac isn't asleep. Having been disturbed by the arrival of her father and his accountant, Christian Saint-Clair, she's decided to stay put without making her presence known. She's been lying there for several minutes now, buried beneath the enormous third volume of the *Universal Dictionary of Trade and Commerce,* trying to grasp the meaning of the tense conversation taking place in the office below.

"I cannot sleep, Saint-Clair. I've had so many long and restless nights."

"You mustn't lose sleep, Monsieur Bassac, you have nothing to fear," replies the young accountant, a reassuring smile detectable in his voice.

"But it's all I have," sighs Bassac. "All I have in the world, along with this house, these few pieces of furniture. And my daughter."

"And four hundred hectares of plantation land in Saint-Domingue," adds Saint-Clair. "And one hundred and fifty slaves working for you there."

Bassac doesn't reply. Amelie hears the floorboards creaking beneath her father's feet.

"What if someone had found it?" he continues.

"You know how careful we've been. It's hardly noticeable, anyway. No one will see it."

"Hardly noticeable?" Bassac thunders.

"I'm telling you, we managed to fit everything in four or five chests, each only a foot tall."

Amelie listens carefully. She has no idea what they're talking about. What precious thing could possibly fit in a set of boxes no taller than a stack of books?

A few years earlier, after his wife's death, Bassac sold all the family jewels after Amelie swore never to wear any of them. But perhaps there are other valuable keepsakes hidden somewhere? Amelie thinks about all the important papers her father has accumulated: their ancestors' marriage contracts, receipts from the little grocery shop her grandfather used to run in the village.

"Not even Captain Gardel knows," says Saint-Clair. "There's

only one man in the entire crew who knows about it. He'll keep us up to date."

"Is he trustworthy? You still haven't told me his name. Four and a half tons! How do you expect—"

The shipowner is interrupted mid-sentence by someone bursting into the room. It's Madame de Lô, Amelie's formidable tutor. She's managed to open both of the double doors with one shoulder. Carried by her own momentum, she slides across the floorboards, not stopping until she reaches Bassac.

"I'm terribly sorry to interrupt," she says.

"Are you looking for something, Madame?"

"No."

"No?"

Madame de Lô tries to catch her breath.

"I . . . just . . . a book . . . "

Saint-Clair looks at the short, breathless woman standing before them, eyes sparkling. Her enormous bouffant makes her look twice her actual height. Her dress is a century behind the latest fashions, with leafy green embroidery and ribbons lifting the fabric on each side.

"Monsieur," she says, addressing Bassac. "As I'm here, I just wanted to let you know . . . "

Madame de Lô glances over Bassac's shoulder. Up above him, Amelie ducks out of sight.

" . . . I wanted to let you know that your meal is being served in the conservatory."

"Is my daughter there already?"

"I . . . I don't know. I'm sure she is, yes."

"All right, I'm coming," says Bassac. He turns to his accountant.

"Tell me, Saint-Clair, you haven't received anything since the first letter from Lisbon?"

"Nothing yet. Our contact will send word with another ship once they arrive in Africa. We'll also be receiving the official letters from Lazarus Gardel. For now, all we can do is wait."

Bassac sighs.

"You've made me lose my appetite. Come back tomorrow with good news, please."

The door creaks and slams shut. The room is silent once more. Amelie hears footsteps on the landing.

She waits for a moment. Finally, she gets up, puts the dictionary away and descends the spiral staircase leading downstairs from the gallery. She walks over to her father's desk, her bare feet sinking into the plush carpet.

There's a huge model of a ship hanging from the ceiling. It's *The Purple Rose*, Bassac's first ship, lost at sea a long time ago. The model is hung by a pulley system that keeps it suspended above the desk, making the room feel like the open sea.

When she was younger, Amelie would untie the strings, slowly lower *The Purple Rose* onto the leather desktop, and let her eyes wander through all the little openings inside the hull.

But this morning, there's nothing but a square piece of paper on the desk with a few words scribbled on it.

"Amelie?"

She turns around to see Christian Saint-Clair standing by the window.

He's been here the whole time. He decided to stay when he heard her coming down from the gallery.

"I believe they're expecting you in the conservatory. Your governess—"

"Tutor. She doesn't govern anyone, Monsieur."

He smiles.

"She was looking for you, though she wouldn't admit it. She looked as though she was about to have an apoplectic stroke!"

Amelie doesn't move from her spot. Leaning against the desk, her hands behind her back, she looks Saint-Clair in the eye. She's furious at herself for letting this man see her barefoot. She digs her big toe into the wool of the carpet.

"And don't call me Amelie,"

This man is in love with her. She can tell. She doesn't like people who are in love. In fact, she doesn't think much of love—or people—at all.

The only person she loves is her father. He's the only one who stirs up any kind of emotion in her.

Him and Madame de Lô. Because although her tutor is a little peculiar in her ways, she knows all about chemistry, Greek, English, arithmetic, and all the important aspects of philosophy and reason. She's also teaching Amelie piano and astronomy. But she certainly isn't her governess. Amelie jokingly says she's her rudder.

"Forgive me, mademoiselle," says Saint-Clair in a feeble voice. "I shall call you mademoiselle."

Besides, this man is a crook. She's seen the accounts he kept for the last ships. Twenty thousand pounds remain unaccounted for on *The African* alone. And on another ship, two crew members and three little enslaved boys were mysteriously wiped from the registers at somewhere between their arrival in Saint-Domingue and the slave market there.

She told her father, who simply laughed and said:

"You don't need to accuse him of theft just so you don't have to marry him! You can do what you like, you know that, but Saint-Clair has talent. He's a promising young man."

Men are always promising. But that's no reason to believe them. Amelie doesn't want anyone touching the Bassac family business.

Each day, she draws up charts with curves indicating the

price of sugar, cotton, and coffee. She counts the number of captives in the registers over and over. She monitors. She forecasts. She calculates the most profitable seasons, tracks the winds and the currents. She would have liked the ship bearing her name to arrive in Saint-Domingue before Christmas to coincide with the sugar harvests, when the price of captives soars.

For as long as she is alive, she won't let anything tarnish the Bassac family business.

"It was your father who asked me to call you Amelie," Saint-Clair explains. "He tells me we're almost the same age."

"The eighth of your age is the square root of mine," says Amelie, with a pretentiousness she immediately regrets. "We're not the same age at all."

"Not quite the eighth, mademoiselle. I believe you were born in December."

Of course. She bites the inside of her cheek. The worst of it all, she thinks, is that he actually *can* do maths. That's why she can't forgive him for the fact that the figures in his account books don't add up.

"Did you know, Saint-Clair, that Madame de Lô writes love letters to you in the bath at night, then hides them in her hair?"

Amelie just blurted out the first thing that comes to her head, as quickly as possible. She wants to take advantage of the man's confusion so she can grab the little piece of paper on the desk behind her.

"Sorry?" says Saint-Clair.

"Nothing. Forget it."

She crumples the paper in her hand and hides it behind her back.

"I thought you said . . . "

"Don't mistake your desires for reality," she says. "Madame de Lô's heart is already taken. She's loyal to her husband, and there's nothing you can do about it, even if it has been over a hundred years since his death and even if he did leave her destitute."

Saint-Clair is flabbergasted. Mission accomplished. He's completely lost. But Amelie isn't finished yet. She rushes towards the door, whispering as she passes him:

"Don't worry, I'll be sure to tell her how you feel."

With her blue and white dress rustling along the waxed wooden floors, her bare feet drumming up a rhythm as she goes, she looks like a little wave galloping onto the shore, not letting anything get in her way.

"Yes, I'll be sure to tell her. You never know," she adds before disappearing into thin air.

On the stairs, she runs one hand over her crumpled dress. That should get rid of him for a while, she thinks to herself.

But she's wrong.

Because Christian Saint-Clair is drunk on love, drowning in the wave she just created. He's so bowled over it looks as though he's about to shatter the window he's leaning against and tumble down into the topiary, or find himself clinging to a climbing rose. He gasps for air. He wants her to love him. She almost makes him want to forget his project—the project he's been preparing for two years.

Saint-Clair tries to take a deep breath. He must remain calm. Everything must be done in the right order.

As she runs down the stairs, Amelie unfolds the piece of paper she took from her father's desk and stops on the bottom stair to read it. Her ears weren't deceiving her. Four and a half tons. That's exactly what's written there. That's what she heard just as her tutor entered the room. What is this four-and-a-half-ton secret? The only way to find out is to search the inventories.

She walks through the vestibule, then the parlour, into the conservatory. Her father is already at the table. The bright October sun streams through the windows, tinting the room shades of green and grey like the moss on the trees in the garden.

"My daughter!" he cries. "There you are."

"Papa," she replies softly.

He rises for a moment as she sits down across the table from him. The butler immediately appears, carrying a dish beneath a silver cloche. A second servant emerges from behind the curtains and places a towel on Amelie's lap. She hates these formalities. They may as well wipe her mouth and adjust her petticoat while they're at it.

"Did you see Saint-Clair?" her father asks.

"No."

"I'm sure he would have been delighted to see you."

"I'm sure he would have."

"What a nice boy he is."

"Don't."

Amelie replies distractedly. Her head is elsewhere. She no longer sees her father, nor the butler standing behind his chair, nor the servant who appears at the table in his white gloves to lift the cloche and serve cream of mushroom soup, nor Madame de Lô who, in the distance, is still searching for Amelie at the bottom of the garden.

Amelie's mind is occupied entirely by questions of physics and geometry.

What is this mysterious load weighing four and a half tons that Saint-Clair said he managed to fit in four boxes, each one only a foot tall? Something about this story doesn't add up. It'd be like keeping an elephant in a hat box.

19

What If It's Them?

The search party has come to a halt. Awoshi is the first to arrive at the edge of the ravine. The horse can't have come from any further than this. This is where the tracks begin, out of the blue, near a chasm filled with vegetation, as though the horse just materialised out of thin air.

Awoshi turns around. Baako and his father are still way behind. They're walking slowly, dropping with exhaustion. They no longer have faith in this impossible quest. For several days, they haven't even been able to see the tracks their young leader is following. They no longer exist. Time has trampled on the horse's hoofmarks.

But Eeko and Baako, terrified by Awoshi, continue to follow him. More than anything, they now feel as though they're following in the footsteps of his madness.

And now, for the first time, standing before this impenetrable ravine, Awoshi feels inclined to agree. He cannot go on like this. He knows that the legend of the last Okos is beginning to consume him. At night, he no longer dreams of the price he'll be able to sell them for, but the exhilaration of finally catching them.

Now that they've finally reached this place, so far from Ashanti territory, he's ready to give up. They have to stop. Awoshi is crouching down on the ground, waiting for his men. He looks down into the ravine filled with thorns. A horse can't just magically appear from between the cliffs.

From afar, the mountain they've just climbed looked like an enormous volcano. The ravine probably just leads to a crater of more stone and thorns. How could anyone be hiding in there?

"Awoshi," says Baako, finally catching up. "My father wants to speak to you."

Weak with fatigue, Eeko trails behind his son.

Awoshi fixes his gaze on the old man.

"There's no need. His eyes say it all. And I understand. It's time to go home."

Baako and his father look at one another.

"We're going home," says Awoshi.

He feels calm. It was reassuring to hear his own voice announce that it's all over. Why did he insist on embarking on such a long expedition? For several moons, they've been wandering through uninhabited lands when his people could have simply sold prisoners of war, thieves, or murderers.

Old Eeko has turned on his heels and is already heading in the other direction.

"Wait!" his son calls after him. "You need to sit down for a while."

"I'm ready," says Eeko. "I want to go home."

Baako helps his father sit down.

"I'm not tired," says the old man.

The two of them sit together. The branches above their heads protect them from the sun. Baako places a hand on his father's knee, laughing at the old man's impatience.

"Just wait and see," says Eeko. "At my age, every second counts."

Awoshi sits apart from them on a flat rock. He listens to them talking, as though they've already arrived, as though they're standing in the shade in front of their house. He can almost hear the voices of the women gathered round them and the children bathing beneath the big tree, jumping into the water from the branches with cries of joy.

Awoshi remembers a time when this kind of contentment was enough for him.

"Shall we go?"

The other men come to join him, and the three of them set off together. Eeko is chirping away like a bird.

"It was my son who was getting tired, you know. Not me. He was using me as an excuse to be able to sit down."

They begin to descend a very steep passage. Their laughter spurs the old man on.

"If it hadn't been for me, he'd have spent the whole night sitting on that canoe. And you, Awoshi, you'd still be sleeping like a baby."

Behind him, Baako continues to laugh. But Awoshi stops in his tracks. He turns to Eeko.

"What did you just say?"

"I was only joking. I said . . . like a baby . . . but—"

"Before that!"

Eeko looks at him timidly.

"What did you say before that?"

"I don't know. I didn't mean—"

"A canoe."

"What?"

"You said something about a canoe."

"In the moss, where we were sitting . . . I think . . . but I can't be sure. It looked like the bottom of a canoe."

Awoshi runs back up the slope. By the time the others reach him, he's already rolled the hollow tree trunk over. He's running his hand over the wood, which has been stripped of its bark.

"Who would bring a canoe up into the mountains?" Baako asks, laughing. "Where are these giants hiding?"

It is, indeed, a little canoe covered in moss.

Baako is speaking loudly. He's trying to get the group's spirits back up again. He gives the hollow wood a kick, and the sound echoes. But behind him, Awoshi is already heading towards the ravine full of prickly bushes, brambles, and thorns.

"At some point, there was water running through here."

Baako goes over to him.

"Come on," he says. "We said it was time to stop."

"The horse must have come out of the water."

"Come on . . ."

Baako tries to take him by the arm, but Awoshi pulls away.

"The horse didn't just fall out of the sky," he says. "It must have come from somewhere."

Baako pulls him again, a little harder this time. Awoshi throws him to the ground. He points the barrel of his rifle in Baako's face.

"Do you think I'm going to stop now I've finally found the way?"

"You didn't find anything!" Baako shouts. "You're crazy, Awoshi! I don't care if you kill me, it needs to be said. Do you think canoes can sail through forests?"

The young man is lying in the dust in tears.

"My son is right," says Eeko. "There may have been water, a long time ago. But we can't just wait here for the rains to come back."

"No, we won't wait," says Awoshi, regaining composure. "We won't wait for the rain."

Slowly, he lowers his rifle. The two men are begging him now.

"You're crazy!" cries Baako. "What are you going to do, attach wings to the canoe?"

"Come back with us," Eeko implores. "It's time to go home."

Awoshi is looking at the ravine. He rubs a little black powder from his rifle between his fingers.

He's always liked to go against the grain. If he's following a horse's tracks, he prefers to go backwards. When Moses Shackle points him in one direction, he takes the opposite path. And when it seems that the only way through is via water . . .

"Fire," says Nao, standing in front of her house. "There's a fire."

She's alone. Smoke is rising from the cliffs in the distance. Soum has gone to put it out. The day is coming to an end. Nao stayed behind by the fig tree, tired from the day's trials and from carrying the baby in her belly.

What if it's Mosi, Lam and Alma coming home? What if it's them?

20

Scattered

They'd only ever seen one fire in the valley, and it broke out just after Alma was born. The whole savanna was ablaze. It was a stormy night. Antelope came bounding through the night in flames like leaping torches. Birds of prey hunted along the line of fire. Even the sky was burning.

This time, the fire is up on the cliffs of the ravine. The pure white smoke rises up into the sky before tumbling down to the bottom of the cliffs in a shower of black rain.

Since the three of them disappeared within hours of one another—Lam, Alma, then Mosi—Nao has felt as though her entire life is in flames. If everything burns, what will she be left with? She's standing by the door, where her husband's left his spear. She's cradling her belly in her arms like a calabash.

With her back against the house, Nao slides down to the ground. Her eyelids droop along with her. She falls asleep, crouched against the wall. The fire for their meal continues to burn in a hole in the ground in front of her. Above the roof, in the branches of the sycamore fig tree, the two little monkeys cover their eyes.

Night has fallen. Nao wakes up. The fire seems to be under control. There's no more light coming from the ravine. The smell of charred wood cooling hangs in the air, carried along by the southerly wind.

Nao gets up slowly. She throws a branch into the dying fire and goes into the house.

In the darkness of the room, she wants nothing more than to see all of her children together, to hear the little noises they make as they roll over in their sleep.

Since the others left, Nao and Soum have grown closer. For years, Alma and Lam have each had half of their mother, leaving nothing for their big brother. But in the space of just a few moons, Nao's silent son has become much more than just her guardian. He's all she has left. His is the only shoulder she has to cry on.

She calls out to him. Why hasn't he returned? From the back of the house, she looks towards the little square of light where the door is and listens. She hears the sound of footsteps rustling in the grasses just outside. The baby in her belly curls up tight.

"Lilim, is that you? Lilim?"

The name she calls each of her children when she's alone with them is also the word for the shade of the trees in her language.

"Is that you?"

As soon as she crosses the threshold, she stops.

There's something sharp poking her behind the ear. Someone is holding Mosi's spear to her neck.

"You're speaking the Oko language," a voice says. Nao doesn't answer.

"Are you alone?"

"Yes."

She replies in Fante to try and cover her tracks.

"You're all alone in this valley?"

Silently she prays to the talisman around her ankle and the ancestors in the ground below her feet. She begs them to keep Soum safely hidden somewhere. They mustn't find him.

"Why are you saying there's nobody else here? Don't lie."

"All right, I am lying."

"What?"

"I'm expecting a baby."

Awoshi lowers the spear slightly for a moment, walks round to face her and holds it up again, right in the middle of her throat.

He mustn't allow himself to get distracted by her beauty or by this child. If anything, this revelation has just doubled the price of his prisoner.

He cannot take any risks.

"Move. Walk towards me."

She walks forward. If the man takes her away right now, Soum will escape this fate. He retracts the spear slightly. Nao only wishes she could turn around and take one last look at the shadow of the big tree holding their home in its embrace.

"Wait," says Awoshi.

He picks up a piece of wood from the fire and throws it on the roof. The stacks of grass burst into flames. Nao closes her eyes.

The house is burning. Flames are licking at the leaves of the tree.

"There. Moses Shackle wasn't lying after all," says Awoshi.

"Who?" says Nao, with a start.

"A man who told us we'd find a field of ashes and burnt trees here."

Nao turns her head suddenly away from the light of the fire.

Awoshi is walking behind her.

"If you really are alone in this valley . . ."

"I am alone."

They begin to walk. Awoshi takes his time, savouring his victory, as though driving a pregnant woman from her home at spearpoint were anything to be proud of.

"If you really are alone," he continues, "then where did the smiling mute come from? The one my fellow hunters trapped just over there?"

Just then, a cloud of hummingbirds escapes from the burning tree, and descends towards them in a vertical line.

"What was that?" asks Awoshi.

The birds disappear into the darkness.

As she walks towards the ravine, Nao thinks of her family: the last living Okos. They're like a handful of wheat grains, ripped from the ear that kept them together, about to be scattered.

21

The Horse and the Moon

Alma suppresses a cry of joy. She falls to her elbows to inspect the quarry of red earth beneath her. She's dropping with exhaustion, worn out by the endless trek. But now, finally, she finds what she's been looking for all this time: Cloud. There he is. A smudge of white rearing up on his hind legs in a little clearing of red earth.

Alma has been walking for miles through patches of wheat and fields of rice and peanuts. She's been on her guard the whole time. It's the neatness of this landscape that makes her suspect there are people living here.

The land is arranged in perfectly straight strips of all different colours. There are lanes filled with grasses and butterflies and enormous trees sitting obediently in their places, lining the paths. She could never have imagined such a big garden.

At home, her father used to grow wheat mixed with wet clover. It grew in a little circle by their house, which seemed big to Alma and Lam when they used it as a spot for hide and seek, even though it was possible to cross the patch in just a few strides.

The landscape she's walking across now looks like a patchwork quilt, made up of dozens of gardens, stretching as far as the eye can see.

Gradually, over the weeks, Alma's perception of the world has begun to change. She once thought the whole universe was there in her valley. But now she understands that the valley only seems big in her memory because she was so small. The world she's discovering is endless; the horizon retreats further into the distance each time she moves towards it.

After so many days of walking through arid scrubland, she's discovered a new landscape made up of every shade of green imaginable, from the softest to the deepest, a landscape where gazelles with legs as thin as twigs watch her as she walks. Finally, after climbing a little trail, she's reached this new valley: the quarry of red earth where she found Cloud.

She realises suddenly that the horse has been captured. He's tied to a pole planted in the centre of the clearing. The rope is covered in earth and blends into the red backdrop. Cloud is pacing around in circles. His coat is completely white from the upper body to the knee. The rope shortens each time he goes round the pole. He becomes even more agitated when he senses Alma's presence.

"Cloud," she whispers.

She's about to rush over to him, but just before she jumps up, she realises there's a girl crouching by the horse's side, her eyes glued to him. Alma has never seen another little girl before. This one is around nine or ten—Lam's age. She must have been knocked to the ground several times while trying to get close to Cloud. That would explain why she has streaks of red earth on her legs and shoulders. She's wearing nothing but two large pewter bracelets on her wrists and a string of seashells around her waist.

The little girl gets up. She's so dainty, she almost fades into the background. Even her face is streaked in red earth. She makes one final attempt to go and touch Cloud, but the horse turns towards her, rearing up on his hind legs. Furious, she starts to shout at him, crying and shaking her fists. She says some things to the horse that Alma doesn't understand. Then she leaves without noticing Alma at all.

Once again, Alma goes to rush over and free Cloud. Once again, something stops her. She thinks of Lam. Whoever captured Cloud must have found Lam, too. She has to follow the girl to find out.

Alma skirts the edge of the quarry. She walks past a structure with a straw roof that seems to be used for storing the earth for building houses. But now that night is falling, there's nobody there.

Alma discreetly follows the girl, keeping her in sight at all times. She's thinking about Cloud. He must have felt her presence. He must be wondering why she didn't even go over to see him.

Alma follows the girl for a few minutes until a river emerges from behind some large trees that have fallen across a bend in the path. The river seems so wide and fast as it flows between the black rocks. Alma has never seen such a large body of water before.

By the time Alma turns back, the little girl has disappeared. Alma looks around for her. Eventually, she spots her a little further along and finds a hiding place to watch her from. The girl climbs down the riverbank and dives into the current. There's a bird on a sandbank watching the girl's shoulders wriggling in the water as she washes her neck. She comes out all clean, her skin having gone from the colour of yam root to near black. She drips dry beneath the trees before continuing down the path along the river.

The little girl isn't moving very quickly. Alma has to force herself to slow down to remain unnoticed. She can hear the girl crying little sobs of anger all by herself. Since leaving the valley, Alma has discovered her uncanny ability to hunt prey without being seen, always ready to spring into action, even when she's exhausted.

Suddenly she stops. Just around a bend, shadows begin to appear on the other side of the river. Alma sees one house appear, then another, then ten, then a hundred. A whole stack of mud and thatch houses. She doesn't understand why they've been packed together at the water's edge. Instead, a tree could have been chosen for each one, along with two little monkeys for every roof and savanna stretching as far as the eye can see. There's a wall rising up in the distance, just beyond the farthest houses, which are not protected by the river. Slender figures of all different sizes are moving from one place to the next or waiting around for something. Night is beginning to fall. Canoes are being brought to shore. People are lighting fires. The only sound that can be heard is the low, steady beat of a drum creating ripples in the water's surface.

Alma watches the little girl wade into the water and resurface near the houses on the other side. The water isn't deep enough to swim in but she has to push her hips against the current so she doesn't get swept away. She lifts her hands above her head, elbows raised as though they might melt away in the water.

Alma stays where she is. She won't be able to follow the girl any further than this.

She watches the girl step out of the water between the canoes, but she doesn't hear when another child starts calling the girl's name:

"Sirim! Sirim!"

Alma goes to leave. She's heading back to the quarry.

Not allowing herself to be distracted, Sirim walks up a narrow passage carved out by the rain. She weaves through the labyrinth of houses, startling the hens as she crosses the courtyards. She continues up towards the tallest building, which looks like a termite mound. Sirim stops in front of this mud palace and leans against the wall with its low doors and square windows. She's thinking about the horse she's been given, the horse she always dreamed of having. The horse is uncontrollable and refuses to bow to her will.

At first, her father refused to give in. He'd had bad experiences with horses. But he ended up with the animal on his hands as the result of an exchange with some traffickers who were passing through. He didn't know what to do with it.

Sirim swore to him in tears that she would tame the horse before the full moon. If she wasn't able to, her father could do what he wanted with it. But time has passed too quickly. Soon it'll be too late. The full moon is tonight. The horse is no tamer than before, and the day is already beginning to fade.

Sirim is the daughter of the King and Queen of Bussa, a kingdom on the edge of Yorubaland blessed by the bountiful River Quorra. The people of the desert call the Quorra the Niger, which means "river of rivers". The Kingdom of Bussa doesn't get involved with wars and trade, despite the processions of captives constantly passing by, the heavy flow of canoes on the river and the kingdom's frequent brushes with the Fulani warriors who come from the north to plunder neighbouring regions.

Now Sirim, the Princess of Bussa, is heading into the palace, a series of ordinary houses plastered with dung and connected by covered passages and small courtyards.

There's an assembly taking place in the first room Sirim walks through. The voices of the attendees are muffled by the earth on the walls and floor. Sirim knows her father must be here somewhere, overseeing all these men debating at length, but she doesn't manage to spot him in the darkness of the room. She's able to deduce that they're discussing an issue regarding a herd of goats, but she doesn't stick around for details. She goes through another room into a succession of open-air corridors. She has more important business to deal with than these adults and their stolen goats.

"Sirim!"

Her mother is sitting in the main courtyard. They almost look as though they could be the same age, but when Sirim's mother sees her daughter, a mixture of tenderness and concern appears in her eyes. It's the same look that all mothers have.

Two little girls sit cross-legged on the floor, fanning their queen with palm leaves, partly to create a breeze and partly to keep the mosquitoes from the river at bay.

Sirim collapses onto her mother's lap. Her mother covers her with a corner of her robe and hugs her tightly.

"Is it your little horse? Is that why you're upset?"

There are eight coral bracelets jangling on her wrist. She gestures for the two girls to leave. The inhabitants of Bussa call their queen "the Midiki." They've embraced her as their ruler even though she comes from a faraway coastal region. She's taught her daughter her native language: Fante.

"Your father is only looking out for you," she tells Sirim. "He won't hurt the horse. He'll let it go. You haven't even given it a name yet."

She places a hand on her daughter's back.

Darkness has fallen upon the palace courtyard. There are women making a fire in one of the rooms nearby. At night-time, the animated voices have a different ring to them, just like the laughter in the street and the clicking of the lizards on the walls.

In the distance, the drum begins to beat faster.

"There'll be other horses," Sirim's mother says, tenderly.

"No, there won't be others."

Between sobs, Sirim wonders if there might be a way to stop the full moon from rising. She thinks of last summer's eclipse, of all the miracles that could still happen. Then she falls asleep. In her dreams, a horse covered in red earth is eating from the palm of her hand.

When she opens her eyes, the courtyard is bathed in pink moonlight. She hears the sound of voices coming up from the town and her mother's voice coming from above her.

"I think something's happening. They're heading towards the river."

Sirim watches the shadows go by. She hears the sound of hurried footsteps within the palace.

"Is there a war?" asks Sirim, groggily.

"No. I don't know what's happening. Come. I keep hearing the same words."

"What words?"

"The horse and the moon."

22

The Grand Entrance

Sirim and her mother make their way down to the river amongst the crowd. There are people bumping into them, scrambling to get up on the wall. The kingdom has always been able to protect itself from enemies. Peasants, artisans, and fishermen alike transform into warriors the moment the alert is sounded. They know that an attack from one side often precedes an ambush from behind. But Sirim isn't afraid. There's a murmur of excitement in the air all around.

"Look!" says Sirim's mother, pointing to the horizon.

The gigantic moon alone could be responsible for this commotion. It's risen from the other side of the river, blood red. In Sirim's world, the phases of the moon give life its rhythm. The moon is the ruler of time, of their gardens, their bodies. But as they get closer to the river, Sirim and her mother sense that there's something more than just the moon causing a stir.

When the townspeople see them coming, they respectfully step aside, making way for the Midiki and her daughter to approach the river. There are people everywhere: sitting in the grasses, crammed into canoes, knee-deep in the river. Everyone's looking in the same direction.

The queen squeezes her daughter's hand.

"I've seen," says Sirim.

"Is it him?"

"Yes."

There in the river, near the opposite bank, there's a white horse standing perfectly still. The red moon is shining so brightly, it looks as though it's the middle of the day. On the horse's back sits a rider covered from head to toe in red earth. There's a group of men standing in the rapids, taking aim at her. Some have rifles in their hands, others have spears.

Alma remains still. She's sitting up perfectly straight, red like the saffron stalk of a white crocus. Her face is covered in a mask of red earth, leaving only the black and white of her eyes visible.

"Let them through," says the queen.

The warriors do not lower their weapons. They simply shuffle aside slightly in the current to allow them to pass. The horse and its rider move across the riverbed, leaving the orange reflection of the moon in their wake.

This is precisely what Alma planned. She put on her war paint. She prepared her entrance. And now here she is with her bow on her back. She wasn't expecting to find all these people gathered around her, but as she watches the men lower their weapons to allow the horse to walk through, she knows she's succeeded.

Little Sirim goes down into the water. The queen follows her without hesitating.

The red girl has tamed the wild horse.

Alma is right next to them now. She doesn't know a thing about the organisation of society. She doesn't know the meaning of the word "kingdom." But she could tell right away from the way the crowds looked at these two women that they were the ones she needed to speak to.

The woman addresses her daughter.

"Are you sure it's him?"

Alma replies for her.

"Yes. It's him. Climb up here with me."

She leans down, extending her hand to Sirim.

The queen tries to hold her daughter back. How can the red girl speak Fante? The queen and her daughter are the only ones in the land who speak the language. Only spirits have the ability to address each person in their own language.

But Sirim grabs the red girl's hand and climbs up behind her without a second thought. Slowly, they emerge from the river on Cloud's back with the queen escorting them. They begin to make their way through the crowd together. The town slowly begins to hum with noise again. The horse weaves its way up through the houses with a throng of people in tow. Alma holds onto Cloud's leather collar with one hand. Her other hand hangs at her side.

"Who are you?" whispers Sirim from behind her.

Alma looks straight ahead of her, not knowing how to respond. Suddenly, she feels the girl's arms around her and remembers how Lam clung to her as they galloped together on Cloud's back. She decides to take a risk. She tells the truth.

"My name is Alma," she begins, her throat tightening. "I need your help. I need to stay here for a while. I'm tired."

Sirim glances at her mother, who is trying to work out what the two riders are saying to each other. But Sirim has already made her decision.

"Take us over there," she says. "By the house at the foot of the ramparts."

When they arrive, there's another group of men guarding the entrance to the palace. The king was led inside for safety when the alert was sounded. At the first sign of danger, the king is shut away for protection.

Cloud stops on the square in front of the low door of the palace. The queen enters alone. Alma and Sirim wait among the crowd.

Finally, the king emerges. A sudden silence falls upon the square. The king walks up to the horse, followed by his wife. He's dressed all in blue and is wearing a hat made from red cloth.

"Who are you?"

Alma doesn't understand the king, but the little girl behind her answers.

"She's travelled very far. She needs to rest. She's come to give me the horse."

"Do you speak the Fante language? Did you come from over there?"

Sirim whispers a translation into the red girl's ear.

"I don't know where I'm from," says Alma.

The king takes a step closer and grabs the collar that Cloud is still wearing after all this time.

He strokes the horse between his eyes.

"What's your name?" he asks Alma.

"Her name is Alma," replies Sirim.

"And the horse?" asks the king.

Alma guesses what the king is asking about. "Cloud," she replies.

He tries to repeat the name. He smiles because he can't pronounce it.

"See, Sirim? Your horse does have a name," says the queen.

"Cloud," says the little princess.

The king steps aside to let them into the palace. They duck their heads to fit through the entrance on Cloud's back. A flock of servants rushes to their aid, and the horde moves together slowly through the hallways. Women appear with blankets, even though it's a warm night. Some rub the horse's flank. They begin preparing a meal for Alma and heating water over the flames to wash her with. The two girls are still clinging to one another on Cloud's back. Above them, a flock of tiny birds has landed on the climbing flowers of a terrace.

Alma is overcome with exhaustion. If only her little brother were tucked away in this house somewhere. If only he'd been there, hiding in the reeds of the river, to witness her grand entrance.

23
Sunny Spells

It's been two weeks since Alma arrived in Bussa. She hasn't told anyone about Lam. Not even Sirim, who never leaves her side.

She's waiting for the right time.

The first night, when she slid down from the horse's back onto the mud floor of the palace, three women came up to wash her with soap, surrounding her like a grove of limba trees. They scrubbed her skin rhythmically with handfuls of straw. They put her in a bath to wash away all the red earth covering her skin, all that dirt that had been keeping her upright. The women laughed at how dirty the water was. Alma let the hands and the laughter wash over her. She came out in a daze, no longer able to walk. She fell asleep before she even reached the rug where Sirim was waiting for her.

Over the course of the following days, Alma has slowly begun to get her strength back. She's been fed all the different foods the kingdom has to offer: ash cakes, partridge, hippo meat, and butter tree caterpillars roasted on an open fire. She's beginning to get back on her feet. She's discovering a whole new world. When Sirim places some salt in her hand, brought back by her father from a lake ten days north of Bussa, Alma puts it on her tongue. Her eyes light up with pleasure. She remembers tasting something similar once when she bit her brother's neck one hot day when they were playfighting.

Every day at the same time, Alma takes Sirim to Cloud, then turns to go, pretending not to be interested in them.

"Can't you just help us?!" Sirim cries furiously.

But Alma leaves them to tame each other. She makes out as if she's doing something else. Sirim and Cloud look at one another, slowly inching closer together. Then, one morning, the Princess of Bussa is finally able to mount the horse by herself.

This is when Alma's plan begins to fall into place. She tells Sirim that their training is not over, that she wants to see them riding together. She spends several days accompanying them to every last nook of the town, through all the surrounding land and along the banks of the river. Sitting behind Sirim, Alma discreetly looks for Lam everywhere they go.

The people of Bussa watch as they pass by: the princess and her shadow. They think of Alma as a sort of chaperone, caretaker, or lady in waiting. But really, it's Sirim who's been looking out for Alma all along.

She still hasn't found her brother on the banks of the River Quorra. Instead, she's found a girl his age who crouches down by her side, showing her how to crush wild black pepper. Even when Alma wakes up in the middle of the night, she can feel the little girl watching over her.

"Are you thirsty?"

She's never asked what Alma is doing there, nor where she came from. With her piercing black stare and her head held high, Sirim immediately silences anyone who asks questions.

For several nights now, they've been pulling their rugs out into a small courtyard covered in fallen white petals. They sleep outside to be close to Cloud when the moon goes into hiding, causing him to scratch at the ground with his hooves. They're lying together beneath the black sky.

Emboldened by the silence and the darkness, Alma finally begins to tell her story. She doesn't tell Sirim everything. She doesn't mention the faraway valley or the rest of her family. She only talks about her brother and Cloud the horse. She talks about the journey she made to find him.

When she finishes her story, the pair lie together listening to Cloud's breathing.

"I think I saw your brother," says Sirim.

"Where?"

"Does he come up to about your shoulder?"

Alma trembles.

"Yes."

"Describe him in more detail, just so I can be sure," says Sirim.

Alma doesn't know what to say. She doesn't know how to distinguish him from anyone else in the world because she doesn't really know anyone else. Should she tell Sirim that Lam's belly button looks like the small hill that a raindrop makes the moment it touches the water's surface?

"He's not like anyone else," says Alma.

"Then it might have been him," says Sirim.

They hear the sound of bare feet shuffling along the ground somewhere inside the palace and wait for them to pass. The sky is overcast, the night pitch black. There's nothing to see but the jasmine flowers that turn into shooting stars as they tumble down from their stalks.

"They came from the west," says Sirim. "They weren't proper

hunters. They were just taking whatever they could find. They had six elephant tusks, the horse, and a child. They spent one night further along the river."

"When?"

"Two moons ago, maybe four."

Sirim is just like Lam, Alma thinks, providing dates that fall somewhere within a period that spans three whole moons. For them, time is meant to be whiled away, not counted unnecessarily on fingers.

"There were five men," says Sirim. "They were making a canoe to take out to sea. One of our fishermen saw them. He came to address the council. The elders said we should leave them be. They say the river is responsible for washing away the blood shed by these men. It's not the Kingdom of Bussa's business to interfere."

Up to this point, her voice has been filled with the pride of a future queen, but now it falters slightly.

"The fisherman said the child was hungry." Alma nestles further into her blanket.

"There was a long silence in the council," Sirim continues. "Someone suggested that we at least bring the child something to eat. All of the elders agreed. But my father wanted to buy the little captive."

She stops talking. "My father had never wanted to buy a captive until that day."

"Go on," whispers Alma.

"The fisherman accompanied two messengers to the camp. They put forward the king's proposal."

Alma starts trembling again.

"My father promised them canoes, glass beads, a cow . . . whatever they wanted. The traffickers refused. One of the men was very tall. A giant with a severed ear. He said that on the coast, white men were giving out brandy, new rifles, silk parasols with tassels."

Alma listens as Sirim describes the goods. She didn't know that some things could be bought and sold. She's never seen a silk parasol or a tassel.

"They'd tied the horse's legs," Sirim continues. "They laid him down on the ground along with the six elephant tusks. We promised the traffickers a lot of food in exchange for the live horse, as long as they fed the child."

"And then?"

"The giant with the severed ear accepted. My father bought the horse. In any case, the men couldn't take him on the river with them, and an untamed horse isn't worth any more than the meat on its bones. The child ate the yam and the rice in front of our men. The next day I saw him for the first time."

"Where?"

"We saw their canoe sailing down the river, in front of the houses. Everyone saw it. Then it continued on its journey. I remember his eyes."

The two girls are silent.

"He'd got his strength back up, but his arms were tied behind his back with wicker. The other hunters don't tie children up. He must have tried to escape."

"Then it must have been Lam," says Alma.

"He had the same eyes as you."

Sirim senses movement just next to her. The blanket falls onto the rug. Alma is standing up in the darkness.

"They'll be far away, Alma. They might have already reached the sea." Neither of the two girls has ever seen the sea.

"I'm leaving," says Alma.

"Take Cloud with you."

"No. I've seen what the forest is like along the river. The trees are too thick; I'll never be able to get him through."

Sirim gets up, too. "Will he go crazy again if you leave?" she asks.

"He wasn't crazy. There's no such thing. He was just lost."

"And now?"

Alma goes over to Cloud.

"Now he's found you."

Sirim joins them.

"There's a little canoe that I hid in the calmer waters, a little further up the river," says Sirim. "I'm giving it to you."

Their three shadows move silently through the palace. Cloud's hooves unfold slowly on the ground like a cat's paws.

Sirim and Alma arrive at a door that opens up onto the ramparts. They stay close to the wall to make sure the guards at the top don't see them. They leave the kingdom's little capital behind them and head north, towards a bend in the river.

Alma looks up. The sky is clearing up slightly. If they were back in the valley, she'd take Sirim to lie down in the grasses and enjoy the night. They'd listen to the deep, rumbling roar of the lions—a sound so deep you can feel it in the pit of your stomach. These last few days in the Kingdom of Bussa have been so bright. But Alma knows now that sunny spells don't always last.

24
To the Sea

Alma brings Cloud to a sudden stop by leaning back and putting her hand on his rump. With her other arm, she holds on to Sirim, who's sitting in front of her. The night is completely silent apart from the river humming away to their right. They don't move a muscle. Alma's hunting instinct has returned once more.

"Over there," she whispers. "Look."

Slowly, they turn the horse around to face the river. Their eyes try to pierce the darkness. Eventually, they're able to make out pale shapes in the distance, their reflections lighting up the black water. There's not a single voice, not a sound. Only those white streaks in the night. Something's brewing on the other side of the river.

"The Fulani," whispers Sirim.

Dozens of silhouettes of men dressed in white appear. The girls can see them clearly now. They can also make out their horses, some waiting in the water, some on the riverbank. The warriors haven't spotted the two girls.

Alma brings Cloud to a walk and they move away silently. After a few minutes, Sirim is able to speak again.

"There are always little groups that come to plunder the villages. But tonight there are a lot of them. This means war."

"We have to go back," says Alma.

"No. If they surround the town, you won't be able to leave. Go."

"I'm staying with you."

"I won't be alone. You're leaving Cloud with me. Your brother needs you. You have to go. The canoe is at the end of this path underneath a tree."

Alma slides down from Cloud's back.

"Watch out for the whirlpools in the river just outside of Bussa. The waters are dangerous around there," says Sirim, taking her hand.

Cloud sets off again at a slow trot. Alma runs alongside them for a moment.

"Good luck, Sirim," she says.

She's still holding her friend's hand. When she can no longer keep up, she lets Sirim go. Her shadow disappears into another, bigger shadow.

At the end of the path, Alma gropes in the darkness to find the canoe. It's lightweight and looks like the pieces of wood that float by in the streams of the Valley of Isaya during the rainy season. Alma knows that to continue down the river, she'll have to pass the Fulani warriors again. If a war is going to break out in Bussa, she'll also have to get past the village before the fighting starts. She looks around into the pitch-black night.

She pushes the canoe down to the water. She gives the sand a little kick with her foot and grabs the paddle. Sirim was right. The water is peaceful here. There's not even a current to show her which way to go. Alma tries to find her balance in the hollowed-out wood as it rolls this way and that to the chorus of toads. The paddle sinks silently into the water.

She remembers crossing the flooded ravine. Everything she knows about water, she learnt that night when she left her valley after the heavy rains.

This time, there's no moon. The canoe is invisible in the darkness. Alma chooses a direction at random, trying to follow the sound of the current somewhere in the distance. It would make no difference if she were blindfolded. And yet, with just a few strokes of her paddle, she manages to find her way. Now all she has to do is let herself be carried off.

Gliding along the river, she thinks of her little brother. It was along one of these riverbanks that he was being held captive. It was probably here that he tried to escape. She tries to remember the last time she saw him. He was by the fire, in the house under the fig tree. His eyes were closed. But was he really sleeping? Was he only pretending? Even the past has been changed by everything that's happened since. She's willing to fight to keep it intact.

Just then, a little landslide on the riverbank brings her back into the present. A Fulani horse has sent a rock rolling into the river. The men are very close by, silent as before. There seem to be more and more of them. They're waiting for something.

Alma drifts past in silence, lifting the paddle out of the water. She has the night for protection. She thinks she must be safe.

But as she turns her head, she sees a new group of silhouettes appearing in front of her. More men on horseback have moved down from the banks. They're lined up right in the middle of the river, and the canoe is heading straight for them. She doesn't even try to escape. She just lies down in the hollow of the canoe. It's over. She holds her paddle against her with both hands like a sword.

Somewhere, she hears a horse neigh, followed by a loud clap on the water's surface as a commotion breaks out. From the bottom of her canoe, Alma can't make out what's happening. She hears muffled noises, followed by a gunshot. She holds the paddle tighter, waiting to feel the impact. But apart from a slight ripple in the water, nothing sets the canoe off course.

Everything is calm again.

Alma will never know that her saviour came in the form of a half-ton crocodile. A Fulani horse had fallen down in the water. The rider managed to wrestle the animal free from the sixty teeth planted in its leg. That's when he fired the shot. The other men retreated to the shore alongside him, clearing the way for Alma.

When she sits up to look behind her, the darkness has erased everything from the scene.

She can already see the lights of Bussa in the distance. Just in front of the village, the river widens, and the current slows down. Sirim must have managed to warn the inhabitants. Shadows are moving from house to house. Torches are being lit. Alma slows down, letting her eyes wander through the night. She gazes at the calm before the battle, the lights flashing from the top of the town's wall. She hears the sound of feet hitting the ground. She lets the paddle drag through the water.

Suddenly she sees Cloud standing in the middle of the river just in front of her.

The water comes right up to his neck. He watches as she gets closer.

"Cloud!" she says, as she reaches his side.

She grabs his leather collar. The back of the boat swings around, swept along by the current. Alma keeps hold of

Cloud's collar like an anchor, and the canoe stops parallel to the horse's body.

"I'll come and find you when it's all over," she whispers into his ear.

The water roars beneath the canoe as it struggles to resist the current. Alma throws one arm around Cloud's neck.

"Alma! Is that you?"

Sirim is standing at the water's edge. She's climbed down a sand bank to look for Cloud, who has evidently managed to escape. The river is deep. Sirim can't get any closer to them.

"Sirim!" cries Alma.

She looks at her friend, unable to let go of the horse. The current is about to tear the canoe away.

"I'll come back, and I'll bring Lam with me," says Alma. "We'll see each other again!"

Finally, she lets go of the leather collar and lets the river carry her. She becomes smaller and smaller as she plunges into the darkness.

Cloud hasn't moved.

Sirim dives into the water and swims towards him.

"Cloud . . . "

She climbs onto his back, hugs him tightly with her legs and runs her hand over his cheek. She talks to him. Together, their eyes search for Alma one last time in the darkness. But she's already disappeared.

"Come."

The horse hesitates, then takes a step to the side, cutting through the water towards the lights of Bussa.

Off they go into the distance to join the battle that's waiting for them.

Alma has already reached the rapids. She's paddling between

the black rocks. There's water splashing everywhere, dispersed through the air by a flock of little green birds just above, whose wings are beating so fast they seem to disappear.

If we were to go way up above the whirlpools, far above the birds and the tallest treetops, we would see the river stretching for hundreds of miles in front of Alma. And one day, a long time from now, if we were to look down from far above the clouds, we'd see a little canoe gliding through the calm waters that lead to the sea.

25
A Mirage

The Sweet Amelie appears on the horizon, enveloped in smoke each time its cannon is fired. The sound of the detonation reaches the shore a couple of seconds later. Captain Gardel has ordered his crew to cast anchor. Firing the cannons is his way of signalling the ship's arrival.

Perched on the foremast, Joseph Mars is looking out at the village stretching out on each side of a bright white fort. He can just make out the colours of the flag flying from this angular building at the top of a wide, rounded staircase. Fort San Sebastian in Shama was built by the Portuguese but has belonged to the Dutch for over a century. In the bay alongside *The Sweet Amelie*, there are four swaying schooners that have come from Amsterdam. Dozens of forts like this one have been built along the African coast by Europeans vying for control of the slave trade.

Up on his mast, Joseph ties a knot in a final rope to keep the sail tight against the yardarm. He takes a couple of steps as though walking a tightrope, then descends via a rope ladder hanging from the shrouds.

Gardel is beside himself, hoisting the jolly boat Picard has just launched into the water back up onto the ship.

"Aren't we going ashore, Captain?"

"Look what's coming our way!"

Two long canoes have left the shore and are paddling towards a wave forming within range of the ship's cannon. The wave is part of a dangerous rip current that stretches along hundreds of miles of coast, rising like a wall and breaking a few feet from the shore. To get across the wave, you have to learn to tame it. Those who try were either born in a canoe or wish to die in one. Gardel knows the rip current in Shama is not as dangerous as in certain spots along the coast, but he's not taking any risks.

The canoes have just crossed the wave, propelled by fourteen paddles and a few small yellow sails. They're heading for *The Sweet Amelie*.

Abel Lebon looks enviously at Joseph Mars as he climbs down from the shrouds. Jumping down onto the deck, Joseph places a hand on Abel's shoulder, smiling.

"I had nothing to do with it, I promise!"

Joseph has been chosen to go ashore. He has no idea what made the captain grant him this privilege. The governors of the fort are going to be hosting a welcome dinner for the ship's officers. Over the next few days, there'll be discussions on the market conditions for the slave trade in the region, as well as some negotiations.

If he could, he'd gladly let Abel go and do what he's been dreaming of: setting foot on dry land. Joseph would much prefer to stay on board. He doesn't want to leave the captain's quarters unattended. He's still convinced that the gold he's been searching for since Lisbon is in the two locked chests he discovered beneath the captain's bed.

"Will you bring me a handful of earth back in your pocket?" asks Lebon.

Joseph smiles again. How did this boy end up on a ship like this? Just like the poor little seasick piglets plucked from the deck by a wave a few days ago, Abel Lebon seems out of place on the ship. He'd probably be happier to join them at the bottom of the ocean than stay aboard *The Sweet Amelie*.

What the two sailors don't realise is that there's a telescope pointed right at them as they speak.

The governor of the fort is watching them from the ramparts. He observes each of the sailors one by one and scrutinises every last detail of the ship. He's dressed in a frilled shirt and white wig and is whistling an opera tune to himself. There are two bottles of brandy on the table nearby. He notes how tidy the deck is and how well the ropes have been rolled. His gaze lingers on Amelie's sculpted face at the ship's bow, freshly painted yellow over the last few days. This ship is well looked after. Jon Jacobsen is pleased to see that a few officers on deck have dressed up for the occasion.

"The French," he says. "For the past two or three years, they've started coming here again. They made themselves scarce during the war." He's just spotted the silhouette of Lazarus Bartholomew Gardel, a formidable business partner he often hosts in Shama.

"What war?" asks a voice behind him.

"I can tell you've been away for a long time, Moses Shackle. America has gained independence from the British. And guess which side the French picked?"

He lowers his telescope, laughing.

"Believe it or not, they didn't side with the British! You must have been far away if you didn't know that."

"Yes. Very," says Mosi.

"For a long time," Jon Jacobsen continues, "French merchant ships were being targeted by the British, so they stopped coming over. That or they'd turn up in a convoy of warships with two gun decks. Cost a fortune to host them."

The Governor of Shama pauses to take a sip from his silver flask. He studies his visitor.

Mosi cut straight through rivers, savanna, and forests to get to this port on the Gold Coast. From here, he plans to follow the shoreline to Angola—even Zanzibar if necessary—to scour every ship, every convoy, every slave hut, and the dungeons of every fortress, until he finds his son.

"So, Shackle. You come out of retirement, and the first man you come to see is your old friend Jacobsen at Fort Saint Sebastian in Shama."

"I know the best places to come," says Mosi.

The governor gives him a satisfied smirk and puts down the brandy flask. His hand is shaking a little more now as he picks up his telescope again.

"And if I'm not mistaken, I'm the only one still at my post after all this time," says Jacobsen.

He lowers his telescope and bows ever so slightly in a pitiful excuse for a salute.

"His Imperial Highness, Emperor Jacobsen of the Coast!" He laughs to himself.

"Tell me, Shackle. Are you going back into business?"

Mosi watches the canoes, which have now reached the ship. The men are getting the captain, his first mate, the surgeon, and a few others into the canoes.

"I'm looking for one or two captives for a good client."

"That's bad timing. You've come right at the same time as the French. And there are four little schooners coming from

Amsterdam that don't have a single captive on board. But for Moses Shackle, I'm sure I can find one or two exceptional specimens."

"I want to choose. I want to see them all. Every captive you have."

Jon Jacobsen laughs again.

"You haven't changed, Shackle. My advisers and I will have a think. Come back and see us tomorrow."

Without taking his eyes off the ocean, the governor picks up his two little bottles, the only advisers he's ever had. He slips them into his pockets. The canoes are now coming across the rip current with their passengers inside. After waiting for a long time, sheltered in the trough of a wave, suddenly the canoes shoot up a wall of foam.

The boatmen of Shama are renowned from here to Porto-Novo. They're the best boatmen along the whole coast. They play with the waves like kittens with a ball of string.

When Jon Jacobsen finally turns around, Moses Shackle has disappeared.

Mosi is making his way down the steps that lead to the double doors of the fort. He's looking out at the village of Shama. This is where it all began for Mosi. The son of a Fante fishermen, he arrived at the age of twelve and was hired as an oarsman on one of the canoes. Ten years later, he became Moses Shackle. He belonged to a group known as the Gold Takers, the biggest slave traders on the coast.

Mosi is heading towards the beach. A stretch of grey sand in the western part of Shama, where the fishermen and boatmen live, serves as the village square. On the other side of the fort, up on the hill, there's another district, which is home to peasants, craftspeople, and men and women living off the land.

These two worlds have been in conflict since the dawn of time. Governor Jacobsen has learnt to fan the flames of these wars, which enable him to sell more guns and liquor.

The canoes have made it through the rip current. It's still too deep to walk to shore, so the passengers are being transferred to other, smaller canoes to keep their silk stockings and pumps from getting wet.

Mosi feels the cool sand beneath his feet. He watches the arrivals flock towards the fort. As they climb the steps, the doors are opened by two young guards dressed in blue and red with hats that are too big for their heads.

There's one boy being turned away at the door. It's Joseph Mars. His companions leave him behind, sniggering as they go.

A little lost, Joseph lingers near the door under the watchful eyes of the guards, who are barely any older than he is. Finally, he goes back down the steps. He walks down to the beach and sits on a rock next to a small crowd of boatmen who are dragging their canoes onto the carpet of seashells.

Out at sea, the sailors gaze at the land.

A man walks over to Joseph and starts speaking to him in French.

"Was it the clothes they didn't like?

"How did you know?" asks Joseph.

Mosi smiles his first smile in a long time.

"Once upon a time, I knew these people well. They promise a good meal, bring in a hungry cabin boy, then leave him at the door because he doesn't have the right clothes. They think it's funny."

"You really think the governor would have kicked me out just because of my clothes?" asks Joseph.

"It's the only power he has," Mosi explains. "He dresses up his soldiers, has his towers repainted white, drinks, and plays with his twenty cannons. What does he have apart from that? He has to be in control of something. So he demands that his guests wear the clothes of his old country. The country he'll never return to."

"Why won't he ever return?"

"Because he'll die of fever, like all the others."

"Who are you?" asks Joseph.

Mosi looks at the boy in front of him. How old is he? He suddenly thinks of his daughter. This boy must be around Alma's age.

"How many captives do you have aboard?" asks Mosi.

He came to the boy with the sole aim of asking this question.

"I'm not allowed to tell you," Joseph replies.

"Then I have no more to say, either. Goodbye." He goes to leave.

"None!" cries Joseph.

"What?"

"There are no captives aboard. This is the first time we've come ashore."

Mosi nods and carries on walking. Now he knows that Lam isn't on the French ship. He knows the Dutch aren't carrying any cargo, either. All that remains is to check the dungeons of the fort before moving on.

"You still haven't told me who you are," says Joseph, running after him.

Mosi stops.

"My name is Mosi."

He says his real name to make himself feel better, to forget Moses Shackle just for a moment, to erase the hat-wearing shadow on the sand at his feet.

Just then, his gaze is drawn towards the very end of the beach.

There, in the evening light, a thin line has appeared from the mist. It's like a mirage.

26

The Captives

They shuffle forward two by two, taking short, rapid steps. Their ankles are bound together by very short chains. There must be about ten men. Just behind them are three women and two children, jogging along in step with the others but without any chains. There are a few other men escorting the convoy. These men are black, too, armed with rifles and spears.

With the sun at his back, it's as though Mosi is pushing his own shadow along the sand in front of him. He walks towards them. As the group draws closer, he begins to pick up speed.

Joseph has come to a stop behind Mosi. He watches the group of people approach.

These are the captives. For months aboard the ship, the crew has spoken of nothing but the captives. But this is the first time Joseph has seen them. Now he can hear the clinking of the chains mingled with the lapping of the waves on the grey sand.

Mosi has stopped a few steps away from the convoy. His eyes are fixed upon the two silhouettes at the back of the group: the two children bringing up the rear. From a distance, he'd still hoped he might be looking at his son.

But these children are older than Lam. The little boy and girl are looking straight ahead. They're hurrying along in step with the others. For a split second, the girl flashes a glance at Mosi, begging him to pull her away from this fate.

One of the guards has just noticed Mosi approaching them.

"What do you want?" he barks, stopping just in front of him.

"Are you taking them to Fort San Sebastian?"

"No. To the British, three days' walk from here."

"Ah. Okay. I'm waiting for someone."

"Move along."

Somewhat reassured, the guard catches up with the rest of the group. Further along the beach, the boatmen come forward one by one to watch the captives pass by. They've almost reached them.

Joseph Mars is standing stock still. From the beginning, he swore he wouldn't let anything get to him. Captives, middle passage, prime slaves . . . he knows all these words but has never wanted to think about the meanings they hold. Sometimes, when he's speaking with Jacques Dubois, he feels the shell surrounding the words beginning to crack. But this time, it has crumbled to dust. Dust that settles at the feet of those passing in front of him now, mingling with the sand and bits of broken seashell.

All that remain are fifteen human lives moving along the beach. Joseph sees all the little scars on their skin, perhaps from childhood escapades. He sees the marks on the crooks of their necks left by the rice so recently carried home from the fields. He sees haunted eyes that do all they can to avoid thinking, lips that have been bitten raw to fight back the tears. Fifteen whole lives.

Just then, the little group comes to a halt. There's a cry coming from somewhere.

One of the boatmen has come to block their path. The guards are pointing their rifles at him, shouting. The captives take the opportunity to catch their breath. They bend down, clutching their knees. When one man tries to rest his head on his neighbour's shoulder, a guard prods him to make him stand up straight.

The boatman who stopped the convoy has his hands in the air. He's surrounded. But he doesn't want to fight. He just wants to talk to one of the women. The guards exchange a few words. Without lowering their weapons, they allow him to go over to the captive.

"I know her," says the boatman. "She's from my village, ten days from here across the lagoon. She shouldn't be here."

He gets up close to her. She's around thirty years old, thin and petite, with eyes like two black suns.

"What are you doing here?"

When she doesn't reply, he goes to touch her arm, but one of the guards pushes him away. The boatman raises his hands again.

"What happened?" he asks her softly.

She remains silent.

"What happened up there?"

"They came to the village," she says, her eyes shining even more now.

"What about your family? Should I warn them you're here? Your children . . ." His breath catches, and his eyes open wide as though he's suddenly understood.

"And my family . . .?"

They look at each other. She stands up straight. It would be too shameful for her to look away.

"There's no one left to warn," she says.

The man lets out a cry. The guards throw him to the ground. A struggle ensues.

"I know her," he shouts. "I know her!"

His cries are getting louder and louder. The sand is sticking to his skin and face.

His friends come to restrain him. They say his name over and over to calm him down.

The convoy sets off again at the same pace, with the same clanging of chains and bare feet hitting the sand.

The captives are heading along the coastline towards the west. The silhouettes of their backs are visible against the sunlight. As they recede further into the distance, a haze of mist reappears just above their heads.

Joseph doesn't need to speak a word of their language to understand what has happened. He watches the boatman get up from the sand and run across the beach, abandoning everything. He's going home. He knows there's nothing he can do, that it's all over. But he's going home. His feet sink into the sand as he runs. Joseph watches him fall down and get back up several times.

Just then, loud voices come echoing from the fort. The officers of *The Sweet Amelie* are coming down the steps in disarray.

The captain can be heard shouting angrily.

Picard hurries on ahead in Joseph's direction.

"We're leaving," he says. "Get them to put the canoes back in the water. The captain's furious."

"Why?"

"There's not a single captive in all the dungeons of that fort. Jacobsen's a drunk. He wanted to buy some time, settle the accounts for a few services, and use our ship to attract others. But there's not a single captive for sale here."

Palardi joins them.

"There's been peace in this region for three years. I knew it.

There's nothing worse for the slave trade. No wars means no captives. I've said that from the beginning."

"Said what?" says the captain, appearing from behind them. "What have you been saying now, Palardi?"

"That you have a strong intuition, Captain," says the surgeon, pathetically.

Gardel knows the tricks of his trade. He's always sure to discreetly send one of his men to explore the dungeons before getting into any discussions. This time, they didn't find anything.

"I just saved us eight days. This place is a madhouse. Picard, tell the boatmen they're coming with us. We'll need them until we get to Ouidah at least. We'll tow them. Arrange for them to join us for two months. Two canoes and fourteen men, not one less. They can find their way home at their own expense. This Dutchman's a crook, so we're taking his sailors."

The boatmen of Shama are like gold dust on this coast. Picard knows they're also very tough businessmen. He suspects this is why Gardel is sending him to do the bargaining. The captain has a plan. He wants to know Picard is worth his salt if negotiations need to be carried out later down the line.

"What about water? And wood?" asks Savage, a trainee naval officer.

"Not now," barks Gardel. "We're leaving. We have enough water to get to Elmina. If we run out, we'll open the brandy. Whatever happens, don't let the other ships get word of why we're leaving. Tell them Governor Jacobsen doesn't like the French and has been reserving his stocks for his own countrymen. Let them all waste their time hanging around here. I don't want anything to do with them until Christmas."

Picard goes over to the head boatman. The discussions are long-winded. The head boatman seems reluctant. He turns to his men. In reality, they know it's an acceptable offer. The crisis in Shama means it's the best they can hope for at the moment. But there's also one little issue they don't want to bring up. Now that their colleague has left, they're one man short of the fourteen required for the deal.

The clock is ticking. The tide is going out. Picard, who thinks he's getting a bargain, pretends to get angry. He speaks to them in dreadful English, glancing at Gardel.

"Decide now! I don't pay higher. You also take tobacco for each man on Sundays."

Joseph is keeping his distance. He's watching Mosi, who has waded out into the waves. His clothes are in a little pile on the sand. The water is up to Mosi's shoulders. Joseph watches him turn around to look at the group of boatmen. He hesitates for a moment before diving once more into the water. Then he emerges, leaving his clothes on the shore. He goes over to the head boatman, who is still negotiating with Picard.

"If you need an extra man," says Mosi, "I'm here."

"You know this part of the coast?"

"I was born here."

The head boatman nods, turns to Picard, and shakes his hand.

Watching from up near the fort, Gardel understands that a deal has been struck.

Joseph Mars is sitting at the front of one of the canoes. Next to him, Mosi plunges his paddle deep into the water. He paddles even harder than the rest. He's just found the best way to visit all the forts and slave trading posts along the coast, perhaps as far as Bonny and Old Calabar. All he has to do is follow the French ship.

On the beach, a group of children have found his old clothes and are dressing up in them.

Mosi prefers to keep his shoulders and legs bare. He likes to feel the seawater against his skin. His mind drifts back to when he was twelve years old, rowing among the boatmen of Shama. Back to a time when it was impossible to imagine that, one day, he might lose a son to the slave trade.

27

Barbaric Harvest

Since that night on All Saints' Day, 1786, the course of *The Sweet Amelie* has been punctuated by the purchase of captives all along the coast. From port to port, women, children, and men in clusters of seven or eight, sometimes more, sometimes fewer, are traded in for the ship's cargo: cloth, iron, firearms, poor-quality alcohol cut with water, and parasols with golden fringes that have been cluttering up the ship's hold. The beautiful black and yellow boat, with its immaculate sails and figurehead of a young girl in a nightgown is slowly becoming a slave ship.

Villagers light big fires on the beaches to signal to passing ships that there are captives for sale on their shores, but they can't always be trusted. The captain surveys the coastline. He never hangs around for very long. Often, the ship goes by without even stopping.

The first time it does stop, before the tall towers of Elmina Castle, only one man is brought aboard the ship. The first man. He stands straight and proud like a wooden figurine, his jaw clenched and his chin held high. His eyes are red from trying to keep them open for so long. The sailors hoist him up on deck, but not one of them dares look this dignified man in the eye.

Gardel is looking down from the aftcastle. He's beside himself. He was very close to buying a batch of thirty perfectly healthy men in one go. The sale would have been a good omen for the rest of the trip, but then a one-hundred-and-fifty-ton brigantine ship from Liverpool outbid the captain by throwing three kegs of powder into the deal. Instead of thirty captives, he's left with one, too old to bring in more than a thousand pounds.

On the first page of the register, Picard writes down the name he has given this first man: Adam. Next to the name, he writes down how much he cost: a small barrel of brandy, a dozen sheets of fabric, three iron bars, some gun powder and four rifles.

The first man is sitting alone on deck, the rowboat suspended just above him. He's still wearing that heartbreaking smile; his steely gaze seems to be directed within. He doesn't make a sound even when the hot iron brands the skin on his right shoulder with a capital "A" for Amelie, enclosed within a circle.

Joseph has fled to the bowels of the ship so he doesn't have to watch. He's working with Jacques Dubois, who's managed to find all the wood they need. Tavel is with them, too. The cooper has been back on his feet for some time now. He's eternally grateful to Dubois, who saved his life with nothing but fresh air and the cooking water from the rice. Now he won't stop thanking Dubois and never leaves his side.

Alongside his health, Tavel seems to have regained his voice. He never stops talking. It's as though he's afraid that if he does, he might never be able to speak again.

"You know, Monsieur Dubois, I'm currently working on a little study that I think will interest you."

"Is that so?" the carpenter mumbles politely.

"I've noticed that the weight of one human we purchase is roughly equal to the weight of the goods we give in exchange. What an extraordinary coincidence."

"Extraordinary," sighs Dubois.

"That means the ship's waterline barely changes when the ship is filled with captives."

"A happy coincidence indeed!" Dubois shouts, swiftly bringing his mallet down onto a wooden peg. "You might also discover during the journey that the increase in the captain's weight corresponds exactly to the decrease in the captives' weight. Wouldn't that be simply astonishing?"

Tavel thinks for a moment.

"I'll do my calculations," he says. "I can see that you, too, are mathematically minded, Monsieur Dubois. Did you also know that—"

"Say, Tavel? Could you go and get me the mallet I left in the crow's nest up on the mainmast?"

"Yes. Remind me when I get back that there's something else I wanted to tell you. I've thought of a way to find out whether the barrels of brandy have been mixed with water as a trick. I've found rather an impressive method."

"I'm familiar with the method you're talking about. It's called tasting."

"No. It's called weighing, Monsieur Dubois. Would you believe, water is in fact heavier than alcohol?"

He raises his index finger knowingly before continuing.

"All you need is a 250-quart barrel, a scale and—"

"Please, save your bright idea for afterwards, Tavel. Go and find the mallet. We'll be here waiting for you."

"All right. I'll be right back. Hang on!"

"We'll try."

Tavel disappears. The carpenter lets out a sigh of relief.

"Is he really going to go up the mainmast?" asks Joseph.

"No. But this will give us a few moments' peace. Depending on how long it takes him to invent a flying machine or extendable arm."

"Or how long it takes him to realise you can't have left your mallet up there—because it's right there in your hand!"

Tomorrow, *The Sweet Amelie* will cast anchor once again with renewed hope. Of all the forts along the 400-mile stretch that constitutes the Golden Coast, Cape Coast is the most important one belonging to the British. Perched on a wave-battered rock, the fort is surrounded by a swarm of canoes that come and go amidst a handful of hungry brigs and three-masters waiting on the other side of the rip current.

Cape Coast is where Gardel manages to conclude his first real business deals. The prices are too high, and the competition is fierce, but one way or another, the hold must be filled.

And now the ship is finally ready. During the night, Dubois and Joseph completed the barricade that divides the ship's deck in two, using wooden planks they picked up in Elmina. The new palisade, with its two small doors, has been built just in front of the mainmast and is capped with spikes and blades.

Gardel has just bought seven men and one woman. After spending a night in a hut on the beach, they're brought aboard the ship. As they set foot on *The Sweet Amelie,* they stare in astonishment at the single, solitary captive sitting behind a disproportionately large barrier with forty men watching over him. The woman is called up to the aftcastle at the rear of the deck. They write her name in the register as "Eve."

Adam and Eve! Naming the captives is a rare source of joy for the sailors on all slave ships. They clap their hands together, feeling so amused with themselves, so powerful and smart. But to Jacques Dubois, who watches the spectacle from afar, nothing could be more terrible than pretending that this man and woman have just been created. As if they didn't exist before. As if they never had their own names, their own land. By calling these two people Adam and Eve, Gardel's crew are pretending they've given them life, when in fact, the opposite is true. They've destroyed everything the two of them once were.

Joseph is perched up in the masts. Down below, alone on the aftcastle, he sees the woman standing tense and ready to fight. She's just bitten a sailor on the wrist because he tried to force her to sit down. A shower of beatings rains down on her. That's when she becomes acquainted with the weapon that will rule the rest of her life. It's called a cat o' nine tails, a whip with nine cords, each with a knot at the end.

None of the other captives even get to witness this woman's bravery. They're on the other side of the barricade, crowded around the man the whites call Adam. Soon, they won't be able to remember daylight or air. They'll be locked up in the steerage.

The canoe that transported the captives is moored alongside the ship. Joseph catches Mosi's eye as he heads ashore in the other canoe. In the boat with him is Cook, who's convinced Gardel to let him talk with other nearby boats to see if he can exchange some rice and beans for fresh produce. The chicken cages have been empty for a month now, the pigs were swept away by the storm and the meals on board are becoming more dismal by the day.

"You'll see," says Cook. "You won't regret it."

Cook has also promised to find out which of the coastal rivers are the purest, so they can replenish their stock of drinking water. The water they've been drawing from the barrels has turned brown. It smells like a frog has died in there.

Mosi stays with Cook all afternoon. One by one, they board the other ships. While Cook charms the crew with his smile and his perfect English, Mosi discreetly slides his canoe along the hull. Through the portholes, he asks in the lower decks if there's a Lam Lilim of Isaya among them.

These three words begin to spread through the bowels of every ship on the coast, whispered from one invisible captive to the next.

Only a parent could believe that among the tens of thousands of human beings torn from this coast each year, it's possible to find a child by taking to the water with only a canoe and paddle and repeating a name in the steerage of every ship, the dungeons of every fort.

That evening, back on board *The Sweet Amelie*, Cook will be serving morel vol-au-vents made by the chef of a ship called *High Society*, a speedy little vessel that travels directly from La Rochelle to the Gold Coast and back again.

After a few disappointing stops and with barely three dozen captives in the hold, the search will truly begin in Ouidah.

Gardel has decided to keep *The Sweet Amelie* anchored just beyond the rip current in Ouidah until Christmas time. Fort Saint Louis in Ouidah is the hub of French activity along the coast.

During this time, Joseph is not allowed to leave the ship. Gardel fears that he'll ditch them once he's solved Luc de Lerna's riddle and jump aboard one of the other ships swarming around Ouidah.

The crew is divided into three groups.

The first will soon leave to set up camp in Ouidah, led by the captain and accompanied by the surgeon, who is in charge of inspecting the goods. They'll have to negotiate at the fort to get the hundreds of captives they need. The captain will also pay a visit to the King of Dahomey who lives a day from the coast on the other side of the swamps.

The second team will accompany Picard on a mission aboard the rowboat, which is finally set to be launched. They'll go on ahead and start making trade negotiations at the next stops: Porto-Novo and Badagry. This is Gardel's latest plan. Picard will gather captives for *The Sweet Amelie* to pick up later. This will save them a lot of time. Rumour has it that this is where the best deals are being made right now.

One final group will stay on board with Absalom the boatswain and Dubois the carpenter. They'll guard the ship and the few captives already on board. They'll also make any necessary repairs. Gardel has left Cook with them, of course, in the hope that Joseph will get some information from him about Luc de Lerna and his treasure. He's personally entrusted Joseph to Absalom. The rules are strict. Joseph is to stay locked up working in the chart room from dawn until dusk.

And so, one evening, the three teams go their separate ways. *The Sweet Amelie* stays moored. The little rowboat sets off east carrying Picard and his crew of scouts, and the fourteen boatmen of Shama take Gardel, Palardi, and around fifteen other men to continue their barbaric harvest in the Kingdom of Ouidah.

28

Dark Flowers

"What we're living now," says one sailor, "is the life of a castaway. I know; I got stranded for a month on a sandbank just off Bourbon Island."

"The only difference is that we'll be here for two months," remarks another.

"And that I have fifty people to feed twice a day," adds Cook, wearily.

"Please . . . can you all *please* stop talking?" groans Absalom.

The boatswain is lying on the deck with his arms crossed. He's feverish and has a wet handkerchief across his forehead. The others around him aren't faring much better.

The Sweet Amelie has now been anchored off the coast of Ouidah for seven weeks. Tiger sharks circle the ship day and night. The weather is humid and foggy during this season. Everything is white. Submerged in a mist as thick as mashed potatoes, they can't even see the coast. They've lowered the upper parts of the masts to prevent the ship from being swept away in the wind. With its flag and masts lowered, the ship looks like a Roman galley.

The sailors' only distraction is watching the two large canoes emerging from the mist three times a week. Morel and Savage sit proudly at the head of the fourteen boatmen. They gradually empty the cargo from the ship's hold for bartering and cram everything they can into the boats. The larger barrels are tied together, thrown into the water, and pulled ashore. In exchange for the goods, the two trainee officers Morel and Savage give news to those who've remained aboard.

They explain that Lazarus Gardel and his men are staying in Fort Saint-Louis in Ouidah, where they've received a less-than warm welcome from Governor de Montaguère, a crook who's been no help whatsoever. Luckily, the captain has paid the King of Dahomey the required fee to enable him to buy captives. The captives are locked up in shacks built along the beach next to the cargo being unloaded from the ship.

"It's coming along," says Morel vaguely, when the crew ask him how much longer this is likely to go on. "It's coming along."

The sailors aboard *The Sweet Amelie* never get more information than that. The canoes are already leaving, loaded with iron, pipes, fabric from the Indies and red handkerchiefs from western France.

"Tell Joseph Mars he can come out of his cell," says Absalom suddenly. He's still lying on the wooden floorboards of the deck, pale as a ghost. "I forgot about him again."

Since he's been ill, he hasn't been keeping an eye on Joseph. Nobody on board understands what the boy is supposed to be doing all day in that little cabin. Joseph tells them that Gardel has asked him to copy out the logbook several times so he can have it sent to Bassac and his associates. But surely it doesn't take fifty days to do a job like that?

"I'll go," says Cook. "I'll let the boy out."

He makes his way down the ship's ladder, which leads to the door of the chart room. He pushes the door, only to find that Absalom hasn't even bothered to lock it. Joseph has his back to him. He hasn't noticed Cook standing there. Slowly, Cook goes over to him and leans over his shoulder.

"So?" he asks. "Are we going somewhere nice?"

Joseph jumps. He covers up the map he was bent over.

"Looks like you were off in the islands."

"I wish," Joseph replies. "Time passes so slowly here."

"And it's not over yet," Cook laments, walking away.

"Cook!"

He comes back and stands in the doorway.

"Gardel told me to find out more."

"More?"

"About the years you spent with Luc de Lerna."

"Ah."

He shakes his head despondently.

"What does he want to know?"

"I can make do with whatever you tell me."

Cook closes the door and leans against it. He rubs a hand across his forehead. What to tell?

"I was your age when I first set foot aboard *The Hydra*. At the time, Luc de Lerna was sailing not far from here, just off the coast of Sierra Leone. He liked the Windward Coast. There weren't many foreign forts, only the forest tumbling into the ocean. And ships passing in the distance, full to the brim."

"What was he like?"

"He had respect for God and for gold. But nothing else. He would dip smoked meat into liquid gold and break the crust with a hammer when it was time to serve it. He had a little monkey that he dressed in gold chain mail and a red papal hat."

Joseph smiles. Now he's sure that Cook knew the old pirate.

"Why did you leave?"

"I didn't. I was left behind on a British naval ship after a battle. Luc de Lerna went on without me. I spent four years in various prisons in Britain."

"Are you angry with him for doing that?"

Cook doesn't reply. Joseph watches him leave. He feels reassured. This information should be enough to satisfy Gardel a little longer. Cook doesn't seem to miss his pirate years.

Everything is going exactly as it should be. Good old Cook isn't about to scupper Joseph's plans. All that remains is for him to leave the coast of Africa as soon as possible and follow the trade winds to the place where they're expecting him. During this time, he'll have to try and forget the living, breathing beings in the ship's steerage.

A few moments earlier, two captives on the coast just opposite came to sit in the grass below the long avenue of lemon trees lining the fort in Ouidah. They've just arrived from the north. One of their guards carries a dragoon officer's sabre, the other a bush rifle.

"Give her a piece of fruit," Baako says to his father, pointing at the woman.

He's just realised he doesn't know her name, despite having walked with her for two months. She's pregnant. How hasn't she died of exhaustion? He could hear her singing in a low voice as she walked. He doesn't know if she was doing it for herself, for her grown son of twenty years, or for the baby she's carrying. Baako only knows that she sings like no other human on earth.

"Give her a piece of fruit," Baako repeats.

But Eeko doesn't dare take a lemon from a white man's

garden. What if they throw him on a boat, too? What if they mistake him for a captive? He's afraid to be this close to the sea, on the edge of the abyss. What difference is there between him and the other living beings who are thrown onto those ships? He's waiting anxiously for the return of his chief, Awoshi, who's gone to find the governor of the fort.

In the end, Baako picks a lemon himself. He goes over to the woman and gives it to her. She turns it over in her hands. She passes it to Soum, who bites into it, just to break the skin, then gives it back to his mother. She throws her head back and squeezes the fruit over her open mouth. A few drops come falling down. Nao closes her eyes. Her eyelids are moist.

Eeko and Baako hold their breath. They look at each other. She's beautiful. They wish they could turn around, let her escape. They wish they could take her back to that beautiful valley.

For just a few hours, they were able to glimpse its splendour from the threshold, watching the herds of elephants and zebra sketching patterns across brand new landscapes right before their eyes. It was morning. The ashes from the fire had settled. The sun was rising for the first time. The giraffes were dancing and galloping around. Storks and flamingos circled above their heads, waiting for the ground to cool down.

As they left with their captives, the Ashanti warriors felt as though they had trespassed upon a forbidden dream, and that this act of sacrilege would haunt them for a long time.

Awoshi is back. He's accompanied by a white man whose hair is tied back in a ponytail. He's holding his hat under his arm. The frills of his shirt look like a mass of white foam on his chest, spilling out between the lapels of his coat. But he isn't the Governor of Ouidah. It's Lazarus Gardel.

Governor Olivier de Montaguère left this morning on a

diplomatic mission. He was carried off on a hammock stretched between two bamboo canes. He's afraid of the sacred caimans swarming around in the swamps.

Gardel has taken advantage of de Montaguère's absence to follow this young Ashanti into the garden, where he claims he has two captives to sell. The Ashanti only had to say one word to make Gardel follow him through the lemon trees: "Okos." This word still sends a shiver down the spine of the older, more knowledgeable slave traders. Those who have experienced the extraordinary Oko phenomenon first-hand.

"Here," says Awoshi.

He points to Nao and Soum.

"Probably the last two on earth."

"What are their gifts?"

"Hers is the gift of song."

Gardel has only ever heard one Oko with this gift sing. It was a little boy. He'll never forget it.

"And the boy?"

Awoshi goes over to Soum.

"Move."

The boy doesn't budge.

"Move!"

With a hard kick, Awoshi sends Soum rolling across the ground.

"Good Lord!" cries Gardel. "Growth."

"Yes," says Awoshi. "The gift of growth."

Just where Soum was sitting, in the middle of the vast, freshly cut lawn, a little circle of dazzling green grass has grown, along with coiled vines and a bulging flower that makes a crackling noise as it bursts into bloom.

Gardel rubs his face. He sucks his tongue as though it were a fruit sweet.

"Are they fragile?"

"No."

"They're always fragile."

"They walked two months to get here. And the woman is pregnant. You actually have three Okos sitting in front of you," says Awoshi.

Gardel knows the five gifts of the Oko. There's the gift of growth, the gift of song . . . then there are the gifts of healing and hunting. Which one will this child possess? All of them are invaluable. There's only one gift he's afraid of, because he's seen it cause ships to burn down or explode: the gift of war.

"Well?" says Awoshi. "If you're not interested, I'll speak to the Portuguese."

Baako and Eeko admire their chief's confidence.

Gardel goes over to Awoshi and whispers in his ear for a long time. He's quietly listing off all the goods he can trade. He's never offered this much for captives before.

"That's all I have to offer you."

Awoshi turns to face him. "That will cover the unborn child. But what are you offering for these two here?"

Gardel sighs. Beads of sweat from his forehead are rolling down into his eyes. It's obvious he's willing to give anything.

"I'll give you double for the others."

"For each one?"

"Yes," he says, as though under a spell.

"And the canoe to take the goods upriver to the hills of Kumasi."

"Okay. You can take the canoe, as well."

"And three good rifles for protection."

Gardel doesn't even recognise himself anymore. "Yes."

Awoshi goes over the trials of these last days in his mind.

The endless road. Now he can go home. He'll be welcomed back like a prince.

"Put them in my room in the fort," says Gardel, still feverish. "I have two men there who will keep an eye on them. I'll bring them aboard later this evening."

Gardel is worried about de Montaguère's return. The French governor of Ouidah always keeps the best batches for his son-in-law, who does business in the region. Whatever happens, he must not find out about the Okos.

"Go to the beach depot for your payment," says Gardel, going over to the Okos.

Soum jumps up and huddles against his mother. She puts her arm around him for protection. Beneath their tangled bodies, small, dark flowers begin to unfurl.

29
The Sea

Night has fallen. Mosi is walking on the beach alongside the cages full of captives. He looks carefully at each one. Many are still wearing iron collars or are chained to one another by the ankles. Children move around between the curled-up bodies.

When his name was Moses Shackle, Mosi never looked at the captives he took. Just like when you pick a handful of tall grasses while walking through a meadow. You chew on the end of one and throw the rest away, scattering them in a trail behind you. Do you know how many you've plucked from the ground? No. You were thinking about something else.

Mosi has searched all the dungeons of William's Fort, which belongs to the British, just opposite Fort Saint-Louis in Ouidah. A few days ago, he did the same at the nearby Portuguese trading post. All the captives had been brought out of the caves to be washed and shaved. He walked among them, asking to look at the children. He didn't find his son.

Mosi can't wait any longer. Lam is somewhere along this coast, waiting to be taken aboard one of the ships. *The Sweet Amelie* has been anchored for several weeks now. Mosi will continue on foot. He'll travel to Porto-Novo in three days' time and won't stop until he finds Lam. There are only a few moons left until the rain opens up the valley again. They'll cross the ravine together. It'll be nighttime, perhaps. He'll see their house from a distance. He'll wake up Lam, who'll be sleeping on his shoulders.

"We're home."

He'll lift him down and take his hand.

No one will hear them tiptoe in. Mosi is sure Alma will be the first to wake up.

"Is that you?"

The head of the Shama boatmen is sitting with his men around a fire in the sand, far away from the captives. Mosi sits down next to him. The head boatman acts as though he hasn't noticed him.

"I know what you're going to say," he says, after a while.

Mosi listens, watching the embers.

"I've been watching you every day. You're the best of them. You know the waves. But I can tell you're not here for that."

"For what?"

"For the waves."

"No. I'm not here for the waves."

"You're leaving."

"Yes."

"Wait a while. Stay the night. The sea is treacherous. We still have two captives to take onto the boat. I need you."

Mosi lifts his head.

"Two captives?"

"The ones the captain bought."

"Where are they?"

"At Fort Saint-Louis."

A glimmer of hope reappears in Mosi's eye. The tiny flicker that reignites in him each time he arrives somewhere new.

"Some Ashanti hunters brought them here today."

Mosi turns to him. "Since when do Ashanti hunters come as far as the sea?"

The head boatman doesn't reply.

"Was there a child?"

"Yes," the man says, smiling.

"Around ten years old?" asks Mosi.

"Younger. So much younger, it hasn't even been born yet."

Mosi gets to his feet. The light in his eye has gone out. The head boatman calls after him.

"Wait! There's a pregnant woman and her grown son. Wait a little longer, and I'll pay you afterwards."

"I don't want you to pay me. I'm leaving. You don't owe me anything."

Mosi slips into the darkness, unwittingly turning his back on the two beloved faces he came so close to seeing tonight.

Later, when the boatmen arrive at the ship with the two Okos, they're surprised to find that the rowboat has returned from its mission and has already been moored alongside *The Sweet Amelie*.

Picard and his men have worked miracles. There are two hundred captives waiting on the Porto-Novo beach a few miles away. All that remains is to settle the bill. The goods promised in exchange for the captives are still aboard the ship. The traders are even keeping Abel Lebon and Tavel the cooper as collateral. They'll be released as soon as the payment is made.

Upon hearing this good news, Gardel decides it's time to leave. Early in the morning, he starts loading the captives he bought from Ouidah onto the ship. There are too many to bring aboard using only the canoes from Shama. Gardel commissions other boats to take several trips across the rip current. The whole crew is put to work. Even Joseph Mars.

The sun has only just begun to rise. It's raining. It's been so long since Joseph last left *The Sweet Amelie*. He's sitting in the front of one of the canoes.

In the endless string of tragedies caused by the slave trade, this has to be one of the most heartbreaking moments of all.

Slowly, shadows begin to appear on the beach. The captives are brought to the sea in small groups. They begin to make their way through the water. Almost all of them are chained together. Heavy and shackled, they're unable to climb aboard the canoes as they're jostled by the waves. The sailors surround them, shouting.

The captives cling to one another in the rain. They look back towards the land. Heavy blows fall upon their shoulders. This is the first time most of them have seen the sea. The waves break, preventing them from climbing aboard. They can still feel the sand beneath their feet. Their feet slip and sink in the sand beneath the water. But they're still there. Each time one person falls down, those who are chained on either side savour the extra few seconds they're able to linger on the shore. Then the sailors pull them aboard by force. Their feet slip. They're torn from the earth. They can't feel anything beneath them anymore.

They're pushed into the canoes.

It's over.

The white shores of their continent begin to drift away. Between the trees, they see the glow of millions of fireflies: the eyes of their ancestors watching them go.

Some try to jump from the canoes into the water.

Their fear of sharks is nothing compared to their fear of the unknown.

Where are we going? What's going to happen to us?

The Sweet Amelie appears, glistening in the rain. The towering masts have been put back up. The pink light of the dawn illuminates the sea. One last glimmer before everything is extinguished by the darkness of the steerage.

It's still raining at midday. Gardel's crew has brought out the sails that have been stowed away for the duration of the long stopover. They're heavy, sticking together with the rain. Dozens of men are up on the yardarms, hoisting them up. They're anxious to set sail.

Slowly, the ship shudders back to life and resumes its course.

The next day, in the protected anchorage of Porto-Novo, the two hundred captives purchased by Picard are brought onto the ship. This time, the crew thinks it's all over. The boatmen of Shama have gone home. By gathering captives in Ouidah and Porto-Novo at the same time, Captain Gardel has saved them nearly two months. There are five hundred and seven prisoners aboard the ship. So far, an epidemic hasn't broken out in the steerage. Hardly any of them have fallen victim to the bad weather conditions of the previous months. It's unusual. They have to take advantage of their head start.

Gardel summons his officers to his quarters.

They're expecting him to show them the route he's mapped out across the ocean. But the beginning of winter is no time for getting creative. Everyone knows the only possible route is directly to the islands, in the straightest line possible. It doesn't do to try and outsmart geometry. So what pressing fancy has led the captain to call this meeting? What does he want to discuss?

Gardel has laid a strip of paper on top of the large map

of the Atlantic spread out across the table. It's a plan of the ship. He places his finger at the ship's bow, just in front of the foremast.

"What's this?" he asks.

"The ship's store," replies Morel, like a teacher's pet.

"And what's in the ship's store?"

"The crew's food, Captain. Three months of food to last us until Saint-Domingue."

"Empty it."

"Sorry?"

"Bring it all up a level, onto the forecastle."

"What for?"

"The ship's store is about thirteen square feet, isn't it?"

"But what do you want to put inside?" asks Picard.

"Captives."

To the captain's right, Savage starts counting. "We could take twenty-five out of the steerage. That would give them a little more space," he says.

"We'll put at least fifty in there," says Gardel, "but we won't be emptying the steerage."

"Pardon me, Captain?"

"I want fifty more captives on this ship."

Even Picard is beginning to despair.

"There's no ventilation in the ship's store, Captain. We've already exceeded the five hundred agreed upon with Bassac."

"How are you going to find food to feed five hundred and fifty captives?" asks Cook.

"We'll make sure we stay at least thirty days ahead of schedule," says Gardel. "A month's worth of supplies is more than enough to feed fifty new captives."

Gardel has been doing his calculations. He knows that with fifty more captives, he can increase his earnings by ten percent.

That's a bonus of over three thousand pounds. It's the monthly salary of a regular sailor.

"But there's not a single captive left for purchase along the whole coast, Captain."

"That's why we're going further afield, gentlemen."

"Where?"

He traces a line across the map with his finger, then slams his fist down somewhere over to the east, where the River Niger flows into the sea.

"Bonny! Weigh anchor and take me to Bonny."

At the exact spot where Lazarus Bartholomew Gardel has planted his fist lies the small, grey sandy beach where Alma has just run her canoe aground. For days, the river has been forking off in different directions and widening until, finally, its banks disappeared.

Alma is standing there on the sand. She's looking out at an endless expanse in front of her, unlike anything she's ever seen, black and white beneath the stormy sky.

It's the sea.

30

Saint-Clair

A few hours later, in the dead of night, a shadow dotted with lanterns appears, taller than the houses along the docks, and moves into the port of La Rochelle. It hasn't started snowing yet, but a cold snap has gripped the city. There are a few figures walking through the icy streets in the dark. Everything is silent. It doesn't feel like Christmas Eve.

The only activity in the whole port is coming from the entrance, near one of the fortified towers, where the shadow is approaching without a sound. The two-masted vessel completes its manoeuvre before mooring on the dock. The whole city seems to be sleeping.

But just on the other side of the port, near the old houses lining the Maubec canal, lies the pillared doorway of the Saint-Sauveur church. The path leading to the entrance is slippery. The door creaks open, and suddenly there's a dazzling light, a big crowd, the smell of burning incense and candle smoke, the rustling of dresses, the sound of the organ being played, hushed whispers, the creaking of benches and warm, damp air . . . It's the beginning of midnight mass.

The first row is where the city's best dressed can be found. The ladies take advantage of the warmth coming off the candles and bodies to show off the latest tropical fashions, baring their skin from their shoulders right down to their lower backs. The priest, perhaps a little more sensitive to the cold, matches their elegance with his layered robes lined with lace. He wouldn't be out of place at a dance.

Children slide down from the prayer stools onto the floor to play with their mothers' slippers, which have been slid off surreptitiously beneath their petticoats. The men are wearing brocade jackets with as many buttons as there are pieces in their backgammon sets.

Full to the very last row, the church has been transformed into a theatre. There are the sailors standing at the back, followed by the little black servants waiting on their mistresses, the older women who have been there since midday, wearing white peasant bonnets with long flaps at the side that make them look like cocker spaniels.

In the third row, Amelie Bassac is sitting with her tutor, Madame de Lô. Amelie isn't scantily clad like the others. Not a single fleck of her skin is visible. She's wearing a deep red cape, buttoned under the chin with the hood drooping over her forehead. Next to her, tiny Madame de Lô is blocking everyone's view with her enormous, tiered hairstyle.

Every now and then, they exchange a knowing glance. They notice when the priest employs a rare construction in Latin that interests them, or when he uses the singular vocative *deus* (which did not exist in Roman times), among other little linguistic curiosities.

Truth be told, Amelie would rather be saying her own private prayer. Since childhood, she's always loved Christmas Eve, the one little flame flickering in the dead of winter. And even though it was on Christmas night that her mother was taken from her a few years ago, she anticipates the arrival of this holiday as soon as the nights start to draw in, without really knowing why.

But tonight, as though to spoil her celebrations, her father's accountant, Christian Saint-Clair, is sitting a few feet to her right next to a column. He keeps gazing over at her intensely. To avoid catching his eye, she stares fixedly at one of the choir boys, who is a little younger than her. The boy can feel her eyes on him; his cheeks have turned the same shade of scarlet as his robes.

Saint-Clair came to speak to Amelie before the mass began. He wanted to pay her his respects. She didn't take off her glove to shake his hand.

"Where's your father?"

"He isn't here," replied Amelie.

"He's unwell," Madame de Lô added from beside her. "It's nothing serious. He caught a cold in the garden on Sunday."

"Poor man."

Saint-Clair took his leave. He knew that these few words were all he could hope to get out of Amelie. He also knew she wouldn't offer him the empty seat next to her, in the specially reserved pew with the Bassac name engraved upon it.

Amelie thinks of her father, all alone under his eiderdown quilt.

Feeling too unwell to attend himself, he sent everyone else to mass. It's a tradition Amelie's mother began. She would allow all of her staff to take leave from the evening of December 24 until Christmas morning, provided she saw them all communing at midnight mass. Ferdinand Bassac has kept up the tradition. And so, that evening, every member of his staff from the groom to the linen maid dashed out of the door all at once.

For perhaps the first time in his life, Bassac has been left alone in the big house without any servants. Amelie can imagine him there, his head resting on the pillows, unable to move. He can't even make himself a cup of tea. He's never stepped foot in the kitchen. All he can do is stay in his bed, shivering and coughing, listening to the clock ticking away.

Just as the priest starts making his way to the pulpit at the centre of the church, Amelie takes a quick glance from beneath her hood in Christian Saint-Clair's direction and sees a blonde boy leaning over to speak to him. Within an instant, they've both vanished behind the column. Only the accountant's hat remains on the pew.

He's gone. Amelie feels a sudden wave of relief as she hears the sound of "Gloria" resonating through the church.

Saint-Clair is walking along the deserted dock.

"Watch out for the ice," says the boy accompanying him, pulling his red cap over his ears.

"What's the name of the ship?"

"*High Society*. It's a brig. Less than two hundred tons. It's just arrived from Africa. And I knew you were waiting for something, so . . . "

"I've been waiting a long time."

"That's what I thought. And I knew you'd be at mass."

"Did you see the letter?

"I didn't see it," says the young man. "But someone aboard the ship said your name. And I knew that—"

"I get it."

They've reached the end of the dock. Just as the boy described, there's a two-masted brig waiting there with icicles dangling from its yardarms. The crew is growing restless in the cold. They're happy to be back in time for Christmas, but entering the port like this in the middle of the night means there won't be any cheers or young girls waiting for them, jumping up and down on the dock.

"Where's the captain?"

A sailor points to a small group of people standing to one side. Saint-Clair recognises these men as the customs officers and a representative of the port authorities. There's also another man swaying slightly on the pavement, like all sailors who have just spent months at sea.

Saint-Clair goes over to them, followed by the guide in the red cap, who's waiting for his tip.

"Are you the captain of *High Society*?"

"I was until one hour ago."

Saint-Clair shakes his hand. They introduce themselves.

"Christian Saint-Clair."

The captain nods his head and takes an envelope from his pocket.

"I told your colleague back there on the coast it would take a month. But I wasn't counting on three weeks of dead calm at sea. It's now been almost two months. The wind's more temperamental than a post horse. Here."

"Where were you given the letter?"

"Cape Coast, just after All Saints' Day."

"Thank you."

The two men quickly part. A customs officer is tugging the captain by the sleeve. The boy in the red hat runs after Saint-Clair.

"See! I knew I'd heard your name. And I knew . . . "

"All right, I get it. Here. You can go now."

He places two coins in the boy's hand. The boy tries to count his earnings in the dark as Saint-Clair heads towards a petrol lamp hanging between two shelters on the dock. He tears open the envelope and hastily reads the letter.

Around him, the sailors are talking about money and their extravagant plans for the night. They're happy to have made it back alive. When they arrived, they were greeted by the father of one of the three sailors who died on their journey home. The old man could see that his son wasn't there. They handed him the boy's wages, the contents of his little suitcase and the money they got for his clothes. After the death of a sailor, his clothes are sold in an auction held beneath the ship's mainmast, in the middle of the ocean. The price of the clothes skyrockets. The crew think of their colleague, sewn into his hammock and thrown into the waves. Penniless sailors will spend a fortune on a threadbare shirt, pea coat or old breeches, just to fill up the kitty that will be handed to the family of the deceased.

Behind the sailors, oblivious to everything going on around him, Saint-Clair folds the letter up carefully. He lifts up his head in the lamplight. His face is beaming. He's had excellent news. And quite unexpected.

When Saint-Clair knocks at the courtyard door, Ferdinand Bassac is sitting at his desk in a pink dressing gown, little gauze rags stuck in his ears. He doesn't hear a thing. He's been up for a long time, tormented by this head cold and his anxieties. Sometimes, even the most minor of illnesses can be life-threatening. He knows that a fever can transport a man to the strangest of places, the way hot air can make humans fly around in balloons these days.

Ferdinand Bassac is looking at the papers on the desk in front of him. He's brought the lamp in from his bedroom and put it on the desk. Hanging just above him, the model of *The Purple Rose* casts a long shadow on the ceiling. The ship bears the name of the wife he lost: Rose. They were still engaged then, and she blushed every time he spoke to her about the future. *The Purple Rose* was the first vessel the young shipowner ever sent out to sea.

It's cold. Bassac feels as though he's surrounded by ghosts. He hasn't been able to get the fire going again in the fireplace. He's looking at the numbers on the page.

When he finally hears a knocking at the door, he jumps, takes out one of his earplugs to listen, and jumps again when he hears another knock.

It's one o'clock in the morning. Who could it be?

He gets up from his chair and walks over to the window to try and listen. But the visitor is directly below him, and Bassac can't see who it is. In any case, if they came through the carriage entrance from the street, it must be someone from the house who's forgotten their keys. Bassac groans. Amelie won't be back before two o'clock. He's alone. He'll have to go.

The old shipowner adjusts his dressing gown, pulling the knot of the belt tight. He picks up his lantern and goes towards the office door. Holding on to the banister, he begins his painful descent down the stairs.

"Coming, coming," he mumbles to the visitor, who probably can't hear him.

There's another knock.

The fire is still burning in the entrance hall. Bassac spends a long time fiddling with the lock, which he doesn't understand how to use, until finally the door opens a crack. He sticks his congested nose out into the winter air.

"Good God! Saint-Clair!"

31

The Conversation

"I'm terribly sorry to bother you, Monsieur Bassac. Where are your staff?"

"At mass. Why aren't you there? How did you get through the gate?"

"I climbed the garden wall."

Bassac's eyes widen.

"What are you doing here, Saint-Clair?"

"I have news."

"What news?"

"News from the coast."

Bassac studies his accountant's face. For a moment, he'd feared a marriage proposal might be imminent—that or some other extravagant gesture that would warrant a visitor climbing the garden wall at midnight. Now he feels reassured.

The young man seems to be in a good mood. Perhaps there's a glimmer of hope yet in this hellish night.

"Come in, then."

He directs Saint-Clair into the house, closing the door behind him.

"Follow me."

There's a shuffling of slippers on the stone floor as Bassac attempts to tackle the staircase on the north wing of the house. In his dressing gown, lamp in hand, he looks like an innkeeper who's been awoken by a traveller in the middle of the night.

"Forgive me. I'll show you upstairs, but you'll have to see yourself out. I don't have the strength. This has almost finished me off."

When they get to the office, Bassac points at the fireplace.

"Could you do something about that fire?" Saint-Clair gets on his knees and blows on the logs. Little sparks shoot out from the embers. The shipowner walks over to the table and puts down his lamp. He collapses in his chair and pulls out his handkerchief.

"I didn't want to wait," says Saint-Clair, still leaning over the fire. "I know you're worried about the matter."

"I'm not worried," replies Bassac, blowing his nose. "I'm positively terrified."

He hears Saint-Clair's laughter echoing in the chimney. It's a comforting laugh that sounds like it belongs to a teenager.

"Laugh all you want!" groans Bassac.

"I shall," he says, getting up. "Monsieur Bassac, your endeavours are invariably a success. Why, you even succeed in scaring yourself."

"To this day, my fears have never been unwarranted."

Ferdinand Bassac thinks back to his wife's illness, to the dizzy spells that only he was ever worried about.

"I have some news for you," says the accountant. Bassac has both elbows on the desk. Saint-Clair remains by the fireplace, seated in a green velvet chair.

"Our contact has written to us," he says. "The letter arrived this evening."

"Our contact?"

"Yes."

"Any word from Gardel? Why on earth is my own captain not writing to me?"

"Gardel must have sent his letter on a slower ship. There was no wind off the coast of Spain."

"Go on."

"He says *The Sweet Amelie* . . ."

Saint-Clair pauses. His heart skips a beat each time he utters her name. He repeats it, just to experience the feeling again.

"He says *The Sweet Amelie* has arrived on the Gold Coast."

"Ah!"

"Everything is going splendidly. The trading, and everything else. Nobody suspects a thing with regard to you-know-what."

"Not even Gardel?"

"He's too engrossed in trading."

"I can't believe he doesn't even have an inkling . . . What about the crew?"

"Neither the officers nor the sailors have any idea. There's just . . ."

"What?"

"He mentioned a boy who isn't on our books."

"See! You told me you were going to check everything! Every last human being on that ship! Every detail about their past, their families, every last one of their acquaintances!"

"And I did. He's the only one who slipped through the net. Apparently he boarded the ship by accident at the last minute in Lisbon. He's only fourteen years old."

"And what about the other one? The carpenter Gardel wrote to us about from Lisbon?"

Bassac's expression darkens as he tries to remember the name.

"Dubois," says the accountant.

"You know, Saint-Clair, I have never been able to get over what happened to the previous carpenter, Bassompierre, and his apprentice. Falling into the port. Poor things. The apprentice was only fifteen."

"They'd been drinking," says the accountant, reproachfully.

"How do you know they'd been drinking?" yelps Bassac.

"You don't just fall into the port by accident."

"That is precisely what troubles me, my friend. You *don't* just fall into the port by accident."

The shipowner repeats the words slowly, looking directly into Saint-Clair's eyes. But the accountant pretends not to notice. He hastily resumes his story.

"Our contact said the boy's name is Joseph Mars, and he has an arrangement with Gardel."

"Good God. I thought you said you had good news?"

"The arrangement is nothing of any importance, but apparently it's difficult to explain. Fortunately, our contact said he's managed to get close enough to the boy to observe him. He appears to be perfectly harmless. There's nothing to worry about."

"You say 'our contact,' but in reality, he's your contact. Do you still trust him?"

"Yes."

"Yet you still don't want to tell me his name?"

"Monsieur Bassac, once again, your cargo is perfectly safe aboard your own vessel."

"Then why don't you want to give me the name of your contact?"

"He asked me not to."

Bassac leans back in his chair. He looks at his accountant.

"I have something to tell you, my friend."

A sense of foreboding washes over Saint-Clair.

"The thing is," the shipowner begins, "I've had a terrible few days."

"My dear Bassac—"

"You're doing me a great service," he interrupts. "I have to laud your intelligence, my friend, and your knack for business matters. But the decision we made—"

"You made the decision."

"And I don't want to regret it. I put my entire fortune aboard that ship for your American investments."

"They aren't my investments. They're yours. That country is giving you the opportunity to lend them money."

"Opportunity?"

"Yes, opportunity! You'll get it all back, ten times over."

"One day, yes. But why offer such an opportunity?"

"Gratitude. America is grateful that our country helped them gain independence."

"As far as I'm concerned, they can keep their gratitude. And what about the last few months of salary I owe you that you still haven't paid yourself?"

"Don't worry about that. It works out well for me. I'll pay myself in good time."

"Monsieur Saint-Clair, I don't like this one bit."

Bassac searches for his handkerchief up his sleeve. Saint-Clair sees his opportunity to attack.

"So withdraw if you that's what you want. Monsieur Beaumont will be more than happy to lend his money to America. Or it'll be your friend Roussillon who gets to triple his fleet and land. They'll be all over this offer like vermin. The country is fifteen times bigger than ours. The prospects are extraordinary. America must be rebuilt entirely after the war. If you're afraid of getting rich, then by all means, withdraw immediately!"

"You see?" sighs Bassac. "Every time I listen to you, you end up convincing me. That's why I ought not to decide anything for myself."

Saint-Clair sits up slightly in his chair. Bassac puts his handkerchief back in his pocket.

Then finally, hoping to bring the conversation to a close, he adds: "I've decided to speak to my daughter about all this tomorrow."

32
The Last Snowflakes

"Amelie?"

"I'm aware of your . . . fraternal affections for her," says Bassac, mischievously. "But you'd be surprised at her aptitude for business. You're shrewd as a cat, but she's more of a tiger. Two well-bred felines. You might just be able to come to an agreement. Our gold may well be able to continue on its course to America, just as you were hoping."

Saint-Clair jumps up from his seat. He grips the back of the wooden chair he was sitting on with both hands.

"Monsieur Bassac, I would advise you not to speak to anyone about this."

"I haven't."

"This must remain between us."

"My daughter and I are one and the same when it comes to matters of business."

The accountant slams the chair down on the wooden floor. He's holding it firmly between his fingers. Bassac freezes to the spot behind his desk.

Saint-Clair tries to regain his composure. He takes a deep breath and continues in a low voice.

"Monsieur Bassac, I implore you. Don't do something you'll later regret."

Bassac is at his calmest at moments like these. He's built his fortune upon tense situations. He replies in a voice that's almost light-hearted, sitting calmly in his chair, one eyebrow raised.

"Tell me, Saint-Clair, is that a threat?"

The accountant doesn't reply. The fire begins to pick up again, crackling loudly in the fireplace.

Bassac remains lost in his thoughts for a moment, then looks up and gestures to the ship above him. It's like a ghost ship. It's almost a metre long, made entirely of walnut and rosewood. The hull is glowing in the light of the flames.

"*The Purple Rose*. You weren't even born then. Two masts, one hundred and fifty tons. My first vessel."

He takes a deep breath.

"Everything I know, I learnt with that ship. Accounting, planning, earning people's respect. But the morning of the ship's departure, I realised my captain wasn't loyal to me. He failed to mention the detail of a stopover he was planning to make. One hour later, *The Purple Rose* left without him."

Bassac looks at his accountant and says, gravely:

"Do you hear me, Saint-Clair? Without him!"

Saint-Clair can't hear anything. He's gripping the back of the chair with both hands.

He can just only see Bassac's lips moving, his eyes peering at him with the calm, strict expression of a father.

Saint-Clair turns in a full circle to gather momentum, then throws the chair with all his might. Slowly, it turns through the air, right in the direction of *The Purple Rose*.

When Amelie returns to her pew after communion, he's back again. Saint-Clair! He's returned just as quickly as he disappeared. Now he's lost in prayer, his eyes closed, kneeling in front of his hat, which is still lying on the pew. Saint-Clair, like a well-behaved child at his first communion, has come back to his seat in the church. Where did he come from?

Now that his eyes are closed, Amelie can look at him more freely. She imagines herself sitting next to him one day on the pew. They would certainly look nice together, shoulder to shoulder, kneeling in prayer. But Amelie hates anything that's nice. She likes things that are dazzling, things that are so beautiful they hurt her eyes. So beautiful, they're almost frightening.

When mass is over, Madame de Lô grabs Amelie by the arm. This is where her job really begins. She has to try and get Amelie across the church square without being stopped. With all those beautiful people gathered there, the square is a minefield. Partners, neighbours, suppliers, and suitors will all think of some excuse to pounce on the Bassac girl.

So it's up to Madame de Lô to take over. She keeps a firm grip on the young girl's arm. After all, she's supposed to be her rudder. Amelie walks beside her, her hood still covering her eyes. They start by doing a lap of the church to throw the congregation off. A few followers, trying to be discreet, are hot on their tails. Madame de Lô pretends to be taking out her rosary in front of a statue of the Virgin Mary, before quickly tugging Amelie towards the door without warning.

There, an ambush is waiting for them. Three women are stationed in the passage with their grown-up sons. With exceptional skill, Madame de Lô manages to cling on to Amelie and spin her in the other direction the moment they approach. They look inside the church, pretending to admire

the choir without stopping for one second. They continue to walk towards the exit, this time in reverse, focused as ever, looking up towards the arch. They manage to break through the wall of nuisances. As soon as they get out, they take a slight turn in the direction of the bell tower, skimming the wall as they go.

Finally, they reach an alleyway that runs alongside the church towards the north. They've made it. They've saved themselves, and they're absolutely thrilled.

"The one I'm surprised at," says Madame de Lô, breathlessly, "is your friend Christian Saint-Clair. I can't believe he didn't try to follow us."

"He's not my friend, he's yours."

The old tutor chuckles into her fur collar.

"You have to admit, he's veritably pulchritudinous."

"Sorry?"

Madame de Lô can't help herself from trying to improve her young charge's vocabulary. "I mean he's handsome," she says. "I've seen angels depicted in the paintings at Versailles with the same blonde curls."

"Look," says Amelie. "It's snowing."

"We must get home."

"No. I want to watch the snow falling in the public gardens."

"Your father will be waiting for you."

"He's fast asleep!"

"I suppose," the tutor concedes.

"There's no doubt about it," laughs Amelie. "You should have seen him wrapped up in his blankets before we left. Poor thing. Like a limp, lifeless, white animal."

"Like a ball of dough wrapped up in a cloth!" Madame de Lô looks at Amelie, blushing at her own insolence.

"Let's go!"

They head towards the gardens, staggering beneath the falling snow.

"The cook will take care of him," says Madame de Lô, to make up for her comment. "She told me she'd go back after mass. Her three sons are at sea. She doesn't want to take any leave."

"What about you?"

"Me? Take leave?"

"Yes, you!"

At the end of the road, they disappear around a corner. Now only Madame de Lô's voice can be heard.

"What would you do? You'd need twelve grenadiers on horseback to replace me!"

Their laughter rings out until it becomes muffled by the same snow covering their footsteps behind them.

When they arrive at the Bassac family home an hour later, the carriage entrance door is wide open. Just in front of the house, a deep layer of snow has already settled and been trampled on. There are two carriages parked in the streets, and another two in the courtyard. The horses are steaming in the cold.

Amelie and Madame de Lô enter the house, their shoulders coated in white. What's happening? There are men going up and down the stairs. The cook is in tears on a bench in front of the hallway fireplace. She's been given a blanket to wipe her face with.

Madame de Lô goes over to her.

"Monsieur Bassac," sobs the woman when she sees her. "Monsieur Bassac . . . " She can't manage to say anything else.

Madame de Lô turns to Amelie, but the young girl is already at the top of the stairs. The police are trying to prevent her from entering. She forces her way past and goes into the office. As she stops and removes her hood, snowflakes fall down onto the carpet.

Her father is sitting in his armchair, his head resting on the table. *The Purple Rose* is in pieces all around him. The blood has spilt onto the floor.

A policeman goes over to Amelie with his hat in his hand.

"The pulley system broke. The cook discovered your father an hour ago when she came back from mass."

Amelie walks slowly towards the desk.

"It was a terrible accident, mademoiselle."

She feels the last remaining snowflakes melting on her cheeks.

33

So Close, Yet So Far

A sudden gust of wind comes in from the east, bringing with it a stale smell. It's the sad smell of elephant flesh.

Alma is sitting on the beach in the mist. She's just finished digging a hole for her canoe and her bow. She's covered them completely with sand. She lifts her nose up again to breathe in the air, like an animal hunting.

For months now, Alma has been crossing whole forests of different smells. She first started perceiving these overwhelming wafts of scent when she left the valley. She knows there's a mongoose around before she sees it. The same goes for every bird hiding along the riverbank, every agouti, every chimpanzee. If a snake tumbles into the canoe from the branches above, she can catch it and throw it out with her bare hands. She can harpoon fish with a spear cut from a reed. She can shoot an arrow with her eyes closed. While she was making her way down the river, it was this instinct that saved her. It's the reason she didn't die of starvation.

While crossing a mangrove swamp over the last few days,

her feet in the water amongst an expanse of tangled trees, she began to detect the salty taste of the sea. Brand new smells emerged from this labyrinth: the smells of turtles and manatees coming up to the surface to breathe.

Finally, Alma discovered the sea. She's been following the coastline for days now, hauling Sirim's canoe up onto the sand at night and sleeping beneath the stars.

On the second night, she saw a ship sailing by in the distance. She didn't know what it was. It was like an enormous white bird. A bird that doesn't exist. She'd never seen anything like it.

Then finally, this morning, when she woke up in the grassy dunes of a long, misty beach, there they were: two of the same birds bobbing on the surface just beyond the waves, their square wings outstretched. They were floating one behind the other, perfectly aligned by the wind. They, too, were ships. Their silhouettes mingled as they swayed, and at some point, they must have closed their wings, because the white came tumbling down all at once. But their skeletons remained there in the ocean, and when the mist cleared for a moment, Alma thought she saw little living creatures moving at their feet. She thought of the stories she used to tell Lam, the ones of giant houses with white wings.

Alma had been watching these strange shapes through the haze for hours, when suddenly that familiar smell came wafting in from the east. She recognised it right away. She remembers the time the carcass of an old elephant appeared in the Valley of Isaya. The vultures and hyenas fought over the dead beast for a whole month. By the time peace was finally restored, not even the bones remained in the grasses.

Alma marks the spot where she's buried her canoe. She starts to run in the direction the breeze is coming from. She knows why the smell is calling her. She forbids herself to hope.

Suddenly, a gust of wind frees the beach from the grip of the remaining mist. Alma throws herself to the ground. She feels her heart beating against the sand. It's exactly what she thought.

Just a hundred yards away, she sees a row of elephant tusks lined up on the beach. She lies as flat as possible to the ground. There are six tusks in total and two men guarding them. These are the men who took Lam. She's sure of it. Where did her little brother go? And what about the other men Sirim told her about? Where is the giant with the severed ear?

"What are you doing?"

There's a voice coming from just behind her.

Alma turns around. There are two children looking at her. A boy and a girl, both of them smiling. Each of them has an ear of corn in their hand, covered in their teeth marks.

"Are you afraid?"

She doesn't reply. Of course she's afraid. She didn't sense them coming. They came with their sweet, childlike scent from the direction the wind wasn't blowing in, and the rustling of the grasses must have hidden the sound of their footsteps.

"We want to show you something," says the little boy. "Follow us!"

"Are you coming?" asks the girl.

"All right."

The two children laugh. They repeat "all right" in Alma's accent.

"You're from Nembe!"

"Yes," says Alma, who doesn't know what Nembe is, but is happy to come from wherever they like, as long as they don't ask any more questions.

The girl holds out her hand to help Alma up.

"You're very skinny. Did you forget to eat?"

She hands over her ear of corn. Alma takes a bite.

"Are there elephants in Nembe?"

"Yes."

Alma sets off with them, the sand still sticking to her skin.

"Do you say yes to everything?"

"No."

The little girl laughs again. Alma stops for a moment to look at the men the children are taking her to. She gives the little girl her corn back.

"Are you afraid?"

She doesn't reply.

"Come on."

The two men are lying down beside the elephant tusks. They don't move when the little explorers crouch down next to them.

"Don't touch," says one of the men.

The boy puts on a dignified expression.

"My father can find you a boat that'll buy the lot," he says.

The men prop themselves up on their elbows. They're talking to each other in another language.

"Do you want to speak to my father?" asks the boy.

"Maybe. But you'll have to wait for the others. They're on the French ship. They'll tell you whether or not they want to speak to your father."

They point in the direction of the ships.

"There they are, look!"

In front of the huge, winged canoes, another, tiny wingless one tries to make its way to the shore against the rising tide.

The two men get up.

"What were they doing there?" asks the boy.

"They went to sell captives."

"How many?"

"Two. One boy of your age and another."

"My father could have bought them."

"It looks like you're too late. Look. They've already been sold."

The man looks at the little canoe and its two rowers with a satisfied expression.

Alma also looks out at the sea so they don't notice the emotion on her face. The canoe is getting closer.

"The other day, I saw a very tall man. A giant with a severed ear. Was he with you?"

Everyone looks at Alma. She asked the question as nonchalantly as possible.

"Yes, he was with us," replies one of the men.

Of course, Alma has never seen this giant before. She just wanted to be sure that these men were the ones who kidnapped Lam. She continues to look out at the horizon.

"Why were you asking about the giant?"

She scrunches up her nose as she replies. "Does it hurt, his ear?"

"No. It happened a long time ago. When the giant was a boy."

The two men look at each other. Perhaps they're thinking back to when the giant was a boy.

Alma gathers her courage and tries to find out more.

"Which boat did they go on?"

"The first. The French one with three masts. The other one's British. It's mostly the British who come here. But the French pay more."

Alma doesn't know any of these words. "French," "English," "masts," "pay" . . . But she's understood everything she needs to know. Her brother is there, just beyond the waves. If she were to make a fire, he might even see it. If she were to shout her heart out, he would hear her.

The children go back to playing with the ivory, touching it and then snatching their hands away quickly as if it were dirty or burning hot.

"Clear off," says one of the men. "We'll tell you if we need you."

The children go to sit nearby and begin drawing pictures in the sand.

"What do they do with the tusks?" asks Alma.

"They put them on the boats," says the girl.

"And then?"

"The boats go."

"Go where?"

"They just go."

The canoe has just arrived ashore. Its two passengers join the others on the beach. From the corner of her eye, Alma watches the silhouettes from afar. Sirim said there were five men who took Lam. Now there are only four. The giant with the severed ear is no longer there.

One of the men is looking at the black, tempestuous sky. He's heading towards the children.

"You'd better go," he says as he approaches them. "We don't need anything. We'll sell the tusks to the French. Off you go. There's a storm coming."

The three children get up and leave, dragging their feet as they go. They move along the beach in single file and head into the grasses, which are swirling in the wind.

The clouds gallop along above them.

"Where did she go?" the boy asks suddenly.

"Who?"

"The girl who was with us."

The two children look around them. The girl from Nembe is gone.

"She was right in front of me. I only looked up for a second to see the clouds."

"She's vanished."

None of the grasses around them have been trampled down. They look at each other, smiling.

"Or maybe she never existed! She might have been a ghost."

"Stop it!"

They open their eyes as wide as they can to frighten each other, before walking away calmly beneath the tumultuous sky, taking their time, pretending not to be afraid of storms or ghosts.

At midnight that same evening, Alma reappears not far from the spot where she vanished. She digs up her bow and canoe. The wind is howling. The rain begins to fall.

Earlier that day, hidden away in the sand dunes, she watched how the men manoeuvred their canoes towards the French ship. She watched how they rode through the wave as though it were a tunnel. Then she watched them return to the coast. They didn't have the elephant tusks with them anymore.

It's nighttime, and Alma is alone on the beach. She pulls her canoe onto the sand. She knows she can't wait. The first white bird is about to take off. The other might fly away, too.

Alma walks into the sea through the rolling waves and heaves herself into her flimsy little canoe.

She aims for the flashing yellow light she can see ahead of her. The waves are rising so high, she suddenly feels sheltered from the wind. The largest wave continues to roll above her

like a roof, but just before it closes, engulfing her completely, the sea hesitates, gives up, and rolls back, curling in on itself before finally subsiding. That's when the canoe really takes off, buoyed on the round back of the beast. For a moment, Alma paddles through the calm water of the crest, before the beast turns its head towards her, its mouth agape. The little canoe is carried away by the choppy waters, and the whole thing starts again.

And so, on this January night in 1787, Alma heads off into the darkness. She can no longer feel her arms. Out at sea, the speck of light coming from the ship shows her the way. She never loses sight of it. It's so close, yet so far.

PART THREE

34
Clandestine

Joseph holds the lamp up high in spite of the storm. He's on the platform halfway up the mainmast, soaking wet, with one arm wrapped around the wood to stop himself from falling. The wind is howling, the rain is lashing down horizontally, and he's frozen to the bone.

"Hold up the light, my boy! Hold it up!"

Jacques Dubois, the carpenter, is suspended in mid-air, his bag of tools flapping away at his belt. Joseph leans over even further. Every now and then, he almost thinks he can see little green birds with silver beaks flying towards him, attracted by the light. Dubois has been working on the repairs for four hours. Just above them, the boom is swaying back and forth like the needle of a metronome in slow motion.

"Come on, hold it up!"

Dubois saw a storm coming right from the start of the day. He begged the captain to let him do the work necessary for the ship to leave. But Gardel had different priorities. He wanted the carpenter to hang nets along the deck to prevent the captives from throwing themselves into the sea once the weather improves and they're eventually let out. Many of them try to jump into the water as soon as they leave the coast, driven by a frail hope that they might escape, followed only by despair as their world disappears on the horizon before their eyes.

"I don't like tossing my goods overboard," said Gardel. "Put those nets up first. You can do the rest of the repairs at dawn. We'll set sail at noon."

"If the storm breaks, Captain, you won't even be able to weigh anchor and sail to shelter."

The captain laughed at Dubois, pointing towards the sky.

"A storm? On this coast? On January 1? That'll be the day! The devil himself would have to be aboard for that to happen."

But lo and behold, at eight o'clock that evening, a roaring storm broke out. The devil was indeed on board *The Sweet Amelie*. Some might have even said he was dressed in the captain's frock coat.

Now it's one o'clock in the morning, and the two anchors are skidding along the mud and shells at the bottom of the sea. The ship is getting dangerously close to the shore. And Jacques Dubois is at work, roped to the mast as it dances in the night.

Meanwhile, at the ship's aft, Gardel's pride is preventing him from acknowledging his mistake. He's gathered all his men in the shelter of the aftcastle. With his thumbs in his waistcoat pockets, he shows them the manoeuvres they will have to make: weigh anchor as soon as Dubois gives the signal from above, set the sails and head southwest.

Picard finds the courage to raise his hand. Once again, he suggests leaving before the work is complete.

"Let's do the repairs later, Captain. The other sails will be enough. With the foresail alone we'll get up to at least fifteen knots."

Gardel silences his first mate. He refuses to leave on a ship that's falling apart. When the time comes for them to leave Africa, he wants his departure to be triumphant.

The sailors stand in silence before him. The storm alone could explain why their faces are so pale. But in reality, the wave tossing their hearts to and fro in their chests is coming from beneath their feet. It's the murmuring coming from the bowels of the ship. Neither Gardel's voice, nor the whistling of the wind and the creaking of the wood can cover the moans and groans coming from beneath the deck.

There are now five hundred and fifty captives locked up in the hold.

Three for every ten square feet. With forty thousand gallons of fresh water on board and enough barrels of peas and rice for two months, the water level on the hull has risen right up to the cannons. To prevent the ship from flooding, they've even blocked up the three portholes, the only openings letting air into the steerage.

None of the captives are able to lie down on their backs. They have to lie on their sides. Some of them have to remain squatting the whole time. Gardel is expecting some space to be freed up by those who don't survive the crossing.

"Listen," says Gardel suddenly, looking up with a finger in the air. "Listen carefully."

He speaks as though he's just recognised the tune being played on a harpsichord by a neighbour downstairs. He looks closely at his men.

This is what he's gathered them here for. He wants them to hear the groaning and sobbing. Not so that the men will feel moved, or even to get them used to the sound. No. He wants them to feel the force of the threat that will accompany them for the whole journey. They have to stay on their guard. Sorrow and fury make anything possible.

"In the Paris and London salons, they're debating whether these are human beings we're transporting. But let me tell you one thing for certain. Their rage will be superhuman when they realise we're leaving."

Outside, the deck is completely deserted. Only Abel Lebon is left, straddling the bowsprit that sticks out at the front of the ship just above the figurehead. He's been put there to watch the two anchors and the ship's centreboard. Even without touching the ropes, he can feel them vibrating. These anchors, each weighing two tons, are no longer planted in the seabed. They're scraping along the sand, pulling the ship back towards the shore

Amidst the waves, Abel can't help but stare at the painted yellow figure below him. They say it's Amelie, the girl the ship was named after. She braves the storms without ever leaving her post. He thinks of the real Amelie, who must be sound asleep somewhere this New Year's Day, wrapped in dry sheets with hot water bottles, a sachet of lavender under her pillow.

Suddenly, Abel is startled by something. He just felt a shock coming from the starboard side. An object must have collided with the hull. It's too late to warn the crew. Leaning forward, he sees a tree trunk floating away, rolling along in the waves. For a split second, Abel thinks it might be an abandoned canoe.

But then the shape disappears into the night. It doesn't seem to have broken anything.

Abel is cold. Rain blends with seawater, lashing him from every side. He wipes his eyes with his hand. At that very same moment, a shadow springs up behind him without him noticing. A little black comet rolling along the deck before disappearing. It's Alma.

"Hey!"

There's a cry coming from the mainmast. Abel Lebon looks up.

He recognises the voice as Dubois's. Joseph is waving the lamp. They've finished their work.

Abel leaves his watchman's post. Bent over against the wind, he heads towards the stern, stepping over the six elephant tusks lined up on the forecastle floorboards. He goes down onto the deck and rattles the door of the barricade. Someone opens it. He joins the rest of the crew, raises his arms in the air and announces through chattering teeth:

"It's all ready, Captain. It's all ready. We can go."

The sailors look at the dripping messenger in relief.

We can go.

Just then, Jacques Dubois and Joseph Mars collapse, exhausted, onto the floor, sheltered by the forecastle in front of them. They've managed to find a spot here in the space that has been turned into the pantry of the ship's store.

Dubois groans as he takes off his tarred cloak.

"Sleep!" he exclaims. "Finally we can sleep a little."

Joseph puts down the lamp. The room is filled with the nauseating odours of the food piled up behind him. The whistling of the wind continues to ring in his ears. Unable to move or take off his sodden clothes, he waits.

The anchors have finally been weighed. The ship is tilting towards the starboard side. *The Sweet Amelie* is no longer resisting the wind. She finally gives in and lets herself be carried out to sea.

For a few seconds, the captives don't make a sound.

"This time, we really are leaving," says Dubois.

He props himself up on one elbow and laughs in a low voice, like a drunkard in the street, barely able to stand. They'll be cosy in here. It's the best place to hide away for a few hours. Outside, the rest of the crew are getting back to work up in the masts and on deck.

"Sleep!" Dubois sighs again. "Blow out the lamp, my boy."

Joseph looks around him, knocked out by the storm. When they left the shores of Europe, almost six months ago, there was space for twenty sailors to hang their hammocks beneath the forecastle for the night. Now, there's only room for these two exhausted bodies lying on the floorboards. There are bags and barrels piled from floor to ceiling.

In the ship's store, at the bow just one level below them, the reserves have been replaced by the last fifty women Gardel picked up on Bonny Island. Along with the one hundred and fifty captives on the starboard side, that makes a total of two hundred women and three hundred and fifty men imprisoned on board.

Women and children usually count for around a third of the captives on slave ships. But the captain has done his calculations. The ship's store is not ventilated at all, making it even less liveable than the rest of the steerage. Gardel is counting on these women being more resistant during the journey. He's sure this will increase his profits more than if he locked away more expensive but less resistant men in the ship's store.

"Put out the lamp," says Dubois.

Joseph extends his hand and lifts up the glass protecting the wick. He leans down low to blow it out, but then he stops, perplexed.

He dabs his finger on the floorboards just next to the burning lantern.

There on his index finger is a dark red spot, perfectly round. He brings it up to his nose to sniff it.

Nearby, Dubois is mumbling something, his eyes closed.

Joseph grabs the lamp and kneels down in front of it. The little drops have fallen in a perfectly straight line. He begins to follow the trail, which continues along a chest.

"Put out the lamp," Dubois grunts again from behind him, pulling his rain hat down over his eyes.

"All right. I'm putting it out," says Joseph.

Instead, he takes the lamp with him as he follows the spots, which get closer and closer together. He walks around three small barrels before standing up straight to step over a sack of flour. Then he crouches down again and shines the light into an empty nook.

"Put out the lamp," Dubois' sleepy voice repeats.

Even if he were to put the lamp out now, he would have enough light to last him a lifetime. Because two small fires have just been lit before Joseph. Alma's eyes.

They look at one another like two survivors at the end of the world. The only two people left who have wandered for a thousand years on opposite sides of a planet in ruins and have finally found each other.

Alma knows she could have killed him three times over already if she'd wanted to.

If he's still alive, it's because she has nothing to fear. This is what she thinks to herself, and her instincts never deceive her.

She's never seen a face like his. A white face with rosy cheeks and nose, surrounded by wild hair. What world does he come from? Does the winged canoe belong to these little ghosts with grey eyes?

Joseph looks at the girl. She's holding one of her shoulders with her right hand. Her body is curled up, and she has her

arms crossed over her knees, which are pressed tightly together beneath her chin. She's clinging to something with one hand in the shadows.

"She's not a captive," says Dubois. Joseph jumps. The carpenter is standing right behind him.

"Look carefully," he adds in a low voice. "She's holding a bow in her right hand."

"She's free," says Joseph.

When he says this word, the porcelain eyes before him flicker slightly.

"What's she doing here?" whispers Dubois.

In the lamplight, Alma's pupils dart from one man to the other, attentively.

"Look," says Joseph, pointing at her shoulder.

"What?"

Alma keeps her hand clasped tightly over her shoulder. There's a red liquid oozing through her fingers.

Alma is clutching at a wound. The blood is running from her wrist all the way down to her elbow. A wave threw her against the hull just as she jumped out of her canoe.

Alma is staring at Dubois. She's trying to read what the eyes of the old ghost have to say. His face resembles the smaller ghost's. It has the same discoloured skin, like the grasses in dry season. Strangely enough, she wasn't afraid when she saw Joseph. But what about this man? What does he want from her?

The boy has turned towards the carpenter and is staring at him, too. He's thinking about this world full of people just trying to survive. A world of obedience and terror.

There's an armed girl aboard. Surely Dubois has to sound the alarm? He'd have to be crazy to risk keeping this clandestine traveller a secret—wouldn't he?

35

Indestructible Freedom

"I know this ship well," whispers Dubois. "It's my job. I've examined every space between the beams, every tiny groove in the floorboards. I can even tell you where Hercules the cat leaves his rat bones and pinpoint the cavity under the planks where someone is hiding a double-barrelled shotgun."

Joseph waits. Jacques Dubois never starts at the beginning. He makes digressions whose meaning only becomes clear long afterwards.

"If there were anywhere," he continues, "where an injured child could remain hidden for the next two months, I would know about it."

He pauses.

"But there's no such place."

Joseph holds his breath. Why does it feel as though his life depends on the next few seconds?

"*Now* will you put out that lamp?"

The moment Joseph finally obeys, he hears a man's footsteps coming into the room. He's holding a little flame that flickers in his hand. It's Cook. He doesn't see the three figures hidden by the pyramids of food.

Cook puts down his lamp and fills a bucket with rice. Then he closes the sack and leaves.

"Listen to me when I ask you to do something," Dubois says to Joseph. "Otherwise, we're as good as dead."

Had Joseph waited a second longer to put out the lamp, the light would have given them away.

The carpenter continues to make his case in the darkness.

"Her shoulder will need stitches, and we'll need to feed her."

They can just make out Alma's shadow, barely thicker than the wood of her bow.

"So what do we do?" asks Joseph.

"What's the difference between the captives and those who are free?"

Dubois always answers questions by asking another question.

"The captives are locked up in the steerage."

"That's not what makes them captives. Soon they'll be brought out into the wind, in the shade of the sails, but they won't be free. One day, they'll be surrounded by birds and sugar cane that towers over them. They'll go to drink from a stream when they come back from the fields, and they'll weep when they breathe the air from the east because it carries their lost country to them. If their masters like them well enough, they might marry. But I promise you they still won't be free."

"Then it's the colour of their skin!" exclaims Joseph.

"Cook is black. Is he a captive? He's a free man just like—"

"Please, just say what you want to say!" pleads Joseph. "We don't have time."

Dubois continues.

"What makes a person a captive is the brand burnt onto their shoulder and the name given to them in the ship's register."

There's a silence.

"That's it," Dubois concludes. "If this girl doesn't have a mark, if her name isn't in the books, she'll remain free."

"But where can we hide her?" asks Joseph.

Until a few moments ago, he'd never met her. His whole existence revolved around a pile of gold stashed under a bed and the task that was assigned to him before his departure. Now he's whining about her like a little wounded dog.

"Please," he says to Dubois one last time. "Tell me where we're going to hide her."

"With the captives."

Joseph is ready to jump up and grab Dubois by the throat.

"We'll put her in the ship's store with the women from Bonny."

"What about her name? The register?"

"Her name will never be written in there. The register will be put away until we get to Saint-Domingue. The captives are counted when they go up on deck in the morning. Then they're counted again when they come back down. She'll go up with them, then go back down again."

"But there's no mark on her skin. The others have had an "A" for *The Sweet Amelie* burnt into their skin with the hot iron. They'll notice she doesn't have it."

Dubois smiles in the darkness.

"Trust me. Nobody will notice. You'll see."

They're silent for a few moments.

"There are just two more problems to solve," says Dubois. "We have a few weeks to solve the first one: how to make her disappear once we arrive. The second is more urgent. How do we get her to understand our plan?"

Then a low whisper comes out of the darkness behind them, a voice Joseph will never forget:

"What about my bow? What are you going to do with my bow?"

Palardi the surgeon is walking across the deck with his little trunk. Dubois has just woken him up and brought him to the other side of the barricade.

"What I don't understand is how you noticed the girl was injured."

"You should just be pleased I managed to get her out of the ship's store. There are fifty women crammed in there. There's not even space to lay a napkin on the floor—imagine what a struggle it is to get people in and out."

"But I was wondering—"

"It was that little thief that helped me in the end. What's his name again?"

"Mars. Joseph Mars."

"That's the one," says Dubois. "Mars. He's a decent lad when he's not rifling through Gardel's pockets."

"But what I can't understand—"

"You can't understand everything in life," says Dubois, firmly.

He grabs the surgeon by the shoulders and looks him straight in the eye beneath the rain.

"That's the problem with doctors. You have no respect for mysteries. Do you hear, Palardi?" he says, his eyes widening.

Palardi nods nervously. He's been afraid of Dubois, as though he were some kind of witch doctor, ever since the carpenter managed to cure Tavel the cooper of his dysentery.

"The girl's in here. We brought her here to keep her out of the rain."

They duck down into the store where they first found Alma. Joseph is watching over her. They've hidden her bow amongst Dubois' tools.

"Does the captain know about this?" Palardi asks when he sees Alma.

"He'll know about it if you don't do a good job. If you sew her up like a sack of potatoes and the wound gets infected, I'll be sure to tell him about the standard of your work. The captain doesn't like waste. And this girl is worth fifteen times your salary for the month of January."

Palardi kneels down, white as a sheet. He lifts up Alma's right arm.

"She's bleeding a lot," he says, pulling a small bottle out of his pocket.

He unscrews the bottle.

"I use the sailors' brandy on the captives. It's cheaper."

"No. Give it to me."

"Why?"

"Because I'm thirsty."

Dubois grabs the brandy and pretends to drink it.

"Use the same thing you'd use to treat your own daughter," says Dubois, wiping his mouth in the crook of his elbow.

"My daughter?"

He doesn't have a daughter.

"Take the most expensive thing you have!" cries Dubois. Palardi reluctantly takes a red vial from his wooden case.

Alma doesn't take her eyes off Joseph as the surgeon stitches her arm up. She doesn't clench her teeth or fists. She doesn't bat an eyelid.

The surgeon is doing a good job. This man would have made a better tailor than doctor. He could have made cuffs or bedsheets and steered clear of the dead bodies.

Once he's finished, Palardi uses part of a clean sheet to bandage Alma's wound.

"Now I'd better brand her other arm," he says.

"Sorry?"

"With the scarring, her brand won't be visible anymore," says the surgeon, taking the iron used for branding captives.

"You're joking, right?"

"She needs to be branded," says Palardi.

Dubois smiles, shaking his head.

"I see . . ."

"What?"

"You know perfectly well what, Monsieur Palardi. Captives marked on the left arm are Captain Gardel's personal purchases. Don't act all innocent. I can see what you're trying to do."

Palardi's eyes are wide as an owl's.

"It's called corruption, Dr. Palardi."

"Now, now, Monsieur Dubois . . ."

"You were hoping to give this captive to Gardel when you know full well she belongs to Monsieur Bassac."

"But—"

"Anything to get back in the captain's good books."

"I assure you—"

"Enough. This little girl is hardly going to fly away. We can discuss the matter once her wound is healed."

Palardi turns pale.

"For now, let's just say you haven't seen a thing," whispers Dubois, as Joseph looks on, dazzled. "There's no need to mention anything. It'll be our little secret."

They hear footsteps approaching. Picard appears below the forecastle.

"Jacques Dubois! The captain is calling for you. He says

you've slept enough, and he wants to speak to you. You too, Joseph Mars."

Picard is with a sailor. The two of them stop dead when they see Alma.

"What's going on here?"

"Look at our surgeon's work!" says Dubois, grasping Alma's arm brusquely and lifting up her bandage.

He shows them the wound, stitched up like a work of art.

"See? In fifteen days it'll all be just a bad memory. Dr. Palardi is a talented man."

Dubois gets up. He hasn't slept a wink. He hasn't even had time to dry off.

"Take the girl down to the storeroom," he says. "I had enough trouble getting her out. Come on, Mars. Let these men get on with their work. The captain needs us."

They leave. Picard stays behind with Alma, Palardi and the sailor.

"What's gotten into you, doctor? I need to know if you're letting the captives out."

Palardi opens his mouth to speak, but Picard barks at him.

"That's the rule! End of story! The captain wants a word with you, too."

Palardi closes his trunk and leaves.

Picard and the sailor lift Alma up. They take her up onto the deck and head towards the forecastle. The young girl goes along without protest. She looks up at the sky. It's raining a little less now, but the wind hasn't died down. It's chasing the clouds across the sky. There's even a star somewhere up there.

"Inside!"

The two men push Alma towards the foremast and into the ship's store. What they don't realise is that what they've just released into that windowless, airless cell is indestructible freedom.

36

A Ticking Time Bomb

Gardel ushers Jacques Dubois into his quarters, leaving Joseph Mars at the door.

"You stay here."

Joseph was hoping to go inside with them. He hasn't been able to enter the captain's quarters for months. He wants to get into the alcove under the bed and examine those chests he's placed so much hope in. The moment he puts his ear up to the wooden door to hear what the two men are talking about, Dr. Palardi appears behind him.

"I was told the captain wanted to speak to me."

"Yes," says Joseph. "He's waiting for you."

The surgeon knocks at the door. Gardel flings the door open.

"Palardi!"

Standing in the doorway, the captain looks back into the room.

"Wait there," Gardel says to Dubois. "I'll come back to you."

The captain remains on the threshold, not allowing the surgeon to enter. Joseph sees the carpenter waiting on a chair in the middle of the room.

"Palardi, you've been very lucky up till now. I didn't blame you for the five captives we lost during our time on the coast."

"That's very kind of you."

"We could have lost more in that climate."

"Even the rats were getting sick," Palardi agrees.

"And yet you're the picture of health."

"Thank you . . . "

Gardel continues. "At least you managed to save the cooper."

The doctor nods modestly, embarrassed that Dubois is there to hear a compliment that's really meant for him. What's worse, he suspects that Gardel's kind words are a prelude to other, less forgiving sentiments.

"Doctor, beneath these floorboards in the powder magazine is a captive who's expecting a child. She was among those who came aboard in Ouidah."

"She has a severe case of anaemia, Captain."

"You're going to get her out of there and put her in the rowboat."

"It's no use. She only has two or three days to live."

The captain calmly grabs the surgeon's ear and begins to lift him off the ground again.

"Doctor," says Gardel, "please be so kind as to make her better."

Dubois is listening carefully. It's so rare for the captain to take interest in the fate of a specific captive.

"If that's what you want," says Palardi, standing on the tips of his toes.

"That's what I want, Monsieur Palardi. So much so that I'm willing to sacrifice a lot to keep her alive."

"Sacrifice?"

"Let me tell you something," whispers Gardel.

Still holding the doctor by the ear, he pulls him close, and breathes:

"If she dies, I'm happy for this ship to continue its course without a surgeon."

Palardi opens and closes his mouth like a fish. Gardel continues. "I'll give you the jolly boat swinging in front of that window with her corpse at your feet. You'll find your own way home together. Do I make myself clear?"

"I believe so."

"Now go and make her better. That's an order."

The doctor's heels fall to the ground with a thump.

"You'll see which one she is. She has *The Sweet Amelie* brand on her left arm."

This is what is known as a venture. The shipowner has granted the captain the right to transport two captives to sell for himself. These goods belong to Gardel personally as a bonus on top of the profit he's due to receive upon arrival. He also has some jars full of beeswax, a small barrel of cola nuts, and some pepper from Guinea. Gardel is essentially protecting this woman in the same way he would protect his coin pouch.

Palardi goes to leave. Joseph hasn't moved. He's trying to remain unnoticed behind the half-open door.

The captain goes back over to the carpenter.

"What about the ivory on deck?" asks Dubois. "Does that belong to you, too, Captain?"

It does indeed belong to him. Gardel is planning to sell the ivory for himself.

"That's precisely what I wanted to talk to you about, Monsieur Dubois. Your habit of asking questions."

"You're going to lose those tusks the next time there's a gale. They're not secured. Three poor creatures will have died for nothing."

"Three?" says Gardel, worried. "There are supposed to be six."

"If I'm not mistaken, you only need three elephants for six tusks. It's a question of biology. You might be confusing elephants with unicorns, Captain."

"Silence!" cries Gardel. "Back to work! Secure the tusks and stop asking questions!"

Dubois gets up.

"Not now!" yells Gardel. "Sit down!"

Dubois sits back down.

"I'm all ears, Captain."

Lazarus Gardel tries to regain his composure. He goes over to Dubois.

"I've been told you've been asking a lot of questions about your predecessor, the ship's former carpenter."

Dubois is sitting on his chair, leaning forward a little, his hands on his thighs. With his elbows spread on either side like handles, he looks like a small, thick, and very sturdy cup.

"Did you know Bassompierre?" asks Gardel.

"I know practically every carpenter from Bristol to Bordeaux. French, English, and Portuguese . . . I even know some Italians, seeing as I spent my best years building church frameworks—"

"I'm asking whether or not you knew Bassompierre."

"Yes."

"When you arrived in Lisbon, did you already know he was dead?"

"I was told by one of your sailors who spent a lot of his time talking and drinking—and I don't mean water. I found out by pure coincidence. It's thanks to him that I put myself forward for the job."

Gardel is slowly beginning to calm down. There's a smile creeping across his face.

"In that case," he says, "explain one thing to me."

"Yes, Captain."

"You saw the captain of *The Phoenix* when he came to have supper with me at this very table, a few weeks ago. Do you remember?"

"Yes. But it was up on deck that I saw him, not at this table, which I've never had the privilege to grace."

"He told me that night that he already knew you."

"I was the second carpenter when he was boatswain on a ship that set sail from Le Havre over twenty years ago."

"Twenty years?"

"Yes."

"He told me he'd seen you much more recently in the port of La Rochelle—the day after *The Sweet Amelie* departed."

Gardel takes a moment to observe Dubois's face before continuing.

"You were at La Rochelle that day. But you joined us in Lisbon only five days later. Another pure coincidence?"

Dubois doesn't reply.

"It takes a lot of effort to get from La Rochelle to Lisbon on land in a matter of days," the captain continues.

"I had some good horses. And it's true, I wanted this job."

"Did you want it enough to inadvertently drown your friend Bassompierre and his apprentice in the port of La Rochelle?"

The captain watches as Dubois's face suddenly becomes flushed with emotion.

"I wouldn't dream of it," he replies fiercely. He looks closely at Gardel. Does the captain really suspect him?

"The carpenter's death was a messy affair. I didn't like it one bit," says Gardel. "I regret having been absent when it happened."

"Where were you?" asks Dubois.

"I'll answer your question, just this once. I was spending

a week in Nantes at the request of Monsieur Bassac. It was a futile trip, but it was imposed upon me by some plantation owners from Martinique. In my eight days of absence, right before our departure, Monsieur Bassompierre had just enough time to finish his work, anchor the ship in the port, and then die. I was extremely vexed that he chose that precise moment to disappear."

"I don't believe it was a choice."

Gardel peers out into the darkness through his bedroom windows.

"No. It's just a turn of phrase."

There's a silence before Gardel continues.

"While I was in Nantes, Bassac sent his accountant, Christian Saint-Clair, to La Rochelle to oversee the construction of *The Sweet Amelie*. That man may well have a good education, glorious blonde curls, and fancy shoes, but he doesn't know the first thing about how to build a three-hundred-ton ship, let alone line its hull and recruit a cook!"

The carpenter lets Gardel speak. If the captain really did suspect him, he wouldn't be talking this much. He wouldn't be telling him any of this.

"You're right. I'm not here by fluke," says Dubois, trying to win the captain's confidence. "I liked Bassompierre a lot."

"Aha!"

"He was my teacher and my friend."

"So you came to finish the job he started."

"Perhaps."

"Right," sneers Gardel. "And I've been sailing for the last fifty years out of love for seagulls and sardines in oil. I don't believe a word of it, Dubois."

Gardel's eyes flicker back to the windowpanes. For a moment he thinks he can see flying fish or small birds brushing past the glass in the darkness. He leans over for a closer look, but there's nothing but a broad, white trail of foam in the ship's wake.

"Now go," he tells Dubois, finally. "We'll speak about this another time. Send Mars in."

Dubois gets up, troubled. He doesn't look at Joseph as they pass one another.

"Enter!" orders Gardel. "And shut the door."

Joseph enters. His hair is still wet from spending all night in the storm. He stands in the doorway.

Gardel pulls a sheet of paper from his pocket, unfolds it and places it against the wall. He takes a few pins from the lapel of his jacket and sticks them into the four corners of Luc de Lerna's riddle.

"Think of me, boy, as a king who summons his noblemen in the middle of the night. Palardi, Dubois, Mars . . . little noblemen who tremble as their names are called."

Gardel pushes in the final pin.

"Each one is afraid His Majesty will banish them from Versailles. But out at sea, our manners are a little less refined. There are no airs and graces. In a few days' time, for example, when all the captives are released onto the deck, I'll dream up a crime that none of them has committed. I'll punish one at random. And then peace will reign for a long time. Sacrificing a man to the sharks can often save money in the long run."

Joseph doesn't react. He's known for a long time that Gardel's little kingdom is held together by fear.

"No," Gardel continues. "This is no place for pomp and ceremony. We're a world apart from Versailles or the British court."

He begins to pace around the room.

"I've thought a lot about the information you got out of Cook."

"He trusts me. It was easy to—"

"Shut up!"

Joseph clasps his hands behind his back, bowing his head like a child who's been scolded. Gardel continues.

"You say he told you about the years he spent with Luc de Lerna."

"Yes."

"That's completely useless."

"Why?"

"He'd already told us that."

"I wanted to be sure," Joseph replies timidly.

Behind his back, Joseph is pulling from his belt a small, thick, black rectangle, no larger than his hand.

"So he told you that the pirate loved gold and was a very religious man."

"Yes."

"Fascinating."

Gardel presses his fist up against the glass, almost breaking it.

"Is there a single person alive who doesn't know that?"

"Sorry?"

"When I was twenty, people had already begun calling the Caribbean 'Brother Luc's font of holy water.'"

Joseph bows his head even lower. Slowly, behind his back, he slides the black rectangle from his belt up into his sleeve.

"Next time we drop anchor," Gardel continues, "we'll be in Saint-Domingue."

"God willing," says Joseph.

"Gardel willing," says the captain, turning his back to Joseph. "If, however, by the time we drop anchor in Saint-Domingue, you haven't found the exact location where the treasure is buried, you'll be tied to that anchor like Christ on the cross when it sinks into the mud."

What Gardel doesn't know is that while his back was turned, Joseph managed to leap forward and return to his spot again in a matter of seconds.

When Gardel turns around again, it's as though Joseph never moved an inch.

The captain makes a little gesture towards Joseph with the back of his hand, as though wafting away a bad smell.

"Now go. This is your last chance."

Gardel is left alone in his quarters. He picks up a black object from the chair where Dubois was sitting.

It's a book. A thick little book with a black leather cover. Dubois must have left it behind.

Gardel turns it over in his hands and reads the words engraved on its cover. His eyes light up.

The Four Gospels.

This is the perfect time for him to take up this kind of reading. Based on what he knows about Luc, the answer must be somewhere in these pages. Why didn't he think of it before?

He'll read it a hundred times over if necessary. He'll find the answer.

Joseph goes to join the other sailors on deck. The rain has stopped. The sky is gradually clearing up behind them.

He obeys orders, working on the sails through the night, but his eyes keep flickering back towards the ship's bow, just like the needle of a compass always points north. He's thinking about the girl in the ship's store.

Back there in the captain's quarters, he's just set in motion the final step of his plan: a ticking time bomb.

37

Chasing Away the Darkness

Alma can sense that daytime has come again. There's a streak of light coming through the cracks of the locked wooden panel above her. The faint glow is gradually spreading across the cell she's been locked inside.

During the night, Alma tried to determine how many women were in there with her. Closing her eyes, she attempted to count the breaths and the sobs.

Now she can see them all in the shadows. Fifty women. They take turns lying down or huddling together on the planks that divide the space in two horizontally. Many of them are forced to remain seated. Piled on top of one another, they try to breathe, keeping their eyes open to feel they're still alive.

"Listen. Do you hear that?"

A tall woman right next to Alma is speaking to her.

"Do you hear that sound?"

There are so many different noises coming from the steerage that Alma doesn't know exactly what she's talking about.

"That's the sound of iron. Listen."

Alma listens carefully. "Yes."

"The men are just behind the wall. They have chains around their ankles. They're attached to one another in pairs."

"How do you know?"

"Because I've been here for over two moons. I was the first. To begin with, they put me with the women being kept at the back of the ship. Yesterday they brought me here to separate me from the others. They don't think I'll be able to understand the Igbo language that the girls from Bonny speak. But we can all understand each other if we really want to."

Alma looks at the woman. She's tall and beautiful. She holds her head high. You can tell her face used to be fuller and plumper.

So it is possible to stay alive.

"Where are they taking us?"

"No one has ever returned to tell us."

The woman smiles. So it is possible to smile.

"Why did they separate you from the others?"

"The whites are afraid of me."

She says this with an air of slight astonishment, rather than pride. How can they be afraid of her? She has nothing but her bare hands and her open eyes.

"I was the first to arrive on the ship. You're the last."

She seems to be implying that fate has brought them together. She takes Alma's hand.

"I'm hungry," says Alma, after a long pause.

"Be patient. When the weather is bad, they never let us out. They bring a little food down here instead."

Alma hears the chains clinking again, louder this time. The men must be getting up. Even if they haven't slept a wink, they try to mark the transition from day to night by moving around a little, saying a few words, making the sounds of an ordinary morning.

"My husband isn't on this ship," says the woman. "It's better that way. I want to be able to imagine him free."

"I'm here, and I'm free," says Alma.

The woman smiles and squeezes her hand tighter. "You're free?" She wouldn't contradict her for anything in the world.

"Yes."

"That's good."

They sit in silence for a moment.

"I'm looking for a little boy I've lost," says Alma. "A boy who's smaller than me."

"The children are with the women at the back of the ship. But there aren't very many. I've only seen three little boys."

"Was there one called Lam?"

"We don't know anybody's name. They give us names that don't exist. The whites call me Eve."

"Eve," says Alma.

"Don't say that name. I don't want the whites to touch my real name. They can call me what they want. But don't you call me that name."

"What is your name?"

"Maybe one day I'll tell you. It's all I have left."

"Listen," says Alma. "I know some men brought a little boy here yesterday."

The woman doesn't reply.

"He's my brother."

The woman shakes her head as though she can't hear.

"Tell me where he is," says Alma.

"No little boy arrived yesterday," says the woman, with great sadness. "I was still back there with the others then. I would have seen him."

Alma repeats herself, fighting back tears.

"A boy arrived here yesterday. He's my little brother."

"You arrived here yesterday. That's quite enough. And earlier on there was a man. And six elephant tusks. That's all."

There's a silence.

"They brought him here," Alma repeats.

"The last women came from Bonny, three days ago. They're all here with us. Then there was the man I told you about. And you."

Alma is choked up. There's not a sound in the ship's store. All the captives have been listening to them. A young girl at the back of the room finally speaks.

"You have to believe the one the whites call Eve. We only saw one man come aboard just before you. We were still outside then. A very tall man."

"Yes!" cries Alma. "That's him, Lam was with him! A giant with a severed ear!"

Alma sits up slightly, almost bumping her head on the ceiling. She stoops into the same position as the rest of the captives.

"The giant came alone," says the young girl on the other side of the ship's store.

Alma covers her ears. She doesn't believe these women. Her hunter's instinct tells her there's a familiar presence on the ship. She felt it as soon as she arrived. Even through the smell of death, she smelt the scent of her valley, her loved ones. Here aboard the ship, there's a piece of the Valley of Isaya. Lam must be here somewhere.

When she takes her hands away from her ears, she hears the women talking among themselves.

"They bought the giant," one woman says, "because he's as tall and strong as four men. But they don't usually take those with damaged faces, bad legs, or missing teeth or ears."

"Well, if you needed somewhere to keep your oil or salt,"

asks a voice from the shadows, "would you buy a cracked pot with a broken handle?"

There's a silence. We might allow ourselves to imagine quiet laughter in the darkness. We might allow ourselves to imagine that some of these women regret not having broken a tooth a long time ago, so they might still be smiling at home. Even with nothing but a single tooth left in their heads, they'd be able to smile, standing at the front door, watching the sun rise. At least they wouldn't be here, crying in this tomb.

"I'd buy it, your broken pot," says the one the whites call Eve. "I'd buy it because anything that's alive is at least a little broken."

There's another silence, heavier this time.

"What are they going to do with us?" a voice whispers.

"Nobody ever came back from over there to tell us."

For the first three days, the women never once see daylight. But the storm has begun to die down. Finally, the shutter covering the minuscule air vent is opened from the outside. The piled-up captives take turns taking a breath and passing along the seasickness that takes hold of them, one after the other. Nobody complains. They know that just on the other side of the partition, each of the men is chained to his neighbour. A sick person can't even move without dragging another, often weaker, man behind him.

Every morning, the double wooden panel opens above the women for a few seconds, and a slop bucket of rice and beans is passed down. They eat from the dish using wooden spoons that have been hung around their necks. When the sailors come back for the empty bucket and water pots, one of the women is responsible for bringing up the metal tubs used as chamber pots in the night. The woman goes up the ladder.

She's like an emissary from the underworld. She goes up on deck, into the blinding light. She empties the buckets overboard and takes a look around her.

When she goes back down, the other captives are waiting for her. The hatch closes again. She sits down in the middle of the ship's store and gives news from up on deck. She tells them how white the sails are. She says the earth is getting thinner and thinner. First it was like a strip of cloth, then a thread of cotton, then a child's eyelash. She tells them there's nothing left to rest one's gaze on. She says the birds have disappeared from the sky. And each day, the women's eyes become a little drier as they listen to her, because even their tears have been exhausted.

In the afternoon, they are given large, brown biscuits that taste like dried earth.

The nights are endless. Fear, sadness, and longing invade the steerage the moment night falls. The air becomes thinner, the stomach aches more agonising. The women hold each other.

None of them ever imagined this. Even those whose villages had been under threat for a long time. Even those whose children were taken by slave catchers when they let them play in the rice fields to keep the birds away. None of them had ever imagined this nightmare.

Muffled sobs can be heard throughout the ship.

Finally, on the fourth day, the hatch opens wide. This time, it's not a bucket of rice and beans, but a man throwing down a ladder and giving orders. The women are to go up on deck.

Alma is one of the last to come out.

The captain had been waiting for land to disappear.

The final tie has been cut. Now there's nothing but the ocean. The captives are floating between two worlds. This is what the whites call the Middle Passage. At least two months between Africa and America without a glimpse of land.

Alma goes up onto the forecastle with the other women from the ship's store. The space is tight, cluttered up by elephant tusks. But finally there's air. The fifty women are seated near the foremast between the big bell and the ship's bow. They look up at the sky above them. The sunlight flickers on the white sails between the passing clouds.

Two armed white men are monitoring the captives from the jib. There's a third man up in the shrouds, hanging like a monkey. Alma can't see the little ghost who found her in her hiding place. The ghost with the big hands isn't there either. How could they just abandon her?

Beyond the rowboat, all she can see is the spiked palisade separating them from the stern of the ship.

"The women I told you about are on the other side," whispers the one the whites call Eve. "There are three times as many of them. They must have been allowed out, too."

They fall silent. For a moment it sounds as though there's singing coming from the stern, but it must have just been the sailors shouting.

"What about the men?" asks Alma.

"They'll never be allowed out at the same time as us. There are a lot of them. We're on the same side of the barrier as them. The whites would never be able to monitor us all."

"How do you know all this?"

"I'm trying to think like them."

On the other side of the windows in the barricade are two little cannons aimed and ready to fire grapeshot at them. Before setting the cannons in their current positions, Gardel fired into the open water to demonstrate the force with which any revolts would be crushed.

Further along the barricade, there are two narrow, double-locked doors connecting the two halves of the ship.

Day by day, Alma will come to discover what life is like on this floating prison: the heat, the stench, the cries during the night, the sick who are isolated, those who are force-fed, those who never return to the steerage, the sharks patiently following in the ship's wake.

Whenever she thinks about why she's there, she thinks of the brave little birds in the valley she sometimes used to see perching on a buffalo's back or between the bright eyes of a crocodile. She wants to be one of them. Alma thinks of Lam. She thinks of her family waiting at home for them both. They're probably under the sycamore tree right now, looking out at the tall grasses dotted with zebras. They're probably dreaming of the moment when their two missing children will come tumbling down on the grasses along with the first rains, soaking wet and cold as the walking dead.

Alma doesn't know that her house no longer exists, that the animals stop every day at the edge of the burnt grass, staring at the great black fig tree as though waiting for someone or something.

Alma doesn't know that her brother Soum is right next to her, chained up on the men's side. He wakes up every morning with a small bed of green moss and forest flowers beneath him that he hurriedly brushes away so that nobody sees.

She doesn't know that her father is following the long strip of the African coast in search of Lam.

Nor does she know that if she were to jump up from the forecastle, leaping high into the air as she does so well, she could land in the rowboat and snuggle up to the tired body of her mother as she sings her songs in a low whisper to survive, to chase away the darkness.

38

Black Ink

"Nothing?"

"As good as nothing," says the solicitor, devastated.

Amelie Bassac is dressed from head to toe in black and is standing in her father's place behind the desk. The old family solicitor is seated across the table. On his knees is a bundle of papers covered in ink that keep slipping onto the floor. On the carpet at his feet, his empty satchel looks like a toad that's been flattened by a carriage.

Monsieur Olivier is a former schoolmate of Amelie's grandfather and has been the family's faithful solicitor, witnessing their successes and sorrows, since the turn of the century. It's impossible to tell how old he is. When people compliment him on how well he's doing for his age, he replies that solicitors don't have the right to die. He claims this is why he stopped ageing fifty years ago.

Christian Saint-Clair is standing nearby. He hasn't taken his eyes off Amelie's fingers, which have landed on the desktop like butterflies.

It was there, on the tobacco-coloured leather, that Ferdinand

Bassac died a fortnight ago. Saint-Clair can't stop thinking about it. He can't look Amelie in the eye.

"I have here," the solicitor continues, "your father's will, which leaves absolutely everything to you, mademoiselle. But the text is five years old. It dates back to just after your poor mother died. And as I said, everything listed: the contents of the coffers, the land, the vineyards, the bank accounts, the buildings in Paris . . ."

The solicitor runs out of breath.

"All of that . . ."

"Yes?"

"It's all gone."

A few hours ago, Monsieur Olivier was certain he could tell Amelie, as her only consolation, that she was the wealthiest heiress in town. Instead, he's just discovered she has nothing left.

"Nothing."

"And how do you explain this?" the young girl asks coldly.

"I believe—"

"That was a question for my father's accountant. How do you explain this, Monsieur Saint-Clair?"

"Saint-Clair?" repeats the solicitor, turning to the young man.

He jumps. He was so lost in his thoughts, he hadn't even realised that Amelie was talking to him. Saint-Clair pulls himself together. He responds with just the right amount of solemnity and emotion.

"Forgive me, but I find it difficult to comprehend that this situation is news to you, Mademoiselle Bassac."

"Believe me, it is," says Amelie.

"I was certain you knew . . ."

"Stop telling me what you thought and explain to me how things stand."

The accountant takes a deep breath.

"When your father took me on two years ago, it was because he was in a dire situation."

"Dire?"

"Your father could not afford the lifestyle he lived."

"What lifestyle are you talking about?" asks Amelie. "My father wore the same outfit every day of the year. He used to take it to rue des Carmes to have it mended. And I've been having the same mourning dress enlarged ever since I was eight and a half. The only real expenses in this household are the encyclopaedias and nautical charts."

"The war with Britain did a lot of damage to your father's business. He had to sail his ships under a foreign flag . . ."

"Don't tell me about my father's business. I know his accounts line by line. Business is excellent. Even during the war in America, none of his ships were ever taken by the British."

"You know what he was making, Mademoiselle Bassac, but you also have to look at what it all cost him."

"True. I don't know anything about that, seeing as the books were always in your hands. I was told a young girl from a good family did not need worry about the small expenses of running a house and the salary of a coachman."

"But you don't understand, Mademoiselle Bassac. I never saw his accounts, either."

"So what were you there for?"

"There's something I want to tell you—"

"Just spit it out rather than announcing what you're going to say."

"Your father hasn't paid me for over a year."

"Is that so?"

"I didn't blame him. I'm fortunate enough to have received

some savings from my mother. I stayed with Monsieur Bassac out of loyalty."

"How touching," says Amelie, though she doesn't believe a word.

"It's true. There's no record of your salary for the past year," confirms the solicitor. "But since when does an accountant agree to work without payment, and above all, without access to half of his client's accounts?"

"Perhaps I should have left, you're right." He pauses for a moment. "But I'm not the sort to abandon a man who's drowning."

Amelie looks away.

"How is it possible," the solicitor asks, "to spend millions within a few years without building castles or parks, without hiring artists and orchestras?"

"I don't know," says Saint-Clair. "Monsieur Bassac must have taken a secret to the grave."

"Excuse me?" says Amelie, with a start. "What secret?"

The solicitor intervenes diplomatically. "I believe what Monsieur Saint-Clair is suggesting is that your father may have had a more complicated life than you might think."

"Women?" cries Amelie. "Mistresses? Illegitimate children?"

The solicitor looks offended. "I wouldn't have dreamed of saying such things, Mademoiselle Bassac."

Amelie paces around the desk.

"Why not say the things that are there on the tip of your tongue? Women. Surely you know the meaning of the word, Monsieur Olivier?" she asks, going over to the old solicitor. "Or do I need to spell it out for you?"

Nearby, Saint-Clair looks at Amelie's ankles below the hem of her black dress. He tries to get a grip on himself.

"Let's all just remain calm," he says, partly to himself.

Amelie goes over to him. “You seem nervous, Saint-Clair. Are you sure *you* are giving us the whole story?”

The accountant manages not to back away from her. Amelie takes a step back.

“Look at what you still have,” says Saint-Clair, softly. “It’s not to be sniffed at, Amelie.”

“Don’t address me by my first name.”

“You have the house in La Rochelle, Mademoiselle Bassac, the plantation in Saint-Domingue, and a ship somewhere in the Atlantic, whose profits will keep you going for a while.”

Upon hearing these words, the solicitor sits up in his chair, paler than ever. A few more papers slide down from his pile. It looks like he’s surrounded by dead leaves. He gives the leather briefcase at his feet a little kick, as though he’s relying on it for courage.

“That’s the thing . . . that’s what I wanted to talk to you about,” he says, almost inaudibly.

Amelie goes back to her seat. “It sounds as though the good news is just going to keep on coming,” she says.

“There are two men waiting in your courtyard. As I’m sure you’re aware, a shipowner never invests in a slave ship alone.”

“I am aware, thank you.”

“These men have invested one hundred thousand pounds in *The Sweet Amelie*’s voyage.”

“Tell them not to worry. They’ll get their money when the ship returns,” says Amelie. “Before the year is out, the ship will be back in La Rochelle. We’ll do the accounts.”

“That’s not what they want.”

“Sorry?”

“There’s a clause in their contract stating that in the event of a business partner’s death, they’re entitled to immediately withdraw the amount invested into the venture.”

"Immediately?"

"As of today."

"You're not telling me that's what they want to do?"

"They have certain doubts regarding—"

"A fourteen-year-old girl's ability to manage her father's affairs? Is that it?"

Amelie goes over to the window.

"I'd like to see these generous souls." She rests her forehead on the glass and looks out into the courtyard.

"Oh! Monsieur Beaumont and his son have come to pay a visit." She turns to face the solicitor. "Don't tell me . . ."

"Yes. It's them. They're here to collect their hundred thousand pounds."

Amelie can't help but laugh. She opens the window in spite of the cold January air.

"Don't wait out there, gentlemen! Come into the warm. We have a fire burning. Tell the servants I'm waiting for you."

From the cobbled courtyard, the two men lift their noses up towards her. From above, all bundled up in their scarves, they look as though they could be twin brothers. Their bewildered eyes widen beneath their identical sealskin hats.

Amelie closes the window. The solicitor coughs.

"I don't think those gentlemen wanted to speak to you in person."

"How sweet. How chivalrous!"

Now Saint-Clair can't keep his eyes off the back of Amelie's neck beneath her tied-up hair. Where does she find this strength? Orphaned, bankrupt, humiliated, yet she's never been so dazzling.

A few moments later, the Beaumonts enter the room. In the excitement of the moment, they've forgotten to take off their hats and coats.

"Leave your pet animals by the fire, otherwise they'll soak the carpet."

It takes a moment for the two men to understand. They look at each other and go to leave their hats in front of the fireplace. They've made a fortune importing sealskins by the million from the islands of Mexico. They wear them in all different shapes and sizes, no matter the season. Rumour has it they even wear sealskin undergarments.

"I won't ask you to take a seat," says Amelie. "I know you're in a hurry."

She smiles at the two men.

"I understand you're concerned about the ship bearing my name. I'm sorry to hear that."

The younger man, Charles, gathers his courage. "My father wishes to collect his money."

"One hundred thousand pounds?"

"One hundred and twenty thousand, including interest," the young man corrects her.

"Yes. You're quite right, young man. After all, a penny saved is a penny earned."

Charles blushes.

"Did you know that three days before Christmas, your father spoke to mine regarding a marriage proposal?"

"A . . . a marriage proposal?"

He blushes again.

"I know," she says. "I, too, wondered why Monsieur Beaumont would want to marry my father. But I believe he was thinking of you and I, Charlie."

She turns to Beaumont senior.

"Have you changed your mind, sir?"

"I want my money," Pierre Beaumont replies. "I never spoke to anyone about a marriage proposal."

"I was hiding under this very desk when you spoke about the matter. I could only see your feet, but I heard every word. I could even tell you which sealskin slippers you were wearing that morning. Your words to my father were: 'One day, we'll have to think about marrying off the children.'"

"Your father told you that story to make you happy."

"That's not the kind of happiness I'm looking for. I've heard the same words uttered by half the town when they come to sign deals with my father. I've grown rather tired of it."

She runs her long fingers over her black dress. "What's changed since Christmas?" Amelie lifts the sides of the skirt a little and looks down at it. "Is it the colour you don't like, Monsieur Beaumont? If the wedding takes place in two or three years, I'm sure I could marry in white."

Panicked, Monsieur Olivier gets up from his chair. "Mademoiselle Bassac is in shock, gentlemen. As the family solicitor, I can tell you her father's paperwork is not yet in order. I think she'd appreciate it if you could give her a few months."

"I want my money," Beaumont repeats.

"Please understand—"

"Monsieur Olivier," interrupts Amelie. "Will I ever have the right to speak on my own behalf? Is it too much to ask now that I'm the only one who bears the family name?"

She turns calmly to her visitors.

"Gentlemen, the Bassac family never keeps creditors waiting, particularly those of the miserly sort. Today is Monday. You'll be paid by Friday. Please take your creatures and leave."

The solicitor and Saint-Clair don't take their eyes off Amelie.

"Mademoiselle Bassac . . ." Charles Beaumont begins. Amelie waves her hand in the direction of the door.

"Go. I said take your things. I don't mean to be rude, but

they're beginning to smell. You'll have your money by Friday morning."

The two men pick up their hats and edge backwards towards the door.

"You're being unreasonable, Amelie," says the solicitor once the men are gone.

"You don't have that money," adds Saint-Clair.

"I have everything I need," she says, gesturing to the room around her. "How much do you think this house is worth?"

"Amelie!" cries the solicitor.

"It'll be worth one hundred and fifty thousand if I have to sell it tomorrow. With that money, I'll reimburse those gentlemen, pay Monsieur Saint-Clair's back-salary and your own fees, Monsieur Olivier, and finally say goodbye to all those who have taken such good care of me over the years."

"And then what?" asks the solicitor, his internal arithmetic machine ticking over in his head. "You won't have much money left if you sell."

"I'll use what's left over to pay for a cabin on a ship to Saint-Domingue."

"Do you mean to say—"

"I need to attend to the only place I have left in the world. And if I understand correctly, all I have left is a sugar cane plantation and a ship somewhere in the middle of the ocean."

She crosses her arms to hide her trembling hands.

"Sell this house, Monsieur Olivier. Along with all the furniture, paintings and tapestries. And now, please leave me alone. I have a lot to do. As my mother always said, the lightest suitcases take the longest to pack."

Christian Saint-Clair and the solicitor leave the room, stunned. When the door closes again, Amelie remains on her feet for a few moments. She waits until she hears footsteps on the stairs. Then she falls cross-legged onto the carpet and dissolves into tears, her dress spreading out around her like a pool of black ink.

39
All the Lost Children

When they arrive at the end of rue de l'Escale, Christian Saint-Clair and Monsieur Olivier shake hands beneath the archways. It's cold and dark out.

"A tragic affair," says the solicitor. "At the very least, we must ensure the girl leaves town with her dignity intact. Such misfortunes must not be made too public. She'll have to marry one of these days, after all."

Then he adds in a low voice: "Though she really would have been better off locking herself up in a convent."

The solicitor notices Saint-Clair's pale face. "Don't worry, young man," he says, pinching his cheek. "You couldn't have saved Bassac from himself. All men carry with them a dark shadow that nobody suspects."

The accountant nods his head mechanically. This last sentence echoes through the wide expanse of Saint-Clair's own dark shadow.

Monsieur Olivier leaves. His wooden heels click as his feet dance along the pavement. Whether they come bearing very good or very bad news, solicitors, judges, and doctors are among the lucky few who are able to go home at the end of the day, put on a pair of slippers, eat the leg of duck that's waiting for them on the stove, and bounce their grandchildren on their knees. For them, life goes on.

Saint-Clair takes a few steps and slips into a narrow passage piled high with rubbish between two small buildings. He's so exhausted, he can no longer stand up straight. It's damp and icy out. The sea air whistles mournfully through the streets.

Saint-Clair is resting against a stone wall. He lifts his head up to breathe. He doesn't even notice the odour of rotten fish around him anymore. He closes his eyes.

None of this was planned. It all happened without him realising. The fortune was put on the ship to increase Bassac's wealth. He'd be willing to swear it. The only part Christian Saint-Clair played was keeping the secret. And when, on Christmas night, that secret was in danger of being revealed, he panicked.

As for Bassac's death, that was an accident. Saint-Clair is not a criminal. Nor is he responsible for the disappearance of Bassompierre the carpenter and his apprentice. Saint-Clair's contact aboard the ship acted without consulting him. Saint-Clair never asked for any of this.

And that's not the worst of it. The worst is that he never meant to keep his silence in Bassac's office when Amelie realised that all was lost. He had meant to tell her about the gold on the ship. Four and a half tons of gold belonging to the Bassac family. Their entire fortune melted down into precious metal. But suddenly, when he came face to face with her, he just couldn't do it. He wanted to be seen. He wanted her to need him.

And for that to happen, she had to lose everything. It was

the only solution: for him to become rich and her to be left with nothing. Then she would love him. She'd have no choice.

He catches his breath. Gradually, he begins to feel less guilty about everything. All that remains is to collect the cargo upon arrival. Amelie will get everything back the day she marries him. In the meantime, he'll be able to take care of the treasure better than a fourteen-year-old girl ever could.

For a long time, Christian Saint-Clair remains there among the foul odours wafting in the wind. He keeps his eyes closed. When he finally opens them again, he sees the rats on the abandoned rubbish pile at his feet staring up at him fearlessly, as though he were one of them.

There's a scratching at Amelie's door.

It's another kind of rodent, belonging to the genus *rattus bibliothecae*, otherwise known as the library rat or black parlour mouse. Little Madame de Lô enters the office. She's been in mourning for her late husband for a long time, but now she's added an extra layer of darkness to her clothing. Her dress is made up of layer upon layer of black, mauve, and grey. Her hair is covered by a kind of mantilla veil that flutters before her eyes like a mesh fence speckled with black cotton flies. And if we had seen her dressing early this morning in her bedroom mirror on the top floor beneath the roofs, we would know that even the panniers beneath her nine skirts are black. They're made from nigra bamboo, a sort of black cane that grows in the forests of China. Madame de Lô has taken mourning to the next level. Being a widow is something she has down to a fine art.

When she sees Amelie collapsed on the carpet, she begins frantically searching for a Greek quote from Arcesilaus or Asclepiades of Bithynia that might offer some consolation, perhaps a few words on resilience in times of hardship. Instead, disarmed by all the tears, she takes Amelie in her arms and shouts the first Latin words she can think of:

"Elixus cuniculus!"

Which, roughly translated, means "wet rabbit."

Madame de Lô is already up to speed on the day's developments. The solicitor—who is not immune to her refined, austere charm—told her everything that happened as he was leaving. She knows Amelie has nothing left. Monsieur Olivier even took the opportunity to mention that if ever the Bassac family were forced to let her go, he'd be delighted for Madame de Lô to give embroidery and dressmaking lessons to his great-granddaughters, who are eight and ten years old. She amiably replied that she was equally clueless about both disciplines, but that she would keep him informed about her plans.

Amelie has never cried in front of anyone before. Her tutor has never held her in her arms. Today has been a day of many firsts.

"You know," Madame de Lô begins, "I was in shock, too, when my husband died. Though of course, it came as much less of a shock than this . . ."

She smiles sadly.

"Firstly, he was my husband and not my father—though he looked as though he could have been the latter. Secondly, I found out the day after my honeymoon that he only married me because he was planning to fleece me."

"And you let him?" asks Amelie between sobs.

"I don't remember anything. I was eighteen. That's when I started studying astronomy. My head was so far up in space that I forgot to keep an eye on my pockets. He took everything my family had, right down to the last silver-gilt teaspoon."

"And what about my father? Did you see this coming too?"

Madame de Lô shrugs her shoulders. "No. But I always have lacked imagination."

Amelie is lost in thought for a moment.

"I don't believe all of this is true," she says. "Christian Saint-Clair must have known something."

Madame de Lô smiles. She hugs Amelie a little tighter. "After I lost all my money, I wanted to find someone to blame, too."

"Someone must be to blame."

"Yes."

"But who?"

Madame de Lô's face falls.

"Back then, I asked myself the same question. What I found out about my husband was much worse than anything I'd been told. Don't dig too deep, my dear, please."

"Saint-Clair—"

"That poor boy is the perfect scapegoat. The only thing he's guilty of is loving you when you don't love him back."

"If I believed he were incompetent, I wouldn't be suspicious of him. But he can't have just let my father bankrupt himself. I heard him talking about a mysterious shipment—"

"Leave him be."

"I'm sure he knows something."

"Soon you'll never have to deal with him again."

"Why?"

"You're leaving."

"They told you?"

"Yes. You know I can't handle hot climates, don't you?"

"I know."

"My parents once took me to the islands on business. We had to leave almost as soon as we arrived. I was like one of those shrivelled little snails you find in the grass in summer. There was barely any life left in me."

The young girl looks up at her tutor in tears.

"In any case, I won't have the money to take you with me."

"It's true. Times are changing. Who would pay for the services of someone who can't even teach girls to dance the minuet or the gavotte?"

Madame de Lô smiles. Amelie looks at her, surprised at her light-heartedness, despite the fact that their time together is ending.

"This is going to be a huge change for me," says Amelie.

"For me, too. I liked my little room. The cook's sorbets. But we'll get through this. You'll see."

She taps the end of Amelie's nose with her index finger.

Amelie's eyes widen. Her room? Sorbets? Is that all her tutor will miss after all their years together? She feels her throat tightening but attempts to feign the same indifference.

"You can write to your cousins in Versailles," she says.

"What cousins?" asks Madame de Lô.

"Those who wanted to put you forward to work at the king's residence. The little princes of the court will all become scholars thanks to you."

"I say! And by what miracle?"

"By taking your lessons."

"My lessons? And how do you propose the princes of Versailles will benefit from my lessons if I'm working full time as a shrivelled snail at your side?"

"A snail?" says Amelie.

"Yes."

"A little shrivelled up snail?"

"That's right. A very badly paid snail."

Amelie starts crying softly again like a three-year-old.

"Are you saying you'll come with me?" she asks.

"There's no question about it."

"Why?"

"Because your piano playing is atrocious, and we haven't even got you started on the Delian problem. I can't let you go out into the world alone like that."

"We have to take the piano?"

"And a trunk of books. Those are my only conditions."

Amelie heaves a long sigh, punctuated by a few last sobs.

In Madame de Lô's arms, after all the tears she's cried, Amelie feels a new strength within her. The need for revenge. A desire to rebuild everything.

But how is it possible that, on that fateful day, such a young, pure brain with its billions of neurons, all closely connected, does not for one second think of the hundred and fifty slaves working on the lands in Saint-Domingue, or the five hundred and fifty captives locked up on *The Sweet Amelie*, or all the others out there? The loss of her family and possessions—the tiny cataclysm that has shaken her world—seems to have done nothing to finally open her eyes to the immense tragedy all these men and women are living through. What about their freedom, their world? What about the millions of houses and families that are being destroyed? What about all the lost children?

40

Rebirth

Alma has been waiting for this day for almost two months. Yet she doesn't reply when he finally speaks to her. The little ghost, whose name she still doesn't know, is standing right behind her.

"Are you okay?" he asks.

Joseph is kneeling under the large jib sail, which is barely moving. He's leaning towards the ground, pretending to be working. Just next to him, Alma is crouching in the sun along with the others. The heat is suffocating. The twenty-five sails hang like badly ironed bedsheets. There hasn't been the faintest breeze in the air for days. And yet they're so close to their destination. If the wind would finally pick up, they could be in Cap-Français, Saint-Domingue in less than a week.

Joseph takes the measurements of the ship store's shutters.

"I couldn't come any sooner," he says, without raising his head so nobody notices him talking to her. "I'm sorry. I'm not allowed near the front of the ship. I was waiting to find a way to come and see you."

Alma is sitting on the forecastle with the other captives,

like every other morning. Today, there's only one guard monitoring them. He's armed with a musket and stationed on the opposite side of the deck, next to the bell. He's all pink and sweaty and has a soaked rag tied around his head. When he brings the women back down to their cell, the men will be able to come out of the steerage and sit up on deck beneath the rowboat.

Alma has never seen any other captives apart from the women with her in the ship's store. She hasn't seen those who are imprisoned at the back of the ship, hidden by the barricade. Nor has she seen any of the men. This strict level of separation, along with the scent of the valley lurking somewhere aboard, give her hope that Lam might still be here, in spite of all she's been told.

The guard has just ordered two women to dance. Another is beating a small drum. All three of them have their eyes closed. They're dancing under the blazing sun.

Each day, the captives are forced to dance. The shipowner came up with this recommendation to keep the captives in good health. Gardel obeys the orders left for him in Bassac's engagement letter, but generally, if the captives are going to be doing exercise, he'd rather they be scrubbing the deck with sand and seawater.

Alma's eyes are fixed on the whiteness of the horizon. She refuses to watch the women dancing. When you're forced to dance at gunpoint, when the heat is stifling and the rhythm of the drum brings back so many memories, every second is painful. Even so, their dancing is deeply moving.

Alma is angry with the boy working nearby. She thought he'd forgotten her. She was so afraid. If he were to disappear, who else would know that she's free?

"You never told me your name," he says. Alma doesn't reply.

"Are you angry with me? I wanted to come, I swear I did. Your wound is healing nicely . . ."

There's another silence. He's right. The wound on her shoulder has almost disappeared.

"Many women have died down there," Alma says finally.

"I know. That's why I'm here. Do you remember the man who was with me when we found you?"

Joseph is trying to speak discreetly through his teeth. He's finished taking his measurements. The guard has risen and is slowly making his way towards Joseph, weaving through the captives.

"Do you remember? The man's name is Dubois," says Joseph, before the guard gets there. "He asked the captain to replace the shutters with a wooden grate to let more air in. So that's what I'm doing."

The guard has almost reached them.

"I'll be back tomorrow. My name is Jo—"

He doesn't have time to say his full name. The guard has grabbed him by the jacket.

"Enough loitering," he says. "And don't leave anything lying around."

He pushes Joseph forward. Alma watches them leave. The little ghost is called Joe.

The following night, as the men fall asleep in the steerage, a woman pushes through the darkness of the ship's store among the tangled bodies. Alma doesn't see her coming.

"You speak their language?"

It's the one the whites call Eve.

"I heard you speaking their language. Come with me."

She holds out her hand to guide the little girl through the night. Alma follows. Doubled over, they grope their way through the darkness. The woman gestures for Alma to squat on a square plank against the wall. She stoops down alongside her, waits a few seconds, then knocks twice on the wall. There are two knocks in response.

Alma watches as the woman places her finger on a black knot in the oak timber, just at the height of her head. Her finger sinks into the wood.

The partition is made of beams at least six inches thick. The heat must have caused the knot in the wood to come loose, because now it's possible to slide it in and out like a cork.

One the other side, someone pulls the wooden cylinder out, leaving a hole the size of a coin between the women's cell and the steerage where the men are imprisoned. Then a voice whispers:

"Is she with you?"

The voice is coming from the men's side.

"Yes," the woman replies. "She's here."

"Can she hear me?"

"She can hear you."

"Tell her to come closer."

Alma leans towards the hole.

"Who is the white boy you've been talking to?"

"I don't know."

"How do you know their language?"

"I don't know. I speak the languages my parents taught me."

"Where are you from?" She doesn't reply.

"This white boy you know . . ."

"I don't know him."

"If he's speaking to you, you know him."

"You're speaking to me, but I don't know you."

The voice stops for a moment.

"I want you to get something for me," says the man. "An object the whites have. I need you to bring it to me."

"Why would I do that?"

"So you can be free."

"I'm already free."

The man is silent again. He says, "I know you're looking for someone."

Alma turns to the one the whites call Eve.

The man continues. "Your brother isn't here. It was me who sold him to another ship off the coast of Bonny."

Alma clenches her fists.

"You're lying," she says. "All the women here know I'm looking for my brother. They told you. You're making up stories about him so I'll do what you say."

"We arrived on the river. We sold your brother to the other ship, the one that was just next to this one. Then we came to sell the elephant tusks to the French."

Alma wants to plug up the hole so she doesn't have to hear any more.

"Why are you locked up with the captives if you're the one who's supposed to sell them?" she asks.

"I was betrayed. My men sold me, even though I was their chief. At the last moment, they traded me for copper and guns."

How can she be sure it's him? That he was with the men who took Lam?

"Prove it," she says.

There's a silence. The woman is still holding her hand.

"Your brother had a bat skull around his neck," the man replies. "About the size of a palm tree seed. He was riding a wild horse with three irons on its hooves."

"Stop."

Alma lets her head rest against the partition. She thinks of her brother, gone for good.

"Are you the giant with the severed ear?" she asks.

"Help me," the voice replies.

"Why should I help you now I know I've lost him."

"He won't be lost if you do as I say."

"You just told me he's gone!"

"The white men's ships all have names. I know the name of the ship he's on. If I give you the name, even though the sea is vast, you'll be able to find out where it went, the day when we're all free."

"I'm already free," says Alma. "Tell me the name."

"Do as I say, and one day I'll tell you."

Alma goes back to her spot. She curls up on her side with her legs bent. She hugs her knees to her chest to make herself smaller, to disappear. For so long, she's been tracking Lam through deserts and forests, along rivers to the sea. But now, for the first time, his tracks are veering away from her and might disappear completely.

Alma wants to be alone. She doesn't want her tears to be lost among all the other tears filling up the ship. She wants to keep hers separate, hold them in her hand or put them around her ankle like precious stones. They're all she has left.

Then she hears a voice coming towards her through the darkness. It's the one the whites call Eve.

"What's happening to us now," she whispers, "is like a drought. A swarm of locusts. A disease passing through the village. One day, it'll all be over. And our people will sit around the fire and recall the year of the locusts, the thirst during the drought, all the ones who were lost."

Alma listens to this woman who took her under her wing in the bowels of the ship when she arrived two moons ago.

"We are all among the lost. Those who stayed behind will try to remember us. But you're different. You're suffering now, but one day you'll be able to look back. Listen to me. You're both things at once. The two halves of your people. The lost and the survivors. One day you'll remember us. One day you'll remember Oumna."

And at that moment, the word etches itself into Alma's memory. The name of the one the whites call Eve. Oumna.

"But to make it through the night, you need to be able to remember. During a drought, we don't eat the food that's been scorched by the sun. We eat the wheat that grew when the earth was flooded. We eat the wheat we took precious care of. Remember those happy times. Your memory is your granary. It will keep you alive."

And so, when Oumna's voice goes silent, Alma delves into the granary where her memories are stored.

All night, she regains her strength, spinning around in front of her house with her little brother, running through the storm, making wicker baskets with her father, watching the little lion cubs search for their mother in the tall grasses. She grazes her knees climbing acacia trees. She spends hours combing her mother's hair. She makes little herds of animals out of the red earth. She hides herself as the gazelles walk by, then jumps out of the bushes, barking like a jackal. She gallops on Cloud's back, falls asleep by the fire, and watches her big brother silently shooting his arrows through the air. She startles the flamingos, sending them soaring through the skies, scrambles down hills in the middle of the night, and washes in the babbling streams. She listens to Lam's voice saying, "Come on, Aam! Aaaam! Let's go!" and her mother telling the little boy, "Leave her in peace, my little meerkat. Let Alma rest."

That night, not even the clamour aboard the ship can drown out the noise of the valley that Alma has brought back to life.

41
The Weight of Secrets

For the next three days, Joseph works alone on the wooden grate for the ship's store. From the moment he begins work to the moment he finishes, there's not a single cloud in the sky, no movement in the sails or the sea whatsoever. The ship has never been hotter. When water is poured onto the deck to stop the wood from cracking, a layer of steam hovers along the floorboards. Joseph keeps his tools in a canvas bag that hangs from his belt. On this side of the barricade, all pointed or sharp objects have to be kept safely out of the captives' reach. That's the golden rule on the ship. Even the barrels are secured with chestnut wood rather than metal so they can't be used as weapons.

Joseph is up on the forecastle at dawn. He takes a break around nine o'clock while the women locked in the ship's store are brought upstairs. He spends the whole time waiting for the girl to appear.

The first day, she ignores him. She sits up on the deck with the others, not far from where he's working. She watches as the sailors roll out a canvas above the captives' heads to give them some shade. The next day, two women collapse in the sun. The girl remains motionless, impervious to the heat. Joseph looks at her skin, completely dry apart from two beads of sweat forming on either side of her nose.

On the second day, a bucket is passed among the captives so they can wash their faces and necks. They can't get enough seawater out of the bucket using only the palms of their hands.

The women wish they could dive into it instead.

There's not even the faintest breeze. The girl looks up at the sails above, unable to tell which direction the wind is blowing. Only her pupils are moving.

"Where's my bow?" she asks suddenly, without looking at him.

Joseph lifts his head. The women all around them don't seem to hear. They're waiting for the water to be passed around.

"Dubois hid it," he replies. "What's your name?"

"Alma."

He repeats her name silently to himself. When he says it, his lips touch ever so slightly. It's as though he's catching his breath.

After a while, he speaks to her again, "You'll get your bow back, Alma."

"You told me I was free, and then you abandoned me. You're just like the rest of them."

This time, he looks into her black eyes. Eyes that don't stop, going far into the distance, leaving Joseph feeling ashamed and helpless. Yes. He is just like the rest of them. He does the same dirty work as everyone else, and the only form of hope he offers these fifty women is a handful of salt water in a bucket.

The wind still hasn't picked up by the third day. Joseph is still working. There are a few sailors heading down into the steerage. While the women are outside, the sailors burn a mixture of sulphur and gunpowder to disinfect their prison, just as they did in the stern the day before. The acrid smell does nothing but mask the poisoned air in those cells. The smoke escapes through the wooden grate that Joseph is working on. With no wind to disperse it, the smoke begins to engulf the captives.

Alma takes this opportunity to go over to Joseph. It's now or never.

"Joe . . . "

Not many people in his life have called him Joe. One was the boy who escaped from the Paris orphanage with him. He went by the name of Flea, and he was like a brother to Joseph. The other is the old man who'll be waiting for Joseph at the end of this voyage.

"I know you're not like the others," says Alma.

He can't see her approaching him through the smoke yet.

"There's so much tragedy aboard this ship," she says.

"I know."

"You don't know anything. Look at that woman. Do you know, for example, what she called the boy she loved? The name that she alone would whisper into his ear? Do you know what she promised him? No. You don't know anything, Joe."

Joseph has stopped working. He looks around for the woman she's talking about.

"But the things that matter," says Alma, "are the things that only one or two people in the world know. The reason why these women exist is because they have secrets."

Alma moves towards him and lets the words fall freely from her lips, just like she did when she was telling her little brother stories.

"Did you know that the woman over there used to talk to the trees when she was little? And that this one liked to bathe in the river while her family slept? You see the pain at the bottom of this ship as though it were one big animal caught in a trap. But there are hundreds of different kinds of pain."

The guards move away from the smoke, coughing. Alma is right next to Joseph now.

"Think of a secret only you know," she whispers.

Joseph forgets to breathe for a moment. He's frozen to the spot.

He's six years old, and he hasn't yet left the orphanage. He tells himself that the laundry lady, the one with the short, brown hair, is his mother. And nobody must know.

She mostly does laundry for the orphanage's director, who believes the children have tainted souls and don't deserve clean clothes. Whenever Joseph passes the laundry lady in the white apron in the hallway, he slows down. She never even looks at him. As she walks, her body swings from side to side, sometimes even touching the walls of the hallway. She smells of soap from head to toe. Joseph is sure that the reason she never speaks to him is because she doesn't want anyone to suspect anything.

Once a year, during the holidays, she washes the children's sheets and gowns, just before the sisters from the convent make their annual visit. After the big laundry day, Joseph pretends to find a letter between the sheets, written by the laundry lady. He doesn't tell anyone, not even his friend Flea. He imagines he's reading the letter each night, even though it's dark and he doesn't know how to read. It always starts with: "My darling Joseph" and ends with "all my love." Joseph folds the imaginary letter up carefully, then digs his nose into the mattress to inhale the clean scent.

Suddenly there's a commotion up on deck. The captives are

beginning to gather. The smoke is getting denser and more pungent. The guards intervene, shouting. The captives are being taken away from the opening. Joseph searches desperately for Alma in between coughs.

She followed the others, turning her back on him. It doesn't matter. It's all over. She got what she wanted.

The sailors emerge from the ship's store with their empty smoke boxes. Calm is restored. The air is still stagnant beneath the sun. Joseph has finished his work. He heads back to the stern, shaken up. He's still having trouble breathing.

The next day, it's still dark when Joseph opens his eyes, lying on his back in his hammock. He wakes up on the starboard side, where he fell asleep barely two hours ago. Something has woken him. A forgotten sound. It's the sound of the waves gently caressing the ship. He gets up and climbs up on deck.

He can feel the breeze in his hair straight away. The wind is rising again. He goes back to the aftcastle and sees the sails stretched taught in the moonlight. A swell sends ripples through the ocean. The ship is back on course.

"While you've been fretting over the captives' comfort, boy, I've been thinking about our deal."

Captain Gardel is standing behind him, hidden by the cages that once held chickens. He's leaning against the railings right at the back of the ship. Joseph didn't notice him there. They're alone.

He immediately notices a change in Gardel's face. His little eyes are wider. His nostrils are quivering. The captain looks down into the eddies forming in the sea, then up at the great white flag floating in the darkness. He occasionally glances at the two men at the helm, on the other side of the empty cages.

"I was told you took three days to build two simple wooden grates in the roof of the ship's store," says Gardel, sniffing the damp breeze.

"It'll save a lot of lives and a lot of money, Captain."

"Are you telling me how to do my job?"

"There was so little air, you couldn't light a candle in that cell. A living captive is worth a thousand pounds. Whereas a dead captive—"

"Shut up. You don't know what you're talking about."

Captain Gardel only has two rules: pile up as many captives as possible and rush to the islands as fast as the ship will take them. It's a tried and tested method, one he's had twenty-five years to perfect. If he increases the quantity of goods and the speed of the ship in equal measures, he knows that regardless of any losses, he can make better overall profits than if an eccentric little sailor takes it upon himself to tend to the captives' creature comforts. There's only one he cares about keeping alive, and that's the pregnant woman in the rowboat. Twice—once in Boston and once in Cartagena—he's seen Okos being sold at auction. The buyers were prepared to do anything to have one as a "skilled slave" or "house slave." They could fetch as much as ten thousand pounds if someone fell in love with the voice of an Oko with the gift of song.

But for the last few hours, Gardel hasn't given the Okos a second thought. He's blinded by another, bigger dream. He can almost smell the old leather as he opens up the treasure chests. He can hear the sound of the gold flowing in between his fingers.

The captain lowers his voice as if someone might be listening. He looks around him.

"Come closer."

Joseph moves towards him. This is a sign that everything

is going according to plan. The fear of being spied on is what gives away all treasure hunters.

Gardel takes the little black book from his pocket. "What's this?" he asks.

"I don't know," says Joseph, leaning towards the book. He pauses for a moment. He's excellent at playing the fool. "Isn't that Jacques Dubois's book?"

"It's the Bible, boy. The Bible."

"He'll be pleased. He was looking everywhere for it."

"Remember the skull between the bull's horns?"

"Yes . . ."

"And remember how north and south had been switched around?"

How could he forget? Joseph listens carefully. Things are getting off to a good start.

"If I turn over the parchment and put north at the top, as I would with any map, the mouth and eyes become figures: XIX, 01, 10."

"So?"

Gardel opens his Bible.

"'And behold, there was a man named Zacchaeus . . .'"

"Sorry?"

"'. . . and he was rich.'"

"Who are you talking about?"

"Luke, chapter XIX, verses 1–10."

"What's that?"

"The bull's head is St. Luke."

Joseph pretends to be working things out painfully slowly.

"Chapter XIX, verses 1–10, in Luke's Gospel: 'And behold, there was a man named Zacchaeus . . .'"

"Zacchaeus."

"'. . . and he was rich.'"

". . . he was rich," Joseph repeats.

He opens his mouth as though he's just understood something, then closes it again and tries to look embarrassed.

"I'm sorry. I don't follow."

Gardel grabs him by the neck. At first, Joseph thinks he's going to be thrown over the taffrail and into the frothy water below, but instead the captain drags him in the other direction, towards the large ladder leading to the cabins. As the captain climbs down the ladder, Joseph's feet miss the bottom rung. Gardel picks him up off the floor and drags him into his room. He opens the two latches. Then he takes Joseph by the neck again, yanking him around like a puppet, and presses the boy's face into the map that's been rolled out on the table. Without saying a word, he places his index finger on a minuscule island east of Saint-Domingue, just off the coast of Puerto Rico.

Despite the flickering of the candle flame, Joseph is able to read the word on the map just an inch from his eyes: Zacchaeus.

Joseph smiles. He's been waiting for this moment. The man standing behind him is as smart as he is monstrous.

"Zacchaeus?"

Joseph wanted the captain to find the location himself. He wanted the process of solving the riddle to be so challenging that nothing would stop Gardel once he had the answer.

"So that's where it is," he says.

"Yes, that's where it is," says Gardel, slowly loosening his grip on the boy's neck. "It's there. Five days from here."

Joseph tries to turn his head towards Gardel. As he does so, he glimpses the shadows of the chests beneath the captain's bed. That's the reason he did all this. It was all for the contents of two chests hidden in an alcove in the middle of the ocean.

Just then, they hear the floorboards behind them creaking. They turn around to find Jacques Dubois standing there, his face as white as a sheet. Neither of them had noticed him.

"I'm looking for Joseph Mars," he says.

As he turns to face the carpenter, Gardel's expression is terrifying. His sky-blue gaze pierces right through Dubois. How much did the carpenter hear?

"I need Mars," Dubois repeats.

The captain lets go of Joseph's head and wipes his hand on the side of his jacket.

"Take him. I don't need him anymore."

"And this?" says Dubois, gesturing towards the book on the table, "I believe it's mine."

"I don't need that anymore, either. Don't leave your things lying around."

Dubois takes the Bible between his large hands. It's been weeks since he lost it.

As Joseph watches this strange encounter between the two men unfold, he thinks back to Alma's words: the things that really matter are those that only one or two people know. He's beginning to feel the ship sinking beneath the weight of all the secrets.

42

A Giant in the Sky

The carpenter leads Joseph to a corner of the hold at the back of the ship. This is where Dubois's workbench is set up.

Despite the curvature of the ship's hull, which puts the whole workshop at an angle, the tools are tidied away perfectly in their compartments. Every last wooden dowel is in its place. There are planks of wood stacked to one side. Any sawdust and wood shavings have been swept up and stored in a half barrel for Cook to use tomorrow to light his stove. Even the carpenter's planer blades are laid flat on a shelf so that if a single one went missing, he would notice immediately.

Dubois invites Joseph to sit on the chest where he keeps his saws.

What's going on? Joseph is expecting the worst. He's eyeing two large chisels stored in their box next to him. If Dubois becomes a problem, he'll have to grab one.

"The gouge," says Dubois finally.

"The gouge?"

"The gouge."

"The gouge . . ." Joseph repeats, as the word begins to bounce around in his head.

Dubois's jaw is tense.

"The gouge . . ." says Joseph again, hoping for a clue.

"The gouge!" yells Dubois. "The gouge!"

Lurking behind them, Captain Gardel flinches. Suspicious of Dubois's sudden appearance and the worried expression on his face, Gardel followed the pair into the hold and is listening in, hidden.

"The gouge," says Joseph, as though endlessly repeating the word might explain everything.

But not even the fire now burning in Dubois's eyes is shedding any light on the mystery at hand.

Just as Joseph is preparing to the grab one of the two chisels, his gaze falls upon the shelf next to them. One of the compartments is empty. He blinks and contemplates the terrible emptiness for a few seconds, just enough time for the carpenter's words to lodge themselves there.

"The gouge!" he says.

"The gouge," Dubois confirms, as calmly as possible.

Finally, Joseph understands what he's talking about. The gouge, that small chisel with a sharp, curved blade that sinks through soft wood like a teaspoon in ice cream.

"I had it yesterday," Joseph stammers. "I'm sure I had it."

Still in his hiding place, Gardel repeats those fateful words to himself: the gouge.

"I found your bag this morning on that chest," says Dubois.

Joseph thinks back to the commotion of the previous day amid the smoke of the ship's store.

"The gouge was missing," explains Dubois.

"The gouge," repeats Joseph.

With this object on the loose, the ship is about as safe as a keg of gunpowder by the fireside. But before they have time to come up with a plan, Dubois and Mars see Gardel emerge from the shadows.

"I have no idea what a gouge is," says the captain through gritted teeth. "But I swear, if I find it, I'll find a way to use it on you that you will never, ever forget."

He disappears, leaving Dubois and Joseph completely dumbfounded.

At that very moment, in the steerage just above their heads, the captives watch as the giant files the large iron shackles around his ankles. For hours, they've been adjusting their breathing to cover the noise of the gouge scraping at the iron. After one night's work, the iron is already well worn down. Soon, he'll be able to snap it in two, and the giant with the severed ear will start a revolt on the ship.

Suddenly, the gouge stops moving. The men's breathing stops. Several loud bangs ring out from the deck.

Outside, Gardel has just taken several shots into the air. The captain turned warlord has assembled his men, awoken the crew sleeping on the starboard side, and begun stomping his feet to scare the captives. He sends two men to lock up Dubois and Mars, then divides the rest of the crew into squadrons of ten to search the three sections of the ship in which the captives are imprisoned.

The gouge, once a refined but unassuming tool, is now a weapon fit for the devil himself.

"Search them all! Bring them out one by one! Inspect their chains. And be careful! Somewhere on this ship is a weapon waiting to be driven right through your hearts."

The men opening up the shutters are armed to the teeth. Day is beginning to break.

Alma is lying down in the ship's store. She began to lose her strength in the middle of the night. Her hope is slowly fading. She's lying on the floorboards, watched over by the one the whites call Eve, whose real name is Oumna. The second she heard the first shot, Alma understood what was happening. The panic sweeping through the steerage plunges her deeper into despair. She can vaguely make out the silhouettes of the sailors dragging the captives in and out of the ship's store.

A few hours earlier, Alma slid the blade through the hole in the partition, and the giant refused to give her what he'd promised.

"I can't trust a girl who speaks to the whites. I'll tell you the name of the ship your brother is on once we're free."

Then he closed the hole back up. Alma continued to knock on the partition, whispering: "I *am* free, I *am* free, I *am* free."

Then she fell into her long night of despair.

The giant with the severed ear can sense danger approaching. The crew are beginning to search the bottom of the hold, inspecting the first captives. They bring them up on deck, one after the other. There are still one hundred men to get through before they reach him. He can still do it. The commotion caused by the search will help him. The cells will already be wide open. Anything will be possible.

His companions all around him are all still. They're forming a resistance. When the ship set sail, these men were Efiks from Old Calabar, or Serers from the Kingdom of Saloum. They called themselves inhabitants of a certain village, or said they were born on the banks of a certain river. Some would say they were from Tinmah, and claim it was the most beautiful city of all. They called out desperately through the steerage to find their people, their fellow villagers. When the ship set sail, one man chose to let himself die because he was the only one on the ship who spoke his language. In the beginning, there was still the presence of those feuds between the Fante and the Chambas, quarrels so old that nobody remembers why they began.

But day by day, all that has changed. They haven't forgotten their homes, but a common enemy has brought them together. They were once people of all different colours. Now they are all black.

They can hear the sailors shaking the numb, sick, injured bodies one by one. A consensus has been reached among the captives. No amount of whipping or caning shall make them move faster. They must take their time. From one end of the ship to the other, they drag their feet. They slow down to give freedom one last chance.

Captain Gardel watches amid the chaos. He's caught on to their little game. He shoots into the air again and whips anyone who slows down proceedings. The more the captives resist, the more urgent the situation becomes. Something is brewing.

A cry echoes through the forecastle. The wooden handle of the gouge has been found. Picard is brandishing it at the bow of the ship. It was hidden somewhere in the ship's store.

"I'm looking for the blade!" yells Gardel from behind. "Not a piece of wood!"

He runs towards the foremast.

"Don't stop what you're doing! Carry on!"

He goes to the entrance of the ship's store and pushes aside the women crowding around the forecastle. He grabs a lantern and descends the rungs with Picard in tow. Gardel covers his nose with his sleeve, which is covered in eau de cologne. The tiny space is completely empty. The captives are all waiting outside. He holds his lamp up to every corner. He skims it along the wooden walls.

"We've already searched here several times," says Picard.

"Shut up. Find the weapon."

"It isn't a weapon, Captain."

"You'll see, Picard, when they use it to take out your other eye, whether or not it's a weapon."

Gardel goes to the back of the tiny cell. He puts his lamp down and runs a finger over a dark knot in the wall.

"Give me your knife."

He gives the black spot a sharp tap. The wooden plug sinks into the wood and falls out the other side.

"Aha," he says. "Go to the back of the men's side! Now! Take fifteen or twenty men if you have to. There's an armed captive just behind the wall who may already be unchained."

The giant doesn't hear a thing. All night, he's been holding the blade in his hands. The handle wouldn't fit through the hole in the partition. His hands are wounded, covered in blood and iron shavings. He can no longer hear the crew approaching, the cracking of the whips. All around him, the wall made of his companions starts to break down.

But he's almost there. Only a scrap of iron, barely the thickness of a fingernail, stands between him and his freedom.

When the iron finally gives way and he gets to his feet, he feels the barrel of a rifle pointing at his giant forehead.

"You move, I'll kill you," says Gardel.

The captives and crew fill up every inch of the deck and fore- and aftcastles. There's a human tide flooding the ship. Everyone is looking at the giant up on the foremast. His body

has been hoisted up and tied to the topgallant mast, up above the tallest sail.

One hundred hours. That's the punishment the captain has decided on. One hundred hours up there with no food or water, in addition to the hundred lashes he's already received. To Gardel, punishment is a refined science—one he likes to think he's mastered perfectly. The giant must serve as an example, but still bring in a profit upon arrival.

Lazarus Bartholomew Gardel stands by the helm. He takes a deep breath. He's managed to avoid the worst. For peace of mind, he orders the crew to lock up all the captives. They won't see the light of day until further notice. These events have also given him a reason to dismiss Dubois and Mars, whom he's been suspicious of all along. It was their own doing. It's the perfect outcome. Now nothing can get in the way of his master plan.

There's just one thing that continues to haunt him. The riddle gave no indication as to the exact location of the treasure. Which shore of Zacchaeus should they cast anchor on?

The wind is picking up. There's a black sky looming in the west. A storm is brewing. The claps of thunder almost sound like a distant naval battle.

Gardel's orders echo through the ship once more. The lower sails have been run down to resist the oncoming wind. Half the crew is manning the deck, while the other half continues to herd the captives. Only one boy is resisting as they try to usher him back into the steerage. It's Soum. He spotted Alma as two women were helping her down into the ship's store. He struggles in silence to get his little sister's attention.

Three times the cat o' nine tails rains down on him, but he doesn't utter a sound.

"Don't strike him!" cries Absalom. "He doesn't know what he's doing. He belongs to the captain."

Finally Soum disappears into the bowels of the ship.

Alma didn't notice her brother. She's weaker than ever. Even if she had seen him, she might not have recognised him.

All she knows is that Joe and the old ghost have been locked up. The only two people who can vouch for her freedom.

Just as she goes down into the ship's store, before falling into a deep, long sleep, she catches a glimpse of something resembling a dark flag flying above the ship. It's the giant in the sky.

43

The Horns of the Bull

The waves are high, and Cook is heading down towards the officers' cabins holding tightly onto a small tin bowl. The soup is so viscous that even if he tipped the bowl upside down, it'd stay firmly put. Cook stops right outside the surgeon's cabin. He balances the soup in one hand as he takes the key out of his pocket and opens the door.

It's been a long time since Palardi was banished from his cabin and had all privileges revoked by the captain on the grounds of incompetence. Now he eats and sleeps with the sailors. He's been assigned all the toughest jobs, such as coating the leaking floors with sheep's grease and filling the emptied barrels with seawater to keep the weight of the ship the same. Meanwhile, his cabin is being used as a cell for Joseph Mars and Jacques Dubois.

When the door opens, the two of them are sitting side by side on the velvet bench. Joseph did everything he could to prevent the carpenter from being punished for his own mistake. But Gardel refused to listen. Dubois was forced to take responsibility and didn't protest as he was being locked away.

"My dear Cook, you're the only one who hasn't forgotten us," says Dubois, taking the bowl. "We'd invite you to dine with us, but I don't think you'd be able to stomach your own cooking."

"True, I'd rather eat at the captain's table," Cook admits.

"So would I," says Dubois. "Only I've never been invited."

"On all the ships I've worked on," says Cook, "the head carpenter was always the most respected of all the officers on board. He earned more than the first mate and got served before him at the captain's table."

"I must be different from the others."

"The captain doesn't like you."

"I've never sought that wretched man's affection. Give us some news from the outside world, Cook. Nobody tells us anything."

Cook's cheeks puff up like a toad as he heaves a long sigh.

"Things are going very badly. The captives are quiet, which worries me. We need to get to Saint-Domingue as soon as possible, but the captain has suddenly decided we're taking a refreshment stop."

Joseph's heart skips a beat.

"A refreshment stop?"

"Where?" asks Dubois. "Puerto Rico?"

"No. On a rock in the ocean with not a living soul on it. The Island of Zacchaeus! Never heard of it. I'm certainly not going to find hens or suckling pigs there."

Jacques Dubois looks surprised. Refreshment stops are common. They often happen before the crossing, in Sao Tome or on Principe, just off the coast of Africa, and sometimes at the end of the voyage, just before they arrive. But these stops are more about appearances than supplies. The idea is to build up the captives' strength, fatten them up, make their skin shine using powder or lemon juice, shave their hair, and dye any greys. Then they leave again. Captains will do anything to increase the price of the captives when they arrive.

These refreshment stops have become a business, one of the many industries created by the slave trade. All that's required are a few huts, some vegetable patches, and some fresh water. But never before has a slave ship taken a refreshment stop on a deserted island like this.

"Maybe Gardel will need a carpenter to construct the buildings," says Dubois.

"I don't know. I have to admit, I don't understand it. I just want to get to Saint-Domingue."

Dubois lifts the lid from the soup. He recoils as the smell escapes.

"It has a strong smell," says Cook. "The water's gone bad. But it tastes all right. Just imagine a few extra mushrooms have been thrown in."

"Perfect!" says the carpenter in mock delight.

"I know the Island of Zacchaeus well," says Joseph suddenly, turning to Cook.

Dubois looks at him, laughing. This boy speaks like the old timers you meet at the inns along the ports. He's seen it all!

"Tell the captain," says Joseph, "that in bad weather, there's sheltered anchorage to the south, between the bull's horns."

"Between the bull's horns!" Dubois chuckles.

"Tell him, Cook. Please. He'll understand."

The two men stare at Joseph, incredulous. Dubois turns to Cook.

"You'd better get back to your dishes. And don't forget to lock the door. I could have escaped three times since you arrived."

"You wouldn't have got far," says Cook. "I've been told to

keep throwing the dirty water and rubbish overboard so that the sharks will follow us right until the end."

"Captain Gardel doesn't leave anything to chance."

"I hope he isn't leaving anything to chance," sighs Cook.

He turns to leave. For the first time, Joseph glimpses an expression on Cook's face he's never seen before. Just as he's leaving the room, his jolly mask falls away for a second, revealing a different man underneath.

Dubois and Mars begin to eat their soup, sharing one spoon between them. For a moment, the cabin is filled with the sounds of them lapping noisily at their soup like puppies, along with the creaking of the ship. Then Dubois wipes his mouth with his sleeve.

"Now we can finally talk."

Joseph looks at him.

"I'll start," says Dubois. "My name is Jacques André Dubois. I'm a carpenter. I was born in Le Havre on Whit Sunday in 1726. Like you, I grew up without a family."

"Like me?"

"Yes, like you. If your name is Joseph Mars, you must have arrived at the orphanage on the 19th of March, Saint Joseph's day. They take the name of the saint on the calendar hanging on the wall of the entrance hall as a first name and the month of the year in French as a last name."

Joseph is stunned. He's never told anyone he was probably born on the streets. Now he realises it's written clear as day in his name. Perhaps this shared history is the reason Dubois has taken him under his wing.

"I grew up without a family. But I had a teacher. His name was Bassompierre. He was the best carpenter there was, and the best boss, too. That was enough for me until I began to get my first grey hairs. Then I had a wife. But not for long. From one May to the next. The lifespan of a butterfly. She left me a son, the only reason I had to go on living once she was gone.

Joseph listens to this life, contained in a few sentences that Dubois tells with his eyes closed to stop his voice from breaking.

"Then last August, I suddenly lost everything I had in the Port of La Rochelle."

Dubois is silent for a moment. He slows down.

"My teacher and my son, both in the same night. Antony was Bassompierre's new apprentice. One was fifteen, the other eighty-four."

Dubois takes a breath.

"Almost a hundred years put together. I'd just received a letter from Bassompierre. He wanted to tell me something. Something important. I left Lucca, where I'd been working, and was in La Rochelle within a matter of days. When I arrived, they were both dead. I was told they'd been drinking, that they'd fallen. Can you believe that? Drinking!"

His eyes begin to well up.

"Bassompierre and Antony were born beneath the timber frameworks of carpenters. They were two trees in a forest. And trees only drink rainwater. I came here to find out who killed them and why. I'm here to find out what they knew. What they never had the chance to tell me."

The two of them remain in silence, unable to look at one another. Joseph feels his eyes stinging with tears, too.

"Now what about you?" the carpenter asks.

Joseph's hands are clasped together in front of his mouth, palm to palm, as though in prayer. For a moment, he wants nothing more than to reciprocate Dubois' openness. He remembers Alma's words and is tempted to share everything. He could make it all exist simply by sharing it with another person. He could talk about the darkness of his childhood, and the light he knows he'll find one day. He could say the name of the person who sent him away on this ship. But he's too close to his goal to give in to the urge.

"What about you?" Dubois repeats.

"Me?" asks Joseph, as though he had only just woken up.

"Yes, you."

"I'd like to be like you."

"Like me?"

"To be able to say that at some point in my life, even for a short while, I had a teacher, a wife, or a child."

"Stop," says Dubois, solemnly. "What are you here for?"

Joseph holds his ground. He'd like to at least say that he thinks he's found a role model in Dubois, a teacher. But he's wary of sentimentality. Share one secret and you might end up revealing more.

"I already told you. I'm looking to make my fortune, just like everyone else."

By saying this, he's able to tell the truth without giving anything away.

And that's when it all starts.

Or perhaps the noise had already started. First, they hear a thumping that sounds like bare heels or elbows gently striking the wood. If there weren't ten people doing the same thing, nobody would hear. But within a few seconds, there are fifty, then one hundred people tapping out the same rhythm.

The ship doesn't vibrate. It's a low noise that's swelling. Now it's reached the women's sections at the bow and the stern. Nobody knows where it began. The beat doesn't stop.

"What is it?" asks Joseph.

Dubois takes a deep breath. He understands what's happening. He's only seen it once before, a long time ago on a

Portuguese ship. It's every captain's nightmare. The beginning of the end.

"The captives are beating out a rhythm. But it's not the sound they're making that matters. They could be crying, refusing to eat, shouting, or even remaining completely silent. It wouldn't change a thing. The important thing is that they're doing it together."

"Why?"

"They're here. There are many of them. They're alive. And they're telling each other so."

The rhythm is steady, never speeding up or slowing down. It seems to be sinking deeper into the ship like a nail being struck endlessly.

"Gardel was wrong," whispers Dubois. "He made a mistake. There's a particular space where a captain has to keep the captives. It's a very narrow space, right between hope and despair. If he wants them to be docile, he can't give them too much hope. Nor can he take it all away."

Joseph understands what Dubois is saying. He's always known what it means to live on little promises. Joseph began hoping when he was four. He was still hoping at six. All he ever did was hope. And even if nothing came, it was always better to hope, to believe.

"It's because of the giant," says Dubois. "The giant up there on the mast. He's like a flag signalling that it's all over, that they can no longer expect anything, that all hope is dead. That was a mistake."

In the shelter of the aftcastle, listening to the captives' rhythm and watching the lightning and rain, Lazarus Bartholomew Gardel is having the exact same thoughts. But he's not about to show any sign of weakness. He knows that the punishment came at the wrong time, when the captives were exhausted from the journey. He knows that the dark shadow looming at the top of the mast is not going to help with his plans.

So he's considering his options. He needs to keep control of the ship a little longer. All he can think of is the treasure.

Cook suddenly appears behind him.

"I took the two prisoners their soup, Captain."

Gardel groans. He'd rather they starve to death.

"Go away."

"The boy wants me to tell you that he knows the Island of Zacchaeus."

The captain turns to Cook.

"Mars?"

"He said there's an anchorage that's protected from the wind, between the bull's horns, in the south."

Gardel freezes.

"He said that?" he murmurs, stone-faced. "Does he think this is news to me?"

He waves Cook aside and heads to his quarters.

How can Joseph Mars be so stupid? Has he just revealed the exact location of the treasure to Cook?

Gardel's anger mingles with excitement. He shuts himself in his room and goes over to the piece of paper stuck to the wooden wall. He takes out three of the four pins and turns the bull's head like a compass. He pins it back up with north at the top. He takes a step back and compares it to the map on the table.

Thanks to that idiot, Joseph Mars, Gardel now knows exactly where he's going. The bull's head is supposed to be read like a map. It just needed to be the right way up. There must be a passage behind the two tapered rocks just to the south of the Island of Zacchaeus, right where the skull is, right between the horns of the bull.

44

Tell Me Who's Singing

The rowboat suspended above the deck is like an island on *The Sweet Amelie*. It's a large boat, almost thirty feet long. When it's in the water, it can fit twelve rowers inside. It's currently hanging from the spare mast. Since the ship left Africa, the rowboat has been used to house sick captives—or rather, the few sick captives the captain wants to get better. But even those who will not survive the journey have found a little peace inside that boat. Because tucked away at the bottom, just beneath the middle bench, there's a voice singing softly.

Each night, the voice becomes more fragile. But it never stops singing. Only in the daytime does it fall silent, gaining the strength to begin once again in the dark hours. When night falls, beneath the tarred canvas that's been stretched out like a tent over the rowboat, the sick huddle around her to listen.

The voice doesn't travel beyond that little stage. Outside of the boat, it's drowned out by the crackling of the rain, the roaring of the wind and waves, and the sound of the captives beating against the ship's skeleton.

Nobody who listens to the voice can tell which language

it's singing in. But like children who understand their mother's lullabies before they learn to speak, they follow every part of the story. The tears that follow do more good than all the surgeon's purges and bloodletting put together.

The voice is Nao's. She's singing to the child she's expecting and to all the children hiding inside the frightened men and women huddled around her.

When the drumming began, Nao didn't hear a thing. She couldn't distinguish the rhythm from the beating of her own pulse in her ear. Then she stopped singing. She listened to the story being told by that thudding beat. It was the same story being told by her own song. The rhythm was taking over from her heart so that she could be carried away.

Now she can stop singing.

Now, she can let herself go. She knows what disease is taking over her body. It's a known affliction among the Oko people, a mortal plague caused by captivity and despair.

"Won't you sing a little longer, little cousin?"

It's midnight. There's a smile floating above her in the storm. An old man is lying on the bench just above Nao. He's bending over to speak to her. He's older than most of the captives. Until that moment, nobody had heard his voice. He hasn't said a word since that first day, when he was brought aboard *The Sweet Amelie*. He's the imperturbable captive, the one the whites call Adam on their register. He was brought to the rowboat with a fever. Over time, the wounds inflicted by the chains around his ankles have become infected. The wounds are growing each day, and the race is on between the two legs to see which side's wound will reach the knee first. But the man never complains. He keeps his smile hanging between his ears like a talisman.

"Won't you sing?"

Nao opens her eyes. The little man has a loud, deep voice that doesn't match his body.

"Listen to them," he says.

The captives' drumming rising towards them despite the roar of the wind.

"I think they're calling you, little cousin."

Three claps of thunder ring out, one after the other. On the men's side, the rolling waves make the bodies slide, pulling on the chains, lacerating the skin. But the captives manage to keep time. At the stern of the ship, the women cling to the wooden pillars. Others, exhausted with seasickness, roll on top of each other, no longer resisting.

A man has begun to sing.

They're listening to him in their hundreds.

"This time, I'm going to crush them!" cries Absalom, jumping from his hammock.

The singing voice is more powerful than anything that might fall upon the ship, whether wind, water, lightning, or fire. It's even more powerful than the captives' drumming. Heavy silences punctuate the phrases. They stop time, making you desperate for more.

"It's coming from the rowboat!" shouts one sailor. Lanterns begin to appear across the deck.

The surgeon is the first to arrive. He lifts a corner of the canvas and plunges his lamp into the rowboat. He freezes. Those aren't silences between the phrases; they're verses that the pregnant woman is weakly singing from under the bench. She's started singing again, her voice more bewitching than ever. And each time she pauses to catch her breath, the little man above carries her song with all his strength into the night.

"What is it?" asks Absalom, standing by the rowboat.

"It's Adam."

When the woman starts singing again, even the boatswain shivers a little as he listens to her.

"This one always sings at night," says the surgeon. "It's not usually bothersome. You can barely hear it."

Clearly the surgeon isn't too bothered by her singing, seeing as he always comes to sit right next to the boat. He stays to listen to her almost every night. When he gets up, icy sweat runs down his back, making his shirt stick to him.

"She doesn't disturb anyone," he repeats, feigning indifference. "But this one, Adam . . ."

The man they call Adam looks at them without stopping.

Absalom cracks his whip. His arm gains momentum, and he throws the cat o' nine tails over his shoulder to strengthen the blow. But a hand grabs his wrist in mid-air.

Captain Gardel snatches the whip from him. His shirt is open, his ponytail in disarray. Absalom looks up at him, lost.

"I wasn't going to touch the woman," he says. "I know she's yours. I was going to give the one who's singing a good hiding."

The captain plays with the whip between his hands.

The two captives continue to take turns singing. Nao's eyes are still closed. The one the whites call Adam starts smiling again. The rowboat's other occupants listen with bated breath.

"Don't you want me to punish him?" asks Absalom.

"Haven't you noticed something?" says Gardel through gritted teeth.

"No."

"Below? Listen, you rapscallion! Listen!" he yells.

Other sailors begin to arrive on deck. They're all listening. When the woman sings, they can't help but listen.

"Well?" says Gardel. "Haven't you noticed anything?"

When Nao pauses, their brains kick into action again.

"The noise!" cries one of the sailors. "Listen!"

Below deck, the drumming has stopped. The lower deck is silent.

"Let them sing," whispers the captain. "I'd rather have two of them singing than six hundred of them cutting us to pieces."

It didn't take long for the captives to organise. On the women's side, behind the men's partition and the new wooden grating of the ship's store, a few captives have been designated as messengers. They listen to the one the whites call Adam. Then they relay the sound of his voice. They're singing for those around them. Others spread the words even further into the bowels of the ship, repeating them and translating them into all the different languages they know: Mandinka, Fula, Kikongo, Akan . . . Their words reach everyone from the Igbo women in the ship's magazine to the men lined up along the floorboards, huddled beneath the scaffolding Dubois built in the steerage.

At first, Nao was singing to get their attention. She wasn't telling them anything in particular, just preparing for the moment when she would have them all in the palm of her hand. Now she's speaking to them directly:

Listen to me, you who weep,

In this forest made of wood and iron.

She likens her song to a canoe in a flood. She describes how her voice is kept afloat on a stream of tears. When she speaks of the branches that hang low over the river, all the captives look up at the ceiling of the steerage and see vines and birds appear in the darkness above their heads.

I give you courage, you who are weary.

As the boat drifts in silence, my song you will hear.

The sailors can't help but listen.

"What's she saying?" asks one sailor.

"Shh!"

The storm continues to rage, but alone in his quarters, all Gardel hears is the newly restored calm beneath his feet.

For a long time, Nao continues to cast her spell. Her song reaches the ears of those who no longer wanted to hear, wakes those who were sleeping, those who had given up on everything.

You may have given up on life, but life does not give up on you.

Memory is our solid ground. Listen.

These words, repeated over and over, spill from the rowboat and gradually slip between the beams, spreading their way through the ship. They linger in the darkness like starlight before they hit the ground.

They come without warning. Nobody realises the words are spinning a story. Then shadows begin to stir. And the story begins. The song is the tale of a unique people. A flourishing population of many, who all lived in freedom.

The Okos.

Freedom is what gives them life; without it, they will die.

Freedom is what cultivates the gifts within them, just as trees can grow as tall as the sky if they aren't chopped down. Freedom becomes the air they breathe.

In a low voice, from the bottom of the boat, Nao sings the word "freedom."

And the word in her language is *alma*.

She sings of the Okos' sophistication, their beautiful gardens, their powerful doctors and griots, their brave warriors. Her people bear the same name as the birds that have always lived among them: okos, little emerald hummingbirds with silver beaks. The birds flock around the roofs of their houses, to the yellow flowers of their acacias.

They never leave the Oko people.

All night long, Nao's song braves the storm, stifles the creaking of the ship, silences the cries and sobs. Slowly, it brings Alma back to life. The spirited, heart-wrenching song tells of damp clothes hanging at the entrances of houses high in the trees, hummingbirds gathering in clusters to drink, the births, the kidnappings, the looting. Life and flight are closely intertwined in the history of the Okos.

Whenever danger strikes in their surroundings, their freedom is at stake. The Okos are now hunted like all the other peoples. They've fled deeper into the land, further up the river.

An Oko who is caught will inevitably die. Not right away. They can survive in irons for as long as they still remember freedom. But the moment hope takes flight, their strength will desert them. They close their eyes. Okos, like hummingbirds, die when the cold strikes, when the night comes, when there are no more flowers. They fall into a state of inertia. Their heartbeat slows. They are no longer truly alive.

Little by little, the number of Okos dwindles, until they are fewer than a scattering of lentils in a bowl, then a sprinkling in the palm of a child's hand . . .

. . . *And now, if the last of the Oko were lentils, those lentils could fit on a fingertip.*

And so, to avoid being captured, the Oko people make themselves invisible. They vanish into the forests.

Each time Nao stops singing and those carrying her voice fall silent, the ship seems to hover above the water for just a few moments. Catching her breath, she begins again. She sings of a people who are dying out, who decide they must preserve their memory.

Hunting, healing, growth, song, and war.

The five gifts of the Oko people.

All the knowledge of the Oko people is shared among the survivors. Each of them is born with one of these gifts so that they'll never be lost.

Hunting, growing, healing, singing, or fighting. Every Oko has one of these powers within them.

The cloud of hummingbirds followed them deeper inland, crossing forests and nesting in the trees where the Okos built their homes, having found a common remedy for their shared fragility: secrecy and freedom.

"Who's singing?" Alma asks feebly when the first night comes to an end.

The singing coming from the rowboat has stopped. Alma can't open her eyes, but they're flooded with tears. She'd never heard this story before, but she recognises the word "Okos."

"Tell me who's singing."

45

The Middle of the Night

For the next two nights, the singing resumes, following long days of silence. Nao is sacrificing the last of her strength. The captives are coming back to life. Water flows in through the portholes during the storm, invading their prison, but Nao's song protects them. It shelters them from everything.

Almost everyone aboard had already heard of the Okos. The drums of the Ibibio people tell their story. The Fante and the griots of the Oyo Empire, too. But now, as they listen to the song spilling over the edges of the rowboat, they begin to hear something of their own history—of the dangerous world they, too, grew up in.

During the daytime, the captives are silent, as though their lives depended on the coming night.

Memory must fight to survive. It must rise up, it must grow.

The fewer Okos remain, the more powerful their gifts become. Their hunters hunt like no one else can. Their healers can heal from afar. Their gardeners can make a garden grow up in the tops of the trees, on trellises of hemp or peat. The fire of persecution has concentrated the age-old spirit of the Okos. Their memory is becoming distilled, condensed like a potent liquid.

But the more powerful their gifts become, the more desirable they are to slave traders. From northern Virginia to the south of Brazil, a single Oko can be sold for the price of a cart holding ten captives.

Nao's story becomes one of escape, choreographed to the rhythm of the hunters' footsteps. Because it's not only slave traders hunting the Okos. Each group, each village has to buy its own survival by handing over neighbouring peoples. Relationships are distorted and damaged. The slave trade has poisoned the entire continent.

Then came the day when just seven remained.

Four men, two women, and a young girl. They arrive at the source of a river, having roamed far and wide. They pitch their final camp in the heights of the forest, where the roots of the tall trees bathe in spring water.

What the Oko people don't realise is that the innocent little birds that follow them will lead to their demise. As the seven fugitives pass from tree to tree without touching the ground to avoid leaving tracks, their birds venture high into the sky and swoop down into the clearings to drink from the lobelia and hibiscus. A manhunter is watching them. He's worked out the link. To track down the survivors, all he has to do is follow the flight of the birds to their feast of flowers.

The hunter has two pistols strapped to his belt, a black coat on his back and a gold-rimmed hat on his head. He's the most ruthless of them all. He's the son of Fante fishermen but he eats at the forts on the coast, at the white men's tables.

His men follow him. They surround the last camp in the middle of the flooded forest.

Four Okos are killed. Two more are captured.

The young girl is the only one who manages to escape. She continues to make her way through the branches.

The hunter pursues her, cutting through the black water below. He's lost his men, who are still struggling to wade through the mud. Some stay behind to guard the captives.

There she goes, up in the trees, a cloud of green birds all around.

It's as though there's not a soul left in the steerage of *The Sweet Amelie.* Their souls are flying in a cloud of birds surrounding the fugitive girl. Their souls smell the hunter advancing behind them. But nobody can predict what will happen next. No drum has ever sung this part of the Oko story. It's a secret only two people on earth know: Nao and Mosi, Alma's parents.

The song doesn't mention their names, but it's about them.

Nao is standing face to face with Mosi. The water reaches up to her waist.

Moments before, Mosi fired a shot into the air. Nao, hit by his bullet, tumbled down from the branches. The birds dispersed into the sky.

Nao tries to stand up despite her injured foot and the mud sucking her into the swamp. Mosi turns his other pistol on her. His men have heard the shot. They're calling him from afar.

The hunter moves closer to her.

"Don't move."

He thinks it's all over.

Lightning hits the deck of *The Sweet Amelie*. Light radiates from the tip of each mast and yardarm. The boatswains up in the shrouds watch on as the masts are lit up with Saint Elmo's fire, a phenomenon that occurs on ships, making them look as though they're on fire—or perhaps inhabited by spirits. There's a clap of thunder, and a fresh bolt of lightning tears through the sky. For a few seconds, Nao's song is lost in the commotion of the storm.

Nobody can hear what's happening between Nao and Mosi at the spring in the forest. But when the voice of the little old man in the rowboat resounds through the ship once more, it describes the hunter cutting through the swamps with the girl on his back. The voices of the other hunters echo through the forest. But Mosi isn't heading towards them. He can feel the girl's chin resting on his shoulder, her cheek against his ear. She has her arms around his neck. He's holding her bleeding foot in his hand. He's running away with her.

Little crocodiles watch on lazily as they pass by. Their eyes float on the surface like the buds of water lilies. But behind them, the hunters are losing their minds. They're shouting their leader's name. They're calling him. If he doesn't answer, he must be dead. They'll avenge him, they'll follow the girl to the desert if they have to, spill the last drop of Oko blood.

It's midnight on the third night. Alma is listening to the story of her people. In a few moments, she'll recognise the two fugitives. She'll hear how they walk for many days and nights, until the arrival of the monsoon, how they cling together beneath a waterfall, how they make a boat from the trunk of a kapok tree, how they cross a ravine between cliffs and fall asleep in a cave with their canoe.

How they wake up under the watchful eye of a leopard to discover that they've arrived in a valley protected from everything.

The little old man's voice falls silent as always after each verse, but this time the silence lasts a little longer than usual. For a few seconds, the captives in the steerage don't think anything of it. The final echoes of their voices reverberate through the ship. They breathe slowly so that the silence

won't feel as long. They clear their throats. They wait. But nothing comes.

It's over. But it's only the middle of the night.

Up in the rowboat, the little old man reaches down to take Nao's hand. He can see she can't take any more. Nao is cradling her belly with one arm.

"Rest, little cousin. But stay with us. I'll hold on to you so you don't slip away."

The man the whites call Adam feels very old. He'd like to be the one to go, to take her place. All he asks of her is that she hold his hand. He'll hold her if she falls. Or he'll go with her.

He feels the woman's pulse beating between his fingers. But something else is beating, too.

The captives have started drumming again. They're calling out.

They're waiting. They've been left hovering above a valley, at the gates of paradise.

Up in the sky, there's a head striking rhythmically against the mainmast.

He's starving, his back lacerated, and he holds his mouth open to catch raindrops on his tongue. But the giant with the severed ear is waiting, too. For the two and a half nights he's spent tied to the mast, the song of the Okos has kept him going.

He's listening.

In the ship below, another voice has just resumed the song, silencing the captives' drumming once again.

The voice tells of a valley, of the lines of elephants dotted in the distance, of the wind making ripples in the grass, the sound of insects, the swaying giraffes. It tells of the birth of children, the passing of moons, the generous rains, the sun. It tells of a zebra with no stripes, and a little boy who runs away.

"Who's singing?" asks Nao.

"We don't know," replies the little old man.

The one the whites call Eve is singing from the ship's store. It's Oumna. Her words are punctuated with the same silences. With her eyes closed, she softly repeats Alma's song.

Alma's voice has suddenly become unrecognisable. It's as though it's coming from far away, enveloping and enchanting everyone aboard the ship.

A few moons ago, Alma acquired the gift of hunting. Now she has the gift of song, the gift her mother has abandoned.

On the lower deck, Soum hears his story being told, the story of his people. He knows he has the gift of growth. It's a gift he uses clumsily, still unsure what to do with it. Each time he touches the soaking wet floor, a sort of tender watercress springs up between his fingers.

Their gifts lay dormant within them for all those years in the valley. They were ready to be awakened when the children left, when they would have to face the outside world.

Part of the Okos' memory is there aboard *The Sweet Amelie*, with Alma and Soum—and in Nao's womb. Because tucked away in the rowboat, Nao is still breathing. She's still there, kept alive by the child she's expecting, who already bears the fourth gift: healing.

But at the ship's stern, something even more extraordinary is happening. Nestled around the red letters that spell out the ship's name and hung in the friezes surrounding the windows of the stern are thousands of tiny birds. They've attached themselves to the side of the ship, hidden from sight. They've been there since the ship set sail. They're not moving. They're okos. Their body temperature has dropped by ten degrees and their heart rates by one thousand beats per minute. They sleep to forget about their hunger, the absence of flowers.

One hundred miles away, there's a second cluster of oko birds perched on the stern of another ship: a small British brig on its way to Louisiana. A young black child has just laid down on the floor in the officers' corridor. Dressed as a valet, with a silk scarf around his neck, the boy has finally been given permission to close his eyes. He's thinking about his mother rocking him to sleep, whispering to him: "Lilim." He's listening to the sound of the harpsichord coming from next door. He's been told to sleep there so that when Captain Harrison's door opens, he can jump up immediately to brew tea, even if it's the middle of the night.

46

Getting Closer

It's two o'clock in the morning. Captain Gardel is at the helm of *The Sweet Amelie.* The silhouette of an island is expanding before him like a mountain floating on the sea. It's the Island of Zacchaeus. The ship has reached the calm at the eye of the storm. The full moon slips in and out of the clouds.

Gardel is oblivious to what's been happening over the last three nights between the rowboat and the rest of the captives. While things remained calm in the steerage, he kept the ship on course through the storm. Until then, *The Sweet Amelie* hadn't once veered from her course. She followed the north coast of Puerto Rico from a distance, as though heading straight for her destination in the port of Saint-Domingue. But now the ship has suddenly swung due south, sailing as close to the wind as possible to reach Zacchaeus and the treasure.

Abel Lebon is standing proudly by the captain's side. He's been selected to travel in the jolly boat with him when *The Sweet Amelie* arrives in the cove between the bull's horns.

Lazarus Gardel would rather have gone alone, but he knows it'll take two to carry the treasure. He's chosen the most naive member of the crew to help him.

He has no intention of taking the treasure right away. He wants to move it somewhere else, to a different location on the island, with Lebon's help. He'll equip a fast vessel himself at a later date and come back then for the treasure.

Abel Lebon is beaming. Gardel has even begun to address him by name. He's designated Lebon as his aide and new carpenter.

The young sailor thinks about his two companions locked up in their cabin. He feels he's paying homage to them by taking their place.

But Lazarus Gardel isn't counting on Abel for any particular skills. All he needs to know is how to handle a shovel and carry a trunk or bags of gold without asking questions. Then he needs to be stupid enough to allow himself to be hit on the back of the head with a log.

All Gardel will have to do is make his way back alone and regretfully tell the story of how the faithful Lebon met his tragic end at the bottom of a crevasse or sinking in quicksand. He'll admit remorsefully that the Island of Zacchaeus is too dangerous a place to make a stop. Then *The Sweet Amelie* will continue on its course towards Cap-Français in Saint-Domingue, where, in a few days' time, the captives will be sold and become slaves.

All in all, the stop will only have cost them a few hours.

The outline of Zacchaeus is forming before them.

"What are we looking for on this island?" asks Lebon.

"Fresh water," says Gardel, without looking at him.

"It'll be my first time in the islands."

"I don't want to hear your life story."

Just then, Palardi appears behind them.

AMERIQUE
MERIDIONALE
PARAGUAY
TUCUMAN
URUGUAY
COSTES DU BRESIL
GUYANE
LIGNE EQUATORIALE
OCEAN
MERIDIONAL
DESERT
DE BARBARIE
NEGRETIE
ETATS DE CONGO

"I think your surgeon wants to see you," says Abel Lebon.

"Who are you talking about?" asks Gardel. "We no longer have a surgeon on board."

Palardi comes forward anyway.

"Captain. It's about the pregnant woman."

Gardel's face drops.

"Is she dead?"

"She's still breathing."

"You know what'll happen to you if she dies."

"The rowboat is full of water. We need to get her out of there."

"And put her where?"

"I'm not sleeping in my cabin anymore."

"Mars and Dubois have already been locked inside."

"The woman could sleep on the bunk. She'll be drier there. They won't bother her."

Palardi doesn't want to admit that he's secretly counting on Dubois healing her. In fact, it's his last hope.

"Do whatever you want. Just make sure she survives."

Gardel goes back to gazing into the distance. He's trying to make out the bull's horns.

Dubois and Mars sit up. An unconscious woman has just been delivered to them.

"She's the one who's been singing for the last few nights from the rowboat," says Palardi.

"What's the matter with her?" asks Joseph.

Palardi shakes his head helplessly. He leaves the room, closing the door behind him.

Joseph Mars and the carpenter are sitting on the floor, leaning against the partition. They look at the pregnant woman lying on the bunk. Her face is turned towards them.

"I spent fifteen years working on ships like this one," Dubois whispers, so as not to wake her. "I stopped almost twenty years ago."

"Why?"

He doesn't reply. The answer is lying right there in front of them on the bunk.

Where did this woman come from? Where will she go if she survives? And what about her child?

All this suffering for a bit of coffee, jam, and chocolate at snack time. All this for the sugar rush gripping the salons all over Europe. This year alone, the colony of Saint-Domingue will swallow up forty thousand new captives on its plantations.

"Now I build barns and churches in Italy," Dubois tells Joseph. "I could show you. It's a wonderful job."

There's a silence.

Joseph's head lolls to one side. He's asleep.

They sit like that for a long time, without moving. The cabin is completely still. There's only the rising and falling of Nao's belly.

Dubois feels the weight of Joseph's head on his shoulder. He's thinking about his son, Antony.

He waits a little longer, listening for Joseph's gentle snoring. When he's sure he's alone, he finally allows himself to cry.

It's half past four in the morning. The captain looks at the two rocks where the opening to the little bay is supposed to be. There's no way through. The bull's horns meet in the middle. The cove he was looking for doesn't exist.

The storm broke again an hour ago. A strong southwesterly wind has swept up all the clouds in the sky and deposited them above *The Sweet Amelie*. Gardel has had a few more sails put away, but the ship is rearing up, its rudder resisting all three men holding it. It's as though Luc de Lerna's ghost is playing tricks on them.

Gardel heads towards the ship's bow, bent over in the rain. If there's no passage, it's all over. He positions himself at the very front of the ship, looking for a way through the black wall.

But no matter what he does, he can't see a thing. The rain and the sea have merged into one.

"Captain!" shouts Morel. "We're heading into the rocks!"

"Keep going! Rudder amidships!" yells Gardel.

Gardel's orders tell the crew to keep the ship on course.

"The storm will blow over in an hour!" says Morel. "We'll have better visibility."

"Shut up. I said rudder amidships!"

The captain's order travels back to the ship's stern. Even with almost all of her sails folded up on the yardarms, *The Sweet Amelie* is travelling at great speed. The wall of rock before them is enormous. The sea is crashing against it, sending white jets all the way up to the top.

"We can still take down the sails at the top," Morel suggests.

"Enough! I need to keep them up to manoeuvre the ship."

All the sailors around him are panicking. There's not even any hope of running aground. The cliffs are vertical. The island is deserted. Nobody would survive a shipwreck.

His hands firmly grasping the wheel, Abel Lebon tries to think of the prayers he used to say as a child.

Suddenly, he looks up to the sky and cries out. He's just seen a shape appear between the two cliffs. It's a tall, pale shape that stands out against the rock and the night sky. It's the passage.

"I told you!" roars the captain from the ship's bow.

The bay is like an almost-closed horseshoe. If they had arrived any further to the west of the island, they would never have seen the opening. But here it is.

Gardel turns to the back of the ship and helps Abel Lebon with the rudder. The passage is narrow. The three-master will struggle to squeeze through.

Just then, in the cabin underneath the captain's feet, Joseph wakes with a start.

"I fell asleep!"

"Don't worry," says Dubois. "I think they've forgotten about us."

He gestures towards the woman lying before them.

"Her breathing's getting better," he says with a smile. "Palardi is going to think I'm a wizard again, but I haven't done anything."

The sea continues to rock the ship from all sides. Joseph slips behind Nao to look out the window. He lifts the curtain.

"Zacchaeus!" he shouts. "It's the Island of Zacchaeus!"

"Calm down," says Dubois. "It's not like there's anything we can do now."

A draft comes in through the window. Dubois takes off his jacket and puts it over the woman.

"Calm down, kid. I was about to tell you why I stopped working on these ships twenty years ago. Just when I thought I was used to the horrors . . ."

Joseph goes back to his place. Dubois is right. There's nothing they can do. All of Joseph's plans can go ahead now without him. All he has to do is be there and listen to Dubois's sad stories.

"This is why I stopped." He pulls the jacket over Nao's shoulders.

"I was on a ship called *Mercy*, a small vessel belonging to a family from Bordeaux. One day, I found three trunks behind a partition I had put up by one of the sections the captives were crammed into."

Dubois furrows his brow whenever he delves into his memories.

"Down in the stench of the hold, I opened up the trunks one by one. I saw that they were full of white linen. Sheets, nightgowns, corsets, petticoats."

Dubois stops for a moment.

"The linen was already perfectly clean, but I'd heard that some families of good standing sent their sheets away because they say the mountain water in Saint-Domingue turns them a more dazzling white. I lifted up all the heavy cotton and lace, and then I heard the cry of a child coming from the women's section, right behind me."

Joseph tries to imagine those sheets, travelling amidst the stench of death, before returning to grace the four-poster beds of Bordeaux's finest mansions.

"So much sophistication and so much horror," says Dubois. "That's what opened my eyes. When I came aboard this ship, the first thing I learnt was that Ferdinand Bassac did the very same thing."

Joseph listens distractedly. He can feel the movements of the ship, the manoeuvres the crew are making. They're preparing to enter the bay. Now everything can begin.

"Nothing's changed in twenty years," Dubois continues. "The same chests full of linen. Only Bassac doesn't keep his in the steerage."

Joseph's eyes suddenly dart to Dubois.

"Where are they?" he asks. "Where are these chests?"

Dubois smiles.

"Where are the chests you're talking about?"

"They're in the only sacred place on the whole ship."

"Where?"

"Beneath the captain's bed!"

Joseph grabs Dubois by the shirt. "Sheets? Those chests can't have sheets in them!"

"Nothing but sheets and linen, kid. Protected like the blessed sacrament."

Joseph jumps over Nao's sleeping body. With a single blow of his elbow, he smashes the window to pieces. He sticks his head and shoulders out and is whipped by the wind and sharp rain. The ship is moving forward through the passageway. Balancing on the windowsill, Joseph leans out. He feels along the side of the ship above him for something to hold onto. There must be something there. He's sure of it. He can feel his hand getting closer.

47
Dead or Alive

Joseph jumps out of the window. Suspended in mid-air above the waves, he grabs onto the first thing his hand touches. It's the rigging securing the ropes attached to the mast at the stern of the ship. By swinging himself back and forth, Joseph manages to grab onto the next mast. Slowly, he makes his way towards the back of the ship.

The sea is doing everything in its power to shake him off. But the ship is leaning in the opposite direction, onto its starboard side, protecting Joseph from the waves but throwing his body brutally against the planks of the hull. The storm is so tumultuous, the wind so violent, that the little bay the ship has entered is like a pot full of sizzling oil making a deep-fried doughnut of the ship.

Joseph has reached the final mast, but his destination is still far off. The captain's quarters are still a yard away. The hull has become slippery, polished over time by wear and tear and seaweed. What can he hold on to get to the window?

Luck. Sometimes, the only thing you can hold on to is luck.

A wave hits the ship's bow at full force, causing the rudder to falter for a moment. The helmsman must have lost control of the wheel. The ship topples sideways, flattened by the wind. Joseph lets go of the shroud and throws himself against the hull.

The port side of the ship is now like a dance floor. Joseph moves along it like a spider. Just before the ship rights itself, he dives through the captain's window, landing amidst shards of glass against the captain's chair. The smell of wastewater and cologne fills the air. He rips off a wooden panel from the wall and brandishes it like a weapon, advancing further into the room.

There's nobody there. The vast room has been deserted. The door is locked. Joseph looks at the little girl with the cotton flower carved into the clock, which is no longer ticking. The captain must be up on deck, manoeuvring the ship. He's left the map on the wall.

Joseph leaps towards the bed. He tears away the mattress to reveal the two chests. The padlocks are so enormous, they could withstand cannon fire at point-blank range. They're enough to discourage even the most seasoned thieves. Joseph has done many things in his fourteen years to survive: brawling, fighting in the streets and on the high seas, pillaging shipwrecks and various other misdemeanours. But never has he considered himself a thief. He decides not to even attempt opening the padlocks.

Instead, he slides the piece of wood in his hands between the wooden slats of the chest, and in one swift movement, pulls the side clean off without even touching the lid. He used this trick often with the bread bin at the orphanage, which was always locked so that nobody could touch the headmaster's fresh loaves. With the help of his friend Flea, he would detach the bottom of the bread bin before carefully replacing it. If they hadn't used this trick during their last years at the orphanage, Joseph and Flea would have died of starvation and been buried somewhere without so much as a name etched into their little headstones.

Joseph plunges his arm inside the chest. He pulls out dozens of sheets, all folded and starched, white underwear in pillowcases, pounds of linen . . . Then he throws it all into the room behind him. He's on the verge of falling apart. He rips open the second chest and does the same thing.

He gets up and heads towards the door. The room behind him is a sea of white. The treasure isn't there.

Lazarus Bartholomew Gardel was expecting a sandy cove, but the little horseshoe bay is surrounded by cliffs. There's just a single stretch of lower rocks covered by a mesh of trees that might be a suitable spot to row the boat through. For now, Gardel doesn't want to drop anchor. Something else seems to be bothering him.

He's immobilised *The Sweet Amelie*, effectively making the ship break down. It was a tricky exercise, just the kind he likes. He's carefully mixed up the different sails so that they each catch the wind at a different angle. They are all working against each other. The ship is champing at the bit like a stray beast that's just been released into an arena.

"Are we leaving?" someone asks.

In the dark of the night, the waves paint the bottoms of the cliffs white.

"No," Gardel replies. "We'll wait."

They crew is preparing for all eventualities. The boatswains are up in the shrouds, ready to roll in the remaining sails if the captain orders them to drop anchor. There are other sailors on deck, holding onto ropes and hoping to get back on course.

Nobody has noticed that Joseph Mars has cropped up in their midst, hidden beneath a rain cloak too wide for him, the hood tied around his neck.

He knows he should make the signal by lighting a lantern at the top of the mast. The signal that says all is lost, everything must be abandoned.

But Joseph is torn. He's thinking about the captives in the ship's steerage. He's thinking about the person in the ship's store, the one he could never leave behind if he has to jump ship.

He starts running towards the bow. Three men are kneeling around the new hatch of the ship's store. They've just realised the lock has been left open. The openings of the grating are too narrow for even the thinnest, most skilful hand to have unlocked it from inside. A guard must have forgotten to lock it.

The three sailors curse the guard and make fun of the captives' stupidity for not having realised. They hurriedly secure the enclosure with a few enormous nails. They'll figure out who was responsible later.

At the ship's stern, the door to Dubois's cell is open. Cook is standing in the door frame, a sack of biscuits in his hand.

Wide-eyed, he looks at the broken window.

"What happened to the boy?" he asks in an unrecognisable voice.

"He went for a little walk," says Dubois.

Cook drops his sack on the floor. He turns on his heels, crushing biscuits into the floor as he goes. A little further along, he discovers that the door to the captain's quarters is wide open. The lock is broken.

He goes inside.

Dozens of white sheets are spread out like ghosts all across the room. Cook goes over to the partition. There's a mysterious piece of paper pinned to the wall in front of him. It's Luc de Lerna's map.

At that very moment, in the port of La Rochelle, Amelie Bassac pulls herself from Madame de Lô's arms.

"Where are you going?"

One hour ago, they embarked on *The Pearl* with their two trunks and a small rosewood piano. They're leaving nothing behind but memories. There's nothing left for them on this continent.

Some of the moorings have already been thrown from the dock. The ship begins to move.

"Please, Captain! Give me one moment!"

Amelie is giving the captain puppy eyes. He can't help but order his men to halt the ship. They help the young lady down onto the dock. She makes her way through the crowd of irritated spectators. They've stayed up late to say goodbye to their loved ones. They might never see them again. Still, they'd be glad to go home and rest now.

"Monsieur?"

Amelie places her hand on the shoulder of a boy who has his back to her. Just next to them, there's another two-master moored beside *The Pearl*.

The boy turns around. He hastily pulls off his red hat when he sees the fourteen-year-old girl in front of him, flushed pink and wrapped up in furs.

She looks at him. He's definitely the one.

"Monsieur, I saw you at church."

The boy smiles apologetically.

"I don't always go to mass, mademoiselle. May my mother and father forgive me, if they're still alive somewhere."

He traces a cross in the air over his chest.

"You were at Saint-Sauveur church on Christmas Eve."

The boy's eyes brighten up a little.

"You spoke to Monsieur Saint-Clair."

"I remember. That was me, He didn't pay me much, the cheapskate."

"What did he pay you for?"

"There was a letter that arrived for him."

"Where did the letter come from?"

"From here."

"From here?"

The boy is delighted to have her attention.

"From this ship. They've just hired me. We set sail tomorrow."

Amelie turns to look at the little two-master brig. The name of the ship is *High Society*.

"So I brought the gentleman here to pick up the letter, and then he left."

"And then?" she asks. "What did the gentleman do with the letter after that?"

"After that? He read it right away. He didn't go back to the church. I followed him for a while; I wasn't happy with the tip he gave me. I left him where the big cobblestones start."

"The big cobblestones?"

"Rue de l'Escale."

Amelie nods slowly.

"What's happened to him?" the boy asks.

"Nothing."

"The captain is right there if you want more information."

Amelie places a gold coin in the boy's hand and goes over to the captain. As she's speaking to him, the colour slowly drains from her cheeks. By the end of their conversation, she's very pale.

Amelie runs back to *The Pearl*, where Madame de Lô is waiting for her. Now all the moorings have been dropped.

"You gave me a terrible fright," says the tutor.

She holds onto Amelie's arm tightly. They watch the docks fade into the distance.

The letter for Saint-Clair was given to the captain of *High Society* on the coast of Africa by a black man working in the kitchen of another ship. He was a free man who went by the name of Cook and spoke with a strong English accent. The captain believes he was the cook aboard *The Sweet Amelie*. The man requested the letter be handed over in person in La Rochelle. Gabriel Cook claimed to have personal business with Christian Saint-Clair.

Four thousand miles from La Rochelle as the crow flies, Cook has broken into a wooden box just in front of the captain's quarters. He pulls out a large pre-loaded flint rifle. Saint-Clair advised him to hide this weapon somewhere in case anything happened.

The carpenter is watching him through the open door of the cabin.

"Don't leave this room," says Cook. "I think your little friend Mars is about to do something very stupid."

Gabriel Cook climbs the big ladder. It opens onto the aftcastle where Gardel is standing by the railing.

The captain looks at him in amazement.

"Captain," says Cook. "Someone has ransacked your quarters."

"My quarters?"

"It was Joseph Mars."

"Where did you get that weapon?"

"It was lying on the floor. I saw Luc de Lerna's map on your wall."

Gardel staggers.

"It's a trap," says Cook.

"A trap?"

"Were you hoping to find treasure? There never was any treasure. It's impossible. If Luc had left any treasure behind, it would have sunk to the bottom of the sea with his coffin the day he died."

"Who are you?"

"The only treasure is this ship. That's what they're after"

Then they hear the first scream coming from up on the yardarm. Gardel spins around.

From a hidden cave that runs along the bottom of the cliff surrounding the bay, shadows are beginning to appear. Dozens of rafts emerge from the band of foam, propelled by gigantic oars.

"Pirates," says Gardel.

He turns towards Cook.

"I'll deal with it. Find Mars."

Only two minutes ago, he would never have imagined asking this man for anything more than a boiled egg or brioche. But his orders are clear.

"Bring him to me, dead or alive."

48

Up on the Mainmast

Joseph Mars is at Dubois's workbench. He's lifted all the floorboards and rummaged through the saw box. But the bow and arrow are nowhere to be found. Joseph's eyes shine in the dim light. Alma must have been here. She's the one who opened the ship's store. She's roaming the deck of *The Sweet Amelie*.

Even from the bottom of the ship, he can hear the chaos breaking out on deck.

When he emerges, he realises all is lost. The rafts are gliding towards the ship. Gardel is barking out new orders to the crew by the second. It's a race against time to get the ship back on course.

Amidst all the commotion on deck, Joseph Mars has become invisible. Nobody is paying attention to him anymore. He removes his cloak and begins to climb the shrouds on the port side.

A few feet away, Cook has just stepped into the rowboat, wielding his enormous rifle. He's looking for Joseph. He won't stop until he's searched every last corner of the ship. He'll even wade through the stinking bilge water collecting in the keel if he has to.

The barrel of his rifle skims the heads of every person in the rowboat. He pushes each of them aside to make sure they're not hiding anyone. He rests the rifle a little longer between the piercing eyes of one girl in particular.

"You don't look sick," he says.

But Cook isn't there to carry out a medical check-up. He pushes Alma's face aside, gets out of the rowboat and jumps onto the aftcastle.

Alma turns to the man next to her, calmly resuming the conversation that's just been interrupted.

"And she didn't tell you how she knew the story she was singing?"

"No. We don't know where she came from," replies the little old man the whites call Adam. "She was expecting a child."

"She must have been seven or eight moons into her pregnancy," says one woman.

"They took her away when she stopped singing."

"Where? Where did they take her?"

"We don't know," the woman replies. "We don't know anything."

"All I know," says the man, "is that my wound hasn't been hurting for several nights now. It's almost completely healed."

Alma stays crouched down in the rowboat for a few moments. The chaos continues all around her. She wanted so badly to see the woman who was telling the story of her people. Now she'll have to go to the women's section at the back of the ship. But first she needs to get up on the mainmast. She needs to speak to the only person in the world still connecting her to Lam: the giant with the severed ear. She takes her bow and plants a kiss on the forehead of the man who's been singing the song of the Okos, sharing all those secrets she didn't know. Then she disappears.

"They almost look like sisters," the man says once she's gone.

Any of the most powerful shipowners in the world, from the Indies to Angola, from the Royal African Company to the privateers, from the ministers of Louis XVI to the Portuguese and British Crowns, any one of these men who've made it their business to command the sea or make their fortune on it would have offered Lazarus Bartholomew Gardel their biggest and best contracts if they'd seen him command *The Sweet Amelie* that morning.

The ship is still behaving like a wild animal in an arena, surrounded by howling wind and the clamour of the pirates besieging them. But the captain handles her like a thoroughbred. He's put a bit in her mouth.

It's as though *The Sweet Amelie* has forgotten about her thousands of tons, her dozens of complicated sails, her exhausted crew. She rears up, launching herself into a dance to get out of the trap. The orders are fired off one by one. Gardel stands on the bench just before the top of the ladder like a conductor. Thanks to his strong instinct for sniffing out pirates, he kept the sails on standby and refrained from casting anchor. The ship was waiting to spring into action. The last thing he wants to do is play at war with his four ornamental cannons. Instead, he sticks to what he does best: speed. He favours a fugue over a military march.

It's six o'clock in the morning, and the day is refusing to break, but the ship is escaping the enemy. She's speeding towards the exit of the trap.

Joseph finds Alma on the mainmast.

She's standing on the long yardarm of the topsail. She still has to climb twenty or twenty-five feet to reach the highest sails, but she's stopped to catch her breath, leaning against the mast. The full moon reappears as a gust of wind blows away a cloud. Alma is carrying her bow across her chest, stretched from one shoulder to the opposite hip.

Behind her is a single, taught sail rippling in the wind. Alma occasionally glances up above her. There, trussed up on the mast, she can see the outline of the giant. He looks barely alive; his head is lolling onto his shoulder.

Joseph is just below Alma on the next mast along. He climbs up the shrouds until he reaches a platform. Then he stops for a moment.

Alma has spotted him from the other side of the void.

They lock eyes, drawn to one another yet confused, like the inhabitants of two separate trees, destined never to cross paths. Alma disappears for a second behind the billowing sail. By the time she's come back into view, she's already started climbing again.

Just then, Joseph notices a rope secured by his feet, around forty feet long and stretching diagonally up to the mainmast. It's the topsail forestay and it's as thick as his arm. It's also a direct pathway to Alma.

Joseph grabs onto the rope as high as his arms can reach and hangs from it with his legs crossed and head swinging below. Then he begins to climb. He inches along slowly, eighty feet above the ship's deck, arms shaking and eyes fixed on his goal.

Cook grins to himself, his cheeks puffed out, as he watches the little circus monkey perform his acrobatics up in the rigging. The first time he saw Joseph Mars months earlier, he was in the middle of the very same act, hanging by his feet from a rope in the Port of Lisbon.

But this time, Cook has a rifle in his hands. He's only made it halfway up the mainmast. But he doesn't particularly want to go higher. He suffers from vertigo and hates exercise.

He cocks his rifle and slowly takes aim. There's no way he can miss the shot. The monkey boy, Joseph Mars, is practically motionless, glowing in the moonlight. Cook concentrates. He has two shots in his rifle and all the time he needs.

In twenty seconds' time, he'll have Gardel wrapped around his little finger for the rest of the trip. More importantly, by saving Saint-Clair's treasure, he'll gain the accountant's respect for life.

Gabriel Cook takes a deep breath, still aiming.

The first arrow that falls from the sky hits him in the wrist, paralysing the index finger that was about to pull the trigger. The second is planted immediately after in the cartilage of his shoulder, where the butt of the rifle was resting moments before. This time, his whole arm falls down by his side like a discarded sock. The rifle slides from Cook's grasp and bounces off something below. It fires a first shot halfway down, then a second when it hits the ground.

If it hadn't been for the first shot, nobody would have batted an eyelid. Nobody would have seen Cook lying on the platform or Joseph Mars climbing the topsail forestay. If it hadn't been for the second shot, Gardel wouldn't be lying on the floor, his eyes rolling back into his head, blood oozing down onto his foot. The second shot hit Gardel in his right leg, just below the knee.

Ten men rush over to him, but he beats them back with his whip. He crawls towards the barricade, leaving a trail of blood on the floor. Then he spots Alma putting her bow back on her shoulder. He points up at her, swirling his whip around him.

"Climb the mainmast!" he yells. "Shoot them!"

Standing on her tiptoes, Alma is attempting to untie the giant. He opens his eyes and looks at her.

"Is that you?" he asks. "I imagined you to be taller."

He hasn't eaten for four days. He's survived one hundred lashes and three or four storms.

"Have you come about your brother?"

"Yes," she says, tugging at the ropes in vain. "Now tell me the name of the ship."

"Even if they'd left me up here for the rest of my days, I would've stayed alive to answer your question."

"Why?"

"I heard the song. I know it was your story being sung."

She looks up at the giant.

"Remember this name," he says. "*The Brothers*. It's headed for New Orleans, Louisiana."

These words are nothing but a string of sounds to Alma, but she'll never forget them. *The Brothers*. New Orleans. Louisiana.

Another shot rings out below them. Two armed men have arrived at the spot where Cook collapsed. The first gunman punctures one of the sails with the lead shot from his rifle, while the other prepares himself. They're aiming at the girl. She's the one they need to get first. In his current position, Joseph Mars looks about as dangerous as a clothes peg on a washing line.

Joseph spots the two men and glances up to see how far he has left to go. He works out how high the mast is above the men aiming for Alma. Then he takes the knife from his belt and slashes the rope just below his feet.

He lets himself fall, holding tightly to the remaining rope. He swings through the air, right in the direction he's aiming for. With his feet stretched out in front of him, he kicks the two gunmen, sending them flying through the air.

Joseph swings in the other direction like a pendulum, lets go of the rope, launches himself at the convex sail and slides down it. He grabs on to the shrouds of the topsail on his way down.

He lets out a wild yell and hastily scrambles to the top of the mast to Alma.

She grabs Joseph's knife and slashes the ropes the giant is tied up with.

Below them, there's a thud as the two gunmen fall onto the deck. Nearby, Palardi looks down in horror at the captain's mangled leg.

"Not you!" says Gardel to Palardi. "Take me to the table in my quarters. Free the carpenter. I need Dubois. Tell him to prepare his tools."

By the time *The Sweet Amelie* finally breaks free from the trap, there's a strong gust of wind waiting to ambush her just beyond the bulls' horns. The ship tips violently to one side.

Then she rights herself. Everything seems to be in order. Except the three figures that were up on the mainmast have now disappeared.

49

There Will Be Light

There's a long line of men making their way through the forest.

Watching them walk quietly, in single file, you'd never suspect that they're pirates. Yet they're descendants of that great, terrifying family that every navy in the world wanted eradicated fifty years prior.

There must be eighty of them crossing the jungle in a thin line. They're all mismatched, as pirates always are, but they're too independent to remain faithful to the image that's been invented for them. There are no gold hoops hanging from their ears, no scars on display like trophies, no black eye patches covering gouged-out eyes.

Some of them are old enough to have crossed paths with Charles Vane or Olivier la Bouche. Others look like children dressed up as adults with their missing teeth and jaundiced skin. This morning, they don't even have that famous jovial pirate spirit—the conviction that justice has been served and it's all been a blast. This morning they're walking in silence.

Leading the penitents' procession are four men. Instead

of the usual loot, they're carrying two stretchers holding two small bodies. A black girl and a white boy.

To the left of the stretcher, by the girl's side, there's a giant with a severed ear. To the right, with one hand resting on the boy's arm, walks an old pirate.

This man has seen everything. He was first mate to the infamous Black Bart when he died on *The Royal Fortune* off the coast of Africa in 1722. At the age of twenty, he inherited his former captain's golden toothpicks and black flag. He's been declared dead, hanged, and decapitated so many times that he named his ship after the mythological monster whose heads grow back each time they're cut off: The Hydra of Lerna.

His name is Luc de Lerna.

Lying on his stretcher, Joseph opens his eyes.

"The black giant saved both of your lives," says the pirate. "You swallowed a lot of water. And the little girl can't swim any better than you can, Joe."

Joseph turns towards Alma and sees her lying next to him, her nostrils quivering. He's overcome with an inexplicable sense of joy. He tries to prop himself up on his elbow a little to look at her, but he immediately falls back down.

"Don't move."

Luc de Lerna walks next to him in silence.

"The birds were there, too," he says.

"What birds?"

"A little flock of birds hovering above you in the waves. It's thanks to them that my men found you."

The old pirate steadies himself to step over a tree trunk blocking the path.

"I messed it all up," says Joseph.

"It was me who messed up."

Luc lowers his voice. He doesn't want to admit his failures in front of his men.

"That scumbag, Gardel, kept his sails out. He was preparing to leave. What we needed was more time, old boy. I should have blocked the passageway through the horns once he was in. If I had, this stretcher would be carrying five tons of gold, and we'd be on our way to bury it in the forest."

Luc de Lerna imagines the ghosts of his old comrades howling with laughter at his mistake.

"The gold wasn't on board," says Joseph.

"Don't try to console me, old boy."

Luc de Lerna calls everyone "old boy." Perhaps that's how he manages to stay so young himself.

"I looked for months," says Joseph. "I'm telling you, the gold was not on board."

"And I'm telling you it was. It still is. Four and a half tons of pure gold."

"But where?"

"I don't know. But I have proof. Who's the girl?"

Joseph doesn't answer.

He's thinking about all the others. Those who are still locked in the hold. They're the reason he didn't make the signal. Even if there was no treasure, he wanted Luc de Lerna to take the ship. Because the old pirate doesn't sell the captives on the ships he takes. He gives them back their freedom.

As they walk deeper into the forest, the trees around them become interspersed with ferns and orchids. A fine rain begins to fall upon the forest. The oko birds must be having a feast up there, getting their fill from the flowers.

"Who is this girl?" the pirate asks again.

"I don't know."

Through the branches, a black shape begins to appear at the

top of the trees. It's the shadow of *The Hydra,* Luc de Lerna's four-master. The pirate has rigged the ship's vast hull high up among the trees. He transferred it there, plank by plank. He removed all the masts and the yardarms and used them to make rafts. Now he lives above the forest with his men. Banished from the seven seas, he now has to make do with the sky.

"She can stay here if she wants to," says Luc.

"Who?"

"The girl."

"Never," says Alma's deep voice from Joseph's side. "Where's my bow?"

At that very moment, Lam is watching a girl who's just come into the ship's kitchen.

The Brothers, a little brig belonging to the Jones brothers from Liverpool, is gliding towards the Gulf of Mexico, then on to Louisiana, leaving behind her the dust of the Caribbean islands.

For a while now, Lam has been watching this girl. She has much darker skin than him. They must be around the same age. Anyone who crosses her path can see that there's a certain poise about her, even if she's only half their size.

She doesn't live in the steerage like the other captives. Nor does she work at the ship's stern like Lam, serving the ship's officers. The girl lives alone somewhere beneath the forecastle on the other side of the barricade.

Lam has noticed that certain captives are given special roles so that others will want their job and behave well in the hope of getting it. Lam never wanted to be Captain Harrison's valet. He doesn't even know what the word "valet" means. He just puts on the ridiculous clothes he's been given and does what's asked of him. He listens to the captain when he locks himself in his quarters to play the harpsichord, issuing orders to the crew without so much as stepping outside.

Lam watches as the cook's assistant hands the girl a bucket of corn.

"It's a shame to give all this to you. It's good corn. The maggots haven't even got into it."

The cook gestures for her to go. She doesn't move. He pretends not to understand. "Are you waiting for flour, too?"

She doesn't even bother to answer. He goes to get her a second bucket.

"Now go."

She doesn't move, just nods her chin towards Lam, who stares at her, his eyes widening.

"You! Help her carry the buckets."

Lam goes over and takes one of the buckets. When she doesn't react, he takes the second one, as well. She starts walking in front of him. The soles of her bare feet make a high-pitched noise as they hit the ground. She has long legs for such a small girl. She stops just in front of the doors to the barricade. One of the guards opens it.

"I'll be waiting here for you," he tells Lam. "Take the buckets and come straight back."

The pair walk across the empty deck beneath the beating sun. The wet floorboards burn the soles of their feet. Just below, where the men are being kept, the heat must be unbearable. Captain Harrison had some air vents put in, but they're useless.

The two children make their way beneath the aftcastle and stop in the shade outside the double door. The girl crouches down. She tugs on Lam's jacket, signalling for him to do the same.

With her head bowed, she pretends to be sorting the corn.

"I know who you are," she says.

Lam realises she's speaking his father's language.

"I saw those men taking you away down the river. I come from Bussa. The river you were on was the Quorra."

Lam holds his breath. He knows he mustn't trust anyone.

"Your sister loves you. She's looking for you. You'll never know how much she loves you, how much she wants to find you,"

This time, Lam's heart begins to melt, pouring out onto the floorboards in front of him.

"Your name is Lam. I'm Sirim."

He's crying.

"Your sister is called Alma. She's my friend. My village was burnt down when she left. Fifty of my kingdom's warriors were captured by the Fulani. They usually only take our men and sell them. But this time they took me, too."

"Why?" asks Lam.

She gets up, and he follows suit. She pushes one of the big doors open. Lam enters.

"To take care of him," says Sirim. He can smell him before he sees him.

Cloud.

Lam is still holding the two buckets in his hands. He walks forward and presses his wet face to the horse's cheek.

A streak of golden sunlight shines through the half-open door. Cloud begins to rummage through one of the buckets that Lam is still holding in his hand. A big puff of flour shoots up into the air.

Sirim looks at the boy and the horse surrounded by white.

She's standing just a few steps behind them. She tells herself that one day, happier times will return. One day, there will be light.